ON

A Novel of King Richard III

By
Richard Unwin

A doubtful throne is ice on summer seas,
Ye come from Arthur's court,
Victor his men report him!
Yea, but think ye this king –
So many those that hate him, and so strong,
So few his knights, however brave they be
Have body enow to hold his foemen down?

The Coming Of Arthur
From Idylls of the King
by Alfred Lord Tennyson.

CONTENTS

PROLOGUE

The Court was its usual boisterous self as it was whenever the nobles got together for a banquet. It was the Yoolis feast and the frugal fare of winter hardly mattered to the Court, although there were some limitations. No venison, but fowl and fish aplenty along with other meats and delicacies and an inexhaustible quantity of wine. This was all the more frantic because afterwards the winter would continue to limit what food was available, and before the largesse of spring would be the period of Lent when they would have to fast again until Easter. The hall was alive with chatter, though most, even while conversing with intimates, kept a watchful eye on the top table where duke Francis, the second of Brittany, sat with his mistress Antoinette de Maignelais. She had been discreet while the Duchess Margaret of Brittany had lived, but now that Francis was a widower she had brought a welcome brightness to his court as well as the three children she had given him. Dozens of torches blazed in the sconces around the hall. These were replaced as soon as they burned down and before they began to smoulder. In the centre was a huge brazier where the wood fire it contained warmed the hall and contributed to the smoky atmosphere. The rafters were invisible, obscured in a haze of smoke that was finding a way through the ventilation slots in the roof. Fortunately, the smoke layer maintained itself a few feet above the heads of the players in the minstrels' gallery, otherwise the music they were providing would have been brought to an ignominious finish.

Not everyone, though, was given to the joy of the occasion. Two men, who were seated far down one of the side tables, hardly cared to join in the revelry. They were waiting for a summons to attend the duke. They had no idea what he wanted of them, but when his grace issued a request, it became a command so far as his personal armourer and his eldest son were concerned. Both the elder and the younger were dressed in the livery of Brittany with tabards that displayed the duke's coat of arms – ermine on a pale blue ground. They were curious and anxious as might be expected. The duke's champion, Sir Gervaise Montaine, had told them to make themselves available this evening. Normally they would be

6

stuffing themselves with the best of the viands, as their companions were, but neither would have much appetite until they found out what was wanted of them.

Presently there was a stir throughout the whole company as Antoinette de Maignelais rose from her seat to leave the revels. Francis stood and bowed graciously as she curtsied to him before sweeping out of the hall attended by her ladies. Francis remained standing and indicated with a wave of his hand that the feast should continue. He walked to the side of the hall and engaged in conversation with one of his men at arms, his champion, Sir Gervaise Montaine. Sir Gervaise beckoned over a lackey and spoke a few words. The lackey hurried away and trotted towards the low table where the armourer and his son were seated, watching duke Francis' every move.

"His grace wishes to speak with you, Simon and your son Laurence," the lackey informed them peremptorily. Lackeys always spoke this way when carrying out instructions from a lord, as if some of the nobleman's authority somehow devolved to them. The two men clambered over the bench where they had been sitting and followed the lackey who bowed low in front of Sir Gervaise and the duke. "Simon the armourer and his son Laurence," he announced. Sir Gervaise waved him away. The duke stood by his side regarding with intelligent interest the two armourers who had both fallen to their knees and bowed their heads.

Sir Gervaise gave a nod towards Laurence. "Simon, his grace understands that your son wishes to spread his wings and move away from us here at Nantes?"

"That is indeed so, my lord, though it is not entirely my wish," said Simon raising his head but remaining in his kneeling position in front of the duke. The duke was an elegant man, more so dressed as he was now in his court dress. His hose was of fine dark blue silk and his burgundy coat was richly embroidered with gold and silver thread while the collar showed fine silk embroidery. Around his neck was a thick gold chain from which dangled a simple gold cross. He wore his dark brown hair long and straight except for the bottom, which was carefully curled and protruded from under a tapered hat. His shoes, which were the part of his dress that the two

7

armourers obviously noticed first, were studded with jewels and had extended points that equalled the length of his feet.

"You may stand," said the duke raising a hand. Both men got to their feet. "I am very pleased with your work as my armourer Simon. Sir Gervaise tells me that your son Laurence is also a fine craftsman." He regarded Laurence quizzically. "I have seen some of your work for myself and you show great ability. Why do you wish to leave us, Laurence?"

"I am not unhappy here, your grace, it is just that I feel I need to travel more widely and see something of the world."

The duke recognised a lame excuse when he heard one and adopted a stern expression, which he exchanged with Sir Gervaise. "I suppose your wish to deprive us of your craftsmanship has nothing to do with a certain wench, has it?" Laurence reddened and began to shuffle his feet uncomfortably. "Sir Gervaise, I believe you know something of this young man's behaviour?"

"Yes, your grace," said Sir Gervaise. "There is a certain Helena, daughter of the castle butcher who finds herself enamoured of master Laurence. Her father claims that she has been deflowered by him and that he should marry her."

"Do you know of this, Simon?" asked the duke, sternly.

"Your grace, I do and may I say that Laurence would make her a fine catch, except her family is not one I wish to join to mine."

"And why is that? Do I employ felons to supply my kitchens?"

"No, no your grace, it is just that butchering is a low trade while mine is highly regarded. I have the honour to serve your grace personally, and Laurence has made many fine pieces of armour for your men at arms. He has a good future and the girl has been set on him by her father, who hopes to use her to improve his own standing."

Simon was a little puzzled by the moral stance that duke Francis seemed to be taking. Francis had deflowered many of his own servant girls while his mistress, Antoinette de Maignelais, had three of her own bastards here at court. Still, it didn't do to question a lord as they had the right of life or death over anyone who displeased them. He had the feeling all this was leading somewhere and he hoped that they both might escape from their predicament without too much trouble.

"If this is just a question of a deflowered virgin, then why not just pay the man off? There is no reason for Laurence to marry the girl just because of a tumble or two." The duke turned his attention to the young armourer. "Laurence, perhaps you could explain?"

Laurence was beginning to feel that the duke already knew the whole story, and that he was being played with.

"There have been problems, your grace. The girl has three brothers and they have been causing trouble for me in the town. Though I can take care of myself in a fight, these three are part of an extended gang and they are a threat to me and to my family. As you may know, I have a younger brother and he too has been threatened. I think that if I make myself scarce for a while matters will calm down once the butcher knows his scheming can come to nothing."

"I see," mused the duke. "And where were you thinking of going?"

"To Tournai," replied Laurence. "We have family there and I can always find work as an armourer. My uncle, my mother's brother has been told to expect me."

The duke looked at Sir Gervaise who acknowledged his glance with a conspiratorial smile.

"I have a certain task that you can help me with. Go with Sir Gervaise now and he will tell you all about it." The duke turned to Sir Gervaise. "Have a word with the castle butcher and let him know that I do not wish the family of my armourer to be distracted in their service to me. I can replace a butcher easier that I can find a good armourer." Sir Gervaise bowed his head in acceptance. Duke Francis then spoke to Simon. "You can go about your business in peace. I have something I wish your son to do in service to me. It will, indeed involve him moving away from Nantes for a while."

Sir Gervaise paused while the duke returned to his place at the high table, then beckoned them to follow him.

"Simon, you may return to table. Laurence, you come with me." Simon, intensely curious, returned to the table with a better appetite than he left it. His immediate companions were desperate in their attempts to get him to say what had gone on and he was the object of a hundred pairs of eyes and ears. When he made it clear that duke Francis would not wish his business discussed with them, they all returned to the feast leaving Simon the subject of intense speculation.

Sir Gervaise took Laurence along a corridor from the main hall and into a small chamber. He signed to Laurence to close the heavy oak door. The chamber contained a table and a couple of chairs. Heavy tapestries hung around its walls, which, Laurence knew, tended to muffle the sound of speech and thus allowed a measure of security from prying ears. The knight settled himself into one of the chairs and indicated to Laurence that he should sit in the other. Laurence knew Sir Gervaise fairly well, particularly as he was the duke's champion and was always at the forges discussing the many aspects of the armourer's art, for that is what Laurence and his father considered it to be. Physically Sir Gervaise was typical of a successful man at arms. Short, with a broad chest and heavily muscled torso, he had developed the strength to carry a lance, or hack and hew at his opponents from horseback with a variety of weapons. Few could oppose him in a straight fight. For the moment he was in his court dress, which did not entirely suit his stocky frame. His beard was neatly trimmed and his hair had been oiled and curled; nevertheless nothing could disguise the animal strength of the man.

"You armourers are pretty knowledgeable when it comes to great affairs," he began, "so you will be aware of the problems we are having here in Brittany with Louis the eleventh of France." It was a statement requiring no particular answer, so Laurence gave a nod of understanding. He knew that the French king coveted duke Francis' lands, and had not, as yet, worked out how he was going to wrest them from him. One stumbling block was duke Charles of Burgundy, who was also disputing with Louis and whose ambitions were engaging the immediate attention of the French king.

Sir Gervaise continued: "Edward of England is presently in exile in Burgundy, having been chased out of that troublesome country by his erstwhile friend the earl of Warwick, Richard Neville and his own brother, the duke of Clarence. For the moment, then, he is no longer *King* Edward. Warwick has replaced the previously deposed monarch, Henry the sixth on the throne and is now controlling events in England, though his position is far from secure."

"Yes, I have heard this," said Laurence, anxious to display his knowledge of events to the knight. "Also, Margaret of Anjou, along with her and Henry's son, the Prince of Wales is in France with Louis's support and is hoping for his help in invading England to join with Warwick."

"Quite so," said the knight. "She has more balls than her husband, who, though he might be Henry the sixth, king of England, has too few wits remaining to him to oppose her. This is, then, a dangerous situation for us here in Brittany. If Queen Margaret invades, with Warwick's support she will effectively rule through her son, king Henry being of little account. We need not concern ourselves with that, except if it should happen, then England will become an ally of France, having an obligation to Louis. France will then be able to call on England for help in dealing with Burgundy, and if duke Charles falls, then Louis will turn his attention to us."

"I understand, but I cannot see how we can do anything to influence matters," said Laurence quizzically.

"We cannot, directly. For one thing we do not want to be seen to be taking sides. In fact, we must not do so because the game has not been played out. Everything depends on who invades England first. If Queen Margaret, then with Warwick in support it is most likely they will control England. However, if Edward gets there first, he might well take back his crown." Sir Gervaise paused and looked around. On the table was a flask and some wine beakers. He indicated that Laurence should serve him. He took up the flask and poured wine into a beaker and handed it to the knight. Then, to Laurence's surprise Sir Gervaise indicated that he should pour some for himself. Laurence did so with some trepidation. A knight of Sir Gervaise' rank would not normally consider sharing a drink with an artisan, even a well-favoured one, ale perhaps on campaign, and then only at the forge, but here in duke Francis' chateau? Unthinkable!

Sir Gervaise leaned forward conspiratorially. "Something has happened to change things. Until now, duke Charles has reluctantly tolerated Edward's exile in Burgundy. Like us, he had not wanted to back Edward in case the Warwick faction manipulated king Henry into supporting Louis. It is only because his wife is Edward's sister that he has had anything to do with him. However, Louis has taken matters into his own hands – he has

11

invaded Burgundy! Now," he said quietly, " while Charles has the strength to resist France for the time being, he can no longer remain neutral so far as England is concerned. He has offered to lend Edward the money he needs to pay for an invasion army. Should this succeed, then England will be indebted to Burgundy and therefore under an obligation to offer military aid to Charles against Louis, who is supporting Queen Margaret, Edward's chief enemy." Sir Gervaise leaned back in his chair and observed Laurence's reaction.

Laurence sipped at his wine to give himself time to think. He could not, for the life of him, figure out where this was leading or how he could possibly have a part in it.

"I can see how this affects Burgundy, and surely, if Louis is engaged there he is, at least for the moment, no threat to Brittany?"

"Well, everything depends on the situation in England," replied Sir Gervaise. "Edward is keen to get his crown back and he has his formidable brother Richard, duke of Gloucester with him. Both of them are clever and hard fighting men, though Gloucester is somewhat young and has yet to prove himself in battle. They only have a small force and must rely on recruiting a bigger one in England if they are to have any chance of beating the Warwick faction. Remember Warwick controls king Henry, and he can therefore raise levees against Edward in the king's name. Also, if Queen Margaret invades too, Edward is in serious trouble."

"Then the situation is in the hands of God. I cannot see what we here in Brittany can do about it." Laurence shifted uncomfortably in his seat and wondered what was coming next.

"You are correct. There is nothing we can do for the moment. Yet whatever happens is bound to affect Brittany sooner or later. What is needed is information. Good solid information that can be relied on, so that duke Francis can plan his diplomatic strategy."

Laurence understood that few matters between princes were decided on the battlefield. In the long term it was diplomacy and the grand game played out by manipulating opposing factions that decided the fate of nations. Much depended on alliances formed by marriage and the lands that came as a result and mutual agreements between princes.

Sir Gervaise continued. "It is convenient that you wish to leave Nantes. I want you to join with Edward's army, which is currently at Flushing. You will be given a letter of introduction to one Nicholas Olds, who is Edward's personal armourer. He and your father know of each other, though I believe they have never met. He will be short of skilled armourers and it will be a good opportunity for you to join him. That will get you close to Edward and those nobles who are with him. I believe that lord Hastings and earl Rivers are presently assembling the ships making preparation for embarking an army."

"I have heard of them – I think that earl Rivers is the brother of Edward's wife, queen Elizabeth?"

"Yes, and Hastings is Edward's chief councillor. You will have to tread carefully where these two are concerned. Hastings cannot stand Rivers, or indeed any of queen Elizabeth's family. They are united in a common cause, but little else."

"It seems that you are expecting Edward to regain his crown," Laurence said carefully, testing the knight's opinion.

"I expect nothing, but I hope he will. Obviously it would be better for Brittany if that happens, but in any case you must find the means of attaching yourself to someone close to the throne, whoever may be sitting on it. As an armourer with considerable skill, and seeing that you will be in the company of Nicholas Olds, you should be able to find appropriate employment with someone at the English court. This is, in fact, why you have been chosen. Your father is armourer to duke Francis and as his son, taught by him, you have a close association with the making of fine armour. English men-at-arms will recognise this and be keen to engage your services. The fact that you will have arrived in England with an invading force matters little. You have no personal attachments to anyone there and as a skilled artisan it is your craft that will be in demand, not your personal loyalty."

Laurence realised that for all this to happen a considerable number of obstacles would have to be overcome. First there was the first contact with Nicholas Olds. If Edward's armourer rejected him, then the plan was stillborn. Next there was the small matter of the invasion itself. There was bound to be serious fighting and it sounded as though Edward's army would be insufficient to ensure success on its own. On the other hand, armourers would remain with the baggage train and not be expected to take part in a battle, which was fine in theory. With just a small force at his command, it is likely that Edward would call on all able-bodied men to take up arms. Laurence was not too averse to this, yet with such unequal odds, if he failed to survive a fight, then again the plan would come to nothing. Laurence made these points to Sir Gervaise.

"Of course, I realise all that, but I consider that you have the best chance of getting into a convenient position and maintaining it once you get there. As a native of Brittany, you can adopt allegiance to any of the disputing factions in England without having to compromise your loyalty. The very fact that you have no allegiances there will tend to encourage the confidence of whoever it is you end up attached to."

There was much sense in this, though Laurence well understood what was not being said. A nobleman could not be sent on such an errand because he would have to take sides and thus be of limited use if his side lost. Moreover, and again Laurence did not expect Sir Gervaise to admit it, nobles could never be trusted as they were susceptible to bribes and would alter their loyalties to suit their own factions at home. There was a considerable amount of freedom of choice for Laurence, and he was beginning to realise the potential for himself in the scheme. He would have a secure home base in Brittany while being able to exploit the opportunities for advancement in his trade and status in England. Whoever he became attached to in England would have his personal loyalty, even though he was also secretly in the service of duke Francis. Francis had no particular enemies in England and so Laurence would be comfortable in his service to both, having no requirement for treachery. He comforted himself with the thought that he was to go to England as Francis' informant, not as a subversive spy.

"If I am able to establish myself in England how am I to communicate with duke Francis?"

Sir Gervaise gave a smile of approval. Clearly Laurence had accepted the scheme and now needed to find out the practical details. "First of all, I understand that you speak some English."

"A little, my mother is English and though we never use it at home, she has taught me enough to get by."

"I wouldn't be too sure of that," replied the knight, "English is a barbaric tongue and even Englishmen cannot make up their minds how to speak it."

Laurence thought of the Breton dialect and how different it was from the French spoken at Court, though he knew a Breton could speak perfectly well with a Cornishman. In fact, Laurence could converse in Breton and French too, because his family had professional dealings with Francis' men at arms and courtiers. Most Bretons would have difficulty speaking the rough native French of Burgundy, or even France itself, so it was not only England where variety of language hampered communication. However, French was the universal courtly language so provided he could become an armourer for an English man at arms, then he could speak French to him at least and hope that his limited English would get him by with others when necessary.

"You can write, I believe?" said Sir Gervaise.

"Only in French. I have some Latin and my written English is worse than my speech."

"French is all that is required for writing, though I expect that even this will be limited. It is never a good idea to put anything in writing, unless absolutely necessary." Sir Gervaise looked at him directly. "I want you to remember this name: Cornelius Quirke. Repeat the name."

"Cornelius Quirke."

"Can you fix that in your memory?"

"Of course."

Sir Gervaise gave a nod of approval. "Cornelius Quirke is an apothecary in London. You will find his shop by the Cripplegate. As soon as you are able you will contact him. He will be expecting you. Report to him directly. He will give you any instructions we might wish you to have and you will answer all his questions. In addition, if there is anything he has overlooked you think would be useful to duke Francis, then tell it to him. He will communicate with us here at Nantes.

"Is that all you want of me?" asked Laurence, wondering exactly what was in store for him.

"Don't you think that is enough for now?" replied the knight. "You will have to become established at or near the English Court first. That will be difficult enough. If you succeed, and I expect you to, then Cornelius will let you know if we want anything from you other than information. We might or we might not – it depends on how events unfold and who wins the seat of power in England, and how firmly they are seated there."

"Very good, Sir Gervaise, Laurence said. "How am I to get to where king Edward is assembling his army?"

"You will leave here for St. Malo, then take a certain vessel whose captain has instructions to put you ashore at the mouth of the Somme. We cannot safely get you to Flushing by sea as the pas-de-Calais is too dangerous, being infested with pirates of several countries. You will be given money to purchase a horse and enough for you to pay your way, then you will travel to your uncle's house in Tournai. As you say, he is already expecting you there because your mother has made arrangements with him. He thinks you are escaping the clutches of the fair Helene, which you are, of course. Once there you will prepare yourself for the journey to Flushing. How you get there is up to you."

"One problem," said Laurence. "If I am to practice my trade I shall need my tools. Master Olds will not provide me with any, besides, my tools are part of me. I need my own if I am to work properly. No armourer would travel without his own personal set."

"Then you will need to take those you need with you. I presume you will not be taking a forge and anvil along too?"

"No, Sir Gervaise," laughed Laurence. "I shall select only those tools that are essential to me and hope to purchase anything more I might need when established in England." Laurence raised his eyebrows quizzically in the expectation that the knight might offer the money to buy them.

"When you are established in England, you will be in the pay of whoever's household you are servant to. No doubt he will pay you for your services and you can buy what you need then." Sir Gervaise got to his feet, indicating that the interview was at an end. Laurence placed the wine cup on the table and stood also. "You may send a message by your uncle when you leave Tournai for Flushing. After that, I shall expect to hear only from Cornelius Quirke when you are in London."

Sir Gervaise gave Laurence a slight nod of his head and strode to the door. Laurence hurried over and opened it for him. The knight passed through and returned to the revels. Laurence stood for a moment framed in the doorway, then closing the door softly, as if to slam it would betray a secret, he too returned to the banquet, hoping that there would be enough food remaining to satisfy his rapidly developing hunger.

Chapter 1 – Flushing, March 1471

The road to Flushing had been bad enough, but the quagmire churned up by the army bustling outside its walls and around the harbour caused wheels to sink deeply into the mud. The cart fortunately was small, and the driver walked beside the weary horse that was dragging it along. Both were tired and bedraggled, spattered by mud and panting clouds of vapour into the cold air. The camp was a huddle of tents and shelters interspersed with small fires whose smoke was soon dispersed in the damp, fitful wind that came from the sea. What appeared to be a couple of guards, designated as such by the halberds they held, rose up from their squat position by a small iron brazier and moved into the path of the cart.

"State your business!" grunted one in English, the shaft of the halberd held at an upward angle, ready but not particularly threatening. The other placed the butt of his weapon on the ground and leant on it indifferently. The man stopped the cart and threw the short rein over the back of the horse.

"I come offer my service your king," he said in broken English.

"And what might that be?" asked the soldier.

"I am armourer, I have letter for Nicholas Olds."

"He's asking for Old Nick," the soldier chortled to his companion.

"Your name?" demanded the soldier, "and where do you come from?"

"Laurence de la Halle," said the armourer. "I come from Tournai."

The soldier thought for a few moments. He had no real idea of where Tournai was but it was miserable standing here in the chill wind and he knew that skilled workers were in short supply. It was not long before he made his mind up.

"Call the boy over and he can take him to the forges."

The other soldier shouted to a group of huddled soldiery who were busy cooking something in a pot over a fire and a skinny looking youth stood up and came over.

"Take this man to Old Nick at the forges and wait until Nick has decided what to do with him, then come back here." The boy nodded and with a longing glance at the cooking pot where his companions were, trudged off into the camp. The soldier indicated with a jerk of his head that Laurence should follow the boy. The armourer took hold of the horse's bridle and led it with the cart into the camp after the boy. He took him to where a bank of earth provided a defence before the ditch that surrounded the walls of the town. A series of lean-to sheds had been erected against the slope of the earthwork. Laurence could tell by the acrid smell and the sound of hammering that this was where the forges were located.

The boy led him past the first of the forges where smiths were beating away at the metal sparking on their anvils. Fires blazed as bellows were pumped and clouds of steam plumed the cold air as hot metal was quenched in water. There was a grinding shed where blades were being honed and another where harness was being polished. It looked as if peasant workers from the surrounding country had been engaged to turn the grinding wheels and pump bellows. Most of the work seemed to be the making of horseshoes and arrow tips. He noted with interest that the latter were the narrow tapered type rather than the twin-bladed armour-piercing quarrel heads. In another of the sheds several smiths were weaving mail and hammering the individual links with rivets to close them, though he noted that these seemed to be repairs rather than the making of new mail.

As they came to the middle section of the work sheds the boy stopped and spoke to a youth who was heating metal rod and cutting it over an iron stake fitted into an anvil. Laurence could see that these were going to end up as arming nails for jointing armour so he reckoned he had reached the armoury. A couple of other men were working away and the two forges in the shed were blazing away furiously. The youth looked curiously at Laurence, then turned and slouched over to where a man of about middle age was using callipers to measure the internal dimensions of a bascinet. He was wearing a cap and apron, both of leather, and he held his head to one side to hear what the youth was saying to him. Laurence guessed he was hard of hearing, an affliction common among those who spent their lives working in the incessant din of a forge. He looked to where Laurence was standing then after a moment beckoned him over. Laurence came up to him and bowed his head respectfully.

"I have been told to ask for Nicholas Olds," Laurence said. "You are he, I hope?"

"Aye," grunted Olds. "What is it you want?"

"I am armourer and I wish to serve the English king. My name is Laurence de la Halle"

Olds looked at him suspiciously. Close up Laurence could see that he was quite an old man, though his arms were sinewy and still well muscled. His hands bore the scars that years of working hot metal inevitably produced. The youth who was standing just behind him was staring open mouthed until Olds noticed he was idle and impatiently waved him away. As the youth hurried back to his work, Olds turned his full attention to Laurence.

"And which English king would that be? We have two of them," he said with a narrowing of his eyes. "Who do you mean?"

"King Edward. I think he is king is he not?"

"Well that is a question we intend to settle. Who was it sent you to me?"

Laurence dug into an oiled leather wallet that hung by his side and took out a folded paper, which he opened and presented to Olds evidently in the expectation that all questions would be answered satisfactorily. Olds looked at the letter having little difficulty in understanding the French.

"You have your Guild papers? You will not be accepted without them."

"*Oui, par ici.*" Laurence reached into the wallet and produced a further document. Olds scrutinised it then passed it back.

"I know something of your father and I know who Sir Gervaise Montaine is," he growled, "but this letter does not state why you are here."

Laurence spoke up: "I have many skill and I wish to work in England. There is too much trouble here to make a life."

"There is plenty of trouble in England, too. That's why we are here getting ready to invade and win the crown back for Edward." Olds looked alternately at the letter then at Laurence clearly wondering what to do. He saw a young fellow of average height in his early twenties who had the rough appearance of a traveller. He had wrapped himself in a worn woollen cloak with a hood, which gave some protection from the elements. He had thrown the hood back and the hem of his cloak was spattered with mud. He had on a

20

leather belt, which held a pair of iron keys on a ring and a dagger in a scabbard. His black hair was dishevelled and his chin either needed to be shaved, or something of a beard cultivated. His eyes were dark with a hint of desperation in them, but not that of a dangerous felon, rather vulnerable he thought. He was well muscled and had the hardened hands of someone who worked manually for a living. Finally he made up his mind.

For a moment he diverted his attention to the youth, and the boy who had brought Lawrence to the forge. They were chattering to one another and one of them should be working.

"You, boy – clear off! I'll deal with this. And you, Peter, get back to work!" The boy scurried off the way he had come and the youth Peter took up his work, though still watching what was going on with Laurence. Olds realised, too that the others in the forge had also slackened their work-pace but they suddenly increased their efforts before the master turned on them.

Olds well knew that those who called themselves armourer were often little more than smiths who could do rough work but had not the skill for working fine arms. "I had better see what you can do." Olds looked about him and his gaze rested on a cuisse that was lying on a bench. He took it up and offered it to Laurence.

"This is not a good fit for the new owner and some adjustments need to be made. See here where the metal is too thin. It will not sustain a hard blow. We need to thicken the metal and change the dimensions to suit the slimmer thigh of the new owner. Show me how you would do that."

Laurence examined the cuisse, which was intended to protect the thigh of the owner. It was not very well made and by its style looked as if it was fairly old. It had probably been taken from the battlefield and who knows how many owners it had served before turning up here.

"I need my hammers from my cart."

Olds nodded and they both walked out of the shed to where the cart was, the horse still standing patiently waiting for its master. Laurence lifted the sacking in the well of the cart and selected a couple of hammers. Olds noticed with professional satisfaction that the striking surfaces were smooth and polished, essential to prevent any blemishes transferring to the surface of the work. Next, Laurence pulled out a curiously shaped lump of iron that

21

incorporated a square tapered shaft. Olds placed a hand on Laurence's arm.

"Never mind that. I have plenty of stakes that you can pick from." Laurence unfastened his travelling cloak and threw it into the cart. Back in the forge, Laurence selected a "T" headed stake and set it into the square of an iron stake plate and took up the cuisse.

"I think this might work cold," he said, placing the cuisse over the "T" stake. He proceeded to carefully hammer around the thin part of the metal, letting it flow gradually over the forming stake until some of the surrounding metal had been moved into the thin section, gradually thickening it. He controlled the strike of the hammer, and worked so that the surface of the metal became smooth and hard. Olds watched him as he worked, noting the careful control of the hammer blows and the way in which he blended the marks of the blows together to present a hardly blemished surface that would require little in the way of smoothing.

"It seems you have the skill," said Olds after watching him work for a while. Let me take you to Master Caxton, who is helping to organise the army supply train. He will take a look at your letter." He regarded Laurence's appearance critically. "You cannot go in that condition. Get yourself cleaned up. Have you any better clothes than what you are standing up in?" Laurence was dressed for the road with a high-neck leather jerkin over a linen shirt. His breeches were of coarse wool stuffed into calf-high boots.

"I have good hose and doublet in my baggage, *mais malhereusement* these are the only boots I have." He looked down at his feet, his arms spread in a gesture of hopelessness. His boots were of reasonable repair but heavily coated with road mud to above his ankles.

"Master Caxton is an important man, you must clean yourself up and change into better clothes if you have them. The boots will do if you wipe the mud off and give them a good brushing. I expect they will soon get into a mess again when we go into the town."

Laurence went to his cart and tugged out a wooded chest that had a secure lock. He took out a key from a ring around his belt and opened it. Inside he had a few clothes and other belongings. He took out a worn but good quality doublet and fairly new woollen breeches. He sat on the back of his cart and changed his clothes.

22

He had folded the cloak and placed it in the wooden chest, which he locked. The boots cleaned up fairly well and soon he was able to present himself before Nicholas Olds in a rather better condition than when he had first arrived. He noted that Olds, too, had changed. His leather apron was hanging from a post and now he had on a brown surplice under a fine woollen cloak. He wore a cap with ribbon that played over his right shoulder and he had on a pair of brown leather boots. These garments had apparently been taken from a space to one side of the forge, where a curtain obscured whatever lay behind, Laurence guessed the armourer's sleeping quarters.

Nicholas Olds gave a series of orders to one of his workmen, telling him that he was going into the town and would return later. He ordered the youth Peter to attend to Laurence's horse and cart then beckoned to Laurence to follow him. They walked through the camp where business was well under way for embarkation of the army into the dozens of ships that were either anchored or tied up inside the harbour that was the principal reason for the location of the town of Flushing. Everywhere men were working on the preparations. Fletchers were attaching flights and tips to arrows, while bowyers were making bowstrings then stringing bows to ensure they were taut enough before removing the strings for waxing and storage. Saddlers were stitching away while farriers attended to the shoes of the horses. Here and there the household men of the nobles attended to the cleaning of plate armour while others ensured that the blazons of the owners were painted clearly for identification in battle. Horses were everywhere, not just those of the nobility, where each man at arms would have four horses to carry into England, but also for the wagons and as draught animals too. Even so, Laurence had noted as he had made his approach that morning, the army was pitifully small for an invasion force.

Laurence and Nicholas entered the town through one of its gates. Nicholas was clearly familiar with the guards because they let the two men through with scarcely a nod. They walked a short distance through the narrow streets, stepping over the ordure that was a feature of any town, until they reached what looked to be the house of a wealthy merchant where Nicholas banged upon a shuttered grill in the heavy door that was the only opening on to the street. Laurence noted that windows were placed in the upper storeys, which appeared to number three floors, but sensibly none in the lower reaches of the house. A small flap behind the grill opened and a bearded face appeared. When the face saw Nicholas he closed the flap and the sound of bolts being withdrawn could be heard. Presently the door opened and the man, who must have been working in the office of a porter, indicated that they should come inside. Once inside the porter closed the door and shot the bolts home.

"Good day Master Olds," he said.

"Good day, Humphrey," Olds replied. "Is Master Caxton at home?"

"That he is, Master Olds. He is with my lords Rivers and Hastings. Shall I tell him you are here?" The man looked quizzically at Laurence.

"Tell him I am here and that I have someone with me I would like him to meet."

They were standing in a room that had plastered walls, white with lime wash. Light came in from a window high up above the door and a side window that looked out onto a courtyard. There were two other doors, one of which let on to the courtyard, and another that must have been the means of entering the ground floor rooms of the house. To the left a staircase with intricately carved banisters led upwards. The man Humphrey bowed and hurried up the staircase. Presently he clattered down the stairs and said:

"The master will see you. He is in his solar. Please come this way." He turned back to the staircase and led the way upward. They climbed to the third floor and were led towards a room at the back of the house. Humphrey opened the door and both men entered through. Humphrey closed the door but remained in the room, taking a discreet position to one side.

William Caxton was seated at a table directly in front of a large window that looked out from the back of the house. On either side were two men who were examining documents on the table. The table was piled with papers and, Laurence noticed unusually a book, which lay open. Caxton held a pen and had been writing something when he turned and looked at them. He was about fifty years old, but not obviously afflicted by age as many others of his years often were. A chest crammed with papers lay open by the side of his table and there was a padded chair beside the plain

wooden one he was presently sitting on. There was a good fire in
the room. Clearly he liked his comfort and had the money to pay
for it. His simple gown was black and he wore a woollen cap with
flaps that hung loosely by his ears. Laurence saw that Caxton
screwed up his eyes when regarding them, probably because he
had just turned from a lighted window but perhaps his eyesight
was becoming dim. The other two men gave the newcomers a
cursory glance then returned their attention to the papers they were
scrutinising on the table.

"Good day, Master Olds. I hope you are well?" he said slowly
getting to his feet. "My bones are beginning to creak somewhat.
The cold penetrates this house and I do not have the advantage of
your forge fires to keep the chill out."

Nicholas gave a chuckle. "Unfortunately, forge fires need a good
draught which finds its way around my body before reaching the
forges, so my condition is not much better than yours, Master
Caxton."

Caxton and Nicholas shook hands in a businesslike way and then
Caxton regarded Laurence quizzically. "And who is this?"

Laurence bowed his head respectfully and stepped forward. "My
name is Laurence de la Halle and I have a letter here from Sir
Gervaise Montaine, in the service of Francis, Duke of Brittany."

Caxton raised his eyebrows and gazed at Laurence with some
interest, then turned his attention to the letter. The two men at the
table lifted their heads and began to take interest in what was being
said. William Caxton read through the letter.

"You are a Frenchman, right?" Caxton addressed him in French.
Laurence gave a slight bow in agreement.

"I was born in France, at Tournai, but my family moved to Brittany
when my father won the position of Master Armourer to duke
Francis." I grew up there and think of myself as a Breton."

"It says here that you have been in the employ of your father, who
is indeed armourer to duke Francis," Caxton stated tapping the
paper with an ink-stained index finger. "It seems that Sir Gervaise
has a high opinion of your abilities, so why have you left him to
come here?"

"I wish to strike out on my own. My father was reluctant to let me
go, but I managed to persuade him. Besides, he has my brother
who is just three years younger than me and who will soon take my

25

place. Also, there has been some trouble over a girl and I find I need to make myself scarce for a while."

One of the two men who were with Caxton stepped forward. "Does duke Francis know you are here?" Laurence regarded him carefully. He was clearly of the nobility because of his dress and manner and he spoke courtly French. He had a silk tabard over his tunic, which was of costly material and he wore a gold chain around his neck with a red pendant jewel dangling from it.

"He does, and he has suggested I try my fortune with Edward the fourth of England. He is aware of the present difficulties regarding the English crown and he didn't want me to offer my skills to Louis of France or duke Charles of Burgundy."

"I see." Caxton turned to the other two men in the room. "This is earl Rivers," he said sweeping his arm gracefully to the nearest of the two. "Along with my lord Hastings here, we three are responsible for provisioning the army for England." Rivers took the letter from Caxton's hand and read it through, then questioned Laurence further.

"Why should duke Francis deprive himself of a good armourer? Perhaps your skill is not as useful as you think. We are not carrying extra baggage to England."

"I can show you. Just give me something to make or repair and you can judge for yourself."

"That is out of the question. We have started embarking so we do not have time for examining the work of a tradesman," said the earl, testily. "It says here that your father, Simon is known to Master Olds. Is that correct, Master Olds?"

"I have heard of him, certainly. We master armourers tend to hear of each other's reputation. Simon de la Halle is indeed known to be a fine craftsman." Nicholas replied in French. As a master armourer he needed to converse with his noble patrons so his French was almost as good as his English.

Caxton laid a hand on Rivers' arm. "Perhaps we can discuss this privately." Rivers regarded Laurence suspiciously, but nodded his assent and returned to the table where he placed the letter.

Caxton turned to the man Humphrey. "Take Master Laurence to the kitchen and see that he gets some food and drink. I shall send for him later." Humphrey bowed in obedience and indicated with a wave of his arm the way through the door. As soon as the door closed behind Laurence, Caxton turned to Olds.

"What is your opinion, Nicholas?"

Olds did not reply immediately as he gave himself time to gather his thoughts. "The fact that he is French means little. Though Tournai claims to be neutral, being close to both France and Burgundy the town inclines towards France. Duke Francis, on the other hand, is no friend of king Louis and if this young man is Breton by inclination, he is unlikely to savour the politics of France. His skill as an armourer seems to be genuine enough. I have only given him a very small test, but real skill is impossible to disguise, and his hammer-craft testifies to that. What is more, if he has been armouring for his father in the service of duke Francis of Brittany he must be good enough to work with quality armour."

"If he had been sent by Margaret of York, whom I have the honour of serving, I would have known of it," said William, "so we know he is not connected with her husband, Charles, duke of Burgundy. That means he could be either one of Warwick's men or perhaps king Louis. There is the Tournai connection to consider."

"Or he might just be who he says he is, someone who wishes to make a new life for himself in England."

"If only life were that simple." Nicholas stared into the fire and William left him to his thoughts. Presently he came to a decision.

"I know that he has the skill of an armourer and that is something I am very short of. I can make good use of him for the moment. Let him cross with us to England. Who knows what will happen when Edward lands. If we are defeated this conversation is of no account. If we are victorious, and Edward regains his crown, then everything changes and we shall have to see what happens. There is one thing we can be sure of, if Laurence de la Halle is working for anyone other than himself, sooner or later he will have to show his hand. Let's worry about that later. For the present we are bound for England. Let that be enough."

"I think you are probably right in what you say," agreed William. "I will make some enquiries with Margaret at the court of Charles. Meanwhile, use him to good account, but keep a close watch."

"Do not worry about that. I shall work him so hard he will have no time for anything but my business."

27

Laurence was sitting on a stool at a bench where the light allowed him to manipulate the armoured joint he was repairing. He had creased the lower lame of the poleyn, the shaped part that protected the knee, which he had made new to replace a damaged one and was preparing to attach it to the poleyn itself. He checked that the lame was able to fit snugly under the poleyn, then fitted it in place with arming nails either side and checked again that it could pivot freely. He slipped a slim spacer around the arming nail between the lame and the poleyn, then proceeded to hammer the nails until each was formed into a neat flattened dome. He then removed the spacer and checked the movement of the joint, noticing with satisfaction its smoothness. This was simple work for a master armourer and he felt some resentment at having been given this and similar tasks by Nicholas Olds. It was due, in part, to the influence of Jack Snipe, Nicholas' assistant, who seemed to resent the presence of the newcomer at the forge. Snipe was a skilled armourer, though Laurence had noted he lacked finesse when it came to fine detailed work and ornamentation. This type of work was done by Nicholas Olds himself. That was not unusual; it was Nicholas who dealt with the knights and nobles who came to the forge for their arming needs. His was the reputation that was at stake if the work was not up to a high standard.

Laurence's work on the poleyn was the last job he would do before packing away his tools and helping with the dismantling of the portable forges for transporting by sea. He had been at the forges for three days, enough time to acquaint himself with his fellow armourers and to gain the taciturn approval of Nicholas Olds. The boy Peter had attached himself to Laurence, that is when he managed to escape the notice of Jack Snipe. It turned out that he was the son of one of Nicholas Olds' nephews who had been lost to plague along with his mother, leaving the boy destitute, and Nicholas had taken him in. Normally there would have been a fee to the master armourer for taking an apprentice so it was a mark of generosity that a place had been found for him. This fact was not lost on Jack Snipe who felt that this made the boy a charity case who could be worked and abused according to his will. Laurence had done no more that to talk kindly to the boy and correct his basic French, the boy speaking English as his native tongue. Once he had shown him how to close up an arming nail, but this was enough to incur the displeasure of Snipe who felt that he alone had the instruction of the boy. Laurence noted that Snipe habitually prefaced any instruction he gave with the remark "a good armourer will do it this way." The implication was that he, Snipe, was thus a "good" armourer, though Laurence had noted this before in certain craftsmen. When in the company of their fellows they often fail to stand out, so impressing a boy while instructing him was a way of satisfying an inflated ego. Naturally this caused Snipe to believe that when instructing the boy, Laurence was in some way usurping his position, yet another bone of contention.

Just as he finished work on the joint, Peter came over to him and asked to see how the lames fitted into the poleyn. Laurence explained to him the necessity of fitting the lames with the minimum gap, yet with enough clearance to allow the knee joint to move within the armour. Peter was examining the joint with interest when Snape spotted him. He strode over and gave the boy a clout behind his head that sent him sprawling onto the floor of the forge. Laurence was taken back by the unnecessary severity of the blow. Snape reached down and hauled the boy to his feet. Peter was clearly disorientated and stood shakily on his feet. Snape lifted his arm to deliver another blow when he felt his wrist seized in an iron grip. Laurence had taken hold of him and pulled him away from the boy. Snape, who was a strong man, staggered backwards and tripped over a box of arrow heads that were waiting to be taken to the ships in the harbour. As he fell he began to twist sideways and Laurence realised that if he held on to him, Snape would likely end up with a broken arm, so he released him. This let Snape recover slightly, but the momentum of his fall made him do a comical backward trot across the floor before fetching up against an anvil and tumbling head and shoulders over it. The other armourers and a couple of peasant labourers who witnessed the spectacle could not contain their laughter. Snape, his face contorted with rage, got to his feet and hurled himself at Laurence, who deftly stood aside. Again, the unlucky Snape tripped, this time over Laurence's foot, and found himself on his hands and knees in the roadway outside the forge.

29

Snape hauled himself to his feet, his whole body shaking with fury, but this time his recent experience stopped his immediate attack. His eyes darted about the forge and then he found what he was looking for. He took up a heavy hammer that had a long shaft fitted with a square head. He hefted the hammer and began to advance menacingly on Laurence. He was not going to rush at him again; he had been unfortunate and made to look foolish so he was about to get some respect back. He noted with satisfaction that the laughter had stopped.

Laurence had no immediate means of defence. If he were to escape without serious injury he would have to think quickly. He backed rapidly into the forge, desperately looking for something to stop the swing of a heavy hammer. Most of the forge equipment had been packed into boxes or wrapped in oiled cloth. He moved behind an anvil that was still mounted on its stand. Unfortunately this placed his back against the wall and he could retreat no further. His brain was racing for a way out of his predicament when a sudden idea came to him. He feigned a stumble and leaned suddenly forward for support placing his hand flat down invitingly upon the anvil. Snipe, seeing an opportunity to cripple his adversary could not resist swinging and striking down with the hammer. Had he thought about it he would have realised the trap, but spontaneity had worked in Laurence's favour. He swung the hammer and instead of crushing bone he heard it ring as it contacted the bare metal surface of the anvil. Laurence had moved his hand away at the last moment, and Snipe's blow had placed the head of the hammer within grasping distance. Laurence gripped the shaft of the hammer just below the head and heaved it towards him. Snipe, taken off balance by the action of his own blow was jerked towards Laurence who head-butted him in the face. He felt Snape's nose smash under the force of the contact. Laurence grabbed further down the handle of the hammer and twisted it from Snipe's grip. He then reversed the shaft and drove it into his opponent's abdomen. Snape went down into a heap and lay curled up in agony, one hand covering his smashed nose and blood trickling through his fingers.

"That is quite enough!" Shouted a furious Nicholas Olds. He had seen everything from his side closet where he had been attending to his bodily needs. He was hurrying towards the two combatants while desperately tying up his hose. It had all happened so quickly that he hardly had time to get his hose pulled up.

"I think master Snipe would agree with you," said Laurence wryly. Snipe twisted around and glared up with intense hatred at Laurence. He struggled to his feet and sat down on the anvil, clutching his stomach. Olds glared at Laurence.

"Do you not realise how short we are of skilled armourers, to say nothing of fighting men, which you may have to become before long? Here you are, brawling like the common soldiery."

"I merely wished to stop Snipe beating the boy, who had done nothing to deserve such treatment."

"Shut up," replied Olds. "My apprentice is under the charge of Jack Snipe, not you. You had no right to interfere. As it happens Peter had been told to help with embarkation at the docks, not loiter around here. If he had done as he was instructed none of this would have happened."

"I have warned you about this Frenchman," growled Snipe.

"And I have warned you about your brutality to the boy, so don't think I am letting you off the hook," snapped Olds. Snipe grimaced and gave Laurence a foul look. "Besides, if you had not been beaten there might have been murder committed and then I would have lost two armourers." Olds glanced around the forge and his gaze fell on the boy Peter, who had been standing dazed and overawed by what had happened. "You! Get yourself down to our wagons at the docks and attend to your duties as you have been told to do. Laurence, you had better go with him and supervise their proper stowage. Jack, get yourself cleaned up."

"But it is my job to supervise stowage" bleated Snipe, his voice snuffling through blood and damaged gristle. "I would be there now if the Frenchman had not interfered.

"You can supervise your own treatment and recovery. You are in no state to properly attend to my business as you are."

Snipe knew this was true. His guts were aching so much he could hardly stand upright, his head was buzzing like a bee-hive and the blood was still pouring from his smashed nose. He would have to see one of the camp women to set it as straight as possible, though he knew he would carry the marks of his encounter with Laurence for the rest of his life. He determined to serve the same to his adversary at the first convenient opportunity.

Chapter 2 – Invasion

Laurence the Armourer stood patiently on the quay watching with interest the embarkation of the horses into the invasion ships. He noted how horses and the sea are mutually incompatible. They might enjoy a gallop along the fringes of the shore, but that is the absolute extent of their recreational involvement. Transportation of horses by sea was fraught with problems from panicking animals, and damage done to individuals who could all too easily fall foul of lashing hooves and gnashing teeth. For this reason the horses were always loaded immediately before sailing. This reduced the time they would have to spend in the ships and also conserved the limited rations of fodder they required for the voyage. The few remaining beasts were still in temporary stalls along the quayside of Flushing harbour. The fleet had been delayed for some days due to bad weather but now, on the 11th March 1471 the final embarkation of the horses was well under way. This involved the use of block and tackle with dockside hoists to lift them in slings before lowering them into the hold of a ship. Once inside the ship they were placed in stalls close beside one another and head-to-head. Most animals when suspended hung in pitiful dejection especially when their eyes were covered with sacking, but there were always some that lashed out, particularly the more spirited war-horses, which made their stowage difficult and dangerous.

Everything else was stowed on the ships ready for the expedition to England, where Edward the fourth of that nation would attempt to regain the crown he had ignominiously lost due to the machinations of his own brother, George, Duke of Clarence along with Richard Neville, Earl of Warwick – the very man who had previously assisted him to the throne of England by deposing Henry the sixth. This feat had earned him the epithet "Warwick the Kingmaker" and he was demonstrating that he believed he could unmake kings too. These two had placed the ineffective and mentally weak Henry back on the throne while his wife, Margaret of Anjou, presently in France, was preparing an invasion fleet of her own to come to the aid of her husband. She, along with her son the Prince of Wales, intended joining with Warwick and Clarence to defeat Edward's force. After the victory she expected to rule through her son, though Warwick and Clarence might have other ideas. King Louis of France was aiding her and it was decidedly uncertain which of the two expeditions would reach England first. Edward, of course, had the added problem of raising support in England to swell the ranks of the small army of English and Flemish mercenaries he had managed to assemble at Flushing.

For the moment the quay was busy with animals, and a host of hawkers selling their wares. Conspicuous amongst these were the peddlers of holy relics. Some were monks, while other hawkers sold such relics along with their various trinkets. Holy relics were always a good trade where there was an army; they offered divine protection against injury and disease or, if calamity should befall the owner, a direct path through purgatory into heaven. Laurence knew that most of these were counterfeit and was grateful that he already had proper protection of his own. He fingered the small silver capsule that he wore around his neck suspended on a strong leather thong. It contained metal filings from the nail that had held Christ's feet to the cross and was one of a pair, the other belonging to his father. It was comforting to think that a worker in the metal trades should have such appropriate protection.

The vessel in which he was to embark was flying a pennant displaying the White Boar badge of the duke of Gloucester, Richard Plantagenet the king's younger brother. He was only eighteen and had not yet proved himself in battle but was fiercely loyal to his brother. Beside this pennant was that of King Edward himself, denoting that the ship was part of his expeditionary fleet. Gloucester, though, was not on board this ship; he would sail with his captains in another vessel along with close-packed soldiery, not in a horse transport. Indeed, he was already on board and his ship was anchored out in the harbour ready to sail. Nevertheless Laurence was part of Gloucester's tiny flotilla, and after landfall, sooner or later his skills as an armourer would be required. This being so, he was somewhat discomfited that Nicholas Olds, along with Jack Snipe and the boy Peter were in the same vessel as Gloucester while he and the other armourers, along with some smiths and farriers were merely to sail in company with them. He supposed that this was Olds way of rebuking him for the brawl with Snipe, who had gloated through his blackened eyes when they had been issued with their sailing orders. It also moved him further from the nobility whom he needed to impress to gain future preferment, something not lost on Jack Snipe.

He felt decidedly uneasy about the outcome of the expedition. From what he could see around him, the king was far from convincingly equipped. He estimated there could be no more than 2000 men, and that head-count was based more on optimism than accuracy. If Edward was beaten, Laurence had devised some remote idea that he would somehow escape the battlefield and offer his services to the first noble he could find. This was risky, of course, but he had no better plan. The fact that he was not English might work in his favour because he could rightfully claim he was part of the expedition merely as an armourer and not particularly as one of Edward's committed followers. He held to the belief that fortune is fickle and circumstance often gave some odd results, provided you were in the game. Duke Francis had tasked him with getting close to the English Court, so it was not necessary to unconditionally attach himself to the fortune of a single protagonist in the English wars.

"If you intend to go into England with Edward, it's about time you were aboard your ship." He turned to the speaker, William Caxton, who had come to satisfy himself that everything he had procured for Edward was safely stowed on the invasion vessels.

"I am waiting until the last moment. The sea is not my natural element," he said lugubriously. He was remembering the sea passage he had recently taken from St. Malo to the mouth of the Somme in the storm-wracked channel around the Cherbourg peninsula. "It seems, though, that I cannot put it off any longer."

"In some ways I wish I was going with you. I was born in Kent, you know, and few Englishmen like to stay away from home for too long."

"Yes, I feel that way too about Brittany."

"Well, my work here is done for now and Edward's sister, the duchess Margaret, is sending me to Cologne on some business for Burgundy after which I shall return to my house in Bruges. If Edward is successful, then hopefully I can safely come into England. After working for the Yorkist interest at Charles' court I do not suppose to be welcome there else."

"What do you think of the king's chances?" asked Laurence. He knew that Caxton, as a confidante of duchess Margaret would have a well-informed opinion.

"The latest news is that king Louis of France has attacked Burgundy and is, at the moment, making inroads into duke Charles' territory around Amiens."

Laurence recalled his conversation with Sir Gervaise Montaine and realised that this was one of duke Francis' fears. If Louis gained Burgundy, he would have the resources to invade Brittany.

"Is it likely king Louis will be victorious?"

Caxton thought for a moment, regarding Laurence carefully as if wondering how much he should tell. However, as the news was bound to be spread through Edward's host anyway he finally considered it did no harm to voice his thoughts aloud.

"Louis' strike is, I think somewhat premature. Warwick has made a promise to Louis to supply men and arms to help in the campaign against Burgundy, he and duke Charles being deadly enemies. However, the threat of King Edward's invasion of England is causing him to hold back his forces, so that is bound to affect Louis and help Burgundy. Warwick will not move until Margaret of Anjou invades with her forces. Then the woman who is the legitimate queen of England along with her son the Prince of Wales, will oppose Edward while Warwick aids France. If Margaret defeats Edward, then with her husband king Henry the sixth on the throne, having his queen and his heir beside him, Warwick will be redundant. It must be remembered that it was Warwick, along with Edward, who deposed Henry and drove queen Margaret out of England in the first place. They are dubious allies. This is why Warwick is hesitating – he dare not go and he dare not stay. Without the extra boost his promised army would give Louis, there is a good chance that the fighting in Burgundy will peter out."

Laurence began to realise the extent of duke Francis' fears. If Warwick was allied to Louis of France along with Margaret and her son, then sooner or later they would pay their debt to Louis by helping him invade Burgundy with the likelihood of success, then Louis would be in an even stronger position to overrun Brittany, his long-term ambition. If Edward wins back his crown, he will be indebted to Charles and England will be once again opposed to France and allied to Burgundy.

"It seems that many fortunes are hanging in the wind," said Laurence.

"Just so. I wish you *bon voyage* and my prayers for a good landfall." Laurence wondered if Caxton was offering a personal benediction or merely expressing his general hopes for the success of the expedition. Nevertheless, prayers were always useful, and fingering the reliquary hanging around his neck, he knew that soon he would be adding a few of his own.

The carrack was moving sluggishly at the quay as Laurence crossed by the gangplank into the vessel where the sailors were fixing down the moveable planking over the hold where the horses had been loaded. He noted the location of a pair of guns on the deck before the forecastle. These had been covered with canvas to keep the spray off. Merchant vessels such as this one often had to deal with pirates in the narrow seas between England and the continent. The other vessels in the group would be similarly armed and these also carried the gunners, archers and pike-men of the invasion force eliminating any possibility of attack. It would take a fleet of armed vessels to stop them now.

The air on deck was cold and damp, but for the moment, preferable to the stifling conditions below, where the horses and men were crammed together. Laurence had already picked himself a place to spread his sleeping blanket along with the other armourers and his personal belongings were safely locked in his chest and stowed with the portable forge equipment. He wrapped his travelling cloak around him and hoisted the satchel he was carrying over his shoulder. This contained some cheese and black bread, which would probably be all he would have to eat during the voyage, which should be less than two days. Dried meat would have been welcome but it was the period of Lent and thus prohibited. He also had a flagon of small beer, but that was unlikely to last more than a day. After that he would have to rely on the ship's own water supply which, if there were rain, would probably be cleaner and fresher than the foul water offered on land. His purse was safely tucked away inside his tunic where it would not be noticed. It was much depleted now but he expected to earn something just as the other adventurers did, either by plunder or ransom, providing he was lucky enough to capture a wealthy prisoner.

He found himself being roughly shoved aside as the mariners ran along the deck heaving on the hempen tackle to hoist the square top sail on the main mast and the smaller sail on the fore mast for leaving harbour. Once under way, the huge square main sail would be unfurled followed by the lateen sail on the mizzen mast to balance the rig. The last of the ropes that had secured the vessel to the quay were being carefully wound on deck as the sails caught the wind and the huge vessel began to move slowly out into the waters of the harbour. He could see the other ships in the fleet getting under way with that of King Edward in the vanguard closely followed now by the Duke of Gloucester in his own flotilla. They were a brave sight, their colourful banners and long pennants streaming forward from the main mast of each ship.

As they gained way the taut rigging on the windward side began to hum while the sound of the bow wave and the pounding of the first choppy waves added to the first few moments of optimism that setting sail often brings. For the first time Laurence felt a frisson of expectation and excitement. The expedition might not be overwhelming in numbers, but it was well organised and equipped. If they could establish a sound landing and recruit rapidly more followers to Edward's cause perhaps it would not be as hopeless as he had at first supposed.

As the flotilla moved out of the harbour and into the open sea, the movement of the vessel began to increase and soon spray was lashing across the deck. Laurence decided that it was about time to go below where his companions were huddled in the hold.

They were crammed into what looked like a stall for stacking goods. A single candle burned in a lantern hooked to a deck beam and another had been fixed by its own melted tallow to a bracket in a corner of the stall. The smell of horses and stagnant bilge water pervaded the whole of the ship under the deck. Laurence wondered what cargo it had previously carried and kept a wary eye open for rats. The horses could be heard nervously stomping and whickering in the darkness of the hold. It was too dangerous to provide light where there were horses as it was all too easy for a light to be knocked over into the straw pens. In any case, the horses were calmer in the dark. So long as they could hear the presence of men in the ship, they would be sufficiently comforted to prevent any panic breaking out. Already ale flagons had been produced and the atmosphere was one of resigned camaraderie.

"Welcome, brother," said John Fisher, who was a master armourer. He was a man of small ambition who worked well but had no desire other than to work for someone else. It let him visit the taverns and bawdy houses without compunction, spending his earnings freely and having no responsibilities. The others were Genase Monk and Will Belknap, skilled smiths who did the mundane work around the forge. Two other men, whom Laurence recognised as farriers, had joined the company. The whole group were cheerfully chatting and drinking in spite of the increasingly violent movement of the vessel. Laurence produced his own flagon of ale and the men made a space for him to sit with them on the bare deck. As none of the men spoke French, he had to make do with his limited English.

"*Merci, mes amis*," he ventured. "Thank you my friends."

"What part of France do you come from?" asked one of the farriers having heard his accent.

"I am not from France, I am Breton." Laurence settled himself down and waved his ale flagon in greeting and took a drink from it. The others took a swig from their own bottles to confirm they were now a social group.

"Fought against the French, and with them too before now," said Genase Monk who had been a soldier as well as a smith. He had reckoned there was more chance of plunder as a soldier while a smith might not be paid if he turned out to be on the losing side.

"Will you be wading in with the king, then?" asked one of the farriers.

"Not if I can help it; too old. I shall stay with the baggage and hope for the best."

"That might not be a good idea. Baggage trains have been attacked before now, even if it is against the articles of war and you won't get much defence from boys and women." The speaker was Genase's fellow smith, Will Belknap. "I have some mail and a breastplate and that is what I shall be wearing when we land."

"I think we will all have des chapeles-de-fer, will we not?" said Laurence.

38

"I certainly have one," replied Will.

"So should we all," interjected John Fisher. "I have made enough of them in my time."

Laurence was only too familiar with the standard head protection, the chapel-de-fer. Like John Fisher he had made hundreds of them as an apprentice. It was skilled work raising the domed metal helmet from a single sheet of iron and shaping an elegant curve to the brim, but wearyingly repetitious for an apprentice armourer who was yearning to engage in more refined work. The bascinet, as head protection for nobles, was much more complex and making one was the ambition of all young armourers, but required the development of much skill before they would be allowed to do so.

The vessel gave a sudden lurch as it met a wave beam on indicating either a change of course or in wave pattern. Either way the movement was becoming more violent and Laurence was starting to feel slightly ill. Normally this was as bad as he got and he hoped that he would not feel any worse.

The other men stowed their flagons and settled themselves as best they could against the sides of the ship. The horses nearest to the men were showing the whites of their eyes, just discernible in the faint light from the candles. Presently, one of the ship's boys came down and filled a leather bucket with oats from a bin and skipped back and forth along the central passage between the horses, pouring the feed into the canvas bag located at each stall. The horses quietened down as they munched away, contented by the establishment of their feeding routine.

Laurence wrapped his travelling cloak around him and attempted to doze. All around the noises of the vessel made sleep difficult and soon he was imagining all sorts of problems with the ship. Timbers creaked as though they were about to split and let the cold grey sea in, and was the cargo shifting? The forge equipment was well stowed but there were heavy cannon in there somewhere and if one should break free it could knock the bottom out of the boat! He could feel the breaking of the seas against the side of the ship and the trembling of the timbers as they took the strain of the sheets that controlled the sails. Every now and again there would be an almighty thump as the vessel breasted a particularly heavy wave. He could tell when night came as the few chinks of light around the hatchway faded. He had eaten a few mouthfuls of bread washed down with the last of his ale, but found he had no real appetite for food.

He dozed fitfully through the night and was only dimly aware of the shipboard life around him. Every now and again one of his companions would stagger over to the stalls and piss into the straw, then return and slump down again in his place. He could hear the calls of the watch on deck and the murmured conversation of those of his companions who were awake. He imagined the other ships in the expedition spread out across the sea with their stern and mast lanterns gleaming to show their positions relative to each other. He was heading towards his mother's homeland and he felt he knew something of what it was like there. The people she had described were hard-working and sometimes savage, but there was an underlying kindness that gave them a strong sense of justice. This was why they were so easily stirred to rebellion. She had told him of the peoples' revolt that came about after the great plague of the last century. The disease had wiped out nearly half the population and those who were left began demanding more for their labour. The king and the nobility put down that revolt by a combination of guile and cruelty, but gradually the condition of the people had improved. The present wars in England were the result of squabbling between the noble houses defined by either the white rose of York or the red rose of Lancaster. He knew that the half-witted Henry the sixth was of Lancaster while Edward was of York, which, of course, only mattered to the English. His liege lord, Francis II of Brittany would deal equally with either house, as would the king of France and duke Charles of Burgundy. It all depended on the fate of this expedition.

The morning had come an hour or so before he realised it. Already the mariners were straining for the first glimpse of land and he was wakened by their calls. Climbing on deck he was at first disorientated by the bleakness of his surroundings, the heaving grey sea and the threatening sky that blended into it as if sea and sky met somewhere on the horizon. He looked to where the mariners were pointing and could just make out a smudge that seemed to him hardly discernable from cloud. He asked one of the mariners where they were, but as he was German, this being a vessel on hire from the Hanse towns, he could not make out his reply. In the far distance he could just see other ships, which he assumed were part of the invasion fleet. He looked around at the stern castle where the captain stood with another, a soldier well clad who carried an air of authority about him. There were several men-at-arms in the vessel and they had been quartered in the stern cabin. Soon they began to spill out on to the deck, attracted by the calls of the mast lookout. The soldier on the stern castle waved one of them into the shrouds with orders to give an account of what was happening with the rest of the fleet.

One of the men-at-arms hurried across the deck and threw up over the side. After an interval when he seemed to be assured there were no more stomach contents to discharge, he turned and lurched towards the main mast and grasped one of the pins that secured the shrouds. He was dressed in mail under an armoured breast-plate, with cuisses, poleyn and greaves on his legs. His arms were protected only by a padded tunic with no external armour. Over all he had a tabard bearing the emblem of the White Boar, the badge of Gloucester. Laurence understood that his outdated armour proclaimed him to be of the lower nobility. Probably the pieces of armour he wore were trophies picked up from past battles. The belt suspended around his waist had a scabbard where the worn hilt of a sword could be seen. There was also a murderer at his belt, a long-bladed dagger that he would use in his left hand if he managed to get through an opponents guard, a manoeuvre known as the *main gauche*. He wore his mail aventail with the head cover down, and Laurence supposed he would have some sort of helmet that he would don before going into a fight.

"Have you any idea where we are?" Laurence asked him. The man swallowed and looked for a moment at the leeward gunwale of the vessel wondering if he needed to make another dash for the side. He regarded Laurence through red-rimmed eyes and gripped tighter to the ropes as if that would constrain his stomach muscles.

"Somewhere off the Norfolk coast. Hopefully Cromer is over there somewhere." He freed up an arm and waved towards the smudge that Laurence now realised was England. "The king will send a landing party ashore and if it is safe we shall follow soon afterwards."

"Not a moment too soon for me," said Laurence.

"Me neither." The man offered Laurence his hand. "James Tyrell."

"Laurence de la Halle." They shook hands firmly.

Laurence looked over to where the king's ships were anchored. The captain was steering a course directly for the anchored ships and presumably they too would anchor before the order to discharge into Cromer came.

"Can you make out what is happening? Why are the king's ships not standing into harbour?" said Tyrell.

"I think I can make out a landing party of boats returning to the fleet," replied Laurence. "It is strange that all of them are coming back, I would have expected just one to carry a message telling us where we can unload."

"If there are hostile forces at Cromer then we are in trouble. It means that Warwick is ready for us and has been successful in using the king's name to raise the men of Norfolk." Laurence noted Tyrell's slip – he had mentioned the king, meaning the feeble Henry the sixth, rather than his own Lord, Edward Plantagenet. These Englishmen have too many kings, he thought.

Suddenly there was a flurry of activity as the mariners caused the vessel to heave to followed by the dropping of the bow anchors. Soon they were lifting the canvas from the ship's boat and, having rigged a pair of hoists began lowering it over the side. Presently the soldier who had been standing with the captain came down the companionway from the stern castle and, taking four oarsmen with him, clambered down into the boat and cast off. The boat moved with difficulty in the choppy sea but soon closed on the king's ship where he clambered aboard.

"Who is that soldier?" asked Laurence.

"Richard Ratcliffe," replied Tyrell, "He is one of the duke of Gloucester's most trusted captains." Laurence thought he detected a note of cynicism in his voice.

Laurence and Tyrell stood about the deck chatting to the other men at arms, worrying about the delay in landing. Presently a lookout shouted that the boat was returning. As soon as it came alongside, Ratcliffe clambered up on to the deck. His fellow men-at-arms clustered around him. Laurence noted that he wore little in the way of armour, probably because he had sensibly shed some of it while he crossed between the ships. Laurence stood in the group and managed to catch what Ratcliffe was saying.

"It seems there are hostile forces along this coast so we cannot land here. We shall sail further north and put the Humber estuary between us, then we should be able to land safely."

Judging by the miserable faces of the soldiers this announcement was less than encouraging. Laurence and Tyrell exchanged glances, neither of them looking forward to the continuance of the voyage. Not only that, but there was a great deal of black tumultuous cloud to the north, the very direction they were heading. Laurence could see squalls hanging like black veils where bands of rain connected the evil-looking clouds to the sea. Tyrell clamped Laurence on the shoulder in resignation then tramped off to join his fellows in the stern castle. Laurence climbed resignedly down the ladder into the hold where his former companions were eager to know what was happening.

"We are heading in the wrong direction if we are to win back the crown," said John Fisher.

"I suppose that my lord Gloucester might be somewhat happier, though. He has much support in the north." This was from Genase Monk who seemed to have an ambivalent attitude to the fortunes of war. "I expect that Warwick will be much further south as his expectation has been to meet up with Margaret's force."

They felt the vessel shudder as it got under way and butted its blunt bow against the rising seas. Laurence pressed himself as tightly as he could against the ship's timbers and buried himself in his cloak. The others all did the same and soon all that could be seen was a series of black humps topped with tousled hair and increasingly desperate eyes that glowering in the darkened hold. The horses were fretting, suspended in slings to stop them sliding around, adding to the nervousness that pervaded the ship.

Through the night and all the next day they sailed on, the weather getting worse and the ship bucking wildly in what was clearly a storm. Water spilled down into the hold from the deck, indicating that waves were breaking inboard and washing across the deck. Matters were not improved when some of the mariners scrambled down into the hold and assembled levers into what transpired to be a pump and began pumping the bilges of the ship. After a while they kicked at the armourers and indicated that they were to take a turn at the pumps. They struggled to their feet and began pumping,

43

glad of something to do while the ship ran onwards into the teeth of the gale.

After his spell at the pumps Laurence huddled back down into his niche in the hold, crossed himself and began to pray. He fingered the reliquary hung around his neck and began asking the Blessed Virgin to keep them afloat. He also appealed to his own special patron, Saint Barbara, to preserve them from lightning strike, as it was clear they were struggling through a severe storm. He was struggling to contain the panic that kept rising in his breast and imagined the sudden burst of sea should the timbers give way, the frantic thrashing of the horses and the screams of men as they tried to gain the deck, each one pulling the other down in their frenzy to get out of the hold. He had to get out first!

Scrambling wide-eyed onto the deck he was shocked by how dark it was. Somehow he imagined rather than saw the base of the main mast and he passed his right arm through the ropes that were secured there and held on. The sea seemed very close, and soon a wave broke inboard and swilled across the deck, drenching his legs. He could see nothing but the dirty grey waves and frothing white where their tops were torn away by the wind. The big main sail had been furled and they were scudding along under the topsail, foresail and mizzen. Suddenly, all around were flashes of lightning and once again he began muttering prayers to the Holy Barbara. She was the Patron Saint of armourers and gunners. Her pagan father had been the one who martyred her and he had been stuck down by lightning in retribution. Since then she offered protection against lightening for her followers and promised that they would not die without first being confessed. As there was no priest in the vessel, Laurence felt sure he would come through providing he prayed to her hard enough.

From his position on the deck Laurence could not see if they were still in company with the other ships. White flecks of spume that had been torn from the wave tops scudded past the ship and the notion came into his mind that hidden amongst them were demons that had come to tear at the sails and rip them apart before dragging them all to a watery doom. He was sure he could hear them calling to each other in the screeching of the wind as their unholy fingers plucked at the rigging. The mariners around the

44

stormy waters of Brittany told tales of Kelpies – water spirits that took the form of horses and which delighted in drowning their victims. There were great whales and other monsters lurking in the waves waiting to batten on the victims of great storms such as this.

Towards evening the waves seemed to abate their anger somewhat and Laurence braved a look out from the side of the ship. To port, he could just make out a grizzled shoreline and he realised they were turning towards it. He could see five other ships some distance away, but where were the rest of them? Thirty-six vessels had set out from Flushing harbour three days ago. The rain was still coming down and now they were heading directly for a long sandy beach, which was visible ahead pressed down under low grey clouds.

Anchored together, it was a relieved force that struggled ashore in boats. The men and horses had been badly frightened and even though they had no idea what waited for them landwards, they knew that there was no more hope of getting anywhere by sea. The horses were slung overboard and swum ashore while boats shuttled backwards and forwards disembarking men and equipment. Already Laurence was busy helping to assemble the wagons so that the forges and armaments could be transported. They were working on the stony ground back from the beach. Soon he was joined by Nicholas Olds, Jack Snipe and the boy Peter. Obviously Gloucester's ship was one of those that had made it to this desolate spot on the English shore. The soldiers and men-at-arms were already forming up ready for the march inland. Laurence saw James Tyrell with his troop, all horsed, and as they moved off both men had time to give each other a wave, knowing that each were overjoyed just to be on firm ground. Tyrell was leading a detachment of prickers to find out exactly where they had landed and if any hostile forces were in the area.

Nicholas Olds was looking decidedly ill and Jack Snipe was not in a much better state. The boy Peter was full of energy, the only one amongst them who seemed to have thrived on the sea journey. Olds was busy with Jack Snipe checking that the forge equipment was all present as most of it had been in Laurence's ship. The forge wagons were now ready to move off, except for the horses they would need to pull them. Peter, busily tying down the canvas covers, worked his way towards Laurence, and was clearly pleased to see him.

"We had a hard time of it in the ship," he informed Laurence. "They stuffed us in the hold like fish in a barrel." Master Olds was in the stern cabin with the captains, but master Snipe was put in with the soldiers."

"Where you with him?"

"No, I was with the other boys – those with the gunners."

"So you had a bad time?"

"Well, not so bad. There were many who were seasick so couldn't eat. We sneaked away with their food. All the boys ate very well, except one who we thought might die. He didn't, though." Laurence laughed. He knew that apprentices were always hungry and no doubt their recent experience had been a rare opportunity for them to get one over on their masters. "Let us see if we can find a couple of draught horses then we can get this wagon on the road, once the soldiery moves off."

A group of captains were gathered together in conference. All of them had been dressed in harness on the beach by their squires, ready for combat. Richard Ratcliffe was with them and they were conversing with a slight figure clad in black harness who seemed to be in command. This must be Richard, duke of Gloucester. He was only eighteen years of age and Laurence wondered how they would fare under such a young general. More and more soldiers gathered around the group, those without squires helping each other to fasten themselves into harness. A banner with the white boar emblem was unfurled to whip in the wind. Most of them were looking out to sea. It was apparent that they were wondering about the whereabouts of the other ships in the invasion force.

Gloucester's Master of Horse had charge of the animals on the beach. They were lucky that only two had been lost due to broken limbs as they had panicked in their stalls. Fortunately these were warhorses, not those used to draw wagons. The butchers had already cut them up and placed their expensive meat in barrels ready for loading into the supply train. Laurence and Peter were given a pair of horses as soon as it became known they were to draw the armoury wagons.

The small force was as ready as it could be but had to wait on the shore until the scouting party returned. Presently the prickers returned with Tyrell at their head and he cantered up to Gloucester and climbed down from the saddle. Kneeling in front of his general he gave a report that seemed satisfactory. Gloucester called for his own horse and along with Ratcliffe and his other his captains, climbed into the saddle and headed inland. The herald with the banner of the White Boar closed in behind Gloucester while Tyrell and his group of prickers fell in also, ready to ride off at a moments notice to report upon the land ahead. The men-at-arms marched on foot after them followed by the rest of the soldiery and finally, the small supply train. They were about three hundred and desperately needed to find the rest of the army before the forces of Warwick discovered their whereabouts.

* * *

To their great relief they met up with Edward's force at Ravenspur, where most of the remaining ships had managed to disembark along the sand banks of the Humber estuary. The port itself was being rapidly lost to the sea, but there was enough left of it to aid with the disembarkation of the army. Earl Rivers had also fetched up along the Humber with three of his ships, though twelve miles further upriver. By the time that Gloucester with his men arrived the following morning, the whole of Edward's army had assembled themselves into some order ready to begin the march inland towards the city of York.

Nicholas Olds had been called into Edward's presence to discuss his armouring needs, but the other armourers remained with the baggage train. The army made slow process over ground that had little potential for forage at this time of year. The baggage train, somewhat larger now, lagged behind the main force, yet soon they caught up as the army in front had come to a stop. Word soon passed down the line that there was a large hostile force barring their way. They had not yet reached Hull.

Laurence looked about him with apprehension. They were in open country with nowhere to hide. He noted that the army ahead was not deploying into a defensive array, so there was some cause for optimism, but the expedition had been halted barely ten miles on its march to York. He climbed down from the back of the wagon he had been riding on and walked forward to where the rear guard were milling around, stretching their necks to try to see what was happening ahead. Presently a captain galloped up to them and ordered them into marching order again. He informed them that the king had entered into negotiations with the leader of about seven thousand militia who was uncertain which side to take. This force was too large to chance a fight with, but Edward had claimed he was merely establishing his rights as duke of York, not as the king. Whether this subterfuge had been convincing or not mattered little. It was enough for them to be given permission to march on, but they learned that Hull had closed its gates to them and Beverley too.

After a hard day's march they made camp near the village of Market Weighton. The tents of the nobles clustered around Edward's pavilion, his banner with its blazing sun raised above the others. As the king's armourer, Nicholas Olds had a tent of his own pitched close to those of the nobles. Nearby were the wagons of the armourers crammed with their portable forges and a variety of arms for the soldiery. No sooner was the camp settled when numerous men-at-arms came along either for help with a repair or to look at the store of weapons. Jack Snipe was doing a brisk trade in maces, daggers and the odd piece of armour while Nicholas was making an adjustment to Edward's helm. The other armourers were working on harness as it was brought to them. The owner of the armour would pay for repairs or modifications directly to the armourer.

Laurence was busy adjusting a pair of sabatons, after taking the foot measurements of the owner who had found them inflexible. He looked up as he heard his name spoken.

"Good e'en, master Laurence." James Tyrell stood grinning down at him. "I hope your stomach has recovered from our recent ordeal by water?" He seemed to have forgotten that he had been the one throwing up. Laurence had been scared almost out of his wits, but he had never been sick. He placed his work aside and stood up to greet the soldier.

"Master Tyrell, give you good e'en." Tyrell was wearing the harness that he had on when they first met. Everyone else had removed theirs for the night.

"I wonder if you can do something with my harness?" Tyrell opened his arms and looked down at the breast plate and the other

48

bits and pieces that clung to his arming jacket. "It has had several owners and though it serves it is not in fighting trim."

"Yes, I can see what you mean." Laurence regarded him critically. "The breast plate is ill fitting. I can't do anything with it here. It needs reshaping and that means forge work. After that, the inside will require repainting and the outside too."

"What about protecting my arms?" Except for his arming coat, he had no other covering. "I have got away with it so far. Having no harness might allow me to be more agile, but I fear it is only a matter of time before I lose a treasured limb."

"Unless you have a deep purse I fear the only answer is mail. I am surprised you have none already."

"I did but it was lost in the hurried trip to Flanders last year." Laurence knew that Edward and his few supporters, Gloucester, Hastings and Rivers had only just managed to get away from Warwick's forces, so Tyrell must have been with them too.

"You will have to ask Jack Snipe to look for some suitable mail from Nicholas' store. You can pay for it, I hope?"

"I have scant funds but I might be able to bargain something out of him."

"Well make sure you don't mention my name or he will charge you double." Tyrell looked at him curiously but made no comment. "Your leg protection is serviceable and as I have seen you mounted it should suffice. Try not to fall out of your saddle and you might survive a fight."

Tyrell laughed and clapped him on the shoulder.

"Thanks for the advice. I shall be sure to take it. Now I can get out of harness and rest. Hopefully we shall get some respite in York, if they let us in, that is."

"If we can spend a few days in York I can work on improving your harness."

"Then I give you good e'en." Tyrell tramped off towards the armourers' wagon, removing the cumbersome breast plate as he went.

Chapter 3 – The Great March

As it turned out, they only had one night in York. At first the city refused to open its gates, but when Edward repeated his previous subterfuge, claiming his rights merely as duke of York, and pledging allegiance to King Henry and the Prince of Wales, he was allowed in with just a few of his men. Later, the city relented and allowed inside his whole force. The city fathers were being cautious. No doubt they were well aware of Edward's intention regarding the crown, but in the event of him failing to win it back, they did not want to fall ill with either Warwick or Queen Margaret. The news was not good. Both the Earl of Northumberland, Henry Percy and Warwick's brother, John Neville the Marquis Montague now commanded armies each larger than Edward's. However, it seemed that Northumberland was sitting back waiting to see who would win in the fight for the crown. The Marquise, though, was using his army near Pontefract to block the road south.

The baggage train, as usual, had become separated from the main body of the army and now struggled to keep up with the rear guard and a few stragglers. The tiny army had turned away from Montague's force and was now marching towards Sandal, the castle there being Yorkist seat and the place near Wakefield where eleven years ago, Edward's father had sallied out with inadequate forces only to be caught and killed by a larger force of Lancastrians. The armourers had talked about this as they huddled around the campfire on the first night of the march from York. With Montague stalking them at their rear it seemed to Laurence that the same fate might well befall the son, and in the same location. At any moment he expected to see Montague's outriders appear and he knew that just a small force of armed men could easily deprive Edward of his supply train.

They had spent two days fording streams and bumping over stony pathways and roads churned to mud by the army marching in front. Travelling with the baggage was no soft option and everyone had to lend a hand getting heavily laden carts and wagons out of potholes or clearing a way through woods and forest. Laurence felt almost as if he had pushed the baggage all the way from York rather than merely riding or walking. It was with some relief that they came upon the high walls and towers of Sandal castle, the family seat of the House of York. The baggage train was drawn up outside the castle walls, but Laurence, with the smiths and the other armourers were allowed to enter the castle. There were permanent forges there and soon they were busy working on those jobs they had put by on the march. The farriers too were soon hard at work replacing worn shoes and checking for loose ones among the horses.

The castle was not in the best of repair, yet it was still a formidable fortress. The whiteness of its walls, bright in the sunshine at a distance, when seen close up was in need of a new coat of lime wash. The lord's apartments were in a tower that stood on a raised mound that looked as if it had once been the base of a motte and bailey structure of a previous period. The high walls, extending out from the tower, encircled a large area within which was a keep. Other rooms and apartments were built against the walls and there were several forges. Only one or two were regularly used, but getting the others going meant that the portable forges would not have to be unloaded. The smiths and armourers could more easily catch up with their forge work.

Laurence had expected, or rather more truthfully hoped that there would be a host of Edward's supporters at Sandal castle, but he was soon to be disappointed. A few retainers were to join them in their continuing march south, but they hardly increased the army to anywhere like the numbers they needed if they had to fight even a modest opposing force. This meant that they had to move on swiftly. Nobody knew quite where Montague's forces were; only that they were somewhere near and Edward was in no state yet to meet with them. Laurence wondered why they had not been attacked before now. Was Montague trailing them so they would be caught between his forces and another army led by Warwick and Clarence, Edward's duplicitous brother?

He considered that Edward's little expedition was doomed to failure. The people of Norfolk had not risen to his aid, forcing the invasion force to sail and land further north. The towns of Beverly and Hull had barred their gates to them and even here in the country of the white rose people were staying close in their homes.

Laurence began to think about how he could extricate himself from the predicament and get to London where he would meet up with the mysterious Cornelius Quirke. Perhaps then he could keep his head down until some kind of new order was established and send a report on the new order to duke Francis. Sooner or later there would be battle and he didn't want to be anywhere near when that happened. It was not that he was in the least afraid of a fight, just that he wanted to give himself the best chance of coming through in one piece. If Edward should be defeated, and so far as he could see that was certain, the victors were likely to engage in an aftermath of slaughter where the non-combatants in the baggage train would hardly expect to escape alive. He decided to add St Jude, the patron saint of lost causes, to his list of intercessors.

James Tyrell was talking to a group of the scouting party that ranged ahead of the main army. He saw Laurence hammering away in one of the forges and came over to him.

"Perhaps you could have a look at my body armour?" he enquired. "I see the forges are lit." Laurence nodded and cast his eye over Tyrell's nondescript body armour. He tugged at the plates and looked around at his back, noting where it needed to be reformed if it were to fit correctly.

"What type of weapon are you using?" he asked.

Tyrell slapped a leather-gloved hand over the hilt of his sword. "Just a sword, though I do swing a mace when there is a need."

"Draw your sword and show me how you use it." Tyrell drew his sword in his right hand and began lashing about, using the normal warm-up exercises."

Laurence studied the movements. "You are usually mounted are you not?" he asked.

"Yes, we have to range far and wide in our scouting duties."

"Then you will have to fight both sides of your horse. Let me see how you work to your left." Laurence noted that the movements were inhibited by the looseness of the plates and the restrictions around the right armpit. "I think I can do something but I need to take your measurements. Remove the plates but leave on your arming jacket." The thick garment was necessary to damp out any blows to the armour plate. Though the armour might prevent cuts to the body, serious bruising and broken bones could easily occur unless suitable padding was worn underneath.

"At least your arming jacket fits properly."

"It is about the only item that was made for me."

Laurence was glad of that. Armour could never fit properly unless the arming jacket was snugly tailored to the body of the wearer. He fetched out a large pair of callipers and proceeded to take measurements of Tyrell's modest frame and recorded them on a slate. He would transfer them to a notebook later against Tyrell's name.

"Once I start work on your armour it will be some days before you can wear it. If we stop here a few days that will be fine, but I think we might be moving on quickly" Both men understood that the armour, once it had been reworked in the forge, would lose its finish and the inside would have to be painted to inhibit rust. This was campaign armour and he knew Tyrell had no squire to keep it polished.

"I have a leather jack I had off an archer. That will suit for my scouting duties, but I will need my armour if we get into a skirmish."

Laurence nodded in understanding. The *jack* Tyrell was referring to was a padded leather coat that gave slight protection. He wondered how Tyrell had come by it. Having it "off an archer" was most likely after the former owner was dead. Perhaps it was not wise to ask.

"I shall have the hot work done today. The rest may take a little longer and the paint will need at least two days to dry properly."

"What colour will be on the outside?" asked Tyrell.

"Dark grey."

"Dark grey! I'm not going to look much in that."

"Exactly," replied Laurence. In a battle it is not a good idea to draw the attention. If you look as though you have wealth then you will be attacked in the hope of ransom."

"That means I would be taken prisoner rather than killed."

"Then I hope your people are rich because if they cannot pay a ransom corresponding to your fine appearance, your captors will cut your throat to prevent you swallowing their expensive food and drink."

"There is no other colour?"

"We have only the dark grey."

Shaking his head and laughing, Tyrell handed the body armour to Laurence.

"I am joking," said Laurence, grinning at him. "We will make the armour bright and polished. You can wear a surcoat over it so that you do not blind your adversaries with your brilliance or let them see you from miles away. I shall quench the metal in oil. We can attend to a better finish once the present difficulties are behind us."

"I shall cover it over with sack cloth. Just remember I am a poor man when you tell me how much it will cost."

"I will need something on account," said Laurence. "The forge coals must be paid for and master Olds will expect his cut." Tyrell drew out a purse and handed him a couple of coins. Laurence gave a nod and slipped the coins into his own purse. "Many thanks, I shall get to work right away."

They stayed at Sandal castle barely long enough to feed the army and rest the horses. Laurence had just enough time to improve Tyrell's body armour and get it burnished by one of the polishers. He decided not to have the inside painted just yet as Tyrell was likely to need the protection of his armour before long. He had removed the old leather straps and replaced them with new ones. The breastplate and back plates had been made to fit their new owner and it was an anxious Tyrell who turned up early at the forges looking for his armour. He was wearing a mail haubergeon rather than the arming jacket, which meant he was expecting to be in a fight.

When Laurence produced the armour Tyrell's eyes lit up. To reduce the size of the breastplate, Laurence had formed two creases that not only corrected the size but also considerably enhanced its strength and appearance. He had also creased lightly around the armpits to remove the previous obstructive shape in these areas. The whole provided a combination of practicality and style with which Tyrell was clearly pleased. Enthusiastically he put on the armour and Laurence strapped him in to it.

"Let me see how you move now," said Laurence. Tyrell moved his arms and pivoted his body. His delighted grin was all the comment needed to signal approval.

"We are leaving immediately to scout the road ahead and I have no idea who we might come up with." As he spoke, one of his

54

mounted scouts, known popularly as prickers, came up leading a horse. "I shall have to get going – the king has ordered us away immediately," he said as he clambered up onto a conveniently placed mounting block. "You had better prepare yourself for the march, the army is about to move onwards towards Nottingham." Tyrell swung his leg over the saddle of his horse and settled himself in. His companion handed him his sword belt and hanger, which he buckled on. He put on his helmet and draped the attached aventail over the neck of the breastplate. "I shall have to chance dazzling the enemy with my brilliance for the moment." It seemed that he had no surcoat to hand and would therefore ride resplendent in his shining armour. Taking the reins he gave Laurence a cheery wave, then tugged his horse's head around and trotted towards the gate. His fellow prickers were mounted in a line waiting for him and as he passed they fell in behind and rode out after him. Laurence was left hoping he came to no harm otherwise, he had just realised, he might never be paid for his work.

"That was fancy work for a churl." Laurence turned to Jack Snipe who had come up while he watched Tyrell ride out. "There are many good men-at-arms who have to make do with mail or a simple plain rig."

"It was the best solution to the problem of making it fit," replied Laurence haughtily. "He is no churl, I think, but a gentleman. Perhaps you should call him churl to his face?"

"It's a question of rank. We can't have churls dressed as nobles, it's against the law."

"Soldiers are allowed to wear captured armour, besides sumptuary law only applies to clothing."

"While you were playing with the decoration of that armour there was other work being neglected. I hope you have charged your friend plenty. Master Olds will not be pleased else."

"Then I shall send master Tyrell to master Olds when he returns and he can charge what he likes and pay me fairly for the work."

"I will see to it that you are paid for necessary work only, not fancy embellishments." Snipe kept his face straight, as if he was merely being business-like without any underlying malice. Laurence decided to change the subject. He would talk to Nicholas Olds about payment without regard for Snipe's prejudice.

55

"Unless we start to assemble for the march none of us will be paid if we are left behind." Having said that, his purse had begun to weigh a little more as he had been paid for various items of work done on the march so far, and not being in town there was nothing to spend his money on. His lodging was a shared tent and his food the sparse camp fare. Laurence walked casually away towards the forges where he had to pack his tools ready for stowing in a wagon.

The march from Sandal to Nottingham was just as tedious as that on the road from York. Each night the small army made camp and the armourers would attend to the many small tasks presented by soldiers anxious to maintain as much protection for their bodies as possible. This did little to calm Laurence's worries and he began to think about getting free of the army at Nottingham. The baggage always lagged behind the army, cutting them off from news of what was happening in the countryside around them. At any time a hostile force could come up with them to either bar their way or attack their rear. At least those soldiers marching in front had some idea of what was happening, though even the prickers had no real idea where the enemy were unless they came within visible distance of them. Edward's little army was surrounded by either indifference in the population or hostility from determined enemies. Unless there were a considerable number of reinforcements at Nottingham, there seemed no way Edward could possibly escape with his life, let alone win back his crown.

The army picked up a few men from Doncaster and others came in ones and twos from far and wide to join Edward. Now he had more archers and yeomen to swell his numbers but they were still far from the force they would need to fight a battle. It was with some relief that Laurence entered Nottingham with the baggage train. The castle towered above the town on its sandstone rock while the houses of merchants and tradesmen, taverns and other businesses clustered around its base further enclosed behind solid walls. The castle was a royal residence and Laurence soon discovered that Edward had installed himself and his immediate retinue in the tower on the west side of the middle bailey. The forges were in the outer bailey so that was where Laurence and the other armourers brought the wagons containing their tools and the small arms of the army. It seemed as if the whole castle was alive with a mass of soldiers and horses, writhing almost as maggots within a rotting corpse. Castle retainers scuttled from place to place according to the demands of the nobles who were with Edward. Farriers were already shoeing horses and grooms were attending to the stabling of the warhorses.

Laurence met up with Will Belknap and John Fisher who informed him that master Olds, along with Jack Snipe had gone to the west tower to be on call should Edward want them. This gave the armourers and the smith a rare opportunity to go into the town to find some entertainment while the nobles enjoyed the comforts of the castle. Laurence was only too glad of the opportunity. He needed to think about the chances of getting out of the present situation with a full skin and a look around Nottingham would be most welcome. They had a word with the sergeant at the gate, letting him know who they were and that they would be returning later. On the way they were joined by the boy Peter, who had also kept out of the way of his masters. It seemed Olds and Snipe were so taken by the need to get close to Edward they had forgotten to give him any instructions. Normally he would have been given some menial task to keep him busy, but now the lure of the taverns had him in thrall.

The quartet tramped down the hill around the base of the castle rock. As they descended they could see the River Trent below, busy with a variety of craft, their sails a pageant of colour in the evening light as they came in for the night. The orange glow of sunset had come as a pleasant change from the glowering skies of their march. Presently they came upon what appeared to be an alehouse. There was a barrel against the door with the legend "The Pilgrim" painted on it and a bunch of dried hops nailed to the doorpost. At first the establishment looked to be impossibly small and what appeared as wattle and daub frontage jutted out from the castle rock by just a few feet. However, stepping inside they found this to be deceptive. The alehouse turned out to have several chambers hewn from the castle rock itself. The place was loud with a raucous crowd of soldiery, which according to the instincts of their calling had been the first of Edward's force to discover where the best ale was. The rock chambers were fitted out with narrow tables and communal benches. The place was dimly lit with rush lamps though here and there candles were burning a little more brightly at the tables of those who were prepared to pay for the extra light. There was a through draught and they discovered that this was due to the fires of the brewing house, which they discovered in one of the rock chambers. The chimney was built at one end of the chamber and appeared to vent up through the rock, no doubt issuing out somewhere above.

They clambered over the benches each side of a table, two either side so they could face each other to hear themselves talk above the alehouse din. A doxy broke free of the clutches of a leering churl and, with a rather bad tempered scowl, asked them their requirements. Laurence gave the others a wink and looked up at her.

"Bring us a flask of your best Rhenish, if you please." The doxy fixed him with a malevolent glare.

"I suppose you think I don't know what Rhenish is?" she snapped. "We get all sorts in here – they come in from the river, along with the rats. Well you can have ale or you can have ale – what'll it be?" She had obviously noted he was not a native by his accent.

"We will take four beakers of your best ale," Laurence said, smiling at her. Without a further word she shoved a drunken soldier out of her way and went to where the ale barrels were ranged at the end of a short chamber. Soon she returned with a jug and four beakers. She thumped these down on the table slopping a little of the ale onto the wood.

"That'll be one penny." She held out her hand for the money. Laurence slipped a silver penny into her hand and added a further halfpenny. She looked at him with interest as her hand disappeared into the folds of her apron where the money was secreted away.

"At that price I hope this is your best ale."

"We only sell ale, which I might say is the best in Nottingham," she replied nodding at the ale jug. Will Belknap had reached for the jug and was busy pouring the ale into the beakers. Her face took on a coquettish look. "Mind you, there is not only ale to be had here. Now there is something I can offer a foreign gentleman such as yourself, where the service is extra special, if you get my meaning." As she spoke she sidled closer to him. He noted that she was quite young, perhaps in her early teens, though it was hard to tell in the dim light. Laurence was not indifferent to her charms.

She was small and rather neat for an alehouse doxy and wore her flaxen hair tied back, which gave her face an elfin appearance.

"Get one for me" piped up the boy Peter. Will Belknap nearly choked on his beer and John Fisher froze with his beaker half way to his mouth. All three of the men burst into spontaneous laughter. Peter took on a hurt expression. "I know what to do," he stated sulkily. The doxy smiled gently at him. She came behind where he was sitting and placed her hands on his shoulders. Gently she massaged his shoulders then slowly slid a hand down his chest and into his hose. Peter's eyebrows shot up somewhere behind his fringe of hair and his eyes nearly bulged out of their sockets. The doxy rummaged around for a while then removed her hand.

"His stones have dropped so I might find a friend for him," she chuckled.

Laurence laughed and reached out for her. She came willingly enough and sat down beside him on the bench. Her name was Anna and she was the stepdaughter of the alehouse keeper. It didn't take Laurence long to extract her history. Her stepfather had married her mother after her father had been killed in tavern brawl. Just a year or so later her mother died of a contagion, the nature of which she could not explain. She asked about Laurence and, with the way of all alehouse wenches, was content to listen to him talk about his family and his home in Brittany.

"There doesn't seem to be anywhere private here, he said, looking around at the rock walls.

"There are caves outside. I can show you. I shall fetch some more ale for your friends and get Lynette to come over and keep the young man company." She climbed over the bench and went over to the barrels to draw more ale. A rough-looking fellow grabbed her arm and, pulling her around so he had his back to them, said something that caused an argument. Her face registered anger, then alarm as he spoke to her. He still held her in his grip and giving her a violent shake, released her. Clearly disturbed, she came back to them with another jug of ale.

"What was that about?" asked Laurence. Will and John who had been talking together had not noticed, but they leaned forward to find out what was happening.

"It was nothing. He is my stepfather and wanted to know why I am sitting with you and not attending to the other customers."

"You mean he is concerned with your maidenly honour?" Laurence saw that she was keeping something back. He looked over to her stepfather who was deep in conversation with a couple of brutish churls. It seemed he was being careful not to look over to where Laurence and his companions were sitting. Presently, the two churls spat on the floor and slouched out of the alehouse door. Laurence decided to turn on his charm and see what he could get out of the girl. He sat her down beside him and took hold of her hand. "You are frightened are you not, mademoiselle? Tell me what is the matter."

"I dare not," she whispered.

"I have been in alehouses and taverns before, you know. I think I shall stay here and not go with you."

"No!" she cried in alarm. "You must come with me."

"Why must I come?"

"I will be beaten if I turn down a good customer such as you."

"Then, ma petit, you will be beaten. Perhaps it will be best for you if you tell me what this is all about?"

"Is he watching?" He thought she looked like a frightened mouse that was being pursued by a cat.

"No, he has his back to us."

Anna dropped her gaze. "I am to take you to the caves where his gang will be waiting. You are to be robbed. They think because of your generosity to me you have money."

"Yes, I suspected something like that. How many of them?"

"Three, sometimes four. They will strike from the shadows without warning and they take no chances. I fear you will be badly hurt."

"Then we shall not go to the caves." Her head shot up and her eyes widened in fear.

"They will know I have warned you!"

Laurence thought for a minute. By now it would be dark outside. If they left the alehouse together and kept to the centre of the street, if what Anna had told them was correct about the louts being cautious of their own skins, they could get back to the castle without incident. In the event they were attacked, an alert trio of men and one boy should be able to dispose of them. Laurence, though, felt concern for Anna. Clearly she would suffer if the robber's plan failed. He felt for his "murderer" which was in its scabbard on his belt. He knew that Will and John had daggers too and Peter had a small knife. Nobody would go unarmed into a strange town at night. Laurence slipped an arm around Anna's waist.

"You had better come up to the castle with us, unless you are really attached to his place?"

"I have often thought of getting away from here, but until now I have had no idea where to go. Will you take care of me?"

"We will sort that out later, first of all we need to leave here without raising suspicion. "Will, John, Peter, you leave first and wait for me a little way up the road. That will appear normal, as if I have succumbed to Anna's charms. If we all leave together with Anna, there might be trouble. We shall follow in two minutes."

The three of them made a show of finishing their drinks and with a few loud and lewd comments left Laurence and Anna at the table. Presently, the couple got to their feet and made for the door. Anna was clinging to Laurence's arm and they were laughing together as they left the alehouse. Outside it was completely dark.

The street rose upwards around the castle rock. To the right was a jumble of houses and shops, all firmly closed and barred for the night. Cloud had returned to obscure the moon and apart from the subdued noise of the alehouse behind them all was silent. He had the impression that there were trees or bushes to the left, growing out from the castle rock.

"Where are the caves you are supposed to be taking me to?" he whispered. He knew that was where the robbers would be lying in wait. He wondered where the others were. They too were keeping silent.

"They are just here in the castle rock."

Suddenly, just up ahead there was a shout and the unmistakeable sound of a fight. Leaving Anna, he ran towards the sound. He could just make out the shapes of a group of men fighting and recognised the voices of Will Belknap and John Fisher. He realised they must have come upon the robbers. Drawing his weapon he rushed upon the group just as the moon came out from behind cloud. He identified one of the churls from the alehouse who had a cudgel raised about to strike John Fisher who was wrestling with another man. Unhesitatingly, Laurence slipped his murderer between the ribs of the felon, who cried out in agony and dropped to the ground. Laurence picked up the cudgel of the man who had been about to brain John Fisher and transferred the murderer to his left hand. John beat down the man he was fighting with and immediately leapt to the aid of Will Belknap who had taken a blow and was staggering as if ready to fall. Leaving John to it, Laurence turned towards another fellow who was coming at him from his left with what looked like a cutlass. He raised the cudgel to ward of the blow and with his left hand raked the fellows ribs with his dagger. With a yell of pain the felon backed away then turned and ran. The one who had first attacked Will Belknap, finding himself alone, ran after him leaving the victors standing with three bodies lying on the ground.

Laurence knew that one of these was the man he had stabbed, another had been beaten to the ground by John and Will. The third was Peter. Ignoring the other two, Laurence knelt down beside Peter. It looked as if he had taken a blow to the head and was unconscious but still breathing. The man who Laurence had stabbed groaned and tried to get up, but then slumped down again. His companion lay unconscious. Anna rushed up to them and looked around her. John Fisher was supporting Will Belknap who was groggy but capable of standing with support. Laurence was standing with the boy Peter in his arms. She gave an indifferent glance at the other two who lay groaning on the ground.

"We had better get away from here before the Watch come along and start making arrests," she said practically. The others did not argue but tramped upwards towards the castle. At the gatehouse the sergeant recognised who they were and, having it explained to him that they had been set upon by robbers, made no further enquiry and let them through. Anna was tending to Peter's wounded head and she too entered the castle without question.

Back in the armourers' quarters beside the forges they laid Peter on a straw pallet and sent for a chirurgeon. While they were waiting Laurence discovered what had happened. The three companions had left the alehouse and were slowly walking up the dark street. Will Belknap and Peter were ahead of John Fisher who was lagging behind waiting for Laurence and Anna to catch them up. In the darkness the robbers had seen Will and Peter apparently alone and, believing the smaller to be Anna attacked Will. John leapt to his aid and the robbers, realising their mistake, started lashing out with their weapons and Peter took a blow to the head. Just then,

Laurence arrived and threw everyone into confusion, but the robbers who had no idea how many they were taking on, fled leaving their wounded companions behind.

Anna tended Peter, wiping the blood from the nasty gash in the side of his head. Laurence looked to Will Belknap's head, where an ugly swelling was rising on his forehead. Presently a scrawny crone bustled her way into the room. She was wearing an ochre coloured wool dress over which was a dirty linen apron. There was a grey woollen shawl draped over her shoulders. At her waist was a belt with a capacious leather bag suspended from it. Grey strands of hair freed themselves from under a leather bonnet, which was tied under her chin. She still had some teeth.

"Wur's th' injured mon?" she cackled. Laurence hardly understood as her dialect was the accursed pagan brogue that his limited English could not comprehend. Anna understood her and she pointed to where Peter was lying. Laurence was unsure how to react. He had met cunning women before and could not make up his mind if one such as this healed by skill or witchcraft. He would take no chances and decided to pray to the Virgin for Peter's recovery. His prayers would thus armour the boy against any possible malevolence. With a great deal of trepidation, but not daring to incur the woman's wrath unnecessarily, he stepped away from the boy. The crone shooed Anna to one side and knelt down beside the lad. She pressed around the wound and muttered something to herself. Next she reached into her bag and took out a small box, and some soft moss. She smeared some of the contents of the box onto the moss and pressed it over the wound. "Here girl, bind that on," she instructed Anna. "The lod's 'ead be not brok but I canno tell if he be reet i'th 'ead 'till he wakkens. Someone has pailt nim weel"

Laurence made the sign of the cross over the boy. "I thought we had sent for a chirurgeon," he ventured.

"Muzzy under a wagon i' th' outer bailey," came the reply. "Anyone else hurtin'?" He thought he understood her question.

"Only Will over there," he replied. The crone went over to where Will Belknap was sitting on a stool with his head in his hands.

"Stan' up" she commanded, "and look into mi een." Will did as he was told. The woman stared into his eyes and passed her hand a couple of times in front of his face. Then she raised a finger and

63

told him to follow its movement with his eyes. Laurence worried that she was casting some sort of spell. "He'll be a'reet in twothri' days. Who's paying me?" He understood that as an open palm was universal sign language.

"How much?" asked Laurence.

"A groat."

"Half a groat it will be," he returned offering her two silver pennies from his purse. "We asked for a chirurgeon not a cunning woman."

"More come to me as go to Jake Wentland," she grumbled taking the money with ill grace. Apparently that was the name of the chirurgeon who was her rival. As she turned to go Laurence had a thought.

"Stay a moment. What is your name?"

"They co' me Mother Malkin."

"You look a bit too old for following the army."

"Aw con manage misel."

"What if I pay you a full groat in return for you taking on a young helper?"

"Tell me your meaning."

"This young woman is in need of an occupation away from here. She could be of much help to you and, what is more, she might even attract customers." Mother Malkin's eyes brightened at the thought. She regarded Anna carefully.

"Let me see how tha fettled that lod's 'ead." She leaned over Peter's pallet and tugged gently at the linen Anna had used to bind the moss to the wound. "Tha's fettled it gradely enow," she straightened up and fixed Anna with a cool eye. "Come wi' me. Tha willno clem but tha must fend for thisen." Laurence gave her two more silver pennies to make up the groat. Mother Malkin placed them in her bag.

"Thank you sir," said Anna.

"Just remember I have two pennies on account when I come to visit you."

"I hope to see you very soon, then." She dropped him a lascivious curtsey and grinned up at him. He took her to one side and whispered in her ear.

"Make sure the old woman doesn't bewitch you. Cunning women are known to enchant the unsuspecting with spells and potions and its hard to tell what this one is saying. She could have you bewitched and you never knowing. Have you a charm against the evil eye?"

Anna was just about to reply when there was a commotion outside. Laurence stepped out to see what it was about.

"There he is! That's the man who kidnapped my daughter." Anna's stepfather was standing between two of the castle guards, one of whom was the gate sergeant. Anna came out and when she saw who was there placed a hand to her mouth in fear. "And there's my daughter." The fellow pointed at Anna. He was an ugly brute, though turning rapidly to fat. His hair was dirty and dishevelled as was his general appearance. The apron he wore had once been white under the beer stains.

The sergeant regarded Laurence and the girl suspiciously.

"You've heard what he said. Also he claims that one of his fellows has been murdered and another cut up badly."

Laurence thought quickly. The alehouse keeper was virtually admitting that his fellows were those who attacked them in the street leading to the castle. He addressed the sergeant at arms.

"I told you we had been attacked and you can see that my companions have been injured. If this man is saying it was his fellows who attacked us, then you should arrest him."

"They were kidnapping my daughter. That's why we tried to stop them in the street," spat the alehouse keeper. The sergeant turned to Anna.

"Is this true? Have you been brought here against your will?"

Her stepfather glared at her and she quailed, clearly afraid of him. Laurence placed a steadying hand on her shoulder. He could feel her trembling.

"I came willingly," she whispered, not daring to look the alehouse keeper in the eye.

"She lies!"

Just then Nicholas Olds and Jack Snipe hurried up to them.

"What is going on here?" demanded Nicholas. The sergeant told him what it was about. Jack Snipe turned on Laurence with a malevolent grimace.

"I have good reason to know that this Frenchman is a violent and dangerous man." He was still showing the vivid signs of his previous encounter with Laurence. "Master Olds here will testify to his aggression." Nicholas Olds frowned at Laurence unsympathetically.

"You have heard the girl," said Laurence, "and the men were already lying in wait for us before we left the alehouse."

"What Laurence is saying is true." John Fisher had joined them. "I was there too and I can testify that we were the ones who were attacked by his ruffians." He pointed at the alehouse keeper. "So can Will Belknap and Peter too, if he recovers. Master Olds, you have known me for years. Do you think I would get involved in a kidnapping?"

Nicholas Olds was shaken to learn of Will and Peter's injuries.

"Is Peter badly injured and what has happened to Will?" he asked, his suspicious frown now turned to one of concern. He was just about to speak when an expression of surprise spread across his face and he suddenly dropped to one knee and bowed his head. "Your grace, he muttered."

They looked around and found themselves under the stern gaze of Richard Duke of Gloucester. All the men fell to their knees in obeisance.

"Stand up all of you and tell me what is going on," said Gloucester. The group hurriedly scrambled to their feet. Laurence had not seen Edward's younger brother close up before. He was dressed in a red gown over which was draped a blue cloak trimmed with sable. Laurence was surprised at how slight and youthful he seemed, yet this was the general who, with Edward Plantagenet, would command the army in battle. Behind him stood four of his retainers, each one smirking at the consternation the duke had caused. Everyone looked to Nicholas Olds to speak first.

"Your grace, it seems that there is a problem between my armourers and an alehouse keeper in the town. I haven't discovered the whole story yet, so perhaps your grace might hear the matter?" Gloucester nodded and surveyed the faces around him.

"I have come here to discuss certain matters concerning my harness and I find all in disarray. Who is it can give me an account of the business?"

"As Laurence de la Halle seems to be the one most deeply involved, I think he should speak first," said Nicholas, beckoning Laurence forward. Laurence dropped to one knee in front of the

66

duke, who signalled him to stand. He gave an account of the doings in The Pilgrim and how Anna had warned him he would be attacked and robbed if he went alone with her to the caves. He explained how Will Belknap and the boy Peter had been mistaken for himself and Anna, and of the fight that ensued. He thought it prudent not to mention the insertion of his blade into the ribs of one of the felons.

"As you can see, your grace, the boy is still unconscious and poor Will has a severe headache."

Gloucester beckoned over the alehouse keeper who was now in a state of panic. He fell to his knees and grovelled before the duke, who was content to let him remain there.

"I only wish to take my daughter home," he whined.

"Did I hear the word murder mentioned?" said Gloucester.

"Indeed, one of my servants was knifed in the fight and has since died. Another has a gash across his body that will take much healing, and another was badly beaten."

"And you say your daughter was kidnapped by these men?"

"Why else would she go off with them, lord?"

Gloucester next addressed Anna.

"Is this man your father?"

"No, your grace," she replied in a tremulous voice, "he is my stepfather."

"And did you go with these men willingly or were you forced by them?"

"No your grace, I came away with master Laurence only. The others left a few minutes before we did."

"Were the men who attacked you in front or did they come from behind?"

"They were in front of us, your grace."

Gloucester regarded the alehouse keeper coldly.

"It seems that there is something very dubious about your version of the tale. I can, of course place the matter into the hands of the town watch and let the local justices deal with it. However, it is unlikely you will succeed in placing the blame for the happenings on to my armourers, and as I need them all with me on the march, I am unwilling to deprive myself of their services. Do you wish to proceed to law?"

"No, no your grace, my lord. As you wish. I am happy that my daughter, stepdaughter, is safe. I am content to leave it there."

"Good, then take yourself off." Gloucester ignored the man as he got to his feet and bowed himself out of his presence before scampering off, laden with his guilt and glad to be free from the repercussions he had nearly brought upon himself. The duke's retainers grinned in self-satisfaction at each other, as if they had themselves discomfited the alehouse keeper.

"It seems remarkable to me," said Gloucester to Laurence, "that three men and a boy should be able to cause so much injury to the king's subjects, seeing that you were at a disadvantage?"

"Your grace, we were prepared up to a point," replied Laurence. "The girl Anna had warned us what to expect and we have taken injury ourselves."

"Yet how did three men, in company with a boy and a mere girl manage to kill one man, wound another and beat yet another into insensibility, or does the alehouse keeper lie?"

"We are smiths and armourers, your grace. Each of us is strong in the arm, especially in the right arm. It was dark and we could close with our adversaries. If it had been daylight and as we were without weapons, it might have been a different story." The duke seemed pleased with the explanation. Laurence noted that when the strong right arms of the men were mentioned, his face had taken on a glow of satisfaction.

"Tell me," the duke continued, "are you the one who fitted my henchman Tyrell with a breastplate?"

"I had the honour to do so, your grace."

"Yes, he has taken to strutting around dazzling everyone with his brilliance. I have had to tell him to cover up. The enemy will see us coming for miles." The duke's retainers laughed as if Gloucester was the soul of wit. Laurence smiled his pleasure at the recognition of his handiwork. "I am pleased that we have such skilled artisans amongst our number. Master Olds, a word with you if you please."

Laurence bowed his head as the duke walked of with Nicholas Olds at his elbow and with his sycophantic retainers trailing behind.

"You are in league with the devil," muttered Jack Snipe as the duke and his train entered into the forges. Laurence made the sign of the cross at the accusation and fingered the reliquary around his neck. Snipe glared at him then stalked off after his master.

When Gloucester had retired to the king's apartments Nicholas Olds gathered them together at the forges. "We are marching the day after tomorrow so I suggest everyone gets a good nights rest. Tomorrow will be a busy day. We are expecting a further force of about six hundred men, brought to us by Sir William Parr and Sir James Harrington and doubtless they will have some work for us."

"Thanks to this troublesome Frenchman, we are short of a smith and the boy, so that means more work for us all," interjected Jack Snipe. Nicholas Olds regarded Snipe and Laurence sternly.

"There will probably be smiths with the new force, and an armourer or two if we are lucky, so we should be able to manage." Turning to Laurence and John Fisher he continued: "what has happened was the result of you men wandering off into the town. That might be fine when we are at a permanent base, but on the march from now on we stay together with the army, unless ordered otherwise. Is that clear to you all?" He looked around at the small group.

Everyone nodded in agreement. Laurence shrugged his shoulders in resignation. His encounter with the alehouse keeper of The Pilgrim had persuaded him that he might not prosper very well in Nottingham, so the decision to remain with the army had been made for him. The supplement of another six hundred men was welcome news, but the army, at around 2,000 strong, was still far too small to have any chance of victory in anything more than a local skirmish. Still, it did show that some men were willing to come in under Edward's banner.

The group dispersed and went back to the forges to find somewhere to sleep for the night. Anna and Mother Malkin were standing together, somewhat apart and Laurence went over to them.

"There is always sickness in an army, so I expect you will both be kept busy." I wish you good e'en." Though his remarks were addressed to both women it was Anna who drew his gaze. She smiled promisingly at him. Mother Malkin tugged her shawl over her shoulders and gave the girl an impatient shove, muttering something unintelligible in her regional tongue. The women went off towards the wagons in the outer bailey.

69

The following morning all was confusion. The smiths and the armourers hammered away at their work while wagons from the surrounding countryside rolled in, bringing much needed supplies of food for the army and fodder for the horses. There was much haggling over the cost of the victuals. This was inevitable as there would be little enough in the country at this time of year and prices were therefore high. The castle ovens were working hard and the smell of fresh bread and roasting meat mingled with the smell of men and horses. Knights and men-at-arms were practising swordcraft with wooden batons or hacking with battleaxes at the heavy wooden stakes placed into the ground for the purpose. Of the soldiers, one of these was the duke of Gloucester himself, who curiously was chopping enthusiastically at logs that were to be used for the kitchen fires. The army was well equipped and professional, but it was numbers that counted most in the confusion of battle.

Peter had slept through the night, but awoke as the first wintry light touched the upper towers and ramparts of the castle. He was in pain and unable to keep food down, though he managed some small beer. Will Belknap was beating away over an anvil as if nothing had happened, though there was a nasty-looking bruise on his forehead. Laurence was sitting on a stool carefully filing the hammer marks from a sallet where he had removed an indentation. Everyone in the forges was busy, including Jack Snipe, and Nicholas Olds was carefully crafting latten embellishments on the visor of Edward's bascinet. The rest of his polished harness lay on a bench ready for any last-minute work that the fastidious eye of Nicholas Olds might detect.

Laurence noticed James Tyrell in the milling mass of soldiery and he gave him a friendly wave. Tyrell broke away from the group he had been talking with and came over.

"The armour you made for me has caused quite a stir," he said with a grin. "My lord of Gloucester has commanded me to cover over with a surcoat, as you can see." He was indeed wearing a surcoat, which displayed the badge of Gloucester. "I am riding out in a few minutes. There are reports that enemy forces under the duke of

Exeter and the earl of Oxford are somewhere over Newark way and we need to find them. We are going out in some strength in case we encounter their outriders."

"The army is marching out from Nottingham tomorrow," said Laurence. "Do you think there will be a fight?"

"It is certain that Oxford and Exeter will have to be dealt with, so I should think battle with their force to be inevitable. The problem is we have a rendezvous at Leicester with levees raised from the estates of Lord Hastings, about three thousand or so, which will give us a fighting chance. Unfortunately, the lords Exeter and Oxford are somewhere between and probably outnumber us."

"Is the lord Edward dismayed?"

"The *king* is never dismayed at the prospect of battle." Came the reply. "His enemies know that and his reputation is often enough to scare them away."

"Let us hope so in this case."

Tyrell gave him a friendly slap on the back and returned to his men who were already mounting their horses ready to ride out.

Laurence ruminated on the chances of the expedition coming to a successful conclusion. That could only be decided by battle and even the reinforcements from Leicester, if they reached them, would hardly be sufficient. Somewhere out there was the earl of Warwick known as the Kingmaker. His reputation as a warrior was well known particularly in France and Brittany. Then there was Edward's treacherous brother, George duke of Clarence. He too had a large force in the field, which was allied to Warwick. After this there was Margaret of Anjou, queen to Henry VI and who, with an army financed by Louis XI of France, could be expected to land in England soon, that is if she had not already done so. The considerable army of the earl of Northumberland had not yet committed to either side, though Percy's loyalty technically belonged to the monarch who, at the moment was Henry. The Kingmaker's brother John Neville, the Marquis of Montague was also in the field. They had managed to avoid his force so far, but the range of powerful enemies that could attack Edward at any time soon was formidable. Each of these had an army larger than Edward's and if they had to face a combination of them, then Laurence could not see anything other than total defeat. What he needed was a miracle and fingering the reliquary around his neck, he began praying to the Holy Barbara, patron saint of armourers, for her help in getting him clear of Edward's army.

* * *

It seemed to Laurence that his prayers had been answered, at least in part, which was encouraging.

"They just turned tail and fled when they saw us coming," said Tyrell. He had been out with his prickers near Newark when they suddenly came upon the outriders of the earl of Oxford and the duke of Exeter. "They must have thought we were the whole army."

"Was there a fight?" asked Laurence.

"No, the duke and the earl, hearing of what they thought was Edward's approach, deserted their armies during the night and the soldiers, once they found out their leaders had gone, simply melted away!"

"Well, you did say that Edward could frighten his enemies away without a fight, but I did not expect it to happen." Laurence thought to himself that the Holy Barbara had arranged this; what other possible explanation could there be?

Tyrell beamed at him. "Now we are marching unopposed to Leicester and from there with reinforcements, continue to Coventry where Warwick is holed up. He still has about a thousand more men than we do, but as you have seen, our king will not let that worry him. He has never been beaten in battle."

They had marched out of Nottingham that morning and now were turning west towards Leicester about forty miles away. Tyrell had ridden up with some of his prickers to chivvy the baggage train along as Edward was anxious to get to Coventry and the earl of Warwick before the Kingmaker could be reinforced by the other forces loyal to him. If he could engage Warwick in battle and defeat him, then the others would likely turn away from further conflict. All except Margaret of Anjou, that is. Perhaps Edward expected to be able to defeat her army once Warwick was out of the way. Laurence considered the whole plan was risky in the extreme. Even if Edward managed to defeat Warwick, much depended on the state of his surviving army. Would they be capable of engaging in a further battle; would they have the

72

stomach for it; would others join him once he had defeated the Kingmaker? The fact was that the forces presently opposing them in the country were overwhelming in number. Their only chance was to join battle with these separately, and then they had to win every time. Just one defeat would bring the whole expedition to an end with much slaughter in the aftermath.

Laurence thought it was about time he tended to the condition of his immortal soul, as that might be the only part of him left if he got caught up in battle. He knew where there was a priest travelling with the baggage. He would seek him out and get shriven, not wishing to risk entering purgatory with all his sins still upon him. He now had something substantial to confess, which meant he could overlook mentioning his clandestine arrangement regarding his liege the duke of Brittany. For one thing there was the soul to be paid for of the felon he had stabbed in the fight at Nottingham. However, he knew that priests liked to hear confession of sexual encounters and he might be able to get a lesser penance if he allowed his descriptions full flight. After his visit to Anna the previous night, he expected he would have to provide some salacious tit-bits for the priest. He would keep some of it back, though, just in case the priest took it upon himself to restrict his further activities with her.

Chapter 4 – The Sun Ascendant

The city walls of Coventry bristled with armed men. Edward had pitched his tents in full view of the defenders taunting them to come out and do battle. He had issued a challenge to the earl of Warwick to come out and fight, but the Kingmaker declined, preferring to wait for the reformed armies of Exeter and Oxford to reach him. Also the duke of Clarence was on the way with a further 4,000 men and thus the combined force should easily overwhelm Edward's army, which even with those who had joined him still numbered less than 6,000 fighting men.

Laurence was standing on a wagon looking towards the city when Anna came along and clambered up beside him. The whole of Edward's army spread out before them, just out of range of the ordnance of the city. A festival of coloured pennants and banners fluttered in the breeze, a pageantry that almost disguised the deadly intent of the combatants.

"Is there anything happening yet?" she asked him.

"Not so far as I can see. The cannon have not been unloaded so it does not look like we will be engaging with the enemy here."

"No, not with so many hostile forces around." She surprised him with her perspicacity on matters military.

"You learn quickly, Anna."

"It is surprising what you can pick up just by keeping your ears open. I was putting a splint on the broken arm of a captain of archers yesterday and he told me about the Bastard of Fauconberg." Coming as he did from Brittany, Laurence had heard of Thomas Neville, the Bastard of Fauconberg. Everyone along the channel ports had suffered from his depredations. He was an English pirate and the cousin of the earl of Warwick. "It seems he is cruising the approaches to the Thames River estuary with a large fleet of ships. That makes him well placed to attack London if the Kingmaker orders him to do so."

Her remarks reinforced the feeling of doom that pervaded his thoughts. Here was yet another threat to Edward's bid for the throne. Apart from his brother, the eighteen-year-old Richard of Gloucester, it seemed that Edward had not a single ally of note.

74

Those nobles in his army, earl Rivers and lord Hastings had been chased out of England with him and their fortunes depended on his victory. Though 3,000 had joined Hastings from his estates, they had not managed to raise many more men on the march so far. Edward had gambled on large numbers flocking to his banner with its sun blazon. This had not happened, yet he continued as if he could take on the whole world and win. The man was a fool and they were all embarked upon a mad caper that could only result in disaster.

Laurence sighed despondently and clambered down from the wagon. He held his arms out to Anna and grasping her by the waist, lifted her down. She took the opportunity to slip her arms around his neck and clung to him for a moment. He was swept with a combination of tenderness and apprehension. The feel of a woman in his arms was comforting, but the threat of a hopeless war hung over them and depressed his spirits. It was not as if he were a part of an enterprise and a cause he could identify with. Anna was getting close to him and he really could not allow that, yet he could not bear to thrust her away. He felt vulnerable and needed the comfort she gave. This was not fair on her, he knew, and though he tried telling himself she was just an alehouse doxy, it gave him another burden for the confessional the next time he visited the priest. He gently prised himself from her embrace and looked to the tents of the armourers that were pitched in a circle by the wagons. Anna could sense the tumult of his thoughts and this made her uncertain of his courage. He had shown himself capable in a fight it was true, but how steadfast would he prove only tentatively allied as he was to Edward's cause. She had no particular loyalty to either side in the argument. As with most people she was tired of the incessant fighting of the nobles and the upheaval it had caused. She cared neither for the red rose nor the white. In this she and Laurence were of one mind.

A sudden blare of trumpets sounded from the camp before the city. They looked and saw the standards flying loose before being pulled down to be furled. Here and there tents were collapsing as their fastenings were loosened. A troop of prickers galloped up to the baggage camp. Their leader called for the baggage to be put into train. The army was to march south immediately to confront the forces of the duke of Clarence. Laurence and Anna looked at

75

each other then with a brief kiss, parted and went their separate ways, she to Mother Malkin and he to the armourers' camp.

The armourers' tents were already collapsing and Laurence helped fold them neatly before stowing them in one of the wagons. Someone had kicked out the campfire and the cooking utensils, some still hot, were hurriedly stowed away. Men were frantically running everywhere. The drivers let their cart horses into the traces of the wagons, anxious to get away with the army rather than get left behind at the mercy of the city garrison who, once the army had left, could ride out and set upon them. Already they could see the prickers were away and the first files of Edward's soldiery on the march.

It all seemed so frustrating. They marched barely ten miles before halting and pitching camp again outside the walls of Warwick town. Laurence had feared the worst; a desperate retreat from some superior and unassailable army, but it turned out to be a matter of strategy on Edward's part. Clarence was, indeed, on his way north to join the Kingmaker at Coventry, but now Edward had placed himself between the two allies. Moreover, he now commanded the road to London. If the Kingmaker wished to get to the capital, where king Henry was, then he would have to get through Edward first. Similarly, if Clarence wanted to get to the earl of Warwick at Coventry, he would have to engage Edward's army, which for once, was superior in strength to his. The knowledge did nothing to calm Laurence's nerves, which had undergone severe mangling from the moment they had left Flushing harbour. Clarence to the south and the Kingmaker behind who could storm out of Coventry and catch them between the jaws of a vice. They had heard Oxford and Exeter had reformed their forces and were on the way to reinforce the Kingmaker at Coventry. The Kingmaker's brother, John Neville, Marquise of Montague was also somewhere near with his army.

Laurence fingered the silver reliquary at his neck and, after making the sign of the cross, began praying to the Virgin for deliverance. "*Imperatrix supernorum, superatrix infernorum . . .*"

The prickers returned to the baggage camp, this time with James Tyrell at their head. Edward was calling on all able-bodied men to take up arms and join the main army. Ahead Laurence could see the deployment of men in battle order facing south. That meant the army of the duke of Clarence was close. He had no choice but to join in. It was better to be armed ready to fight rather than remain in the baggage camp, which could be easily overrun if things went badly for Edward's army. Tyrell was resplendent in his shining breastplate. He was wearing the old leg armour, somewhat incongruously Laurence observed, as it was different in style to his body armour. Yet it offered protection and his enemies were unlikely to notice.

Laurence searched through the armourers' wagons for a suitable weapon and chose a long-handled hammer with a square head one side and a short curved axe the other. At the end of the shaft at the head end was a long spike for stabbing an adversary when in company too close packed to swing the hammer. As an armourer he knew what it would be hopeless to attack an armoured man-at-arms with a sword or blade, but a hammer, properly applied, could break apart plate and shatter limbs. The axe could be used at vulnerable spots and his murderer, a long-bladed dagger, would be effective at close quarters. His body protection consisted of a brigandine, a number of small iron plates riveted onto a leather jacket. For his head he had a sallet fitted with a bevor to protect his mouth and neck. His legs were unprotected and he would have to rely on swiftness of movement to get out of trouble. If the army broke and ran, Laurence was confident he could be well to the fore. The others had also raided the armourers' wagons for weapons and whatever armour they could procure. They were a motley crew. Genase Monk had on a padded jupon topped by a chapel-de-fer. Around his waist was a thick leather belt with a sword and scabbard suspended from hangers. He also had a dagger tucked into the top of one of his high leather boots. An experienced soldier as well as a skilled smith, he wore light boots that permitted rapid movement, essential if he were to avoid the onslaught of heavily armoured men-at-arms. Will Belknap had on a haubergeon covered over by a breastplate. He also had a chapel-de-fer on his head and his favoured weapon was a pike. Peter, who had recovered from his head wound, was attired as Genase Monk, his weapon was a pike and he also wore a dagger in a scabbard at his belt. Laurence stood with them and wondered how they were to deploy, having had no further orders.

"That is poor harness for an armourer." Tyrell had ridden across and was grinning fiercely down at him. "It is rather more make-piece than mine."

"I make armour for others, not myself. This is all I can find for the moment, from the dregs of master Olds stock."

"You probably won't need it, as it happens," said Tyrell. "Which, looking at you is, perhaps, fortunate. The heralds are away and it is expected that Clarence will join with us against Warwick."

"Why should he do that? I know that he and the king are brothers, but the forces arraigned against us are far superior and I am led to believe that Clarence intends to be on the winning side."

"If you were Clarence, how would you define the 'winning' side? If Warwick defeats king Edward, then he expects to rule England through the simple-minded Henry, leaving Clarence out in the cold. Similarly, when Margaret of Anjou returns with the Prince of Wales, then it will be she that rules through Henry and she is mother to his son and heir who will become king after him. That destroys any ideas Clarence might have of wielding power in the land."

"But surely, when Margaret returns then Warwick's ambitions will be confounded too. Margaret and Warwick are reluctant allies, after all. Wouldn't Clarence be better off as an ally of the Kingmaker? If together they can defeat Edward, then they might be able to serve the same to Margaret of Anjou when she arrives with her army?"

"There are many possibilities, my friend," said Tyrell. "Much has been going on while Edward has been on the march. Envoys of their sister, Margaret, Duchess of Burgundy, who has been pleading Edward's cause, have approached Clarence. Family ties are strong, and the three brothers have a certain bond, while my lord of Gloucester is the glue which binds them together, and he is firmly on Edward's side."

Laurence's ears picked up as he heard the name of Burgundy. He knew that William Caxton was in the service of the duchess and there was a continuous stream of intelligence passing between Caxton's agents in England and Burgundy's court. His own instructions to make contact with Francis of Brittany's agent in London, Cornelius Quirke, could well compliment the work of Caxton and his agents. At last he was beginning to see a way clear of his present predicament and find useful employment away from the battlefield where the ambitions of the opposing factions could be overturned in a few hours of mortal combat.

"We seem to be in battle array. From what you say this is just show, but I would like to get a view of Clarence's army and be ready to fight if needed," he lied.

"That is not difficult," said Tyrell. "You would actually be attached to my lord of Gloucester's command and he is arrayed to the right of the king on high ground overlooking the Banbury road. Get yourself and your companions over there and you should be able to see what is happening." A sound of trumpets summoned the prickers and Tyrell jerked the head of his horse around and rode off with the rest of his troop towards the army.

The soldiers in the front ranks of Gloucester's battalion were straining to see the activity that was taking place between the two opposing forces. Laurence could see the heralds riding back and forth, meeting with their opposites in the open ground between the armies. Banners and pennants were flying everywhere on both sides in a splendour of pageantry. Presently, a troop of horsemen rode out from Edward's army and a similar troop appeared from Clarence's force. He could easily make out the blazon of the Yorkist sun and the white boar of Gloucester. Edward was resplendent in armour that reflected the light from the real sun, outshining that on his banner. Another clad in similar brightness rode up to meet him. Both men leaned across and embraced, clapping each other as long lost brothers, which indeed they were, this being their reconciliation. The duke of Gloucester was there too, but slightly behind his brother Edward. Then he rode forward and embraced his brother George, duke of Clarence. It was apparent to them all that the three brothers, Edward, George and Richard were as one and the two armies now almost equalled the forces that the Kingmaker had assembled.

The armies gradually broke ranks and horsemen were galloping everywhere. Soon the captains issued orders for the march into the town of Warwick and Laurence, along with his companions returned to the baggage train. They were met by an anxious Anna who had seen them stride out into the army and believed there was to be a battle. He had not given her much thought and wondered what would have happened if there had been a battle lost and he had fled the scene. He supposed that as a tavern whore she might be better equipped to survive such a defeat than he, but that did little to salve his conscience. In fact, his conscience was beginning to bear down on him and he needed a priest to unburden his soul.

The whole camp was bustling and rumour was rife. Nobody had an idea of what was happening except that Clarence had now joined with Edward. Most were relieved that there would not be a battle, though some grumbled about the continuing march that so far had produced no tangible result. Apprehension lay over the army as a dark blanket and few, though contemplating a welcome respite in the town of Warwick, were content with the business. They were about to set off when a troop of horsemen rode by. One of these was Edward's herald resplendent in full shining armour and plumed helmet, his breastplate covered with a surcoat displaying the sun of York with Edward's banner carried by a horseman in front. They were heading directly for Coventry and Laurence supposed that another parley was to take place.

It was evening before the last of the baggage wagons rolled into the market place in Warwick town. The carriages were grouped close together and a guard set to discourage the townspeople from plundering. On the march in, Anna had found a place on one of the wagons for Mother Malkin. She had joined with Laurence and his comrades to walk in together beside the baggage train. Being last to arrive the taverns and alehouses were full of revelling soldiery, those on the duke of Clarence's side eager to strike up an accord with those of Edward and Gloucester who, until that day, they had expected to engage in combat. Neither side had been keen to fight each other so a feeling of intense camaraderie permeated the whole of Edward's combined force. Sensing that his people were in need of a morale boost, the king commanded that ale be supplied for his army, which he paid for from his own meagre resources, counting it money well spent. Whatever happened next, Edward could count on the loyalty of his army.

They had seen nothing of Nicholas Olds. As the king's personal armourer, he had been in close attendance upon Edward since the march from Nottingham and, so long as there was the likelihood of imminent battle, that was where he would remain. The king, along with his retinue and noble brothers, was comfortably housed in Warwick castle and no doubt Nicholas would prefer his accommodation there with him to a tavern in the town. Jack Snipe turned up to ensure that the armourers' wagons were all accounted for and safely parked in the market square. He too had found some accommodation in Warwick castle while the rest of the armourers were to sleep in the wagons, though covered over from the night frost, somewhat worse off than their master. However, it hardly mattered while they could keep good company and get their share of the ale liberally dispensed according to the king's largesse. They had lit a brazier in the market place close to their wagons and had acquired a liberal supply of ale from the nearest tavern. Anna had taken to serving them, running to and fro to the barrel that was located outside the tavern. She also ensured that Mother Malkin got her share too. The crone had brought a small empty water cask and set it down in front of the brazier where she sat and reached out with her gnarled fingers to the fire for warmth. At Anna's command, Laurence took her some warmed ale mixed with spices as she liked it, and handed it to the old woman. Mother Malkin showed her few remaining teeth in a wide grin and raised the beaker to him in thanks. She took a draw of ale and nodded towards Anna.

"Hoo's a reet whisk-tail an no mistake, bu' hoo con mak' a gradely sup o' mulled ale."

Laurence resisted the impulse to cross himself, correctly supposing that the old crone was making a compliment in her outlandish dialect rather than casting some sort of spell. Anna came up to him and slipped her arm through his. The old crone grinned and nodded at them.

"He's a gurt witherin felley bi th' mass," she cackled.

"What is it she is saying?" he enquired of Anna with a worried frown on his face. He had extracted the word 'mass' from her utterance and wondered if she was cursing the Church.

"She is just admiring your body, and I must say she has a good eye, even though she is too old to take advantage of you. It's a good thing I am here to stand in for her."

"I cannot understand a word of what she says. Is she English?"

"Of course she is English. She comes from the north of here in the county of Lancashire."

"Is that not the county of the red rose, of the house of Lancaster?"

"It is."

81

"Then why is she with the army of York?"

"Like so many in England, we follow whoever offers the best hope for the future. Common folk have no abiding loyalty to a noble house unless compelled by service to their lord, and that may alter at any time depending on his ambition. Why, we have just witnessed the duke of Clarence change his allegiance from York to Lancaster and now back to York again."

"You English seem a faithless nation."

"We are not!" she declared angrily. "We are loyal to England represented by our king, whatever house he may be."

"Well you have two kings and your Henry is sitting on the throne in London while your Edward is here in Warwick."

"Henry is a travesty of a king. It is shameful when you think he is the son of our great Henry, the fifth of that name, the victor at Agincourt. His mother Katherine has passed him the mind of her father, king Charles VI of France, who as the world knows was mad. Margaret of Anjou rules Henry. Their whelp, the Prince of Wales, is a disgusting monster that thinks only of hangings and chopping off of heads. It would be a disaster if he should come to rule over us." Anna was flushed and ready to continue her tirade when Laurence held up his hands in surrender.

"I have no wish to offend," he said quietly. "I only want to understand."

Anna relaxed and scowled at him before letting her lips form a pout. He took her hands in his and gazed into her eyes. I think we might find ourselves a comfortable place in one of the wagons for the night. She brightened up and grasped him by his right hand. She had already prepared a place and the two of them disappeared from the ring of light around the brazier. The others grinned at each other and raised their beakers in silent tribute. Mother Malkin dozed in the warmth of the fire with her chin on her chest. All around were the sounds of carousing and with a full moon behind in a clear sky, the turrets of the massive castle stood dark in silhouetted guardianship over the town. Windows and embrasures in the walls and turrets gleamed with yellow candlelight and shadows flitted back and forth as the inhabitants moved around the castle. Above the town only the stars were still.

Before the last of the stars had faded into the dawn the captains were out rousting the army. Many thick heads were being doused in cold water in troughs and buckets to clear them for the day, a day which had started too early for many. Already horsemen, resplendent in full harness, were trotting out of the castle and heading for the town gates. Laurence and his companions broke their fast on bread and cheese washed down with the remnants of last night's ale, the town water being too dangerous to drink. Anna returned with Mother Malkin to their place in the wagon train. They had space in one of the farriers' wagons where Mother Malkin kept her supply of herbs and potions.

It would be some time before the supply train set off, so Laurence decided to acquire a modicum of safety for his immortal soul in the church by the square. He had heard Matins rung just before first light. Now, upon the tolls of the later bell sounding for Prime he hurried into the church and stood with other soldiers who had crowded inside. They stood in silent prayer while the monks chanted the office. Then one of the priests came to them and gave them benediction. While fingering his reliquary, Laurence offered prayers to his patron saint, Barbara and to Jude for good measure, as he still feared Edward's cause was hopeless.

With the cloying smell of incense still in his nostrils, Laurence stood blinking in the bright daylight of the market square observing the frenetic chasing to and fro of the army. Dodging the careless galloping of cavalry, he hurried over to the armourers' wagons and began helping with the draught horses. They had to wait while the bulk of the army marched out of the town otherwise the lumbering baggage train would cause a blockage at the gates. A captain of archers stood close by with his company waiting for his turn to join the marching column. Laurence engaged him in conversation.

"Where are we off to now? He asked hopefully. The captain was bored with waiting and was only too happy to talk.

"We are marching on London. The king has challenged the Kingmaker to come out of Coventry and fight with us, but it seems he is remaining safely behind his walls."

"The Earl must be considering his position now that the duke of Clarence has joined us."

"We know the Kingmaker has reinforcements and he still outnumbers us, but there is other news that has caused our king to move. Margaret of Anjou has set sail from France with her army and the Prince of Wales. Our king wants to secure London before she lands we know not where."

The progress of the army to London suited Laurence very well. However, they had to get there first and it may happen that a battle might alter everything. He needed to get away from the army and fend for himself. At that moment Tyrell rode into the square with his men and indicated with a wave of his arm that the archers get into line of March. The captain of archers immediately turned from his conversation with Laurence and began chivvying his men into formation. Tyrell spotted Laurence and cantered over.

"Get ready to fall in behind the archers," he shouted imperiously. Laurence took hold of the bridle of Tyrell's horse and raised his head.

"I am weary of plodding along with the baggage."

Tyrell had already noted that the armourer could be more useful on the march than with the baggage. He was pleased that Laurence had spoken out, but for now he had other pressing business – getting the army out of Warwick town and on the march to London.

"I cannot help that, my friend. Let us get on the road for now and I shall come and speak with you when I can. I suggest, though, that you get yourself a good mount from one of the farriers in the town. All the horses on the march are spoken for." Laurence had to be content with that and let go of the bridle. Tyrell gave him a brief nod and cantered away followed by his troop.

* * *

Tyrell came up to them as the baggage train rumbled on after the army, which was keeping up reasonably well on the improved highway. He was pleased to see that Laurence had bought himself a good mount. Nicholas Olds was distinctly unhappy about losing his services, but there was little he could do to keep him with the other armourers. Laurence had reassured him that once in London he would seek him out and return to his small band of armourers. He needed to do this in any case because he required transport for his tools, which he could not afford to lose. Will Belknap had promised to look to his tools and John Fisher would take up his few remaining armouring tasks until they reached the capital.

With a lighter purse and an even lighter heart, Laurence led his mount alongside the wagons to let it get used to him. He had to bargain hard with the farrier who sold him the horse. As soon as the man detected a foreign accent, he had tried to palm him off with a nag. Laurence had a good eye for horseflesh and he had chosen a rouncey mare with good wind and a deep chest. The additional cost of bridle and saddle had depleted his meagre money resource to a pitiful amount, yet he was now mobile and could ride off should the need arise.

James Tyrell cantered up beside him, resplendent in a surcoat bearing the blazon of the white boar. His horse was decked with a short, red caparison and Laurence noted that the barding it concealed was of *cuir bouilli*, at least around the face and chest.

"I see you have taken me at my word," he said gaily. "You are to ride with my prickers. It seems that my lord of Gloucester has taken note of you and is willing to let you join us. We are his henchmen and it is a great honour to be one of us."

"Then I shall hope to be worthy," Laurence replied with some trepidation. He began to wonder if he had not jumped from the cooking pot and into the fire.

"Your horse will be caparisoned as ours and we ride out with lance and sword. You will also wear the badge of Gloucester."

Laurence had already wrapped his travelling cloak into a bundle and secured it to his saddle. Two saddlebags contained his water flask and a few items for the road.

"I would like to take leave of my friends."

"Alright, but be quick. We are to ride the road to St. Albans ahead of the army."

Laurence found John Fisher and asked him to explain to Anna where he was going and that he expected they would all meet up again in London. He considered that Anna would bear his departure stoically and if he took himself off somewhere else, she would have little difficulty in attaching herself to another fellow. That might be for the best anyhow. His future plans did not include a female companion. Both men clapped each other on the shoulders and said their farewells. With that Laurence climbed into the saddle and settled himself down for the ride. Trotting over to Tyrell, the two men rode off to where the other prickers were waiting. Pausing at their supply wagon to caparison Laurence's mount, and to equip him with a lance and sword, they found a tabard in Gloucester's livery and watched while he draped it over his shoulders.

They rode alongside the army, passing the splendid retinues and heralds of king Edward and those of his brothers George duke of Clarence and Richard duke of Gloucester. They were on a king's highway, which meant there was plenty of room for the riders beside the marching column, the ground being cleared a bow shot either side of the road. Laurence was forced to consider this a brave show, a far cry from the little band of bedraggled adventurers that had scrambled ashore at Ravenspur. His newfound freedom from the confines of the army gave him a feeling of euphoria and renewed hope. Perhaps this king might win his crown back after all.

They rode ahead of the army and pausing on high ground to get their bearings, looked back towards the marching column, which had the appearance of a jewelled snake, twisting and turning its way along the road, slowly but relentlessly moving forward. Pennants and banners flew everywhere along the column. The bright spring sunshine flashed and glittered like scales of fire reflected from the polished armour of those knights who had squires to buff their harness. Amongst the brightest of these, Laurence could just make out the mounted panoply of the king, with his armour shining behind an enormous banner showing the golden sun blazon of his house.

At Tyrell's command the troop moved onward leaving the army out of sight behind the hill. Now they rode, seemingly alone along the broad highway and, gazing out across the fresh green foliage, the breeze took the blossoms of early spring and swirled them around their heads as if some holy rite was being enacted. The whole country seemed part of an enchantment where the horror of war was unsuspected rather than slowly approaching from all directions. Everywhere in England, armies marched just out of sight, beyond the nearest hill, glittering serpents in the Garden of Eden. All this might have been unrealised by the yeoman population except for the prickers on all sides who rode ahead seeking out the location of their enemy. Soon the armies would find each other and then in a dreadful meeting, their dispute would be prosecuted in blood.

Tyrell's prickers rode unopposed to London where they found the capital in chaos. They stopped at an inn just outside the city walls and made some enquiries before proceeding further. They learned that the previous day, the Archbishop of York, George Neville, along with other prominent Lancastrians had paraded the imbecile king Henry through the streets of London in an attempt to rally the city around their cause. They had tied his legs under his horse to ensure he did not fall off and carried in front the foxtail emblem of his father, Henry V in a desperate attempt to gain support for the son of the victor of Agincourt. Henry VI made a sorry sight, which failed to impress the council of citizens. The mayor of London took to his bed to avoid responsibility and the council decided not to oppose Edward when he arrived.

Tyrell and his men decided it would be safe to enter through the city gates. He gathered them around him. They were twenty in number, not enough to overcome determined resistance, but circumstances seemed to indicate they would be fairly safe if they stuck close together.

"We will spruce ourselves up and ride in as if we own the place, which, when king Edward arrives we probably will. Make sure there is no road dirt on our livery and boots. It is the colours of our king that will impress them now."

Bravely flying the pennants of York on their spears, the caparisons of their horses displaying Edward's sun blazon and resplendent in the livery of the duke of Gloucester, they rode into London. Just inside the gates they were met by a group of aldermen who had been alerted to their presence outside the city and who had hurried to greet them. One of these stepped forward to address the horsemen.

"Greetings to the house of York. I am Edmund Shaa of the Guild of Goldsmiths. May I and these my fellow aldermen welcome you to London."

"Well met, Goodman Shaa," said Tyrell reaching down to grasp the hand of the alderman, who smiled up at him and continued his greeting.

"We believe his Grace the Archbishop of York has informed king Edward that London will submit to his puissance. Already our people, those loyal to York have seized the tower of London and released the Yorkist prisoners held there. The archbishop has king Henry at his palace. Warwick's supporters have either fled the city or are lying low. There is no impediment to your entry into our city."

"The king will rest at St. Albans tonight but will enter his capital on the morrow," Tyrell informed him. "We seek lodging until then and stabling for our horses." The aldermen bowed their heads gracefully as the troop rode into the city and pulled up in a small square where several hostelries were located. The townspeople gathered around to satisfy themselves that these were indeed king Edward's men as denoted by their livery. Soon the hawkers and doxies arrived touting for business, guessing correctly that men who have been on the road with a marching army might have need of their wares.

Laurence was delighted. He had made it to London unscathed and in contact with a company of the duke of Gloucester's henchmen. He would have to remain in their company for now, but he expected an opportunity would soon arise for a visit to the apothecary Cornelius Quirke near the Cripplegate, wherever that was. He was pondering on how he would find the Cripplegate when James Tyrell, seeing him standing apart from the others, came over.

"I have a job for you," he informed him. "We shall go together to the Tower. There is an armoury there that contains some of the best harness in England. With the king's business to do we should be able to pick ourselves some proper pieces. I fear we will have need of them before long. We will need you to fit them properly otherwise we could end up dropping bits of iron all over England."

Laurence was torn between professional delight at the prospect of entering the Tower armoury and apprehension with the idea he might yet be expected to engage in serious combat. He was still trapped in events he had no means of controlling. Tyrell arranged for the lodging of his men and the stabling of their horses then the whole troop mounted to ride through the streets to the Tower. London might be welcoming to Edward's army for the moment, but it was unwise to trust that one or two horsemen in Yorkist livery might escape attack by the remnants of Warwick's supporters.

The troop clattered over the cobbles through the town gate of the Tower of London. The White Tower, built by William the First, known as the Conqueror, stood high and mighty, at once a fortress and a royal palace. A sentry at the gate, eyeing their livery, directed them to the armoury. The two men turned towards St. Thomas' Tower where the armoury was. They tied their horses to iron rings set in the wall and climbed up a wooden stairs to the door of the tower. The room was larger than they expected and crammed with harness suspended on wooden stands. A crabbed old man dressed in a brown smock tied with a hemp rope and with a wooden stump where a leg had been limped his way over to them. His eye flicked between them, the other being missing from its socket.

"Can I be of assistance, masters," he grunted. Tyrell regarded him with some distaste.

"We would like to speak with the master armourer," he said gruffly. "We are here on the king's business." The old man leaned his head to one side and cocked a single eye at them, which notwithstanding its solitary aspect, still managed to convey inquisitiveness.

"The king?"

"Yes, king Edward. Hurry along fellow." The old man showed them his single tooth in a lop-sided grin and limped off, tugging at his forelock, or at least the place where a forelock would have been if he had any hair left other than the few wisps that grew from the sides of his scalp down to his shoulders. He disappeared around the back of the heaps of harness in the room and returned a few moments later with a man of middle years wearing the apparel of a merchant.

"I see you are Gloucester's men by your livery," he said enthusiastically. "I am so pleased that there is to be a Yorkist king again." Laurence could not decide if the man was genuine in his approbation, but it hardly mattered. Edward would be in London tomorrow and the capital was already his in spirit.

"I'm Peterkin Mumby, custodian of the castle armoury stores."

"Yonder fellow," said Tyrell, indicating the old man who was in the process of disappearing into the shadows behind a stack of halberds. "What is his function here?"

"Oh, you mean Limping Lemmy. He was a gunner until he blew out an eye mixing gunpowder here in the tower arsenal. Unfortunately, it was his aiming eye he lost, though he was never a good shot in the first place. He makes himself useful here and we think of him as a pensioner."

"Did the gunpowder blow his leg off, too?"

"No, that was due to a stone cannonball."

"He's seen action then, to get a leg taken off by a cannonball."

"No, not really. He dropped it on his foot, which went bad afterwards. It was the chirurgeon took his leg off."

Tyrell and Laurence exchanged amused glances. Peterkin Mumby kept a perfectly straight face and seemed to see nothing unusual in the tale. Tyrell cleared his throat and decided to get down to business.

"We have come here to equip our men with some decent armour," he said. "There are twenty of us and no two have the same rig. Our tabards cover most of our iron, but as his grace of Gloucester's henchmen in the service of king Edward, it is necessary for us all to don similar harness."

"What exactly are you looking for?" asked Mumby.

"I think hauberk and breastplate." Tyrell turned to Laurence. "What would you suggest?"

"Your prickers are usually engaged in scouting work so they need not be heavily armoured. Besides, they are not knights so a plain rig would be best. A hauberk to cover the body and legs would be fine with cuirass for the upper body, though this need only be breastplate and backplate. I would also suggest gauntlets. An iron fist is a mighty weapon in its own right and the sight of a man in mail with body armour and gauntlets is very intimidating. You might also choose a sallet for head protection and a mail aventail to cover the neck. They might need a jupon under their body armour."

"Yes, my friend, that would give us a very effective fighting force," said Tyrell. "When dressed over in my lord of Gloucester's livery, they will make a splendid sight." Laurence gave the matter some more thought.

"The body armour might have to be altered to suit the individual wearer and for that I need a forge." Mumby nodded in agreement.

"We have some of the best armourers in England here at the Tower. They will soon fit your men into their armour, though most of them should find we can kit them out immediately from my store."

Laurence hardly knew what to think of that. He had supposed he would be doing the work, which would get him out of the fighting troop, at least for a while. However, that would tie him to the forges and he really wanted to try to find Cornelius Quirke.

Tyrell stood deep in thought. "The king will arrive in London tomorrow. We shall not be in his retinue but we will be needed to get the crowd out of the way as he comes through. We had best get the men set up right away, then, and not concern ourselves with the niceties of a good fit until later. You armourers are too fussy."

"I suppose you will be keeping the breastplate I fitted you with?"

"Certainly, that is one of us who need not concern himself with a proper fit." Tyrell grinned and gave Laurence a gentle slap on his arm. "Come, let us get the men in and then we can tend to our stomachs at the tavern."

Chapter 5 – Into Battle

The progress of a king entering his capital is bound to be a splendid sight – it could hardly be anything less. His strength and power is expressed in pageantry and without it he is beggared and disregarded. So it was that in full panoply of state on the 10th of April 1471, Edward the fourth of England rode with his entourage through the gates of London. His army followed behind and would make camp outside the city walls while the king, his brothers, nobles and armed retainers paraded in front of the citizens. First came a body of foot soldiers closely followed by a bevy of chaplains and priests; after came the yeomen servants in the king's livery, then fully armoured men-at-arms. Next marched the banner men, holding high the sun blazon of York along with pennants displaying the white rose. Then came the mounted heralds, their brass trumpets hung with the device of Edward, the three lions of England quartered with the triple fleur-de-lis of France, and blowing a fanfare that announced the coming of the king. Behind these came the king himself, mounted on a black warhorse that was caparisoned to the ground in pure white, decked with brilliant suns embroidered in golden thread.

He rode alone, with a space between those in front and those behind so that everyone in the city could be quite sure who he was. Edward was in full harness without surcoat or tabard; his visor had been removed to show his face. His armour glittered in the light of the late morning and an ornate gold crown encircled his helmet. Ornamental rondels, fashioned in the shape of the rose of York, were fitted to the front of his shoulder joints and there were steel wings extending each couter and poleyn. These had been embellished with latten, embossed and chased with an intricate pattern. He wore a cloak of scarlet embroidered with gold roses which he wore thrown back from his shoulders and arranged over the horse's croupiere, which was assumed to be under the caparison.

His horse had been trained to lift its forelocks in dance and its face was surfaced with a polished chamfron fitted with a spiked rondel to denote its warlike purpose. A white plume topped its face armour while an armoured criniere swept along the arch of its neck, its assembly of protective lames flexing and gleaming in the sunlight. Its chest was adorned with a brilliant peytral that swept around and disappeared beneath the caparison. Red silken reins were chained with silver and held loosely in the jewelled gauntlet of the king's left hand, near to his sword by his side. His right hand rested on the pommel of a dagger held in a ruby-encrusted scabbard.

The king did not ride aloof. He inclined his head majestically at the crowd and smiled down on them. Edward was renowned for his manly appearance and he was not about to disappoint. He raised his hand from his dagger only when he passed by the ladies who had come to see the man that so many of them admired. Edward had intimate knowledge of some of them, and many a husband made a subdued obeisance while their ladies cheered enthusiastically. He was back and they accepted him as their king – the women would see to that. Every now and then, one of the bolder females would run from the crowd and reach out to him. He would lean down and offer his gauntleted hand to be kissed. Edward was a ladies man through and through. If all the hearts in London had been female, then he was king absolute.

Behind the king rode his brother, George, duke of Clarence. He too had his retinue and it was as resplendent as that of the king, though the citizens of London did not seem to regard him with the same enthusiasm as they did Edward. He rode in harness but with his head bared, displaying a surly, arrogant mien that did nothing to endear him to the crowd. In truth, the citizens were inured to such aristocrats as this and simply applauded as he rode by, their cheers exhausted in the passage of the king. Both Clarence and Gloucester rode black mounts caparisoned to the ground in white and embroidered with golden suns just as Edward, with the clear intention of demonstrating their dynastic Plantagenet solidarity.

Parading in his distinctive black harness, the duke of Gloucester fared no better than Clarence. He wore his visor up and a white plume of feathers topped his helmet. Regarded as a northern lord, Richard of Gloucester was held in low esteem in London. An eighteen year old unproved youth of slight frame; he had little of the charisma his brother displayed. His henchmen preceded him, with James Tyrell in front of his troop. They had not, after all, been deployed to part a way through the crowd. Richard had commanded that they accompany him and so that was what they were doing. He had his immediate yeoman servants with him and that was all.

Behind the duke of Gloucester the loyal citizens of London fell in. Their militia came first followed by those aldermen that were loyal to the house of York. Prominent among these was the goldsmith Edmund Shaa. The good men of London appreciated Edward. Previously he had invested in trade goods to increase his wealth and they regarded him as one of themselves, albeit of a more elevated class.

Laurence rode at the rear of Gloucester's prickers. This was the closest he had come to the king and he, in company with the citizens of London, was in thrall. Gloucester was a prince of the blood, yet he was somehow approachable and had a common dimension that an artisan craftsman could converse with without too much of a problem. Edward was different; he had a presence that was unfathomable. His progress through the capital had demonstrated this quality. The commoners took to him easily, even though he was a king, yet his grandness was in no way diminished by his common touch, rather it was enhanced. On the other hand, the great nobles of England feared him. He had never been defeated in battle and even the Kingmaker himself, the mighty earl of Warwick, Richard Neville, was treading carefully, reluctant so far to engage his erstwhile protégé in battle. It was this charisma that had got them to London unscathed. In the nature of things, it could not last.

Edward made his progress to St. Paul's cathedral where he entered with his brothers to give thanks to God for his success so far. This was a somewhat hurried affair and most of their retinues waited outside. Presently, the brothers came out and made their next stop at the archbishop's palace where Henry the sixth was residing in the care of the Kingmaker's brother George Neville, archbishop of York. Except for his immediate retainers, Edward went in alone to speak with Henry. When he came out he beckoned his brother Gloucester over to him. They conversed briefly before Edward mounted his horse and began to move off towards Westminster, where his queen and infant son were waiting. The duke of Gloucester summoned James Tyrell to his side. He issued some

94

instructions then mounted up and joined Edward's retinue on its route to Westminster. Tyrell cantered over to his troop.

"Dismount, men and follow me." He indicated that he wished to speak with Laurence. "As a Frenchman with experience at moving around at a court, I have need of your assistance." Laurence was most curious.

"Of course, what is it you wish me to do?" Tyrell took him by the arm and pulled him to one side.

"We are to escort king Henry to the Tower for safekeeping. As a rough soldier I do not feel able to converse with him properly, but you can address him in French as you would use it at the duke of Brittany's court, which might make his removal from the archbishop's custody somewhat easier."

"I understand, but is there likely to be any trouble with the archbishop's men?"

"There better not be," snarled Tyrell. "Edward is not kindly disposed towards the Nevilles and if the archbishop causes trouble there will be retribution. No, he knows where he stands with Edward. Besides it has already been decided."

As they marched leading their horses to the archbishop's palace, Laurence reflected on the ramifications of his contact with king Henry the sixth. Whatever happened he would be in a position to join in with whichever faction came out on top. If Edward was successful in his attempts to regain his crown permanently, then so much the better. He was already established with the Yorkists, so he could simply continue developing his relationship with them. If Warwick were to defeat Edward, however, then he would attempt to rule through Henry and so would Margaret of Anjou if she came out on top. That made three distinct possible outcomes. If Laurence could establish some sort of bond with Henry, then he was well positioned to find favour with whoever won. Moreover, located in London at the Tower, he would be well away from any fighting. Things were beginning to look up.

On reaching the palace Tyrell and Laurence, along with Gloucester's troop of henchmen marched through the gates and up the steps to the palace. The guards made pretence of resistance, crossing their pikes as they approached the main door. Tyrell did not even bother to address them. He merely halted in front of them and waited while their nerve failed and they stood back to let the troop through. One inside they asked the way to where Henry was being housed. It seemed he was in an annex of the archbishop's personal apartments.

Anyone would have been shocked on a first view of Henry the sixth of England. He had been king from the age of one year and crowned at the age of eight. Now he was fifty years old and broken in mind and spirit. A king habitually displays himself in glorious array, necessary to impress and subdue his subjects. His dress, his demeanour, his impression of power and wealth are the means whereby he controls nobles and commons alike. Yet here was a man sitting cross-legged on a rug in a plain chamber with just a table and a couple of chairs for furniture. Logs blazed in the fireplace. The illumination provided by their flames supplemented the weak light that entered reluctantly through a small lancet window as if even the sun was shamed by the sight. Henry was dressed in a simple grey woollen robe tied with a silk rope at the waist. His legs were covered with fine hose and his shoes were plain leather. His head was bare and his wispy grey hair hung to his shoulders. He had never been stout, but now his cheeks sagged and his bones were clearly delineated in the cloth over his shoulders. His mind had left him in the year 1453 and a protector, Richard, duke of York, Edward's father, was appointed to run the country during his illness. Two years later, when Henry came to his senses the duke of York was summarily dismissed thus provoking a war during which York was killed at the battle of Wakefield. Then, in 1461 Richard of York's heir, Edward took the throne from Henry with the help of the earl of Warwick, who thus earned himself his "Kingmaker" epithet. Now Tyrell and Laurence were about to confront the Kingmaker's brother, the archbishop of York.

The archbishop was standing by the table regarding them with a combination of trepidation and arrogance. He was finely robed in resplendent contrast to the man in his care. George Neville had been forced to acknowledge Edward as king, though he was firmly Lancastrian by choice. He was portly and his cheeks glowed red, either from the effects of rich food and drink, anger, or a combination of both. His hair was dressed and curled where it emerged from under a woollen cap.

Tyrell, with Laurence at his side stepped into the chamber. The rest of the men formed up outside. Tyrell gave the archbishop a desultory bow while Laurence, careful of the wrath of the Church, knelt before him and kissed the hand that the archbishop automatically proffered. The churchman showed some surprise at this yet his lip could not quite reform itself from the curl of disdain that was fixed there. Tyrell too wondered at Laurence's action but as it was entirely correct, decided to ignore it.

"Your grace, may I present Laurence de la Halle who is a visitor here from the court of Francis the second of Brittany." Laurence almost gasped at the audacity of Tyrell's announcement. He had no rank nor was he here with any authority from duke Francis. "He is to escort king Henry to the Tower."

The archbishop gave him a wry look. All he could see was a plain soldier displaying the livery of the duke of Gloucester, not someone who would even think to look at a king directly, even less form part of his escort. These were uncertain times, though, and the churchman decided it might be best to treat these men with contemptible silence rather than provoke something he could not, for the moment, have any control of. He turned away from his perusal of Laurence and went over to where Henry was sitting on his rug, staring at the fire and showing little interest in what was happening.

"Your Grace," said the archbishop leaning down and offering his hand. "Please stand and greet your *guests*. They have come to move us to somewhere more comfortable."

Laurence's mind had been a mass of confusion until now, but gradually his thoughts began to coalesce into a strategy for action. He might as well play the role he had been given, seeing there was no definite opposition to it. One thing he was sure of, he did not want to provoke hostility by either side. He stood and walked over to king Henry then kneeled before him in obeisance.

"My lord, please be assured your needs will be taken care of," he said in his best courtly French. "We are here to escort you to more comfortable apartments in the royal palace at the White Tower."

Henry looked up with sudden interest when addressed in the familiar language of the court. He gave Laurence a faint smile and nodded his head, then momentarily recollecting himself, rose to his feet and stared regally down on the man kneeling at his feet.

"You may rise," he commanded with a semblance of authority. Laurence got to his feet but remained with his head bowed for the moment. The archbishop showed no emotion but placed a hand under the old king's elbow. Tyrell took this as his cue to step forward and take control of the situation. He led them from the chamber, king Henry shuffling along with the archbishop in support. His men formed a guard and they moved off towards the courtyard where a carriage waited on the king. Tyrell grabbed Laurence by the sleeve.

"That was well done. My lord king Edward wants both king Henry and the archbishop where he can keep an eye on them in the Tower. It seems that the archbishop has no intention of leaving king Henry's side unless forced, so it is convenient that they both come with us peacefully."

"I am only too pleased to be of service. What arrangements have been made at the Tower? Is the former king a prisoner?"

"Well yes, I suppose he is, though Edward would prefer to think him as a hostage rather than a prisoner."

"Doesn't that amount to the same thing?" asked Laurence.

"A hostage is a bargaining tool. Edward may yet have need of such, particularly when Margaret of Anjou, Henry's queen, arrives from France with her army. We know she is on her way."

* * *

King Henry the sixth was installed in comfortable royal apartments in the Wakefield Tower at the Tower of London. He had been permitted to retain his body servants and a small retinue of serving men. The archbishop of York, George Neville, occupied apartments nearby, not nearly so grand, but better than some of the chambers that might otherwise have been his residence in the Tower. However, king Henry would not be left alone but was in the immediate care of Laurence de la Halle who sat with him in his chamber under the orders of the duke of Gloucester via the command of king Edward. Henry had remaining to him some of his regal faculties and at first treated Laurence with disdain. Gradually, though, after a few hours he seemed to warm to his companion and the two men talked together almost as confidantes. They conversed comfortably in French.

Laurence was nervous to begin with, and wondered if the king was trying to engage him in friendly conference to affect some stratagem for escape. He soon realised that Henry was not capable of such devices and he began to feel compassion for the man. He knew something of his history from the tales he had heard in Brittany. The nobles of England held Henry in contempt because he had a propensity for donating huge sums of money to the poor, thus depleting the national treasury, and forgiving his enemies. Being pious and the least warlike of kings, the French had taken advantage so that now all of England's possessions in France, secured by his warrior father king Henry V, had been lost and only the town of Calais remained tenuously under English sovereignty. After the death of her husband, Henry V, the English nobles had not entrusted the infant Henry's upbringing to his mother, Katherine of Valois. She was badly treated and formed a liaison with one Owen Tudor and they had a son together named Edmund. When at the age of twenty-four Henry married Margaret of Anjou, at first it had seemed a good match as it was intended to help cement peace between England and France. However, rather than pay a dowry, Henry had given away the lands of Maine and Anjou. This was kept from the English parliament at first but had caused consternation when it was discovered.

Laurence and Henry sat together on fur rugs in front of a blazing fire. It seemed that this was one of Henry's peculiarities, so Laurence had joined him there. Henry was not in good health and felt the cold. Laurence demanded a warm cloak for the king and draped it around Henry's shoulders to keep off the draughts. There was a small table nearby charged with a flagon of wine and some fruit. Two lackeys stood to one side waiting for the command of the king to serve him. This he hardly thought to do and it was left to Laurence to indicate that their goblets be filled. This was done readily for the king but reluctantly for Laurence. Nevertheless, Laurence, warming to his new role, waved them away once they had been served. In truth, he thought that the lackeys might be spies who would report all they heard to someone, probably Tyrell, and though he did not expect anything subversive to enter the conversation, he resented the idea of intrusion.

"I have been king since my first year of life," Henry said suddenly, "and crowned three times, twice in England and once as king of France, yet I have never truly ruled."

"How can that be, my lord?" asked Laurence.

"Well, you see, the duke of Bedford was my regent until I became sixteen, then, during my illness Richard of York took on that role."

"The father of Edward who now wears the crown of England."

"Yes, and then my wife, queen Margaret. She has been a blessing to me in many ways, but she is a determined woman and her mind is so much stronger than mine." Laurence was surprised at Henry's demeanour as he spoke, which was one of gladness where he had expected a more lugubrious aspect. Perhaps Henry was pleased that his wife, leaving him to his thoughts and prayers, had taken much of the burden of kingship away. He spoke as if he were stating a comforting fact rather than lamenting the dilution and loss of his sovereignty.

"You speak without rancour, your grace. Have you no anger towards your enemies?"

"Not really, I never have had. They fight amongst themselves for power then fight even more to keep it. I do not consider it worth the effort. Think you that just because someone is born into a certain station in life that they are automatically suited to the duties of a rank that is imposed on them? It is almighty God who casts us into our moulds; not all of us are shaped to fit that which is chosen by the world."

"I suppose that is true even of those who vie for power," mused Laurence. "Many in the world abuse their positions and thus show themselves unfit to rule. With you on the throne by your right you are preventing the unworthy from sitting there."

"That is very wise and no doubt true, which is why I thank God for Margaret. She will come soon and set things aright."

Laurence looked around to see if any of the lackeys were in earshot, then he leaned over and spoke softly in the king's ear. "Let us hope so, my lord." He regretted his words almost as soon as he had spoken them. He had intended to offer a small crumb of comfort rather than take sides, yet his sympathy for this simple man had provoked the remark. For the moment, though, his loyalty must be with king Edward. It was by his command that he was sitting here now.

His remark seemed not to have registered with Henry who, disturbed by the sound of a settling log, had turned to stare into the flames of the fire. His thoughts, whatever they were, had moved somewhere else. Laurence reached out and took the goblet from Henry's frail grasp and set it down by his side. Soon the old king began to sing quietly to himself. Laurence rose and drew up a chair near the fire and sat down where he could keep watch. The serving men also seated themselves cross-legged on the floor. It was going to be a long vigil.

* * *

Tyrell's men were carousing in a tavern when the news came and spread rapidly through Edward's soldiery. Warwick was on the march with a large army that was following Edward's route to London. The Kingmaker was just two days away and battle was now inevitable. He too had learned that Margaret of Anjou was on her way with an invasion force and at last the Earl had decided he needed to strike, clearly provoked by Edward's march to London and his control of the deposed king Henry. They heard also that the Bastard of Fauconberg was in Kent raising an army there, which would attack Edward in London.

"Why do you look so horrified?" Tyrell demanded of Laurence. He had come to the Tower to instruct Laurence to get Henry ready for the road. He was to accompany the army out of London. Edward had no intention of leaving him behind in the capital where he could be spirited away to be used as a future rallying point.

"It is a Holy Day today and Easter Eve tomorrow, which means a battle on Easter Day. We will lose the blessing of Almighty God for the venture!"

"God will still have to choose between Edward and Warwick whichever day we fight on. The same omen applies as much to our enemy as it does to us."

Laurence fingered the reliquary and shook his head. "It cannot come to any good. We must stay here in London until after Easter."

"By then not only will we have Warwick to contend with, but also the Bastard's army. Then, if Margaret arrives we are lost. We cannot fight all three at once, or even two of them."

101

Laurence flapped his arms and looked about him, desperately casting around in his mind for something that would ameliorate his position. At least he would not be required to fight in the battle. Henry would be kept safely to the rear and afterwards he might be able to remain with the old king even if Warwick was the victor. As a negotiation point, his neutrality was a better bet than joining in a fight on the holiest day of the year. He would pray fervently to the Virgin. Her protection was more certain than either Edward's or Warwick's. Henry was, after all, a thrice-anointed king and being in his company would carry more weight in heaven than anything that the main combatants could offer. The thought deflated his first flights of panic and of course, Henry had his own chaplain. The three had already prayed together that morning and would do so throughout the remaining days of Easter. Travelling with a priest was a necessity for Henry at all times, even more so at Eastertide and an added level of security for the souls and bodies of those in his entourage.

"I shall see that he is made ready," Laurence said at last. Tyrell's countenance arranged itself somewhere between a smile and a grimace.

"We are to move off in a few hours and I have much to do before then. I shall send an escort. You are to march directly behind the king's retinue and only go to the rear when we sight Warwick's army." With that he gave a low bow to Henry and backed out of the chamber.

* * *

Laurence did not hold out much hope for Edward. The king's advanced forces had met with Warwick's prickers in Barnet and although they had driven them away, they now knew something of the Kingmaker's numbers. He had an army of 12,000, which was spread across the Barnet to St Albans road. Moreover he had brought with him a large artillery train that would fire on Edward as his men advanced. Edward had just 9,000 soldiers under him and only a few artillery pieces. Laurence wondered if he should still pray to St. Barbara. She was the patron saint not only of armourers but also artillerymen and the Kingmaker had plenty of

102

those on his side. Perhaps she would take pity on those few in Edward's army and give them her favour?

Warwick's centre was under the Marquis Montague while the duke of Exeter commanded his left. To the west of the road, sheltering behind a line of hedges was a force commanded by the earl of Oxford. The Kingmaker himself commanded the reserves drawn up behind Montague's centre. Warwick had caused his cannon to bear on the Barnet road along which he knew Edward must come.

Edward had with him his chief supporters, those who would have the most to gain by his kingship. Laurence had seen Hastings and others clustered around Edward, Gloucester and Clarence as they contemplated how best to form up the army. Night was drawing in fast and as yet they had not deployed. Tomorrow they would have to face artillery fire before they could come to grips with their enemy, and they were already at a numerical disadvantage.

A pavilion was erected for king Henry, his chaplain and his serving men. Laurence, whom Henry had taken into his favour, was to stay with him. They were well away from the Barnet road behind a small hillock so that they would not provide a rallying sight for the Lancastrian host. They were to remain under guard while the rest of the army moved forward into the night. They had formed up with Hastings on the left, Edward himself with his brother Clarence in the centre with Richard of Gloucester, as yet untried in a major battle on the right flank. This would place the young commander opposite Exeter's force. They could hear the sound of the army in the near distance as it stopped for the night in battle formation, ready for the morrow when the opposing armies could see each other.

Laurence was on his knees praying with Henry when the gunfire began. The night was pitch black with no moon or stars. At first they could see the flashes of the muzzles and it became apparent that Warwick was bombarding Edward's army even though he could not see them in the darkness. Curiously, there came no reply from the king's guns. Though they were fewer than Warwick's they might get lucky and do some damage to the enemy, yet they remained silent.

Laurence decided his prayers would be more profitably directed at the Virgin rather than St. Barbara and he included St. Jude who would be sympathetic to a lost cause. The priest who had been sent to Henry in the office of chaplain was one Father Godwin whose loyalty was with Edward and the House of York, so it was not difficult to get him to tender his more powerful prayers along with those of Laurence. The two men respectfully prayed for Edward's victory by moving apart from Henry. The old king remained at prayer and all three prayed through the night as was fitting before Easter Day. Father Godwin shared Laurence's concern over fighting a battle on a holy day, and he spent the whole time on his knees in front of a portable altar telling his beads. Laurence fingered constantly the reliquary containing the filings from the nail that had fixed Christ's feet to the cross.

When the dawn finally began to break, the battleground was obscured in a dense blanket of fog so even though daylight was coming, still the two armies were invisible to each other. Laurence hardly knew what to make of this. He had climbed to the top of the small hillock to observe what he could of the conflict. Obviously some device of heaven was at work on this holy day. It was as if the sight of battle was so offensive to God that he had caused the fog to hide it from sight. Whatever purpose was to be worked out, it would occur under a fog blanket from which the first noise of engagement could already be heard. It sounded as if Edward's cannon had finally opened fire, as the fitful gunfire was closer to where Laurence and king Henry were pavilioned. A larger but slightly more distant carronade indicated that Warwick's guns, too, had opened fire. Soon the gunfire ceased and the noise of men at arms clashing in the centre could be heard, though there was not, as yet, any sound from the right where the duke of Gloucester should be. Then it came in a distant shout and clash of steel. Now it was apparent that both armies were fully engaged. Occasionally the tips of banners could be glimpsed stirring the upper reaches of the fog before being drawn back down into the melee.

Father Godwin joined Laurence and both men stood beneath a tree that topped the hill overlooking the battlefield. King Henry remained with his personal retainers in his pavilion, unaware of the battle that was now raging nearby.

"Warwick has been firing his ordnance into Edward's ranks all the night," commented Laurence. "Let us pray there were not too many casualties."

Father Godwin made the sign of the cross over the scene. "If God favours the strong, then Warwick has His benediction. Yet we must believe that righteousness is a greater blessing. As the Holy Book tells us, 'the race is not always to the swift, nor the battle to the strong.'" Laurence thought that the Holy Book was unfathomable to men and contained many contradictions. He had never read it, of course, only a priest could do that, but he listened to the lessons ardently and frequently found himself confused where previously he had been clear. He sighed and muttered to himself *"fides ante intellectum* - faith comes before understanding."

They had been standing in anxious watch for some time when suddenly they saw a stream of men running from the mist towards where some horses were tethered. The battle was being fought on foot, of course, the ground being impossible for horses and the fog too impenetrable to manouvre them. They strained their necks to see which side was retreating. The soldiers mounted in panic and spurred their mounts mercilessly away from the fight and along the Barnet road. They had thrown their arms away and as they galloped by the bottom of the hill, Laurence and Father Godwin could clearly see the sun blazon of York on their surcoats. They were soon being pursued by a large body of mounted knights, fully armed and clearly giving chase. The pursuers were wearing the device of the earl of Oxford – a blazing star! The two watchers turned to each other with horrified faces. Edward's left flank, the one opposing Oxford and commanded by the lord Hastings had broken and was in flight. They turned their attention back to the fog-shroud where there seemed no letup in the sounds of battle. It appeared that Edward was, for the moment, unaware that his left had collapsed.

The battle raged on. Apparently the loss of his left wing had not prevented Edward from continuing the fight. All was shrouded in the mystery of the fog. Then the watchers witnessed the earl of Oxford with his retinue ride away down the Barnet road, though they did not look as if they were in flight. Again it seemed to have no affect on the battle. Presently the earl returned in company with those who had chased Hasting's men away. With his banner of the golden star in front streaming its tail across the heavens, he charged with his men headlong into the fog where Hasting's

105

shattered left would be. Surely Edward's left flank would be rolled up and the fight brought to a finish. Soon now, men would run from the battleground in panic, seeking to make their best escape from the retribution that was the fate of an army fleeing away from a lost cause.

"Should we return to King Henry?" asked Laurence, "or would it be best if we made our escape while there is time." Father Godwin stood frozen, his face a moving picture of conflicting emotion as if a flock of birds of ill omen had flown by and passed their shadows over him. Laurence realised that he was not going to get any meaningful spiritual or any other kind of guidance from the priest for the moment so he took a tight grip on his whirling thoughts. He could ride to London and announce Edward's defeat, then hide away in the streets until the consequences of the change of fortune asserted itself. Then, perhaps it would be better to remain with King Henry? After all, the earl of Warwick would want to parade the Lancastrian king through the streets of the capital in triumph – a Kingmaker once more. Those in his immediate retinue would be unlikely to come to any harm. He was pondering on his options when he detected a change in the sounds coming from the battlefield. The clash of arms was much reduced; there was a lot of shouting and he thought he could detect cries of "treason!" From his vantage point he saw, far in the distant right, men were running away from the fog bank. At first there were just a few but more followed in what was obviously a full-scale rout. These could only be Warwick's men and they were in full flight!

Father Godwin suddenly came to his senses and dropped to his knees, his hands clasped and wringing thanks to God for Edward's victory. Laurence thought it expedient to kneel beside him, yet he wondered at how Edward could have won when the odds had been so much against him. Even the early destruction of the left wing of his outnumbered army had not affected the outcome. Laurence hoped that this was due to the will of God, though he was not about to rule out the idea that sorcery had a hand in it. The mystery of the all-concealing fog, and the seeming invincibility of the victor were just as likely to be devices of one in league with the Devil than of Heaven. His suspicions were not mollified as he noticed the fog was fast clearing to reveal the bloody field. Its purpose, whatever that had been, was done and the spell had

106

expired. These thoughts, however, had no immediate place. Already men were moving in all directions from the scene of carnage and the walking wounded were struggling along the Barnet road looking for help. The clash of steel had been replaced by the cries of dying men while here and there victorious armoured knights had found their horses and were galloping over the field looking for prisoners they could take for ransom. He noted the first and boldest of the human scavengers were already moving among the dead looking for loot. He wondered where these came from; they had been well hidden while the battle raged. He supposed they were like maggots in a rotting corpse, which just appeared from nowhere.

There in the centre where the piles of bodies lay deepest flew the triumphant banner of York, its golden sun mocking the heavenly sun that was even now struggling to shine through the grey clouds that loured over the scene. Suddenly another appeared beside it and the blazon of the White Boar unfurled above the field. The eighteen-year-old Richard, duke of Gloucester had survived his first battle and his standard now fluttered beside that of his brother, king Edward the fourth. Almost as an afterthought, that of Clarence was raised too and the three banners flew there in the bloody centre of the field proclaiming the allied family power of Plantagenet.

Chapter 6 – Cornelius Quirke

"Some believe Elizabeth Wydville, Queen of England, is a witch," said Cornelius Quirke as he sat back and regarded the young man sitting opposite at the table. Laurence had been giving an account of the battle of Barnet and mentioned the unquiet thoughts that had been in his mind afterwards. As soon as king Henry had been brought back to London, Laurence had been relieved of his duty as guardian and had taken the opportunity to seek out the apothecary at his shop by the Cripplegate.

"The Kingmaker is dead who was once Edward's mentor, caught and killed as he stalked away from the battlefield;" stated Laurence, "murdered I have heard by some of Clarence's men."

"That was clearly by human intent rather than witchcraft, though it must be said a skilled necromancer can create the conditions for murder to occur. Queen Elizabeth certainly hated Warwick so one of her chief enemies has been removed." The apothecary nodded sagely as he spoke letting Laurence draw his own conclusions.

"King Edward gave orders for Warwick's capture, though it seems the order came too late to save him."

"Perhaps by the same power that brought down the fog?"

"Which brings us back to the Queen. All night Warwick's cannon were firing at where they imagined Edward's army to be. Not one shot counted; all passed over their heads to land harmlessly at their rear. Then in the dawn, soon after the battle began, there can be no doubt that if Edward's soldiers had witnessed the collapse of their left wing, then all would have been lost. Moreover, when the earl of Oxford returned to the fight, being unable to see that the battle line had rotated, he charged through the fog into the rear of his own men. They, mistaking Oxford's banner of the star for the sun of York, cried treason and began fighting among themselves."

"By what enchantment had they thought the star banner to be the sun of York?" intoned Cornelius.

"Were it not for that then Edward could not have withstood the renewed onslaught, if indeed the battle had not already been lost. It was then that he shattered the Lancastrian centre and with the duke of Gloucester rolling up the Lancastrian left wing, the battle was won."

"It is not the first time that Edward's fortune has depended upon celestial intervention," said Cornelius conspiratorially. "It was at the battle of Mortimer's Cross that the event occurred where he received his banner of the sun. At that time Elizabeth Wydville had not yet come into his life, though we might suspect that even then, she had designs upon him. Edward was the earl of March then – back in 1461 and Warwick was yet to earn the title 'Kingmaker.'"

"I know nothing of this," Laurence replied and leaned forward in expectation. Cornelius too leaned forward until their faces were just inches apart. In a low voice he continued his tale.

"Forces led by Jasper Tudor, earl of Pembroke were invading from Wales to support Queen Margaret of Anjou, who was leading an army out of Scotland and pillaging England from the north."

"The same Queen Margaret we are currently in expectation of arriving with an invasion force?"

"The very same. She had gone to Scotland to enlist help in her fight against the Yorkist faction and let her army plunder and rape as if England was an enemy country rather than she being queen of it. Mind you, being French herself, she has no regard for England so what can you expect?" Laurence decided to take this comment on the chin as he too was half French, though his country was Brittany, not France.

"To continue, just a few days before Edward's father, the duke of York and Margaret's bitterest enemy was caught and killed at the battle of Wakefield. York's youngest son and our Edward's brother, Edmund, was killed with him. The army of Jasper Tudor, earl of Pembroke, met up with the Yorkists under Edward, now duke of York at Mortimer's Cross. It was a cold winter's day in February and the Lancastrian army was reluctant to fight, as were the Yorkists. Then, a strange sight occurred.

When dawn came there was a morning mist through which not one sun rose that day, but three! Edward took this as the sign of the Holy Trinity rising above his army and declared that the hand of God was on the Yorkist side. In the subsequent battle the Lancastrians were defeated. Owen Tudor, Jasper's father was captured and executed but Jasper Tudor escaped by fleeing to France. Margaret could no longer meet up with Pembroke's army and so decided to march on London, pillaging the countryside as she went. It was the depredations of Queen Margaret's army throughout England that finally led to king Henry's removal from the throne and our Edward being proclaimed king. When the two armies finally met, also at Eastertide mark you, on Palm Sunday, Edward defeated Margaret's army at Towton and she fled back to Scotland taking king Henry and their whelp with her."

"So that is how the sign of the three suns has become Edward's emblem?"

"Yes and his motto '*The Sunne in Splendour.*'"

"And rising from out of a mist. Do you think devilry becomes more potent during holy festivals?"

"Perhaps the Almighty has his back turned at such times, who knows other than the Devil himself."

"But who is this Jasper Tudor?" asked Laurence.

"Ah, yes, the Tudors. They are the half brothers of king Henry VI. Owen Tudor their father, a lowly Welshman of no rank was the paramour of Queen Katherine, the widow of Henry the fifth and the present king Henry's mother. Some say they married secretly, but that has never been proved and no marriage agreement has ever been found. There were three sons from the union: Jasper, Edmund and Owen, This last one is a monk and has retired from the world. Edmund is dead but is the only one to produce progeny, a boy named Henry got on Margaret Beaufort, daughter of the duke of Somerset."

"They are of no account, then."

"None – a bastard line."

"You were telling me how Edward's queen, is thought to be a witch?"

"Let the circumstances speak for themselves, said Cornelius. "Elizabeth Wydville was first married to Sir John Grey who was the eldest son of lord Ferrers and through his influence she became one of the Ladies of the Bedchamber to Margaret of Anjou."

"Who is now her deadliest enemy."

"Quite so. Anyhow, her husband was killed at the second battle of St. Albans and as he was clearly on the Lancastrian side she was deprived of her inheritance when Edward took the throne from Henry. She has two sons, Thomas, whom you will now know as the marques of Dorset, and Richard now lord Grey and an extended family too, but we are getting ahead of ourselves. In May of 1464, Edward made a visit to the manor of Jaquetta of Luxenbourg, Elizabeth's mother who was married to Sir Richard Wydville. She was formerly the widow of John, duke of Bedford and has long been suspected of witchcraft herself. As we know, Edward cannot resist a pretty face and it must be said that Jaquetta and sir Richard's daughter, Elizabeth, was and still is one of the most beautiful of women. Predictably Edward was smitten, though Elizabeth was wily enough to play him like a fish. The normal arrangement in such circumstances was for Edward to have his way and then some kind of favour would be awarded, leaving Edward free of an encumbrance and the object of his lust so much the richer. It is well to point out here that the earl of Warwick was at that time in negotiation with Louis of France for the hand of a French princess for Edward with the intention of cementing an alliance with that country; after all, that is why kings marry. Nobody really knows how she did it, but Elizabeth Wydville got Edward to marry her secretly."

"But that is unprecedented!" gasped Laurence. "Was there no objection, no outcry, no celebration as is usual when a king marries? What did the earl of Warwick have to say on the matter?"

"Well, first of all there was no outcry because nobody knew of the marriage. When some time later Warwick found out, he was incandescent with rage and with justification. As the famous Kingmaker, he had been working his own schemes in the expectation that he could influence Edward enough to be the power behind the throne. It was at this point that the close relationship between the earl and the king began to disintegrate. Nothing could be done about it as the king, through the influence of Elizabeth Wydville, had delivered everyone a *fait accompli*. However, Warwick was the one who presented her at Reading Abbey so that her people could do homage to their queen. Some think that this was simply politics on Warwick's part, but we cannot entirely discount the possibility of enchantment. The queen was crowned in the year after her marriage. Matters were not improved when the new queen began to get Edward to prefer members of her family before the established nobility."

Pensively, Laurence tugged at the short beard he had been cultivating. "It certainly seems that the king has been bewitched. The tale is too fantastical to suppose otherwise."

"You can imagine what the nobles at court thought about it, particularly when later they had to endure the conceits of the Wydvilles. She brought with her five brothers and five sisters all expecting royal patronage. Elizabeth Wydville was a commoner and therefore not eligible to marry a royal Prince. She was already the mother of two sons. It was because of the general dissatisfaction amongst the nobles that Warwick, aided by the duke of Clarence who hates the Wydvilles, and in league with Margaret of Anjou was able to drive Edward from the country and the pregnant Elizabeth Wydville into sanctuary. You have witnessed yourself how Edward has managed to return and, against great odds, raise an army and gain victory over Warwick. The queen is proving to be extremely fertile. After her marriage she presented him with daughters. Now, while in sanctuary, she has been delivered of Edward's son and heir, she is unassailable."

"I cannot believe a man, even less a king could be duped so easily, unless some spell had been cast over him."

"Many have fared thus before him. How many of us have been bewitched yet never known of it? There is more to the tale, but I dare not speak of it and it is best you don't know in case you let a careless word slip and destroy yourself."

"We swim in deep waters to be sure." Laurence was thinking of his own case – the butcher's girl at home. She had enchanted her way into his affections and he was lucky his father had stepped in to break the spell. She too had been ambitious for her family. How many women of ambition had caused their men-folk to be promoted from even the most disadvantaged of states to positions of high office? The strange thing was that those men to whom this had occurred were amongst the happiest in their marriages, but that was only to be expected. He pulled out the reliquary from under his shirt and fingering it he recalled some words from his schooling: *venenum in auro bibitur;* poison is drunk from a golden cup.

Thinking on poison brought him back to his present location in the apothecary's shop. He had found the shop easily enough as it was located down a street by the Cripplegate inside the city walls. The

112

area of London by which the gate had its name was actually outside the city walls, its inhabitants excluded from the defence provided by it. Two massive bastions towered above the walls either side of the gate, which also had a portcullis. The gate was heavily guarded and as the Bastard of Fauconberg was expected to try an attack on the city, volunteers from the city militia reinforced its garrison.

A crude daub above the door showing a pestle and mortar was the means by which the apothecary's shop was identified. The door was latched and anyone could enter from the street into a small room having a table and three stools as its only furnishing. At the back on the wall was a number of shelves with pots and bottles, the staple wares of the shop. A strong internally bolted door, that had a spy hole in it through which the apothecary could view his clients, accessed the interior of the premises. If they were thought to be safe he would open the door and enquire as to their business with him. Anyone of dubious character would be ordered to leave and encouraged to do so by the menacing growl of a massive wolfhound that lived in a niche just inside the door.

Laurence had felt the hairs rise on the back of his neck as he had, at first, been subjected to the bloodcurdling snarl of the dog. The effect was all the more terrifying due to the dog being out of sight behind the door and the primitive animal presence worked in his mind so that he could feel it even through stout timbers. He announced himself in reply to the disembodied voice that came from beyond a grill in the door. Presently, muffled commands could be heard and the growl from the dog diminished as the bolts were drawn.

The man who stepped into the room appeared to be of middle years, around thirty-five perhaps, and rather taller than average. He was wearing a long black robe and a wool cap with ear flaps. His face was long and thin with a long greying wispy beard and bright black eyes that scrutinised Laurence's face as if he could read what was written there.

"I have been expecting you ere now." He had said in a deep voice that Laurence thought was out of character with his appearance. "Did you not enter London with Edward's army?" Laurence explained that he had been diverted by his duty in guarding king Henry and that he had witnessed the Battle of Barnet.

113

"You must tell me all about it and I shall tell you what I know of it," the apothecary said showing great interest. "We had a shock here at the first news. Men from lord Hastings force had broken and run from the battle claiming all was lost and Edward defeated. You can imagine the consternation that caused. Only two days before we had allowed him entry to London and freed his queen from sanctuary. Who knows what retribution would have been visited upon us if the news had been true. Fortunately those who ran were premature in their assessment of the situation and now Edward is returned to us."

He turned and beckoned Laurence to follow him through the door. Laurence did so with some trepidation, nervously casting his eyes at the black space behind the door where a dark indefinable presence could be sensed accompanied by a low rumble emanating from something with a deep throat. The apothecary parted a curtain and stood back while Laurence ducked through a low portal into the chamber beyond.

Laurence had been in an apothecary shop before now and this chamber was typical of what could be found in any number of them. He could never enter such a place without first crossing himself, which he did almost unconsciously. Here could be found remedies for all kinds of ills though how much could be attributed to the arcane knowledge of the apothecary and which to the casting of magic spells was uncertain. Some apothecaries could supply a patron with the means of disposing of an enemy or rival without the victim knowing they had been poisoned. Was it the potion, or the spell that accompanied it that did the deadly work? The room was cluttered by a mass of dried herbs, strange roots and body parts few of which could be identified. Hopefully these would be animal parts. They hung from the ceiling and were stuffed onto shelves or lay around on the bench that stretched along one side of the room. A fire blazed providing a flickering light that gave the suspended animal objects a semblance of life as their shadows danced across the walls. One he recognised as a dragon - a small one to be sure, but clearly a dragon. It had an extended tapered snout showing rows of razor-sharp teeth, scaly skin and a long reptilian tail. There were dried bats wings, fins of strange fish and even the horn of a unicorn.

Cornelius Quirk noted Laurence's crossing himself with a disapproving sniff but made no comment. He indicated that Laurence should sit at the table in the centre of the room where a pair of candles had been lit to supplement the light from the fire. There were no windows though there was a door that, Laurence conjectured, would lead to the apothecary's living rooms. Cornelius drew out a chair for himself and waited while his guest seated himself. This placed Laurence with his back to the curtained entrance just beyond which lurked the hound.

Their preliminary conversation revealed that Cornelius Quirke, as well as being an apothecary, operated a courier service and distribution point for information of all kinds. He began with news of Laurence's family in Brittany and at Tournai. All was well and there had been no repercussions from the butcher's family, though he learned that the daughter had caught herself a husband, a farrier's son who had no idea that a girl who was clearly showing just two months after he had impregnated her might not be entirely honest with regard to the identity of the father. Perhaps a horse had kicked his head.

The nature of the apothecary's clandestine business was responsible for the peculiar layout of his shop and the dramatic security precautions. It was impossible for an unwanted person to enter this chamber or to overhear any conversation that might take place. Persons of great importance and influence would use his services to get messages to whomever they wished with the greatest confidence. In a world where even a trusted retainer could be bought, his confidential and anonymous couriers, having no household loyalties, were well paid and often gained certain advantages for themselves when discreet information was fed to them, so that they could gain profit from knowledge unattainable elsewhere. It was a fine balance but Cornelius Quirke had mastered the subtleties of control over information.

Laurence had been recommended by duke Francis as one of Cornelius' agents to keep watch on events and report back on his behalf. The normal use of bribery and corruption would suffice for the purpose of contemporary plotting, but Cornelius managed a longer term and more trusted method. Those who used him knew that he would not disclose anything of their business, even though they suspected he offered the same discretionary service to their enemy and probably had information that they would dearly like to buy. Yet he would not reveal anything pertaining to that enemy either, no matter how much was offered in payment. It was this quality that, frustrating as it might be, kept him in business. He worked in complete isolation to all other considerations, solely for the individual who engaged him.

"So my liege duke Francis has asked you for information regarding events in England. Why are you unable to comply?" asked Laurence.

"I informed duke Francis that I had no reliable single source, though, of course, I have agents out there. Events in England and in Europe are too complex and are moving too fast for me to sift what information I have to obtain a reliable opinion. The situation with Edward the fourth is peculiar. As you know he has two brothers and a wife with a seemingly limitless family all of whom have influence on events. I have informants near some of these but nobody close to either the duke of Gloucester or the duke of Clarence. Clarence is not too much of a problem. His plotting is clumsy and transparent, mainly because of his own inability to keep his mouth shut. Richard of Gloucester is more difficult. For one thing he despises plotting and hardly engages in it himself. His personal motto is *Loyaulté Me Lie,* Loyalty Binds Me and that means he is largely predictable where politics are concerned."

"You mean he will always side with Edward?"

"Yes, which tells me that I need someone close to him."

"I don't understand your reasoning."

"Richard is close to the king, but tends to keep his personal opinion to himself, which makes it hard to discover. As a prince of the realm he can have much influence on events though, as yet, he has shown little interest in doing so. He rather lets his brother the king act as he wishes. As he matures this will not always be so. Apart from anything else, the machinations of his other brother, George, duke of Clarence are bound to involve him at some point. We know that Clarence has a propensity towards treason and is jealous of Edward's kingship."

"Though Edward is the older brother and thus the legitimate king?" Cornelius drummed his fingers on the table and plunged into deep thought. He looked carefully at Laurence and seemed on the verge

116

of telling him something, then, with an almost imperceptible shake of his head changed his mind.

"To one such as Clarence there are always temptations. Most particularly there is the matter of royal succession."

"Well now that Edward has a son, surely that is taken care of, unless the infant should die? Even so, the queen is fertile and may yet produce more sons."

"Remember the very events you have just witnessed for yourself. Why did Clarence turn his coat and return to Edward when he was recently in league with Margaret of Anjou and the earl of Warwick?" Cornelius answered his own question. "He was tempted by an Act of the Lancastrian parliament last year that proclaimed Clarence heir to the throne after Margaret and Henry's son the Prince of Wales. That was after Edward and Richard had been driven out of England to Flanders, where you first encountered them."

"But both Henry the sixth and Edward, Prince of Wales are still alive. In fact, if Margaret is yet successful in her invasion attempt, then Clarence will be no nearer the throne than he is now."

"If you were Clarence, how would you rate your chances with that Lancastrian brood? After all, Edward Prince of Wales is married to Warwick's daughter Anne, sister to Clarence's own wife Isabella. As yet the marriage is unconsummated, but if eventually she bears the prince a son then Clarence will be right out in the cold."

"So although Clarence is clearly better off allied to his own brother the king, yet his path to what he considers his throne by Act of Parliament is still barred."

"Which, to one of Clarence's stamp will always rankle in his mind. What we have to consider is how things will turn out should the king defeat Margaret's army when she arrives." Cornelius looked directly at Laurence and raised his eyebrows inquisitively.

"That is far from certain," replied Laurence. "Not only will he have to contend with Margaret, but also her ally, the Bastard of Fauconberg who is, at this very moment, planning an attack on London. These are not favourable odds."

Cornelius gave a laugh and sat back in his chair. "Who knows which side Fortune will come down on? We have tried to work out whose side God is on and which side the Devil and come to no firm conclusion."

117

Laurence shifted uncomfortably in his chair. The apothecary was getting close to blasphemy, yet he too could not make up his mind either between God and Devil. One only had to look at the events that had occurred to see plainly sorcery was at work somewhere.

"You say there is no need to get close to Clarence?"

"Of course not, his mind is open for all to read and in any case I already have the means for obtaining information from those he confers with. No, depending on how events work out it is likely Richard of Gloucester will be the pivotal point. He is aware of brother George's weakness and blames the Lancastrians for manipulating him. His loyalty extends to both his brothers, though in the final analysis he will favour Edward. We need to get close to Gloucester. Of course, in the coming battles with Margaret and the Bastard all may change. In that event you will attempt to move into the household of king Henry. You have already established some rapport with him so that is all to the good. Henry will require little in the way of armour, but his son the Prince of Wales fancies himself as a general. You are well placed to make something of that. Your father is a respected armourer and under his tutelage you have clearly inherited his skills."

"All this seems very fluid. I can see no purpose in it."

"This is the point," stated Cornelius. "We need not concern ourselves with purpose. Events will work themselves out despite anything we can do. It is our job merely to report on them. Others will use the information we provide as they wish."

Just then a whine came from the canine presence outside. Cornelius got up and parted the curtain to look through the spy hole. Whoever it was must have been familiar to the household because the dog made no commotion as the bolts of the shop door were withdrawn. He heard the door open and then close again and the bolts shoot home. His curiosity arose as he detected the lilt of a female voice. The curtain was pulled away and Cornelius came into the room followed by a young girl. Laurence was at once struck as if by lightening by her beauty. She was of moderate height, slim and plainly dressed in a brown dress over which was draped a black cloak with a hood open to reveal a pretty elfin face framed by the blackest hair. Her eyes sparkled in the light from the candles, as black as night and wide with curiosity as she noticed Laurence. Cornelius turned to him.

"May I present my daughter; Joan, this is Laurence de la Halle of Brittany."

Laurence swept her a bow and murmured "*Je suis très heureux de vous rencontrer, mademoiselle.*" He would gladly have spoken more gallantly but he had been taken aback by her appearance and now found himself lost for words.

She dipped him a curtsy and said: "Give you good den, sir," making it plain she either did not understand French or wished to converse in English.

"Joan has some news," said Cornelius looking expectantly at his daughter.

"Margaret of Anjou has landed at Weymouth along with a large army." She spoke excitedly as if she could not get the words out fast enough. "They arrived the day after the Battle of Barnet, though the news has only just come through to us. She has the Prince of Wales with her. Already the king is issuing orders to get ready for the immediate march of his army to confront her. The city is in turmoil. The Bastard of Fauconberg has mustered a force in Kent and he has a fleet ready to attack London."

"I shall have to return to the armoury at the Tower of London," said Laurence to Cornelius, tearing his eyes away from the raven-haired beauty.

"I think you must. Take care and good fortune." Cornelius held back the curtain at the portal and led him through the bolted door to the shop. Laurence just had time to look back where he saw Joan removing her cloak and hanging it on a peg by the fireplace. Even so mundane an action was accomplished with a simple grace of movement, he thought.

Laurence was in a daze. He found himself on the London street outside the apothecary's shop wondering how he had got there. One moment he had encountered the sudden and ravishing beauty of Cornelius' daughter, the next, having hardly the chance to speak to her, he was out on the street being bustled along by a throng of citizens all shouting in confusion. Her form had imprinted itself in his eyes, as by a flash of light, and he had trouble gathering his thoughts.

By the time he reached the Tower armoury he had, in part, come to his senses. The whole place was alive with soldiery and everywhere men were gathering together arms and cannon ready to move out once the king's prickers had determined where Margaret was. He discovered Nicholas Olds conversing with Peterkin Mumby. As Olds spied Laurence walking towards him his brows knit in a frown of disapproval.

"Where have you been? We are all busy on the king's business getting his army ready for the march and you have deigned to absent yourself."

"You should remember that I have been seconded to Tyrell's troop under the duke of Gloucester and no longer subject to your discipline."

Olds glowered, his face red with fury. "You are an armourer and that means, if you are to be a part of Edward's army, you are subject to me. Besides, Tyrell is not here. He is busy with his prickers scouting for the location of the enemy."

"Well here I am," said Laurence defiantly. "What would you have of me?" Nicholas Olds, having a massive work-load of last-minute tasks in getting the army on to the march was forced to contain his anger. The truth was he had few armourers as skilled as Laurence had proved to be. His main problem was in satisfying the demands of the nobles. They insisted that their harness be not only functional, yet fine enough to define their rank. That meant either he had to do the work himself or delegate it to another. Jack Snipe was one of these but the really fine work, he knew, was beyond Snipe. Laurence was an artist. There was nowhere in England that manufactured complete harness and his training in Europe had exposed him to methods in armoury that were up-to-date and fashionable. Moreover, he could measure the contours of a knight almost just by looking at him and all those who had used his skills on the great march had praised his work. Tyrell had been one of these and he had the ear of the duke of Gloucester. It had been a serious loss to Olds when Laurence rode off with Tyrell and then a greater disappointment when he had been diverted to the service of guarding king Henry. Now that he was back at the forges Olds would do his best to keep him. He regretted his earlier strategy of giving him low-grade work. That might have put him in his place during times of peace, but now the demands of war meant that Olds could not afford to hold him back. Even so, he felt the need to establish his authority.

"You will attend upon his lordship the earl Rivers who will instruct you as to his requirements." Olds felt that that should do the trick. The earl, Anthony Rivers, brother to the queen was a noted jouster and most particular regarding his harness. Many armourers had fallen foul of his finicky demands and Olds had no doubt Laurence de la Halle would fare no better. This was a most sensible decision. He could satisfy the demands of one of the most difficult nobles and free his other armourers to the immediate task in hand, that of getting the army into the field. Laurence would be fully engaged in the service of earl Rivers, which absolved Olds from concern with an onerous client while preserving his obligation to the ruling house of York.

* * *

Earl Rivers, Anthony Wydville, had impressed Laurence at their first meeting. The earl had taken rooms in the Tower of London in anticipation of the coming conflict with the Bastard of Fauconberg. Edward the fourth was about to march off with his army to seek out the forces of Margaret of Anjou and her son the Prince of Wales who were tramping over England somewhere near the border with Wales. The old king, Henry, was safely in his chambers within the Tower. Laurence conversed naturally in courtly French with earl Rivers and the two men immediately took to each other – one an armourer from a family accomplished in the art, the other a nobleman who appreciated the aesthetics of the craft. They had previously met, of course, in Flanders when earl Rivers had been dismissive of Laurence. He pretended to have forgotten that first meeting, hardly recognising the young man who now presented himself in good clothes and who now had a neatly-trimmed beard. Laurence reminded him of their first meeting and the two laughed together.

Rivers was no fool when it came to judgement of fine armour. He had reports of Laurence's work and had already examined some of it, simple though it was under Olds reluctant embrace. He stood now in a padded jupon, head raised while Laurence stood back examining his form and stayed so while the armourer walked around him. He responded enthusiastically to Laurence's commands to move his arms, or place his legs in a particular stance. He answered fully every question regarding his favoured weapons and obeyed every instruction while measurements were taken.

Laurence asked to see his current armour and indicated to the earl's servants to fit him into his harness. As soon as the earl was fully harnessed the instructions of stance were repeated and Laurence tugged here and there at the metal, noting its fit and seeking out any vulnerable places. Earl Rivers bore all this with the greatest patience, though in other respects this was not one of his virtues. Finally Laurence nodded to the earl's retainers to remove the harness and presently, dressed in fine hose and jacket, the earl relaxed and took up a goblet from a side table. A lackey immediately filled it with wine and at the earl's behest filled another and gave it to Laurence. He placed the tablet where he had noted the earl's measurements on a side table and waited on River's command. The earl waved him to a chair and both sat facing each other in front of a blazing fire set under a stone mantle.

"I see that your armour is in the Milanese style, my lord," ventured Laurence.

"Indeed, imported at great expense," Rivers drawled laconically. "I had it made there to my measurements and, I must say, when I first tried it on it fitted surprisingly well. Some minor adjustments were necessary of course, and I had some small changes made of my own devising, but the Milan craftsmen are superlative, think you not?"

"I believe I can recognise the work of the Missiglian family. They export all over Europe and we have come across many examples of their work in Brittany. My father in particular worked for a while under Paolo of Venice, one of their nephews who had a forge and armoury there for a while. My father taught me and I have copied examples of it myself."

"Give me your opinion on the effectiveness of my harness," demanded Rivers as he leaned back in his chair and stretched out his legs before the fire. Laurence considered the question carefully. He had already noted certain points but hardly knew how the earl would receive his observations. Earl Rivers was a flamboyant knight who loved the joust and his harness reflected that.

"Your harness is designed for the tilt yard, my lord, and has some limitations in a serious battle." The earl placed his goblet of wine on the side table, put his finger tips together and looked at Laurence pensively."

"Do go on," he said quietly.

"Let us start at the top, my lord. Your head protection, the *armet á rondelle*; the visor has a narrow eye slit, which is fine when jousting with a lance as it reduces the chance of a splinter entering. It also reduces the field of vision and that could be fatal when surrounded by enemies. In the joust you have just one opponent to deal with and he will always be coming directly at you. In battle your enemies will be looking for your blind spot and come at you from the side." Earl Rivers nodded his understanding and remained silent waiting for Laurence to continue. "The armour is heavier on the left side than the right, as is usual because we assume an opponent to be right handed so the left side is where harder contact will be made. However, the left pauldron over the shoulder is fitted with an additional gardebrace to reinforce the harness at this point. Again, that is sensible in the joust but it does restrict some movement of the left arm. You might consider reducing the weight of armour here for the sake of better movement."

"My weapons will be wielded in my right hand, so I can afford some small restriction on the left, but your point is well made."

"Which brings me to the shoulder protection, the pauldron of the right arm," Laurence slipped in. "You have a notched bracket there that is the support for your lance. Unfortunately this prevents full armour under the armpit and is thus a vulnerable spot that will not go unnoticed by an enemy intent on bringing you to your death. I know that a pin secures the lance rest, which allows it to be removed, but that exposes the armpit on the right side of your body. I think we will need to increase the length of the right pauldron and provide the individual lames with good articulation so that you can still use your weapons effectively."

Rivers held up a hand as a signal for him to stop speaking. "I am very fond of my armour as it is and I am loath to have it changed too much; but please go on."

"I am only making observations, your lordship, but if you are to have proper protection on the battlefield then there are certain considerations I can point out that you might like to think on. For instance, your leg protection is fine for fighting on foot, or for limited use on horseback. The complete enclosure of the leg does

123

restrict movement, though, and on campaign would be very uncomfortable if you are to be in the saddle for any length of time. In any case the horse and saddle mainly protect the backs of the legs. Perhaps two sets of greaves would be advisable – one without backs for horse riding and the enclosed greaves you already have for fighting on foot."

"What you say makes sense, though perhaps the front-only protection for the legs would work well on foot too – more agility?"

"As your lordship pleases. Yet may I venture one last point?" The earl nodded his agreement.

"Your Milanese harness is decorated with latten embellishments around the helmet and in certain places on the body and legs. The extra weight is minimal and may not bother you too much, but for battle armour I would favour chase-work rather than latten for decoration."

"Why so?"

"Because a severe blow can loosen latten strips and while that would not in itself be a problem, because latten has no reinforcing component, yet dangling strips of latten can become a distraction and potentially fatal in battle."

"You seem also to be familiar with the work of the Negroli family of Italy who, I believe, favour chase and repoussé work?"

"You lordship is extremely knowledgeable."

"I try to keep up with current fashions. It appears to me that I should have a second harness of more practical use. Your suggestions, though eminently sensible, would deny me my best harness for jousting."

"I have your measurements, my lord. I can fashion a new harness that will be at once elegant, strong enough for battle conditions and in the Milanese style. Do you wish me to proceed?"

"You may, but let us discuss what you have in mind before you begin work." Laurence reached for his tablet and charcoal. Turning over his notes he began sketching on the back.

Rain was falling and an awning had been erected over the naked bodies of the earl of Warwick and his brother the marquis Montague where they lay on public view in front of St Paul's cathedral. The crowd that had pushed and shoved to get a sight of the dead nobles had diminished during the two days they had lain there and today just a few passers-by paused at the sight. No doubt, now that everyone had proof the two were actually dead, the bodies would be removed and interred as directed by the king. Laurence had been one of the first who, two days previously, wished to see for himself these men brought to mere clay who had held power for so long. They had been in the forefront of events for years and thus in his thoughts during the long march, so his curiosity had the better of him. Death had not only robbed them of their life force, but also the aura of dread authority they once had. He recalled a day some years ago when in Brittany, the hunt came home after the bringing down of a magnificent stag. The body of the beast was brought in on a cart and even in death it retained its aura of strength, nobility and grandeur. Looking at these men he felt not a vestige of residual power coming from the bloated white corpses. In life he would have bowed before them; now he merely wished to hurry by to get out of the rain and reclaim his tools from the warehouse where they were stored while he had been with king Henry.

He found his tool chest easily enough and released the lock with his key. Everything seemed to be there so he shut the lid and locked the chest again. He sought out the keeper of the warehouse, paid him his due and also something extra to transport the heavy tool chest to the forges at the Tower. He had learned Peterkin Mumby was the guild master of the armourers at the Tower of London and Laurence needed his permission to make and sell harness. Documents confirming his guild status in Brittany were secure in his tool chest and once he had produced these and completed certain formalities, hopefully Mumby would allow him to set up in business for himself. Until now Nicholas Olds had taken a percentage of his earnings and though he had built up a small amount of capital he did not have nearly enough to fully equip a forge and workshop. He might have had more, but his time spent with king Henry had not been rewarded so he had been deprived of any income he might have earned mending harness for Edward's men-at-arms. He expected to be well rewarded for making harness for earl Rivers, but Nicholas Olds would take a good percentage of that unless he was able to set up and work independently.

Hurrying back to the Tower he was brought to a sudden stop by a female voice speaking his name behind him. Turning around he came face-to-face with Anna. She was regarding him with a wry smile on her face. She had on her usual fawn dress and apron covered over with a grey woollen cloak, which she wore open.

"I have been wondering about you," she said. "After you rode off with master Tyrell I expected you would return to the army at some point."

"I was diverted to other duties," he replied, noting her neat appearance. "You seem to be managing well enough." He found he was pleased to see her, yet there was something missing. The dark beauty of Joan Quirke came into his mind, a woman he had seen for just a few moments and had no time even to engage in conversation. "Your work with the old witch Mother Malkin must be paying well?"

"Hardly, yet she does well enough. There is enough sickness and injury in an army to keep her occupied. She has been good to me. I have been well fed and cared for. You do her an injustice when you think of her as a witch; she is a wise woman who I have only ever seen do good. If those who call themselves chirurgeon would heal as many as her, then they could command their fees from princes, yet because she is just a wise woman she is tainted by the suspicion of witchcraft and paid a pittance, and that grudgingly."

Laurence was not entirely convinced about that, yet he too found he could not think of the old woman as evil.

"There is much sorcery in the world, as I have discovered. Who knows where she gets her power from?" He was thinking that if a queen could command a mist to rise over her husband's army, anything was possible. Anna's face clouded over with anger.

"If Mother Malkin was taken as a witch, tell me true - you would not raise a finger in her defence. Not only you, but those she has healed and relieved of pain would not hesitate to condemn her either!"

"Holy Church has the means of deciding on those things," he replied lamely. "Such matters are best left in the hands of God." Anna snorted in disdain and regarded him with contempt. Laurence, for his part, was wondering how he had got into this argument. He had merely asked after Anna's welfare and used the word witch without thought, as everyone did. Perhaps he should change the subject.

"The army is to move out soon, when Edward discovers queen Margaret's whereabouts. I am to remain here in London where the earl Rivers is to watch the king's back and guard the city from attack."

"What have you to do with the earl Rivers?" she asked with interest.

"Oh, I am making him new harness," he replied casually. "That means I shall remain in London when the army marches out. What will you do?"

"Mother Malkin is getting too old for the march. She is planning to stop in London too. As for myself, I have hopes for a position in the household of a high noble." She spoke as if that was the most natural thing in the world, for an alehouse doxy to graduate into the house of a noble. She was very pretty, however, and a fair face can often find favour where a plain maid cannot. Nevertheless he felt a pang of concern for her and wondered if she was placing herself in danger.

"And who has given you that idea?" he asked, a note of caution in his voice.

"I have an admirer who works as a cook in the kitchens of my lord the duke of Clarence. He is speaking for me." She eyed him with amused defiance.

"Well it didn't take you long to find a protector."

"Why not. Did you think I would wait upon your casual attendance?"

"No, I suppose not, but be careful. A kitchen maid is regarded as fair game in such houses."

"Unless she has a protector," she inserted. Laurence felt a stab of jealousy though he had no particular rights over the girl's affections. He had used her as a casual lay who could be abandoned at any time. They had begun to form a bond on the march, though it was one soon forgotten when other duties intervened. He had not given her much thought since riding off with Tyrell and even less since his recent encounter with Joan Quirke. His jealousy, he knew, was irrational.

"No doubt the duke will be taking his cooks along on the march. Are you going too?"

127

"I hope not. Barrett is to remain here in London where the lady Isabel is in residence."

"The duchess, Clarence's wife. Yes, I suppose she will need her household servants while Clarence is away." He had noted the name of Anna's new friend but decided to ignore it. "I wonder what she is feeling now as the daughter of the earl of Warwick. Her father's body lies naked on the steps of St Paul's over there and her husband is about to march off with his brother, the enemy that brought the Kingmaker down."

"I believe she cries a lot, but who knows how the high and mighty feel. They are not as us and none of them marry for anything other than advantage to themselves."

They are not as us, she had said, indicating some tenderness of heart. He mused that Anna must have hopes and dreams of her own, yet all had been suppressed by her circumstances. First had been the cruelty and indifference of her stepfather, which led to her readiness to escape with himself and Edward's army when the situation presented itself. Then he, who had taken an interest in her, had ridden off without a further thought. Whoever this Barrat was he represented some sort of future to her and he hoped he would turn out right for her. Knowing the world as he did, he was unconvinced about that and found himself more concerned for her than he should be.

"It seems we are both to remain in London. Perhaps we might run into one another again and you can introduce me to this Barrett?" She looked into his eyes and for a moment he saw great disappointment there. It was fleeting and gone as quickly she smiled up at him.

"Yes, I hope so." She pulled her cloak around her and turned away from him. "My way is over there." She nodded across the road to a side street. "Farewell, Laurence," she said with a note of finality in her voice.

"*Au revoir*, Anna," he replied as she stepped across the road and hurried away.

Chapter 7 – The Bastard of Fauconberg

The armoury in the Tower of London was working at full capacity. Laurence had been allocated some limited space and the use of the forges when he required them. He had been lucky in that Will Belknap was there with him. Both Will and Genase Monk had remained at the Tower armoury when the army went off to gather under Edward's command at Windsor. Nicholas Olds and the other armourers had gone to Windsor with the king. Genase was engaged in general smith work while Will had been seconded as support for the skilled armourers. Laurence had asked him to make up some chasing tools to his own design. These were for the engraving work on earl Rivers' armour. The tools had to be formed then hardened at their tips and ground to shape before they could be used and Will Belknap had made a fine job of them.

London was in a state of fearful suspense. April had given way to May and the month was warm and mild. Out in the Thames estuary, ships of Thomas Neville, the Bastard of Fauconberg were pirating honest merchantmen, and some of these, notably those of Portugal, were blaming Edward IV of England for their losses. Meanwhile in Kent, reports were steadily coming in of the forces being assembled there ready for an assault on the capital. Although the Bastard would know of the Kingmaker's defeat and death, yet he was still determined to carry on with the assault. Margaret of Anjou had an army in the field and she had with her the forces of the duke of Somerset and the earl of Devonshire along with Lord Wenlock. Their combined effort should be more than enough to topple Edward from the throne he had only just regained.

Laurence leaned back and scrutinised the design he had been chasing around the edge of the armet á rondelle he had fashioned. The helmet was almost ready for its final polish, except he would wait until he had finished work on the visor, which he had yet to complete. Earl Rivers had been a frequent visitor to the armoury while his harness was being made. It had been through his influence that Peterkin Mumby had come up with a few pieces of

Milanese armour that could be refashioned into a new set. The rest Laurence would have to make himself, but the provision of back and breastplates, pauldrons, rerebraces, vambraces and couters for the arms, and fine articulated faulds had brought the work forward somewhat. The Tower Armoury also had a small stock of Milanese plate, which Laurence had obtained again due to the influence of the earl. Unfortunately Rivers' influence did not extend to the Armourers' Guild. Mumby had refused permission for Laurence to set up a workshop in the city. He suspected this had been due to objections by Nicholas Olds. Laurence had decided not to force the issue. He could probably get his father to exert some influence on the Guild Masters, but as yet he did not have enough capital to set up for himself and the work for earl Rivers would, at least, gain him something of a reputation. Mumby could not refuse him forever. In any case, he had no idea what his position would be should Edward be defeated. Perhaps Mumby's attitude was fortuitous.

"Word in the town has it that the king has set off in pursuit of Margaret," said Will Belknap. "She has the Prince of Wales with her and many from the west-country have joined her army."

"We can expect an attack on London very soon once Thomas the Bastard knows Edward is away," replied Laurence gloomily.

"Thankfully we are in the Tower, which is a secure fortress. I would not like to be in the city if the Bastard's army break in. They are not likely to make fine distinctions between friend and foe."

"I have heard that most of them are either mercenaries who will be relying on plunder for payment, or rebels with a grudge against the Lord Mayor. I know of Fauconberg; he has been a threat within the narrow seas for years. His cousin, the earl of Warwick was not much better; both have been captains of Calais at some time. We Bretons have many a score to settle with Fauconberg."

"These wars are impossible to work out. Thomas the Bastard was one of those, along with Warwick, who helped Edward to the throne, now he is threatening to take it from him. Mind you, he was always Warwick's man."

"Though not Margaret's."

"That is true; but he has an army of rovers to satisfy. I doubt he can stop now even if he wanted to. Is there never to be an end to war?" Will lamented.

"If the day ever comes when there is no more fighting, you and I will be out of business my friend."

"You could always turn your hand to plain smithing, like me," laughed Will.

"But where would we get an order for ten thousand door latches?" responded Laurence. "Which reminds me, do you not have a few dozen crossbow prods to temper?" Will grinned and nodded as he turned back to his forge.

As Laurence ruminated on the current situation, earl Rivers appeared, anxious to see how soon his new harness would be ready.

"Just another day should have the work finished, my lord. I have tempered the body armour, which is being worked by the polishers at this moment. I have only your helm to finish then we can proceed to a fitting."

"I must have my armour soon. Hostile ships have been sighted approaching London along the Thames and the Bastard of Fauconberg is rapidly filling Southwark with his army. The Lord Mayor, John Stockton is preparing his militia and I shall be required to direct the city's defences. The people of Kent have a grudge against the Lord Mayor for raising taxes on the sale of their goods, so he is sharp about the business of defence."

The two men were talking about the new harness when a servant in the earl's livery hurried up to them.

"My lord," he gasped, bowing low and raising his eyes to his master, "News has just come of a great victory! The king has defeated Margaret of Anjou's army at Tewksbury and there has been a great rout of Lancastrians." Anthony Rivers clenched his fists in joy and beamed down at his servant.

"What more?"

"Very little at present, my lord. Margaret herself has not yet been found, but the reports are that the Prince of Wales is killed!" Rivers face became grim. The death of the prince was worrying. It sounded as if the battle had been a desperate one and he wondered what casualties there would be on the Yorkist side.

"Yet the king is safe?"

"Yes, my lord. He has moved to Coventry from where his messengers have come. No doubt there will be more news as events unfold. The king's messenger is waiting on you to give a full report."

Laurence had been listening carefully to what had happened and the thought came to him that he should visit Cornelius Quirke to see if anything more could be discovered. He knew that Cornelius had his own means of obtaining information, besides, Joan might be with him and the possibility of seeing her made up his mind. A preoccupied earl Rivers hurried away with his servant without a word to Laurence, so he decided now would be a good time to make his way to the apothecary's shop by the Cripplegate.

He walked rather than saddle up his horse and force a way through the busy streets. As Laurence stepped into the street-room of the apothecary's shop, his heart was gladdened by the sight of Joan sitting at the table sorting through a quantity of simples, herbs that would no doubt be used for healing. She gave him a nod of recognition as he swept her a bow.

"Have you heard the news of the king's victory?" he asked her.

"Yes, we knew of it earlier today. Father is not here at the moment. He is attending with a doctor to a sick man but he should be home soon." Laurence repeated what he had heard of the battle.

"Can you tell me anything more?" he said, his voice modulated with his best attempt at charm. She leaned back in her chair and regarded him carefully. He was struck once again by the brightness in the blackest pair of eyes he had ever seen.

"Please sit and I shall tell you what I know, but I warn you there is more to come and first reports are not to be relied upon. Remember the first riders from Barnett spread fear and alarm before the true result of that battle was discovered."

"*Mais oui, je comprend* – I understand," he blurted out, reverting momentarily to his natural tongue before realising she did not understand him.

"King Edward, after a series of hard marches, caught up with Margaret of Anjou's army at Tewksbury. She had made many attempts to divert him so she could march on London, but Edward has good scouts and was too clever for her. Anyhow, both armies were exhausted when they met and Edward, as seems usual for him, was outnumbered. Both armies rested overnight, then, on the morning of the 4th of May the battle began."

"Was there a mist that morning?" asked Laurence.

132

"Whatever makes you ask that?" she replied in astonishment. "What a strange thing to say."

"No signs appeared in the sky?"

"I cannot think what you mean?"

"Pardon, mademoiselle, please continue." She regarded him with a puzzled frown and paused for a moment before resuming.

"The ground was difficult and both sides struggled with the terrain. The king and the duke of Clarence were in the centre, opposite Lord Wenlock and the Prince of Wales. The duke of Gloucester was on the king's left opposite the duke of Somerset and lord Hastings was on the right, opposite the earl of Devonshire. I think that is correct. Anyway, Somerset tried a flank attack on Gloucester who managed to turn and stop him. Edward had positioned a few spears on horseback in a wood for just this eventuality and they attacked, routing Somerset's men who turned and fled. Edward was having a hard time in the centre when something curious happened."

"Yes, I expected something - was it the rising of three suns?"

"I do wish you would stop asking such pointless questions," she snapped in annoyance.

"I apologise."

"No, it was not the rising of three suns. The duke of Somerset became enraged at what he thought was a deliberate act of treason against him when lord Wenlock had failed to come to his aid as his wing collapsed. He rode up to him in fury and, with a single blow of his battle-axe, cleaved lord Wenlock through helmet and skull. Thus was Wenlock struck down by one of their leaders in full sight of his own men. King Edward saw his chance and immediately charged into the centre, which, totally dismayed, broke and ran. Many perished in the pursuit that followed and others fled to Tewksbury Abbey where the Abbot gave them sanctuary."

Laurence nodded in satisfaction but kept his thoughts to himself. Clearly the duke of Somerset had been bewitched to attack one of his own side with such violence. Again Edward had been saved by sorcery. He could detect the hand of Edward's queen in this. He listened intently as she continued her narrative.

"The Prince of Wales galloped from the field pursued by the duke of Clarence and some of his men. They caught the prince and, though the report states he pleaded for his life, yet was he killed on the spot."

More madness, thought Laurence. The Lancastrian heir to the throne was now dead, which left only the frail king Henry who clearly would never sire another child.

"Do you know what has happened to queen Margaret?" he ventured.

"Nothing as yet. She went off before the battle with the prince's wife, the lady Anne, to a place of safety and has not been found. Reports are coming in all the time and it is probable that she has been caught by now."

"If she escapes again I wonder what she will do?"

"There is little she can do now. Perhaps she might seek to return to her husband, king Henry, but I can't see king Edward agreeing to that."

"The world is full of uncertainties," he sighed in his best Gallic manner, trying to gauge the extent of her sensitivity. He was captivated by the simplicity of her beauty. Perhaps it was because her colouring was so different to the girls of Brittany. Her skin was pale, where the frame of black hair around her face enhanced the whiteness of her skin and the red of her lips. To his mind she had the aspect of an armorial device, with plainly drawn lines that delineated the elegance of her form and erased any blemishes that most women had.

"What do you know of queen Elizabeth?" he asked as a way of steering the conversation towards a feminine interest.

"The Wydville woman," she snorted. "She is typical of one who becomes artificially elevated. She can out-queen a queen."

"You do not approve of her?"

"Few women do, but you would."

"How do you know that?"

"Because you are a man. No man can resist a beautiful woman, and when she has the power of a queen, then you are clay to be moulded by her hand."

"That cannot be true," he said simply.

"Why, it is so. Prove to me otherwise."

Laurence thought for a moment, then laughed in exasperation. "I find myself defeated, *mademoiselle*, especially when in the presence of a truly beautiful woman." He bowed in obeisance. She

134

stiffened and looked critically at him, her black eyes sparking as if they had flakes of flint in them.

"I am not a queen, though," she stated.

"But yet a beautiful woman and thus a potential queen of the heart. I am mere clay in your hands."

"You would not speak thus were the queen here also. You are a courtier, sir, and a mere flatterer."

"I am an armourer, which is to say, an *amoureux*."

"A pretty pun, but a lame one. Do not think to practice your sportive tricks on me, *monsieur*." The *monsieur* was delivered sarcastically.

Clearly the conversation was not going the way he had hoped. Normally the kind of banter he had initiated resulted in the woman joining in the game and flirting as a preamble to future developments. This beauty was not of that stamp and he found his passions inflamed further. He was floundering, looking desperately for a way of retrieving the situation when the door opened and Cornelius Quirke entered.

"Ah, Laurence," he said with a note of surprise. "Have you some information for me?"

"No, rather I have come here to find out what is happening abroad. I have been working on harness for earl Rivers and he knows less than I. Mistress Joan has kindly told me more of what is happening with the king."

"Well I have some more news," said Cornelius. "Let us go through to the shop and I can tell you what I know. Based as you are in the White Tower you might be able to discover more." Cornelius opened the shop door and reached down to reassure the great beast, who Laurence had discovered was named Cerberus, that all was safe. Even so, a low growl rumbled from its throat as he passed across the dark passage into the main part of the shop. Joan followed after locking the street door and closing the shop door behind her. Cornelius kicked the embers of the fire into life and threw on a few sticks that soon took and blazed away giving some light. Joan lit a pair of candles and found a flagon of wine and some glasses.

"Queen Margaret is taken," he said as Joan filled his glass. She also filled one for Laurence but scowled as she handed it to him peremptorily. Joan drew up a stool and sat by the fire with them.

This surprised Laurence. He had never been in a situation where a woman would engage with men in serious talk, unless, came the afterthought, she was a queen. "She was found with the lady Anne in a convent near the battlefield. It was lord Stanley who found her and he told her with relish of her army's defeat and her son's death."

"I know queen Margaret is an evil woman, but she must be grieving badly," Joan said sadly.

"No doubt," said Cornelius, "but whether for her lost son or her lost cause, which, I wonder is her greatest loss."

"That is cruel, father."

"Yes, we must not think on such things. However, she will shortly be here in London. Edward has given orders that she be confined in the Tower to await his pleasure."

"What is to happen with the lady Anne?" asked Joan. "She has lost her father, the earl of Warwick, and her husband the Prince of Wales. Not long ago she might have been a queen, now she has nobody."

"She has her sister, the duchess Isabel and I hear that Clarence has taken charge of lady Anne and is to lodge her in his own household with his wife."

"At least she has a sister to comfort her. Queen Margaret has only king Henry and it is unlikely they will be allowed to meet." At this, Joan sank down in her chair and stared pensively into the fire.

"There is more of immediate importance," resumed Cornelius. "After the battle certain Lancastrians fled to Tewkesbury Abbey where they were granted sanctuary. At first king Edward granted this, even though the Abbey is not authorised as a sanctuary. Then he discovered that the duke of Somerset, Edmund Beaumont, was in sanctuary there. He has long been an adversary of York and his younger brother is one of the casualties in the battle otherwise he would have been taken too. The whole brood has been the mainstay of the Lancastrian cause and, so the report goes, Somerset was dragged from sanctuary, tried at Court Marshall by the duke of Gloucester, found guilty of treason and executed forthwith."

"So it is that the whole of the Lancastrian cause is crushed," mused Laurence. "Only king Henry remains alive and he is safely lodged in the Tower."

"Not quite," intoned Cornelius. "Jasper Tudor is still in Wales, though he has no capability of raising a power to oppose Edward, now that Margaret is finished. We need not worry too much about that. Edward is now secure on his throne and no doubt Tudor will either beg favour of him, or quit the realm."

"We still have the Bastard of Fauconberg to worry about. Do you think he will continue with his attack on London? He must be aware that now he is alone."

"He is in a difficult position to be sure. However, his mercenaries will need to be paid and I am guessing he is relying on plunder to satisfy them. You cannot disperse an army of seventeen thousand and a fleet of ships that easily."

"What if he manages to free Henry from the Tower, along with queen Margaret?" said Laurence fearfully. "The whole thing will start all over again."

"That is probably what Thomas the Bastard is thinking, which is the confirmation that he will actually attack us," replied Cornelius. "It may be that is his gamble and with the size of his force the odds are on his side."

"My lord Rivers is here to take charge of the defence of London," said Laurence. "I shall have to return to the Tower."

"The city defences are strong and we should prevail until king Edward comes to our aid, which he surely will," said Cornelius hopefully, looking at his daughter. Laurence looked too, but with different eyes, yet no less committed to her protection.

* * *

The bells of the city rang tocsins for the assembly of the citizens to defend their homes and businesses. A funereal note impressed itself upon his heart. Here he was, safe inside the fortress of the Tower while Joan Quirke was on the other side of the city just beside the Cripplegate, a weak point that the Bastard might decide to attack. He had finished the harness for earl Rivers, though normally there would be some final decoration that circumstances prevented him applying. The earl, usually fastidious about such things, had accepted the harness as it was. He had tested it for fit and freedom of movement and declared it satisfactory. He stated that the harness would next be subjected to the test of battle and expected that it would pass.

Laurence was checking on the condition of his rouncey mare, which he had stabled at the Tower. He had paid one of the stable boys to exercise the beast, which was thus in good condition. The horse seemed to recognise him but he had little opportunity of late to ride. Earl Rivers came over to him followed closely by two lackeys. These sycophants were always at his heels and Laurence gave them little consideration when the earl was present, but should he be diverted to talk to someone else, then they were too ready with their advice. They were, according to their speech, experts in the art of the armourer and instructed him as though they were the earl himself. Of course, he disregarded them, which earned him many a reproachful glare, but they were an annoyance he could do without.

"The bastard has sent a message to the city fathers saying that he wishes to enter London peacefully and take king Henry from the Tower into his own keeping!" snorted earl Rivers.

"You do not believe him?" ventured Laurence, uncertain of the earl's position.

"Of course not, but there are those in the city who would allow him entry. The mayor and the aldermen dare not let him in, but some of the people would."

"Surely nobody wants the wars to continue, which is what would happen if the Bastard Thomas has his way?"

"Fortunately most of the citizens agree with you. Already the Bastard has unloaded guns and is about to fire on the city. He is amassing a force by London Bridge which, I expect, will be his first point of attack, and also at Aldgate and possibly Bishopsgate."

"What about the Cripplegate?" he asked.

"Another weak point."

"I should like to join the garrison at Cripplegate. I have friends in the vicinity and I would be glad of the opportunity of helping them."

"No, I think I shall keep you here for now. The militia under orders from the Lord Mayor, John Stockton and his sheriffs, has reinforced the garrisons at all gates. When the attack begins additional reinforcements will probably have to be despatched as required, so be ready to ride." Laurence had to be satisfied with that and he bowed out of the earl's presence and hurried to a place on the outer walls of the Tower for a view of London Bridge. The old bridge with its business houses along it was the only road into London across the river. If the Bastard's men could get across there they would be well placed to quickly infest the city. However, the roadway was narrow and easily defended, yet if help was needed then men could be quickly despatched from the Tower to ride by Billingsgate and get to their aid.

The city was as prepared as it ever would be. Archers had been stationed along the walls of the city and cannon positioned at intervals ready to fire on the attackers should they attempt to storm the walls. Militiamen, in their chapeles-de-fer and motley collection of body protection were armed mainly with pikes and curtal axes and these clustered together in small groups ready to move as commanded. Heavy stone blocks and other missiles had been heaped on top of the walls ready to be hurled down on the heads of any attackers. Laurence was clad in a mail haubergeon with back and breastplate he had found in the Tower armoury. His head was protected by a sallet to which an aventail was fixed to cover his neck and shoulders. He carried a battleaxe from the armoury and a sword, which was suspended from a belt and hanger.

Laurence had struck up a casual acquaintance with one of the garrison sergeants, named Edmund Carter, who was similarly armed and it was to his troop that he was attached for the immediate defence of London. The two stood atop the Tower walls looking upriver towards London Bridge about half a mile away.

"It seems the attack has begun," said Edmund Carter as they saw the swarm of attackers massed around the entrance to the bridge.

"If they are successful in breaching the gate at London Bridge, then we may have to send reinforcements."

"I doubt they will get in there," replied Edmund. "The bridge is narrow and the buildings on it should prevent the enemy crossing in sufficient numbers to breach the gate. "More seriously, a considerable force has crossed the river and landed to the east of here and is massing at Aldgate and at Bishopsgate.

"If they get in there they can engage the Tower on two sides," mused Laurence. Looking up river, black smoke could be seen rising on the Southwark side of London Bridge. "It looks as if the bridge is on fire. Can you get your runners to report on what is happening?"

The gate captains had already recruited a gang of boys who were stationed in various parts of the city. These would relay messages making communication faster between the defending captains. The Lord Mayor and his sheriffs, Sir John Crosbie and John Ward were already riding between the gates on the north side and earl Rivers was with his men at Aldgate while the earl of Essex was at Bishopsgate.

Gunfire began and great gouts of smoke drifted over the river as the rebel forces at Southwark began to bombard the city across the river. No sooner had they begun when the city ordnance opened up on them which, being more numerous and accurate, soon caused the rebel guns to withdraw. The watchers at the Tower could see flames and smoke coming from the buildings on the Southwark side of London Bridge.

"They will have trouble passing over the bridge now that the south side is on fire," commented Edmund.

"Maybe that was just a diversion," said Laurence as gunfire was now coming from the direction of Aldgate. The two men pushed their way past the soldiers crowding the Tower battlements to get to the north side. The great Abbey of St Clare partly obscured their view, but they could see along the city wall to where the gate was being attacked by the rebel army. One of the messenger boys came panting up to them.

"My lord Rivers commands you attend him at Aldgate," he gasped out between pants. The two men ran down to the stables and while Edmund Carter marshalled his troop, Laurence saddled his horse and joined them. They rode across the drawbridge and galloped the short distance to Aldgate where the defenders were crowded by the portcullis, which was down. The Bastard's men were battering at the outer gate while on the ramparts beside the gate towers, archers were firing down into their mass. Men at arms were mounted and fully harnessed. Laurence saw the familiar harness of earl Rivers and the earl was getting his men into order. Laurence's troop joined those others already mounted and armed with battleaxes. One of earl Rivers' captains rode up to them.

"We are about to raise the portcullis and open the gate. As soon as the gate is open we will charge into the enemy and disperse them.

140

Those rebels who get by us into the city will be dealt with by archers and then the militia. We have cleared either side of the roadway out of the gate with boiling oil and stone missiles. Pikemen will open a way then the men at arms will go out to punch their way into the rebel force. Your job is to follow through and stop those rebels who get past the knights.

Laurence had begun to reflect on how so far he had managed to keep out of the fight for Edward's crown and now he found himself in it whether he wanted to be or not. He should have been safely hammering away in his workshop, not engaging in what was soon to be a pitched battle. He looped the leather thong of the battleaxe around his wrist and gripped the handle, wishing he had thought to acquire a pair of gauntlets. The mail over his arms only extended to the back of his hands, held there by a leather loop around his fingers. Still, he consoled himself with the knowledge that a bare hand had the better grip. His pulse quickened as he saw the portcullis slowly lift into the upper part of the gate tower. Pikemen advanced and filled the narrow passage between the portcullis and the gate with naked steel, spike and axe, those behind holding their weapons between those in front providing a solid wall of impalement.

The gates were unfastened and the press of men outside caused them to burst open and the rebels to rush onto the deadly array of pikes. In the narrow passage there was no escape. Men screamed as the first sudden shock had robbed them of their boldest fighters. The pikes moved forward driving the rebels away from the gate, clambering over the bodies of the dying and wounded. The mounted men-at-arms urged their horses forward and trampled through the injured. The pikes made it through the gate and parted to let them through. Driving into the centre of the attacking force packed around the gate, they hacked about them vigorously and the rebels, having been taken completely by surprise gave way before them. One moment they were clamouring at the gate, the next they were being hewn down by a professional attack force. As horses could not be used to scale walls or force a gate, there were no mounted men to oppose them and the armoured warhorses, with their invincible riders carved a way through the rebels.

Edmund Carter moved his troop into the fray, at first with difficulty due to the confusion of dead and dying in the gate

141

passage and immediately outside. Once clear, though, they could ride more freely. Laying about them with their axes, carving through flesh and bone. Laurence noted that many of the rebels were armed only with pitchforks, staves, scythes and clubs though deadly enough if used aright, and the average churl was very useful with such weapons. What they lacked was armoured protection and though many fought bravely and even managed to bring down a man-at-arms occasionally, inevitably the superior weight of arms and armour in trained hands had deadly effect and they began to run.

Laurence had narrowly missed being speared by a pitchfork, which had been thrust at his face, but he managed to strike it aside and chop into the shoulder of the man who wielded it with a backward swing of his axe as he rode by. The battleaxe proved its worth, as he expected it would, as an armoured rebel, probably one of their leaders, came at him on foot with a sword. He veered away from his first stroke and turned his horse causing the man to follow round. In doing so he stumbled and Laurence managed to strike from his hand his sword, raised to ward off the blow, then follow through with a blow that cut through the helm and into his scull. One thing Laurence knew for certain was how to strike through metal. He twisted the blade free and rode on leaving a crumpled heap of dead humanity behind him.

As the press of rebels tried to retreat the mounted knights slowed and the light troopers caught up with them and all worked together driving the rebels away from the city. Laurence saw that earl Rivers, who was driving the rebels in front of him, was suddenly surrounded by a number of hostile men-at-arms. Soon he was in trouble; his horse had been injured and was sinking to the ground. Others had seen the danger too, but Laurence was nearest to the earl so he spurred his horse forward and rode into the rear of the armoured men. All was a blur of flashing blades as they turned on him. He drove his battleaxe into the shoulder of one and wrenching it free drove the stock of the axe head into the aventail of another, crushing his windpipe. He felt a blow to his helm and was almost stunned but lashed out blindly with his battleaxe at where he imagined his attacker to be. The earl attacked also and between the two of them drove away the remaining men-at-arms who had seen the approach of Rivers' esquires and attempted to get away. The squires went after them and finished them off. One of his squires brought the earl another horse and when he had mounted they turned and made their way back to the city.

Laurence made it back without really knowing how. Someone had taken the reins of his horse and let him ride slumped in his saddle without sense of direction. He came to his wits just as they rode through Aldgate back into the city. Edmund Carter had led him back, seeing that he was disorientated. The earl had ridden back before and was at that moment receiving the accolades of the local aldermen. He saw Laurence arrive and sent one of his lackeys over to him.

"His lordship the earl Rivers wishes to commend your actions in the recent fight and to tell you that his harness stood the test of battle very well."

"Thank his lordship and tell him I wish mine had." The lackey nodded and trotted back to the earl.

Laurence removed his sallet and examined it. There was an indentation and a small gash in the dome. Luckily the weapon that struck him had not penetrated further, though there was a small trickle of blood running down his face. Edmund examined his head and stated that the cut was small and would soon heal. He had been lucky and survived his first fight in the cause of king Edward the fourth of England.

"The earl of Essex has driven off the rebels at Bishopsgate too, though we are expecting an attack at either Moorgate or Cripplegate as these are more lightly defended," Edmund informed him. Panic gripped him. He knew that reinforcements had been hurried to the defence of Aldgate and Bishopsgate, leaving the other gates lightly manned. Without another thought he found his mount and rode off along the inside of the wall towards Cripplegate, which was at the far side of the city beyond both Bishopsgate and Moorgate. At Bishopsgate he had to push his way through the press of soldiers who were tending to the injured, or looking for booty among the dead. The gate had been secured once more and the rebels repelled.

Moorgate was still in a state of anticipation, but as he reached Cripplegate his worst fears were realised. Here they had tried similar tactics as earl Rivers to repel the rebels but without the same success. Rebel forces had managed to break through the gate

143

and were running amock in the surrounding streets. The Moorgate defenders were holding back, expecting an attack at their gate at any moment. The militia at Cripplegate had retreated for a while but had now reformed and were ready to clear the streets of the invader. Laurence dismounted, realising it was impossible to fight on horseback in the narrow streets with such a press of soldiery milling around. The area around the gate was still contested as the city militia battled with the rebels, some of whom were pillaging the shops and businesses of the quarter, hoping for some profit before escaping the consequences of their attack. He worked his way to where the apothecary's shop was located. A lout came at him with a cudgel – he had no idea if he was friend or foe but the man bled his life away in the gutter nevertheless.

The battleaxe he was still grasping was of limited use in these streets. He found the body of a soldier. On whose side he had fought he hardly knew nor cared, but just beyond his outstretched lifeless arm lay a curtal axe, which he knew he could wield more effectively than his battleaxe. Transferring his battleaxe to his left hand, he picked up the curtal axe and felt it for weight. It would suffice.

As he reached the apothecary's shop it was not the sight of the smashed door that caused his heart to falter but the cries that filtered out into the street. He swept the remnants of the wrecked door aside and stepped into the room. His eyes took in the scene immediately and afterwards he would remember it as if it were indelibly etched with acid into his mind. He saw without thinking the still form of the apothecary lying on the floor. Joan was thrown across the table and a churl had her skirts around her waist and his hose around his ankles struggling to mount her. Another held her arms, grinning at his companion. By the wall another lay drenched in blood, his throat in tatters while the instrument of his fate, the hound Cerberus lay on the floor, his entrails trailing from the gash in his belly where he had dragged them in a vain attempt to defend his mistress before his strength had failed him.

The churl who was attempting the rape of Joan never knew what had happened and went to purgatory where his unshriven soul would moan in damnation for eternity, his scull split from crown to chops. The other, the one holding her down was not so fortunate. Laurence swung the curtal axe into his collarbone, rendering him

144

helpless and already mortally wounded. He fell back to the floor and Laurence swept the curved blade across his belly spilling his guts. The man looked on the sight with terrified eyes trying vainly to push them in again, one handed, the other being useless, while his nemesis advanced upon him. Then, with one swipe of the blade, the man's head fell off and rolled onto the floor.

Laurence turned and though his first thought would normally have been for Joan, yet his eyes were drawn to the dog lying on the floor. The beast was yet alive and Laurence saw him for the first time. A great hound with coarse grizzled hair and a massive maw, yet his eyes looked on Laurence as if in approval and at that moment his duty of protection was somehow transferred. The animal's tail gently slapped against the floor. It had always snarled at him, yet now it was almost as if it was making amends. A flash of understanding flowed in the space between man and beast and, as the hound's eyes faded into night, and the flap of its tail diminished, a bond was forged. He looked to Joan and she had seen it too. Nothing would be the same again.

Chapter 8 – The Death of a King

A covering of freshly dug earth marked the spot under a mature yew tree where the body of Cerberus lay. Three people stood in silent tribute, none having appropriate words to utter over the grave of a dog, but each moved by its death. Cornelius Quirke was the first to turn away. Laurence offered his hand to Joan and she slipped hers willingly into it. He had abandoned the conventional language of courtship, which hadn't worked on her anyway, it now being unnecessary. She had been subdued since her ordeal and shocked by its violent aftermath. Laurence spoke little, letting her come to terms with what had happened knowing she would eventually realise matters could have been much worse had he not arrived when he did. He had sent a message to Edmund Carter at the Tower to let him know he was safe after dashing away as he had. Two days had elapsed since the attack on London and he knew he must return to the Tower arsenal soon but he could hardly bear to tear himself away from Joan while she was still in a state of distress.

They walked together back into the house. He had discovered that the passage where Cerberus used to lie led through to a large garden where Joan grew herbs for the various potions brewed by her father. Cornelius stopped and leaned a hand on the doorpost as he reached the house. He was still suffering from vomiting and nausea even though Joan had bathed and bandaged his wounded head. Also, a broken arm had been bound and held in a sling, which handicapped his movements, so he waited while they came along to open the door for him.

The front of the shop had been put back together and scrubbed clean of the blood and mess. Laurence had a local carpenter fix the door and frame, which had been badly damaged. The rebels had not breached the shop itself and Joan helped her father to his chair by the fire while Laurence fed a few sticks to cause it to brighten into life.

Cornelius spoke up quietly. "There are still thousands of rebels beyond the walls, but they are no longer a serious threat, being virtually leaderless and most are already slinking away."

"They say the Bastard of Fauconberg has retired to Sandwich with his ships," said Laurence.

"Yes, the king has sent an advanced guard to disperse the rebels and take prisoners."

"I had better return to the Tower," decided Laurence. "There is still much to do before we can declare a complete victory."

"I have some reports to write," said Cornelius. "I shall inform the duke of Brittany of events here and include a note for your parents, letting them know you are safe."

Laurence turned to Joan who was standing by her father's chair. "I shall return as soon as I can. Is there anything I can do before I go?"

"No, we will be fine. One of our neighbours, goodwife Wood will come if needed though I believe we are settled now and we have our maid Jennet." He noted that her eyes were shadowed with fatigue and he thought she had not slept since the attack on the shop. Goodwife Wood had been much help immediately after the attack in comforting Joan and it had been she who had set Cornelius' broken arm. Joan walked with him to the street door of the shop and when he placed his arms around her she did not resist. They stood for a moment in a quiet embrace, she comforted by his strength, he by her need for the security he offered. He did not kiss her, but drew away simply holding one of her hands in his, then, letting it slip free walked off down the street.

Laurence called at the Bishopsgate to retrieve his horse. The wreckage around the gate had been cleared and repairs were under way. After a few enquiries he found the mare stabled with a local farrier who charged him for looking after the beast. He thought the fellow looked disappointed as he claimed the horse and tackle. He had probably been hoping the owner was lost and, therefore, would acquire the animal by default. He rode back to the Tower and found Edmund Carter on the green supervising the erection of a scaffold and gallows.

"Have you taken many prisoners?" asked Laurence.

"Yes, and quite a number will lose their lives. The first are to be Spysing and Quentin, the Bastard's main captains. They will lose their heads today, others are to be hanged, them who cannot pay ransom that is. The king and his brothers are approaching London and then we will finish off what remains of the Bastard's forces once and for all."

"As soon as the fighting here is over I shall retire to the armoury and take up my duties there."

"You have fought well, my friend," said Edmund Carter, clapping Laurence on the shoulder. "You will be welcome in the guardhouse anytime, especially if you bring ale with you." Laurence thought that he would prefer wine, but these Englishmen drank mainly ale, which was fortunate as their valuable urine was collected for use in the tempering wells where hot armour was quenched.

When he returned to the furnaces he found Will Belknap and Genase Monk looking unusually neat and tidy in their best jacket and hose. Both wore black wool caps with coloured ribbon on one side hanging down over their shoulders.

"What is happening with you both?" enquired Laurence.

"We are off to see the king come into London," said Will, his voice slightly slurred.

"You must come too," said Genase in a voice no less slurred than Wills. The entry of the king into his capital was a festival and obviously both men had started their celebrations early. He thought he would rather be out in the crowd with Joan on his arm, but as she was unlikely to want to join in the festivities he decided to go along with his comrades.

"Let me change into my street clothes." He was wearing the mail haubergeon and helmet, which he had donned for his passage across London. The battleaxe was still in the apothecary's shop where he could retrieve it should the need arise, but the curtal axe was hanging by his belt. He went into the chamber beside the forges where the armourers had their possessions locked away in secure chests and emerged some minutes later bareheaded but dressed in a black leather doublet and crimson hose with his feet inside brown leather boots. Around his waist was a simple leather belt with a scabbard and dagger. Thus equipped, the trio left the Tower to greet the king.

Just a few weeks before, the king had entered London in the splendour of a monarch, but with an undertone of uncertainty. Now he entered as a victor and the parade was organised differently. No longer did the youthful duke of Gloucester bring up the rear, but

148

entered first, as befitted the order of battle that had consolidated Edward's crown. Behind Gloucester rode Lord Hastings and then the king himself. George, duke of Clarence came after the king and then, a miserable Margaret of Anjou, drawn in a simple chariot, her husband, son and cause vanquished. The crowd that had cheered pragmatically before, now hailed their king enthusiastically, no longer reticent with doubt but certain of his power. The taverns and alehouses were brimming with customers and later, the stews would throng with lusty revellers looking to satisfy their lust after slaking their thirsts.

The three comrades had cheered along with the rest as the parade passed by then dived into the nearest tavern. Seated at a bench, Will drew a doxy onto his knee and demanded a kiss before he would pay for the ale she had brought. She complied indifferently then prised herself free to tend to the other customers.

"Has honour been satisfied?" joked Laurence as Will released the girl.

"The strumpet would have been offended had I not bussed her," came the reply. The three laughed and drank each other a health. Someone shouted a pledge to the king, Edward of England! Everyone in the crowd repeated the shout except, Laurence noted, for two fellows seated in a corner. They were wearing the murrey and blue livery of the duke of Clarence and they placed their beakers on the table while everyone else was raising theirs. Nobody had noticed, otherwise an argument would have ensued, but Laurence had and he wondered about them. He was trying to think of a way of approaching them when they were joined by two wenches one of them dark, plump and full breasted and the other fair haired and trim. He placed his hand on Wills arm.

"There is a friend, I think?" Will and Genase followed his gaze.

"Why, that's Anna," exclaimed Genase. "Looks as if you have lost her, Laurence." Genase nor Will knew of Joan but they did know that Laurence and Anna had been bedfellows on the long march.

"No, she is her own woman," whispered Laurence, "but I shall speak with her."

"Be careful," said Will. "Those fellows may not want you to intrude." Laurence went over to the group.

"Hello Anna." He greeted her with a warm smile. She looked up at him with surprise as she recognised his distinctive accent. The two men regarded him suspiciously then looked questioningly at Anna; so did the buxom wench who then turned her head and after scrutinising him lasciviously smiled up at him.

"Hello, Laurence," said Anna carefully. She swept an arm to encompass her companions. "As you can see I have made some new friends."

"I am pleased for you," he replied beaming at the company. "I see you are in the livery of my lord Clarence," he stated looking at the two men, then directing his attention to Anna: "you have a place in his household as you hoped?"

"Yes, I have been engaged to brew ale."

"A most fitting occupation and one you are particularly qualified for."

"A better job she makes of it than this slop and we are paying for it too." The speaker was one of the two men – a gruff looking fellow, dark of mein and similar in type to Laurence himself. There was no aggression in his voice, just curiosity. The other fellow who had a sallow complexion under a tangle of straw-coloured hair placed a proprietary hand on the arm of the buxom female.

"Come and sit with us, sir," said the wench, wriggling along the bench to make room for him. Her companion did not look too happy about this, but let her jostle him nevertheless.

"This is Barrett," said Anna, indicating the gruff fellow with a nod, "and this is Allen . . ."

"I am Angelica," interjected the buxom one. "You are Laurence it seems."

"*Tres hereux de te voir, mademoiselle*," he said automatically responding with his native charm. Angelica gushed and wriggled all the more, setting her ample breasts quivering, much to the chagrin of Allen who was regarding the performance with some annoyance. Laurence had no desire to antagonise the two men so he diverted his gaze to Barrett. "I think that Anna told me you are a cook, m*onsieur*?"

"That is correct, and you sir?" Before he could reply, Anna cut in:

"Laurence rode with James Tyrell's prickers and then was given the task of guarding king Henry before the battle of Barnet," Anna told them hurriedly as if she wished to give him some sort of credence with them.

150

"We have no grudge with my lord of Gloucester," grunted Barrett. "Yet there are others in the king's company who my lord, his grace of Clarence would see gone."

"As for me, I am simply an armourer presently working at the Tower armoury but on the great march with the king I travelled with Nicholas Olds, the king's armourer."

"You told me you were making harness for the earl Rivers, did you not?" said Anna, looking from him to the two men. Both men bristled at the mention of River's name.

"What think you of the earl Rivers?" queried Barrett, his eyes grim under his black eyebrows. Laurence sensed that he would have to tread carefully here. Clearly Rivers name was despised in this company, yet he could only speak according to his own perceptions.

"I found him a most intelligent and courtly gentleman, though I have only dealt with him regarding his harness. I know him to be a brave fighter – I witnessed that for myself outside Aldgate when we drove away the rebels. I know he has a reputation as a fine jouster, a subject in which of course, I have a professional interest. I met him briefly in Flanders when he was helping prepare the king's return expedition, but other than that I know little of him."

Barrett and Allen looked at each other then both returned their gaze to Laurence. Anna sat mute beside Barrett and even Angelica kept silent.

"You have no personal ties to him?" asked Barrett.

"None, other than the business he has put my way."

"My lord of Clarence despises the Wydvilles and we of his household must hold the same opinion, yet we do so willingly. We are loyal to the king, but his queen, the witch Elizabeth, is another matter." Laurence noticed that Anna gasped in exasperation as the word witch was used though he could not help agreeing with Barrett.

"There are others who may use the black arts and better than the Wydville woman," spat Angelica suddenly.

"Be quiet, that is foolish talk," Anna interjected. "I do wish we could get away from this talk of witchcraft. No good will come of it and some may even lose their lives if care is not taken." Angelica reddened and seemed to realise she had spoken hastily. Her two male companions glared at her and she sagged onto the bench and sulked.

"I saw that you didn't drink the king's health earlier. Why was that if you are loyal as you say?" said Laurence, changing the subject.

"The king's is too much under the influence of the Wydville brood and his victories will favour the queen's family more than his own brother."

"You mean Clarence, of course, but what about his other brother Richard of Gloucester; won't he be discomfited too?"

"That he may, and he has no more like of the Wydvilles than our lord, but he does little to combat their ambition."

"He is but a youth and although he has proved himself in battle he has yet to prove himself in government."

"Time will tell us that," replied Barrett. "But you just watch. When the spoils that come from the attainted Lancastrians are divided, it will be Clarence who will gain least and the Wydvilles most; their queen will see to that." Laurence noted how he spoke of *their* queen rather than *our* queen of England.

"Can we have more ale?" whined Allen. Laurence was glad of his intervention. He had contributed nothing to the conversation, but his demand was timely.

Laurence grabbed at a passing doxy and ordered ale for the company. "I am surprised you have no kitchen duties this day," he said to Barrat.

"It is because the duke and duchess are carousing with the king tonight so the kitchen is on light duty. That is an advantage of serving a great lord. He has many servants, each with a particular duty, though we do help out with general tasks when ordered. I am a pastry cook, but I also help bake bread. My family have a bakers shop in the town and when his grace is away at his estates that is where I return."

"You are not fixed to his retinue?"

"No, he has his own cooks, but when he is in London his staff is so large that more of us are needed."

"It is my lady Anne I am sorry for, poor thing," piped up Angelica. "His grace has just brought her into his household. She has not only lost a husband, though that is perhaps fortunate given who he was, but her father Warwick also. She only found out about her father's defeat at Barnet when she landed with queen Margaret's

152

invasion force at Weymouth, and before she could grieve for him her husband was killed too."

"I suppose she will be placed with her sister so they can comfort each other," said Laurence, sympathetically.

"You would think so, but his grace has ordered an apartment for her separate from the duchess Isabel's and in a different part of the house. "She is with the king at the moment, but when she is brought to the house tomorrow, I shall be her only attendant."

Laurence was astonished. "You mean that with all those servants in the house she will just have one - you?"

"That is what I have been told," replied Angelica. "She has no rank and thus cannot demand more. Her husband, Edward the Prince of Wales is dead and declared traitor along with the Kingmaker, her father."

"Yet if the Lancastrians had been victorious, she would have been queen of England when king Henry's heir achieved the throne."

"Instead we have the Wydville," spat Barrett. Laurence considered the whole business to have the taint of evil in it. As the ale arrived he paid the doxy, stood up and drank a health to the company, which replied politely.

"I shall return to my friends, but perhaps we may meet again."

"I hope so," declared Angelica gaily. The two men made no particular gesture other than a raising of their beakers of ale, but Anna smiled up at him and bid him good den."

"That was a cosy arrangement you had going there," said Will as Laurence slid onto the bench beside him.

"Just making friends," he replied. "I am a foreigner here, remember; I need all the friends I can get."

"Strange how most of them seem to be women," grinned Will.

"Not unlike the king himself," jested Genase. Laurence grinned at them and gave his usual helpless shrug.

* * *

Laurence had only one brief glimpse of Margaret of Anjou as she descended from the chariot she had been paraded in before being brought to the Tower of London. This was the woman who had ravaged England and provoked death and destruction for many years, yet she had some justification, being the legitimate queen of an anointed monarch. Laurence could appreciate the great forces within that had driven her. She had chosen the Lancastrian lords as her allies at Henry's court and thus provoked the wars when the Yorkists vied for power. He was surprised how small she was; even more so as the wretched creature, all her ambitions crushed, her husband a prisoner, her son dead and all her supporters either killed or in retreat, was hurried into her chamber in the Tower. She was still wearing the robes of a queen, though soiled by the vicissitudes of the road that had brought her here. He was struck by the bass note of finality when the heavy oak door, studded with iron nails, thudded shut behind her.

A team of Tower guards were swilling down fresh blood from the scaffold on the Tower green. Spysing and Quentin had been decapitated by the Tower axeman and their heads despatched to London Bridge where they would gaze down on the scene of their attack until the crows pecked their skulls clean. The crowd that had been allowed in to watch the spectacle had left and few were there to witness queen Margaret's arrival at her prison while the victors caroused in the city.

As soon as her keepers took charge of the queen, the mounted escort began to dismount. James Tyrell had them in charge and Laurence greeted him as he was still, technically, attached to his troop.

"Give you good den, master Tyrell." Tyrell climbed down from his horse and clapped Laurence on the shoulder, grinning broadly.

"You must call me Sir James now," he said proudly. "The king knighted me on the field of Tewksbury."

"Please accept my congratulations, Sir James," he responded gladly.

"I shall be needing some new harness," said Tyrell. "I suppose you will be expecting to provide it for me?"

"Now that you are Sir James Tyrell, I shall also expect a rather better fee than for the last one," replied Laurence."

"Are there no true friends in the world who would love a man for himself and not expect profit?"

"As you well know, Sir James, love always comes at a price."

"By the mass, I think you would have been better trained as a priest than an armourer. You have a tonsured tongue."

"Then you are fortunate for I might shave some profit for a friend."

"You are too clever for me," laughed Tyrell. "I suppose it will be my purse that is shaved before you are done."

"Are your duties finished, now that queen Margaret is safe in her apartments?"

"No, we rest but for a few minutes. We are to escort the lady Anne, widow of the late Prince of Wales, to the house of the duke of Clarence. His grace of Gloucester has charged me especially with the duty. She is a sad lady though I expect a lodging in her sister's house will help her grieve."

"I suppose that the duke's house is the best place for her, at present." Laurence agreed. "There are still plenty of rebels around and the bastard of Fauconberg's ships remain in the Thames estuary, or so I have heard. What will happen next?"

"The king has some immediate business to attend to here in London, then we are off with him into Kent to arrest the rebel leaders and dispense the king's justice. His grace of Gloucester has already left for Canterbury to arrest the mayor for treason, then on to Sandwich to deal with the Bastard of Fauconberg who has intimated he will surrender to the duke."

"Then it looks as if king Edward is secure on his throne at last, with his most dangerous enemies vanquished. I wonder what will happen to king Henry – exile perhaps or just left here in the Tower? Will he be reunited with his queen now that she is here too?"

"Those are questions for the king to decide," said Tyrell with a tone of mild rebuke in his voice. "The king is considering what to do with the old king right now." With a brief nod of finality, he turned and walked back to where his horse was being fed by a groom.

Laurence clearly was not going to learn anything more for the moment. He thought of the old king locked away in his Tower apartment and wondered how much of his mind was left to him. Did he know his queen was a prisoner nearby and that his son was dead? If his mind was unable to comprehend events, then that would be a blessing, but also a curse for it meant he could be used by anyone against the newly established throne of Edward IV. This had already been the case as he well remembered from his own experience with Henry and in his pavilion before the Battle of Barnet. It had been but a few weeks ago the Lancastrians had brought the feeble king Henry from the Tower and paraded him through the streets in a vain attempt to rally Londoners against king Edward, even though he clearly was in no fit state to rule again. With his unscrupulous queen by his side, however, the whole war could easily revive. The thought depressed his spirits for he could not see a way clear of the problem.

The sun was going down and the shadows from the walls and towers of the old fortress stretched out like black fingers across the Tower green. He could hear the beasts in the menagerie clamouring, growling and spitting as the keepers fed them. Strange beasts they were, but predictable, quite unlike their captors and hardly less savage. He watched as several ravens tore at scraps deliberately thrown down for them. He hated these birds of ill omen for he knew their appearance predicted bad weather and death and thus could not work out why they were encouraged to live in the Tower grounds. One of them, driven away by the others, flew to a corbel of the Wakefield Tower and began croaking at his fellows.

* * *

Forge fires had been damped and the *couvre feu* sounded as Laurence stood by the doorway to the armoury workshops as the fortress closed down for the night. Guards were posted and torches blazed at each gate, but the place was never quiet. Horses whickered at intervals in the various stables and every now and then the bark of a dog would disturb the air. Banners and pennants on the walls and towers snapped in the wind, their lanyards slapping against mast and post. Occasionally a door opened and closed, letting pale light spill out from its portal as people moved around doing their nightly duties; guards murmured together when they met on their spasmodic rounds. Though the day had been clear, night brought lowering cloud and the threat of rain as presaged by the presence of ravens. Laurence fingered the reliquary hanging around his neck having just come from Vespers in a small chapel reserved for the common soldiery. There was something of dread in the air. He told himself that it was because he was a foreigner in this England where the uncertainties of the long march and the hard-fought battles had influenced his thoughts. He looked where he knew the Wakefield Tower to be, though it was hardly more than a black image over the dark cloud. He fancied the saintly Henry VI kneeling at prayer there, as he had seen him in the pavilion outside Barnet. The windows were shuttered though he fancied he could make out a glim from around the edge of one.

He was just about to return to his sleeping quarters adjacent to the forges when he heard something that made the hair stand up at the back of his neck and a tremor run down his spine. There had been a terrible howl of anguish, not loud and almost indiscernible, yet he had heard it. In this place that was no surprise; though it was a royal palace, it had its dungeons and secret places where prisoners would go in but never come out again. The cells were full of rebels at the moment, yet this cry somehow seemed separate from the kind of despair theirs would describe. It had no self-pity in it; just a deep keening sorrow of the kind Our Lord must have felt as he gave up the ghost on the cross. His ears strained to hear more, and he would remember later how silent the Tower had become at that moment. He wondered if he could hear doors slam and feet running, but who could tell what was going on in the labyrinthine passages, apartments and cells. Then the fortress sounds came back and he heard the guttering torch flames fanned by a sudden breeze and saw them brighten momentarily as if a lost soul had just passed by. He stood for a time, fingering his reliquary and praying to the Virgin for he knew not what. There were strange spirits abroad at night and few Christian folk ventured out unless they had to. He kissed the reliquary and tucked it inside his shirt. Looking towards the Wakefield Tower he made the sign of the cross, went inside and found his bed. He hardly slept that night and finally dozed off only as the dawn came. At one point he thought he had detected the sound of horses and the clink of armour, but his sleep was fitful and disturbed with grotesque dreams. He was wakened then by the stirrings of the armourers as they prepared for their day's work.

In the morning, people spoke in hushed tones and went about their duties, careful to avoid being seen gossiping with their fellows. When two or more people did meet there was many a backward glance to discover who else might hear what was being spoken of. King Henry VI of England was dead! Nobody was sure how he had died and rumour was rife in the Tower population. Word had

157

already spread into the city and speculation of some dreadful deed was being noised around. Laurence heard that king Edward had sent some of his nobles to lord Dudley, the Constable of the Tower, with instructions to murder the old king.

Perhaps their arrival was what Laurence had thought he heard during the night. Lord Dudley had announced that king Henry had died of melancholy when he was informed of the death of his son and the capture of his queen. Perhaps the thought of her being here in the Tower, but locked away from him was more than he could bear. Laurence remembered the anguished cry in the night and earlier the croak of the Raven, a bird well known to be the familiar of a witch. At times like this, he knew, you had to be careful what you listened to and talked about. It was unclear who had actually spoken to king Henry regarding the fate of his son and his queen. The nobles claimed that Henry was already dead when they went into his apartment. No one had thought, or dared, to ask why they were there in the first place. His household servants were with him as normal and it could be, that though he had been told the fate of his family earlier in the day, given his mental condition, full realisation of the hopelessness of his state may have come later in the night, causing a seizure and death.

The armourers had just breakfasted when Sir James Tyrell rode up and came over to Laurence.

"You are to ride out with us, master armourer. We are off to Sandwich to join with my lord of Gloucester."

"What about my duties here?" asked Laurence.

"You have proved yourself useful in several ways and the king, at the suggestion of earl Rivers, has ordered that you come with us – so, you come with us."

Laurence thought about this. He wondered why he should be ordered away from his armouring duties at the Tower. The idea came to him that it might have something to do with his earlier involvement with the care of king Henry. Had his natural sympathy for the old king somehow communicated itself to the king? If so, then removing him from the rumour factory that the Tower had become would make sense. It meant he could not be drawn in to idle speculation, a dangerous place to be. In any case, being near to the main protagonists would gain him a better insight regarding events, and this would be most useful to duke Francis in Brittany.

"Do I need to arm myself?"

"It would be sensible. We are showing our strength as well as dispensing the king's justice so the more aggressive we appear the better. You know Thomas Neville as well as the rest of us; would you trust him not to attack us if he felt he could get away with it? The king is to follow us with a larger force and the Bastard will know that. He had been working with his cousin, Warwick and now he is gone there will be little support for the Bastard in the narrow seas. Nevertheless, it is well to expect treachery."

Laurence nodded in agreement. "The death of king Henry has also removed the main focus of the Lancastrian faction. Once we have dealt with the Bastard of Fauconberg Edward will be secure."

"We might hope so. The last of the fighting Lancastrians, Jasper Tudor, escaped Tewksbury and has fled to Pembroke Castle. It is only a matter of time before we go after him. He has Margaret Beaufort's whelp with him and the pair will make a fine sight dangling from the castle walls."

"But they have no legitimate claim to the throne?"

"None, but the Lancastrian cause is in tatters and desperate. Drowning men clutch at straws. Edward will always have to look over his shoulder while any of the Tudor brood live." Tyrell spurred his horse around. "Be ready to ride within the hour," and with that he rode over to the stables where his men were gathering.

Laurence thought of getting a message to Joan and her father and grabbed one of the boys who hung around the Tower begging for scraps. He gave the lad a hastily scribbled note, telling him where to deliver it and with instructions to give the lad something for his trouble. That way he knew the note would be delivered.

Laurence was impressed by the number of ships anchored in the Wantsum Channel along the river into the harbour town of Sandwich. The weather was warm and just a few clouds punctuated the pale blue of the sky as they rode down into the town. Tyrell's men rode into Sandwich ahead of the duke of Gloucester to prepare the route to where Thomas the Bastard was waiting to receive him. The townspeople were sullen, those who were abroad, the majority preferring to keep indoors. Kent had been in the forefront when it came to rising up against Edward and now they knew their defeat would bring retribution.

In the expectation of being hanged, the Mayor of Sandwich, along with most of his Aldermen had fled the town and was hiding somewhere in the countryside. A motley group of local businessmen of lowly rank were all there was to greet them in the harbour. The men clustered apprehensively together in a tight group, their caps in their hands waiting on the arrival of the duke. The town was in a sorry state having hardly recovered from its sacking by the French fourteen years earlier when it was burned to the ground. The harbour was full of ships and one of these, a carrack, was tied to the quay and flying the banner of the *Sunne in Splendour* from its masthead. Clearly this was where the meeting with the Bastard of Fauconberg would be.

As Tyrell and his men clattered onto the quay the crew of the carrack came down from the ship and lined up either side of the gangway. They were a rough lot of rovers, none of them wearing the same dress or armour. As they stood facing each other a man appeared at the top of the gangway and waited alone. He was dressed in a green silk tunic draped with a brown velvet cloak that was trimmed with squirrel fur. He wore a brown velvet cap pointed at the front. He was a tall dark man, heavily built though not yet fat and he displayed a long thin moustache, which gave his mien a strange fierceness. Though dressed as a noble, the trimming of squirrel fur to his cloak normally worn by those of lower rank, offered a hint of humility. He wore nothing ostentatious, no jewels or rings on his fingers.

Laurence wondered how the duke of Gloucester would react on meeting with this brigand, for that is what he was in spite of his bastard Neville nobility. He was the illegitimate son of William Neville, Lord Fauconberg the first Earl of Kent who was the uncle of Warwick the Kingmaker. Laurence had no time for the father who had spent many years pillaging the Breton coast before his death eight years ago. The bastard son had carried on the father's piratical tradition. What did Fauconberg's bastard expect his fate to be? His chief captains had already been summarily executed and their heads now adorned London Bridge. His cousin had been butchered at Barnet and the Prince of Wales was cut down mercilessly at Tewksbury. The young duke Richard had already dragged Edmund Beaumont, the duke of Somerset from Tewksbury Abbey and after a brief trial removed his head from his body. Did Thomas know yet of king Henry's death? Tyrell had told Laurence that Thomas the Bastard was one who, along with his cousin the Kingmaker, had placed Edward on the throne back in 1461. He had fought for York then as his father had. Perhaps he was hoping the youthful Richard of Gloucester would remember that history and be merciful. One thing was sure; nobody in the advance guard was taking bets on the likelihood of his survival.

They would not be long in finding out. The sound of trumpets came from somewhere before the town approaches, announcing the arrival of duke Richard. Tyrell formed his men in a ring around the Bastard's crew, their lances pointing inwards. Presently a cavalcade of men-at-arms rode onto the quay and divided to form up two ranks deep either side of the Fishergate, which was the main entrance to the quay. Richard's banner men rode in next and formed up directly in front of the carrack leaving a space at their centre. The duke of Gloucester, clad in his black armour, rode in and stopped, regarding the Bastard of Fauconberg with an icy stare. His sword remained in its scabbard and his war axe hung by his saddle. Leaning forward and resting an arm on the front of his saddle he said nothing, preferring to wait for the Bastard to make a move. Laurence, being with Tyrell's spearmen, was fascinated by the game that was being played out.

Thomas Neville had no choice but to trot down the gangway and drop to his knees in front of the duke. He spread his arms in supplication and bowed his head. The duke let him stay there a while, being content just to manage his skittish war horse, making it stay in place. The constant fretting of the beast was most disconcerting, as the duke must have known. The rovers that were the Bastard's crew began to fidget nervously and their eyes, previously resolute and hostile began to flicker as they sneaked glances towards their leader.

"Thomas Neville," said the duke in a loud voice that carried to everyone on the quay, "what have you to say to me?"

"Only to crave mercy, your grace."

"In truth, except a quick death, there is nothing else you can ask of me," snarled Richard, his voice dripping with contempt. "You have caused the king's subjects to rise against him, your captains are

161

executed, you have no allies in England. I confess myself surprised that you have the temerity to crave mercy."

"Your grace, I surrender myself gladly to your mercy. I was once a loyal supporter of your father and the king your brother. I can be so again. Just a few years ago I was given the freedom of the City of London for my services in ridding the seas of French pirates. We were not always enemies, your grace. I am a soldier of Fortune but, as you know, Fortune bestows her favours as she will. I have been her captive until now; today I am yours."

The duke of Gloucester looked up from the rebel and gazed along the quayside and down the Wantsum Channel where the Bastard's ships were anchored. His soldiers remained attentive in anticipation, waiting patiently for their orders. Presently he slowly returned his attention to the Bastard.

"You will come with us into Canterbury where we shall meet with the king. I will grant pardon subject to confirmation by the king. You will surrender your ships and men to me." The duke looked around his men. "Sir James Tyrell," he called. Tyrell backed his horse out of the ring of spears around the Bastard's rovers and trotted over to the duke. "Take Thomas Neville along with you. I place him in your charge."

"Very good, your grace." The Bastard remained kneeling until the duke trotted his horse away from the quay, then got stiffly to his feet.

The ring of spears backed away from the rovers who quickly congregated into a group, clearly at a loss as to what to do next.

"You can find a horse for yourself, I hope?" stated Tyrell. The Bastard nodded, his face showing no emotion as he strived to control his inward feelings.

"May I return to my ship to prepare for the ride?" he asked.

"His grace of Gloucester's ship you mean. Yes, but don't be long. We ride within the hour." Tyrell beckoned Laurence over. "Stay with him and make sure he doesn't talk with his men. He speaks French naturally so you are the best one to keep him close."

Laurence had a native dislike for Thomas Neville and certainly did not relish the thought of spending time in his company. The ride to Canterbury, however, would only take half a day so they should get there by evening when, hopefully, he could rid himself of his charge. Laurence was bewildered at how the duke had granted a pardon so readily. No doubt he had his reasons – perhaps the ties of childhood bound him tighter than might be good for him. As a boy, the earl of Warwick and his bastard cousin had been heroes to him and firmly on the side of York.

Next day, the crowd in front of Canterbury cathedral was subdued, quite different from the mood when common felons were to be despatched; then all was festival. Today their Mayor Nicholas Faunt was to be executed for encouraging the people of Kent to rebel against the king. Not only the mayor, but a whole series of rebels were to hang and a scaffold capable of despatching twelve at a time had been erected. King Edward and the duke of Gloucester had placed their men-at-arms in a square around the scaffold. The axe man, the public hangman and his assistants stood ready. Thomas, the bastard of Fauconberg was brought to the front along with Laurence and Sir James Tyrell.

First the mayor was brought up and placed on a stool under a gibbet in the centre of the scaffold. The king's herald stepped forward and announced to the crowd that, by order of the lord our king, the mayor was to suffer the usual penalty for treason: hanging, drawing and quartering, where he would he hanged but not until dead, his genitals would be cut off and burned, his entrails removed before his face and also burned. Then his heart would be removed and burned and his head struck off, after which his body would be divided into four and displayed in various parts of the kingdom. His head would be placed over the main gate into Canterbury for all to see what fate befalls a traitor to the king. With that the herald stepped away and one of the assistants placed a noose around the neck of the mayor. The hangman kicked away the stool he was standing on and let him dangle for a while. As his struggles began to weaken he was taken down and revived before the rest of the sentence was carried out. Finally the axe man raised his axe and with a single blow struck off the head of the mayor. Taking it from the floor of the scaffold the axe man raised it with the exclamation: "behold the head of a traitor." There was no response from the crowd. Laurence noted that the Bastard of Fauconberg, his face ashen, had winced as the axe fell. This was why the king had placed him at the front of the scaffold, so that he could see what would befall him if he ever lapsed in his professed new loyalty to Edward.

163

As the first twelve rebels to be hanged were brought to the scaffold, Laurence reflected on the reason for the pardon granted to Thomas Neville. He had talked to Tyrell about it, at first indignant that the Bastard had not been summarily despatched as he deserved. Tyrell explained that the duke had taken due notice of the number of ships moored at Sandwich out in the channel. If the Bastard had been executed there and then the chances are a fight would have ensued as the rebels and rovers contemplated their own fate. There were too many to handle at that time and Gloucester, nor the king, had enough men to take over and man the ships. The important thing was to get them to disperse so that they could be dealt with separately if necessary. The Bastard had this in mind, which is why he dressed as a nobleman in the expectation of being treated according to his rank. His dress had been carefully understated to proclaim his lineage while being modest enough to denote obeisance to the duke. Both men understood this, which is why the duke of Gloucester granted pardon. How long the pardon would hold depended on the Bastard's future behaviour.

The barrels on which the prisoners stood were kicked away and the twelve rebels pitched into eternity. Laurence contemplated the vagaries of fate as he watched them jerk their lives away. He remembered the invasion of the apothecary's shop and the attempted rape of Joan Quirke, which removed the last vestiges of sympathy from his mind. He had extracted his own retribution for that, but how many others had been molested by the mob and not brought to justice. He never attended public executions as a rule because he understood how men and women could become victims of circumstance. These were paying the price for the others and if any were guiltless of shedding innocent blood, then God would have mercy on them.

After the executions, the king's herald read from a list of names those in the city and surrounding countryside who were to be spared upon the payment of a fine. Some of these were to be held until their families paid ransom. The king declared his intention of returning to London where he would hear any petitions for reduction from the rebels, though few in the crowd considered this to be anything other than an exercise in administration.

The king needed to return to London to consolidate the terms of his government. All the Lancastrian claimants to the throne were now dead, though a messenger had brought some disturbing news that caused king Edward to hurry back on the road to his capital. Jasper Tudor and his nephew, Henry had been trapped in Pembroke castle which Edward had placed under siege by his ally, Morgan Thomas. However, his brother, David Thomas, a friend of Jasper Tudor, temporarily raised the siege, Morgan having been distracted. This had allowed the two Tudors to escape. At first they were thought to be hidden somewhere in Tenby and word was that they had escaped in a vessel bound for France. The mayor of Tenby, Thomas White, was suspected of helping in the escape and it was in one of his ships that the fugitives had sailed. Apparently Tenby was riddled under with tunnels used for the storage of trade goods and it was in one of these that the Tudors were concealed before their flight. Laurence would discuss the implications of this with Cornelius when he too returned to London.

As they readied themselves for the journey back to London, Laurence, to his disgust, saw the treacherous Thomas Neville conversing happily together with the nobles in the king's entourage as if he had never raised a finger against them. It was as if they considered treason a natural condition to be traded rather than a criminal act against the monarch. Maybe the idea lurked at the back of some minds that they, too, might swap allegiance if the conditions were right. Loyalty was a rare commodity. He was not looking forward to the ride to London, but at least he would see Joan and deliver his version of events to Cornelius.

Chapter 9 – Middleham Castle

Laurence had gone to the apothecary's shop soon after his return to London ostensibly to report to Cornelius but in reality to see Joan. As he entered the front of the shop a man emerged from the back room clearly taking his leave of the apothecary. He was plainly dressed and cloaked, the sort you would pass in the street and never notice. Laurence thought there was something surreptitious about him. The two men nodded briefly to each other then the stranger ducked out of the door and into the street. Cornelius, his arm still in a sling, beckoned Laurence through with his good arm and indicated to a chair by the fireside. Before sitting he looked around for Joan and saw her selecting dried herbs and roots from those hanging from the rafters.

Of course, Cornelius knew of the flight of the Tudors as word had reached London as soon as the escape was discovered.

"If the Tudors do get to France," said Cornelius, "then king Louis XI will have a stronger hand against duke Francis of Brittany as well as our king Edward. Duke Francis needs Edward's allegiance badly. Louis is prevented from invading Brittany by the threat of Edward's military support of Francis. He has already attacked Burgundy. Should the Tudors come under his protection in France, then Louis would have a bargaining counter sufficient to stop Edward interfering should he choose to support Burgundy. Once Louis of France controls Burgundy then he thinks he will be in a position to overrun Brittany. After that he will be strong enough to affect English trade with the continent."

"That is why I was sent by duke Francis into England," stated Laurence," to inform my liege lord of affairs here that would affect Brittany. With the Tudors in France, my homeland might well be threatened." He was clearly worried and Cornelius moved to console him.

"You have no immediate need to fear on that count," he smiled. "I have some very good couriers that take regular messages between here and the court of duke Francis. One of them happens to be the captain of a merchant ship that plies regularly to Brittany. It is the same merchant ship that now carries the Tudors. I think you will find that contrary winds will force them into a Breton port where the followers of duke Francis will take them into his care." Laurence breathed a sigh of relief and astonishment at the extent of the apothecary's agency.

"Now, tell me about the situation with Thomas Neville," said Cornelius as he settled himself into his favourite chair. It is difficult for a bastard son, particularly the eldest one, who must find his way in the world, barred from any claim on his father's title or estate," mused Cornelius. "He has the same noble blood in his veins as his sire and it is no wonder so many swap allegiance for gain. The law recognises no filial rights either to him or his children."

"Thomas has displayed a loyalty of sorts though," interjected Joan. "He was true to the house of York while the earl of Warwick helped Edward to the throne and only opposed him when the Kingmaker changed sides. His loyalty to his cousin never wavered, even after Barnet and Tewksbury when he attacked London in an attempt to rescue his dead cousin's cause."

"What could he have achieved if he had defeated Edward?" asked Laurence, staring into the blaze in the fireplace.

"At the time of the attack here on London king Henry was still alive. Remember his first ploy had been to ask the city to free Henry from the Tower. Perhaps he had the idea of getting the old king to declare the late earl of Warwick's son, Edward his heir? Old Henry could never beget another and when he died then Warwick's son would be king!"

"I tried to get that information out of him on the ride back to London," stated Laurence. "He said only that he was a soldier of Fortune and followed a planned course until it was concluded."

"I wonder how long it will be before his loyalty to Edward wavers again? Already the Lancastrians are spreading rumours."

"What do you mean, Joan?" Laurence looked over at her as she spoke. She was standing by a side table mixing something in a bowl. "She gave a little shrug and paused in her work.

"The day you went from London to join the duke of Gloucester, which was the day *after* king Henry died, they chested his body and conducted it in procession to St. Paul's Cathedral for public viewing. His face was uncovered so that the people could see it was actually king Henry the sixth, but as is usual, his body was

167

covered in an embroidered cloth as befits a king. He lay there overnight and the next morning, when they moved the chest to convey the body for internment at Chertsey Abbey, fresh blood was discovered under the chest."

"You mean the king had been wounded and murdered?"

Joan began her mixing again. "I doubt it. How can a body that has been dead for a whole day shed enough blood to soak through wrappings, vestments and the chest lining."

"No," interjected Cornelius, "the blood in his body would be congealed."

"Quite so," continued Joan, "yet the rumour has it that king Henry was *stycked with a dagger* wielded by the duke of Gloucester."

"But he was on the road to Canterbury when Henry died!"

"Perhaps God has caused the blood to flow after death to expose the crime?" ventured Laurence, signing himself as he thought on it.

"Or somebody has poured fresh blood under the chest to induce rumour," said Cornelius quietly. "That would cause people to leap to their own conclusions, something Londoners are adept at. No need then to speak treason and incriminate yourself when all those who saw the blood would make the invention for you."

"On the way to Chertsey, the body lay at Black Friars where there was another show of fresh blood, and once an idea takes root . . .?" Joan let her words hang there.

"*Fama malum quo non aluid velocius ullum*" muttered Cornelius almost to himself. "There is no evil faster than a rumour."

"The point remains that the old king's death was most fortuitous so far as king Edward is concerned," said Laurence. "There is no question of that."

"Which means any attempt to get at the truth of the matter will flounder in controversy," replied Cornelius. Joan stopped stirring the contents of the bowl and placed it on the table.

"What is also true is that king Henry was very frail and ill. If I were contemplating his death I would prefer a quiet suffocation, or perhaps poison – no marks you see, no screams, no telltale blood and wounds. He would have succumbed so easily too. Then there is the question of his servants. His personal servants were in the chamber with him. Either they must have been in on it or made to leave and then silenced, yet there has been nothing said about that. King Edward would have to be very stupid to get rid of Henry is such a manner, besides, now that the Lancastrians cannot combat him militarily, he has plenty of time to decide what to do about the old king while keeping his integrity with the people." Laurence considered her words and had to admit she could be correct, reluctant though he was to dismiss the pointing of a supernatural finger of guilt, and the idea of a scandalous murder was so much more entertaining. There were too many people around Henry to make violent murder a sensible option no matter how much king Edward might want him out of the way.

"Certainly, when contemplating the murder of an anointed king, you would take some pains to disguise the crime," said Cornelius. "Sticking him with a dagger is not the best way to go about it, particularly when dealing with a frail old man. Kings do not normally like to be seen murdering other kings, except in battle of course, and Henry was thrice anointed. We must consider the official version; that he died from melancholy after hearing of the death of his son and his queen's capture. Given his state of health that might well have killed him. Men have died of grief ere now."

"I might speak to Sir James Tyrell about it?" offered Laurence. "He has been close to the duke of Gloucester throughout."

"Best to leave things regarding Gloucester as they are," advised Cornelius. "Nothing can be gained by enquiry; it is unlikely you would get at the truth and only bring yourself into disfavour, which is in nobody's interest. You will learn more just by listening and speaking not." Cornelius paused and appeared to reflect for a few moments. Laurence waited patiently, sensitive to Joan's presence as she busily worked her potions. "You noted that fellow who was leaving as you arrived?"

"I did."

"He had come from Le Herber."

"The duke of Clarence's house here in the city."

"You know the house, then?" Cornelius looked at him in surprise.

"I know some of the servants there. I travelled with one on the great march and I have met others in the tavern. With Joan at his back he considered it politic not to mention that the one he travelled with was a woman."

"That might be useful. I have been asked to keep an eye on Clarence. It seems he is coveting the estate of the countess of Warwick. As you know, due to the treason of the earl this may be

169

forfeit to the king. Both Isabel, Clarence's wife and her sister Anne have a half share each."

"I know that Anne is in Clarence's house, though he is keeping her in separate apartments from those of the countess Isabel. What is more, she only has one servant."

"It seems you know as much as I do. Perhaps, however, you do not know that the duke of Gloucester has been casting a covetous eye over the lady Anne?" Cornelius regarded him with his eyebrows raised quizzically.

"No, I did not know that. In truth, I had no idea that I should have to form an interest in the duke of Clarence's household. I only know one or two of his servants."

"The best information gatherers you could possibly have," declared Cornelius.

"So you think that the two dukes, Richard and George are after the leavings of Warwick's estate?"

"I am certain that George of Clarence is; after all, he is already married to the earl's eldest daughter and if her mother, the countess of Warwick is deprived of her estate Clarence expects the king to award it to his wife. The problem is, in that case, legally Anne is entitled to half."

"Which would go to Gloucester in the event he marries Anne. Do you think that is what he is about?"

Cornelius considered the question. "They are closely related so a papal dispensation would be required for them to marry, though that was not an obstacle when Clarence married Isabel. Richard and Anne know each other very well. As a boy, Richard was under the guardianship of the earl of Warwick at Middleham Castle so he has known Anne from childhood."

"Richard of Gloucester, having been the means of the defeat and deaths of her father and husband might be an obstacle, so far as Anne is concerned."

"Her father perhaps, but Prince Edward was not her choice of husband and it is doubtful if the marriage was consummated anyway. That would not occur until she becomes sixteen and she is barely fifteen now. At the moment she is in great danger of disappearing into a nunnery, if Clarence has anything to say about it."

"Whether she likes it or not, marriage to Richard of Gloucester is the only practical way out of her present sad predicament," inserted Joan. "Clarence will have her inheritance if he can and he is powerful enough to block any other claimant. Richard is the only one to whom her hand and estate would otherwise be awarded by the king. Without an estate she is virtually unmarriageable, at least to anyone of significance."

Laurence stood to take his leave. "There is one thing you should know. Richard of Gloucester is to go northwards. There is trouble on the border with Scotland, as usual, and king Edward is not sure of the loyalty of Henry Percy, earl of Northumberland. It is true that he didn't interfere with king Edward's recent progress through England, but that is more an indication of self-interest rather than of loyalty to Edward. Sir James Tyrell informs me that he is to ride north sometime soon so I shall probably be going too."

Joan began busying herself with taking ingredients from jars on the shelves. "How long do you expect to be away?" she asked unable to quite keep disinterest out of her tone.

"I cannot tell. I am not even sure if I am to go, though the fact that Sir James has spoken to me about it indicates that I shall be called upon."

Cornelius watched them both with interest. He had been wondering what to do about Joan. Her mother had died two years ago of the sweating sickness and it had been a cause of great regret his ministrations had been inadequate to save her. Joan had, in many ways, taken her mother's place in the apothecary shop while he conducted his clandestine affairs under its cover. This young man clearly was interested in her and he would be a good match. His family were high-class artisans with connections in a country that he also had interests in. He had noted how the young armourer had found his way into the company of knights that came to England with king Edward. He was already regarded favourably by some of them, which meant he had a secure future here in England, and he had the natural intelligence to be of use to them in other ways, ways in which he could guide him.

Though barely eighteen years of age, Joan was rapidly becoming old in the marriage market and he was feeling guilty about not seeking out a suitable husband for her. Her usefulness to him had kept her close, but he had to consider how she might fare if something happened to him. There were regular outbreaks of plague in the city, along with many other ills and as an apothecary he was only too aware of the transience of life. The recent attack on London, and the nearly fatal consequences to himself and Joan was another burden of conscience he had to bear. If Laurence was to go north with the duke of Gloucester then it might be a good idea to speak to him before he left so that he could secure his daughter a future. Who knows how long he would be away unless he had some inducement to return soon.

He stood and conducted Laurence through to the front room of the shop. It was with some satisfaction he noted the graceful bow that the young man swept as he took his leave of Joan, and the uncharacteristic coyness as she bobbed him a response.

"I would ask you something, Laurence," he said as they approached the shop door. "Have I detected interest by you in my daughter?" Laurence froze, his heart leaping as he frantically tried to comprehend what was about to be said.

"It would be less than honest of me to say other than I hold her in the highest regard," he replied cautiously.

"Then I wonder if I should write to your father with a marriage proposal, that is if it meets with your approval?" Cornelius hardly needed a response from the young man – his face flushed with joy and he took a few seconds to get command of his voice.

"I should be pleased if you did so, sir. It would be my greatest happiness." He turned as if to go back into the shop and speak with Joan, but the apothecary placed a restraining arm on his.

"Let me speak to her before I write to your father. You must be patient. He might not consider her a good match. These matters are delicate."

"He could not do otherwise than accept, especially as I shall write to him myself telling him of my willingness in the matter."

"Yet I think you know enough of Joan's character to understand she cannot be rushed into something she is unsure about. I would talk to her, though I think there will be no obstacle so far as she is concerned. I have noted her reaction when I mention your name, as I have in you to hers and I feel certain of the outcome; but your father must be consulted before any formalities may be entered into."

Laurence had been reluctant to leave but now he had to force himself through the doorway into the street. It was with lead in his soul that he mounted his horse and rode slowly to the Tower, torn with the sadness of unrequited leave-taking and yet gladness at Cornelius' proposal. He would write to his father today and get Cornelius to include the letter with the one he was sending.

* * *

"Cheer yourself," chirped Sir James Tyrell gaily to his riding companion. "You are not the only one to have left his lady love in London. I have had to leave my wife there as well. This was the first time Laurence had heard Tyrell mention he was actually married. "Consider his grace of Gloucester, he is in a worse state than you!"

The two men were riding together behind the retinue of the duke of Gloucester as they wended their way through the north Yorkshire countryside. They had been on the road for five days, each step one further away from Joan. Laurence had not even had a chance to speak to her before Sir James had bustled him off with a force of men-at-arms with the intention of engaging with the Scottish rebels along the border with England. He had sent a letter to Cornelius Quirke who would include it with his own communications to Brittany. He had pleaded his desire to marry with Joan Quirke and begged that his father would find the alliance acceptable. Simon de la Halle had particular family ambitions for his eldest son when it came to marriage, and Laurence recalled his reaction when the castle butcher had proposed marriage with *his* daughter. That had propelled him into a perilous adventure here in England, and one that was far from over. He hoped that Cornelius had sufficient wealth and position to obtain a favourable reply, but the waiting and uncertainty was getting on his nerves. Not only that, he was missing Joan. He needed to see her and get her response to the idea of becoming his wife. He had to gaze into those diamond-black eyes and see his love reflected in them.

Ahead he could see the banners of Gloucester bright in the early summer sun displaying neither despondency nor melancholy. He wondered if the duke was feeling as he. It was difficult to think what his Grace felt. Tyrell, who had conversed with the duke, thought that Richard was lovesick too, yet who could fathom the workings of such a mind. It was bound to be cluttered with thoughts of advantage, acquisition of lands, benefices and favours to be bestowed and owed. How could such as he love as Laurence did, his mind focused on just his own dear Joan, with thought for no gain other than possession of herself. Yet a Prince still had a heart, which meant the abiding possibility of its loss. Perhaps they both felt the same distress at having their love out there in the world, but unable to cleave to them with so many obstacles between. Laurence had the best of it – there were few barriers between him and Joan other than distance, and a hard ride could easily solve that problem. He looked in front to where the banners flew and pitied the duke, riding before his men, in splendid command of them and yet imprisoned by his rank.

"I wouldn't be too despondent about getting back to London," continued Tyrell when Laurence failed to respond. "His Grace has asked the king formally for the hand of the lady Anne. He knows that Clarence will do all in his power to talk the king out of granting her to him. You know how smooth a tongue Clarence has. It was applied to charm his way back into the king's trust after the nonsense with the earl of Warwick and it will be applied in his own interest at court. Richard is here in the north with no proper idea of what is happening with the king and the lady Anne in Clarence's household. No wonder he is unsettled. He will be anxious to deal with the Scots and return to court. Just get down to the job and the sooner we can be away."

Clarions sounded ahead and the column increased its pace. Just coming into view were the battlements of Middleham Castle, alive with the banners of the king and the duke of Gloucester. They approached from the south by the decayed mound of the former motte and bailey construction that had been superseded by the present castle whose whitened walls rose in shining splendour in the afternoon sun. The castle guard responded with trumpets and a small troop rode around the walls to meet them. The duke passed through the outer courtyard where the castle artisans lived and worked and entered by the east gate, then turned right towards the north range. By the time Tyrell and Laurence entered through the gate and turned to rest under the northeast tower, the duke had already dismounted and was away up the staircase to the great hall

174

followed by his personal retainers and the castellan. As he dismounted, Laurence observed the entrance of the dark-visaged Thomas Neville. The bastard of Fauconberg had been sent by the king with the duke of Gloucester to get him away from London where he would have been well placed to stir up conspiracy. He considered, though, that there was just as much material for treason in the north of England as anywhere else. This castle had been the earl of Warwick's stronghold so there was bound to be a residue of Neville support in the environs of the castle, if not within its walls. Then the earl of Northumberland was of uncertain loyalty and the Scots were causing trouble along the border with England.

The armourer watched as the Bastard dismounted and handed the reins of his mount to a groom to lead away. Beaming heartily, he joined a group of men-at-arms, engaging in merry fellowship, gaining friends and no doubt sharing confidences.

"That fellow must be watched carefully," said Tyrell as he arranged for their horses to be led away to the stables. "I counselled against bringing him along, and his Grace is unhappy too, but it is the king's orders."

"If he is to ride out with your prickers, I should make sure a trusted man is at your back."

"Most assuredly. Now, let us find our quarters. Yours will be near the forge just by here." Tyrell indicated the collection of wattle and daub buildings ranged along the east curtain wall. "At least you will be comfortable there. I am in the great hall and my sleeping space will be on the floor. Hopefully I can get a place near the brazier in the centre."

The armoury was located in the northeast tower conveniently placed near the forges where the castle smiths were busy mending mail and making a variety of metal artefacts needed by the castle. The rougher smithy work, making of horse shoes and nails would be carried out by the smiths located in the outer courtyard. He noted there was a grinding and polishing shed, though the grinding wheels were idle at the moment. Everyone was bustling to make the arrival of duke Richard as comfortable as possible.

There was no master armourer at the castle so it seemed that Laurence would fill that role. He would have to see the castellan to give him authority over the smiths and to ensure he had a workshop of his own. The baggage train, which was following the progress of the small force had his tools, and the few patterns he had made for armour were with them. He felt for the purse hidden under his tunic. Now he was part of duke Richard's retinue he would be paid directly by the castle exchequer for work carried out in addition to the payment he would get as a retainer. His purse was fairly light at the moment and he would need to ensure its increase if he were to take a wife. He had left most of what money he had already earned with Cornelius in London, taking just enough to get by on the road.

On enquiry at the forges he was confronted by the forge-master, Gavin the smith. He was of middle years, short and stocky with the muscled arms characteristic of his trade. He was a rough looking fellow dressed in coarse woollen hose and a leather apron that covered his bare chest, but the completed work Laurence noted lying around was of sound workmanship. Gavin eyed him cautiously, his eyes hooded under a fringe of brown hair. There was no outright hostility in his manner but he was unresponsive to the few questions Laurence directed at him. This was perhaps understandable. Until now he had been in charge of metalworking at the castle, though that would be minimal while the castle was lightly manned and without the duke in residence. Laurence wanted to inform him that he would continue as before, while the armourer would take care of the fine work demanded by the duke and his men-at-arms. Most of this was beyond the skills of the smith who, in any case, was too coarse of speech to converse with a nobleman, let alone measure the dimensions of his body. He decided to say nothing for the moment until the castellan had been consulted. For now Laurence's thoughts were occupied with getting somewhere to lay his head at night. The only response he had so far from his enquiry in this respect was a shrug.

The problem was partly solved by the arrival of the baggage. Laurence's chest and tools were off-loaded and clearly needed some storage.

"Pur i'thup i underdrawin," was the reply when he asked where he could store his chest. Laurence was utterly confounded by the dialect and surmised, by noting the upwards jerk of the man's thumb, that it might be in a loft somewhere. Why couldn't these English speak the same language? Earlier he had tried French, which drew a blank stare as if the smith was looking at an idiot. He saw a ladder reaching up into the roof space of the forge and tentatively climbed it. There was a clutter of objects up there but he thought there would be space for his personal chest and perhaps a little room for his sleeping blanket. A rope and pulley was suspended from the roof beams and he decided to use that to get his chest up there. He had just accomplished this when the castellan arrived looking for him.

Sir Roger Martlett was a picture of elegance, made more so when standing beside the squat form of Gavin the smith. He was wearing a tabard with the badge of the duke of Gloucester over blue and white hose. A heavy leather belt held the castle keys that were his charge. His forked beard was carefully manicured and oiled, as was his blond hair. A pair of pale blue eyes completed the impression of Anglo-Saxon descent. He addressed Laurence haughtily in French, without so much as a nod of the head.

"Sir James Tyrell informs me you are a master armourer attached to the retinue of his Grace of Gloucester." It was a statement rather than a question.

"I have been so since I came over with his Grace from Flanders," he replied in his best courtly French. The castellan looked at him with renewed interest.

"You are his Grace's personal armourer?"

"No, sir, but I have made pieces for his followers and the earl Rivers wears battle armour I made especially for him." He decided that this fellow would be more respectful if he thought Laurence was familiar with persons of rank. "I shall require some work space and the use of a forge. Also I should like to review the armoury to ascertain the condition of the arms kept there." He hoped the arrogance he had assumed would get the fellow to respond. Sir Roger grunted and placed a hand casually on the hilt of the dagger he wore at his belt and hooked the thumb of his other hand into the same. Gazing along the buildings towards the northeast tower he affected to be contemplating the problem while carefully establishing his authority.

"I have levees coming in by order of his Grace to accompany him to the Scottish borders," he said at last. "There is little room in the castle, yet if you can find a corner in the armoury you might work there. For the moment you will have to sleep here. I see you have already found a space." The castellan looked up to the loft space he had seen Laurence climb down from.

"I can manage – for now." Laurence inserted the pause to indicate dissatisfaction with the arrangement. "One more thing. I have been long on the road. Where do I go for something to eat?"

"The kitchen will provide for you. A servant usually brings food for the smiths and I shall instruct one to include provision for you." With that the castellan gave a slight inclination of his head and stalked off. Laurence would seek out the kitchens, though, just to make sure he was not left out when the victuals arrived at the forges.

Tyrell had been wrong if he believed duke Richard to be lovesick for Anne Neville. Laurence was sitting on a stool outside the door to the armoury where he had placed a stake plate. The late morning sunshine gave perfect illumination for working on the delicate ornamentation of the gatlings intended for a pair of gauntlets he was making for one of the duke's men-at-arms. It was the day after his arrival at Middleham Castle when a small retinue comprising half a dozen fore-riders, a lady on a white palfrey and a covered wagon followed by two further armed riders passed through the north gatehouse. The lady was clearly well born, though the veil she wore obscured the bottom part of her face making it difficult to judge her age. The fluid way she moved riding sidesaddle indicated youth. Laurence did not recognise the livery of the fore-riders, but the two behind wore the white boar livery of the duke of Gloucester. Turning to the right, the small group made its way along the north range and disappeared around the corner of the great keep.

He soon forgot the lady in the general confusion of arrivals and departures. Duke Richard was sending couriers out and receiving the reports of others. Armed men and common soldiers were arriving and accommodation for these had extended beyond the castle walls into the outer courtyard where there was space for their tents and pavilions among the habitations of the artisans that served the castle. Provision wagons were trundling in and out of the castle with viands from the village and the rest of the Middleham estate for the duke's table. General soldiery was milling around preparing for the expedition to quell the raiders on the Scottish borders. The castle blacksmiths were busy honing the

178

blades of pikes, war axes and swords while the farriers worked on the shoes of the horses. The forges were bright with heat and emitted the acrid smells of hot charcoal, heated metal and steam from the quenching of red-hot iron and steel. Everywhere was noise from the creaking of wagons, the hammering of the smiths and farriers, the clatter of horse iron on stone all accompanied with the shouting of orders and instructions.

The castle was packed with the duke's retainers and so crammed that the knights were practicing with their arms in the camp outside the castle walls. He knew that this must be serious practice due to the amount of freshly dented shields and harness he had been given to repair. Much of this work was accomplished by the smiths, but the more articulated pieces he took on himself. He had wondered if Gavin the forge master might object to this, but it seemed he was relieved by not having to undertake the more intricate work. Laurence was concerned about the decoration on the armour he was repairing. Normally this would be given to a craftsman who specialised in cloth covering and painting of heraldry, but there seemed to be nobody at Middleham with these talents. Another problem was that there were few paints in any variety of colours that he could find in the armoury. Those he could find would be fine for repainting the duke's armorial devices, but some of the others would have to do with theirs scratched and chipped until they could get to an armoury in a town. As most knights would ride with their harness under a surcoat, this need not be a major concern, but it offended his professional pride to return repaired harness in less than a perfect finished condition. Only plain armour could be polished and finished properly.

His head was bent over his work when a shadow fell across him. He looked up and saw Sir Roger Martlett gazing down at him.

"His Grace the duke would see you in the great hall," he said with his habitual haughtiness. "If you would come this way." Sir Roger spread an arm indicating the direction towards the staircase that led to the great hall in the keep. Laurence stood, placed his work to one side and removed the leather apron he wore over his tunic and accompanied the castellan as requested.

They entered the staircase at the side of the keep by a great oak door and mounted to the upper floor, having passed through two more guarded doors on the way up. The stairs were necessary because the great hall was situated over a capacious under space. It was a long room illuminated on one side by windows set in the massive thick walls of the keep. Today the hall was brightly lit by sunshine, though Laurence guessed it would be rather gloomy when clouds loured over the castle. Tapestries hung along the walls and a great brazier smouldered in the centre, being kept aglow ready for the evening chill when logs would be heaped on and flames fanned into life. At the end of the hall where they had come in he noted an elaborately carved screen that separated the serving area from the tables that were placed along both walls. The high table had a canopied seat where the duke would sit when dining in here.

Sir Roger led him down the hall by the high table and through a portal into an adjacent chamber. Under the windows where the light was strongest scribes were sitting, busily scratching away on parchment. There were several people in the room who were clearly the duke's favoured retainers. Some of these regarded the passage of the two men with bored curiosity and Laurence got the impression they were simply waiting around for the appearance of their lord when they would become sycophantically animated. Rather than a central brazier, this chamber had a fireplace stacked with logs ready to light if the day became chilled. They approached another carved screen at the southern end of the chamber where there was an open door.

Sir Roger stopped and beckoned Laurence forward as a man dressed in a gown of green velvet trimmed with an embroidered edge of gaudy colours stepped into the doorway thus barring passage through the screen into the space beyond.

"You are master armourer Laurence de la Halle?" he asked in French.

"I am." The man stepped back and bid him enter through the portal.

Richard, duke of Gloucester was standing by a window, without a visor but otherwise cap à pied in full harness, swinging a small boy by his arms. The two were laughing together and the boy was clearly at ease. Laurence wondered who he could be: a nephew perhaps? Nearby a plainly dressed woman of middle years stood feigning distress at the boy's usage by the duke. This would be his nurse, no doubt, expressing politic concern for her charge who was obviously in no distress whatsoever. As the duke noted the arrival of the armourer he placed the boy onto his feet and smiled into his face.

"Now John," he said softly. "Go with lady Montgomery back to your mother." The boy's face began to crumble and tears were a second away when the duke held up a finger and stopped the flood. "Remember that knights do not cry and obedience is their attribute." The boy immediately straightened his back and his face took on what he believed to be a stern mien. He stood back and bowed to the duke, then placing a small hand into that of his nurse, let her lead him away through another door that must have led to the duke's private apartments. The duke took up a glass from a table nearby and a servant immediately poured wine into it. He turned to face Laurence who knelt before him and spread his arms in obeisance. Duke Richard bid him rise with a casual wave of his hand.

"As you can see, I am in full harness," he said, opening his arms inviting the armourer's perusal.

"It is fine German armour to be sure, your grace," replied Laurence, wondering what was expected of him. "I would hazard made by the Helmschmid armoury judging by the formation of the plates? The fluting is particularly fine over the pauldrons."

"You know your business, it seems," intoned the duke. "It is fortunate you have considered the pauldrons because that is where my problem lies, at least on my right side." Laurence cast his eye over the harness and studied the pauldrons without detecting a particular fault.

"Can you tell me the problem, your grace?" The duke began to swing his right arm as if wielding a weapon. Laurence could see that the movements were not as smooth as they should be.

"There is some restriction here," the duke grumbled. "The harness was made and fitted two years ago and my frame seems to have altered since." Laurence thought for a moment and considered the occasion in Nottingham Castle where he had observed the duke strangely engaged in chopping wood, something only a low servant would do. He remembered it because it was so unusual, a task unthinkable for one of noble birth.

"Please tell me, your grace: how often do you exercise at arms?"

"Every day."

181

"And your usual weapon?"

"War axe, though of course I am practised in the use of sword and mace."

Laurence's thoughts were in a sudden turmoil. He would have to consider his words carefully if he were to avoid offending the duke. Here was a man of slight build, a Prince of the Blood whose life and position depended on his warrior attributes. It could not have been easy for him to compete with those others, such as his brother Edward and the jousting knights when he was disadvantaged by his size. He could well understand the force that drove him to increase his strength, even by chopping wood as well as practicing arms, in an attempt to take his rightful place among the warrior class of England. These were the sorts of knights who had won renown at Crecy and Agincourt and his own brother had never been defeated in battle in spite of the odds against him. He was part of a warrior bloodline that even when outnumbered several times, still managed to win spectacular victories. In his own lifetime there had been Towton, Barnet and Tewksbury, the last two battles where he had distinguished himself, all fought and won against superior odds.

"I suspect that your right arm and shoulder muscles have increased in size due to your constant exercise, your grace. If you would permit me to take a few measurements I can discover where the problem lies?" He hoped that this combination of flattery and practicality would find favour with the duke. It turned out there was nothing to fear in that respect. Richard nodded his agreement immediately apparently having come to the same conclusion himself.

Encouraged, Laurence thought further on the matter. The original harness must have been fitted to a seventeen years old youth. It would have been adjusted since then, of course, but there were bound to be other parts that were not quite right.

"If your grace would permit, I should like to review the fit of the whole of the harness."

"Of course, master armourer. I am at your command," and the duke laughed heartily while Laurence and the other servants joined in.

* * *

The problem with the duke of Gloucester's armour had not proved simple to resolve. This was due to the German style that incorporated a good deal of fluting. Laurence appreciated that this induced extra strength while being decorative. Normally he would have been pleased to work on this style, but time was short because the duke wanted to tackle the Scots as soon as his levees were fully formed, and that would be in just three days. It had not proved possible simply to alter the existing right pauldron assembly because the fluting prevented the working of the iron to expand its size. Besides that, the thinning of the metal would reduce its strength at a vulnerable part. The correct solution was to make a new pauldron and match the work to the existing harness, mimicking exactly the same form as the rest. Laurence was confident he could do this, but time was his enemy. The harness was heat treated, lightly blackened and burnished so there was the additional problem of matching with the rest of the armour. He had no idea what the original armourer had used to obtain the black finish; each had his own recipe and method. Normally he would have tested his black on scrap metal and that is what he would do in this case, but time was very short.

He had found some plate in the armoury; Milanese plate rather than German but of fine quality, which could be satisfactorily worked and hardened. He had rough-formed the pauldron and was busy cutting strips of metal for the lames when Tyrell came to him. We were correct about Fauconberg," he said triumphantly. "He has been in contact secretly with king James seeking to join his court." Laurence knew something of king James III of Scotland. The man was weak and not in favour with many of his nobles. It was the unrest his vacillations had caused, and his desire to make peace with England against the wishes of some powerful Scottish nobles that had provoked the trouble along the border. That was why the duke of Gloucester was here to deal with it.

"Perhaps the Bastard thinks that there might be scope for troublemaking at that particular court," Laurence replied.

"That is exactly what my lord of Gloucester believes, which is why Fauconberg is to lose his head!"

"It seems a foolish thing to do – to contact the Scottish court so soon after his pardon from king Edward?"

"It was through one of the retainers of the duke of Northumberland he was discovered. Percy has been neutral so far and Fauconberg probably thought it worthwhile trying to offer some sort of deal liasing with the Scottish court. There are still a few disgruntled Lancastrian sympathisers there."

"The Middleham estate was owned by the earl of Warwick until his defeat at Barnet, so perhaps he thought there might be residual loyalty to be exploited in the region."

"No doubt that is true, but his grace of Gloucester has also lived at Middleham; he was brought up here, so he has quite a lot of loyal support in the region too. That was the Bastard's undoing."

"Is it possible that Northumberland's man was put up to test the Bastard's loyalty?" Laurence pondered. "Consider how Fauconberg had ingratiated himself with duke Richard's household knights. It explains why they had accepted him so easily into their ranks. Perhaps they were under instructions so as to loosen his tongue?"

"Knowing his Grace I should think it almost certain," replied Tyrell. "He didn't want Fauconberg here in the first place and now that he has the justification, he hasn't hesitated to pronounce him traitor. The man is to die this afternoon."

"Where is he being held?"

"In the chapel, under heavy guard while he makes his confession and peace with God. His Grace has permitted him that, being a pious man himself. The sentence will be carried out in the outer courtyard and most of the garrison is ordered there to witness it."

Just then Gavin the smith came along with a surly fellow in tow who was dressed in an assortment of rags. They caught the smell of him at twenty paces and Tyrell, giving Laurence an amused grimace, backed away cautiously while his curiosity getting the better of him, encouraged him to remain and discover their business.

"This be Able the Fuller," said the forge master with a nod to his companion. "'E reckons as ow tha's bi takin' t'piss!" Laurence's blank expression testified to his utter confusion.

"I, I have no idea what you are talking about," he stammered.

"Piss fro' guardrobe, 'e reckons as ow tha's bi takin it." Laurence shook his head and looked to Tyrell in desperation.

"I think he means the piss from the buckets in the guardrobe tower, where the latrines are," he chuckled, highly amused by Laurence's discomfiture. "You haven't been walking off with it by any chance?"

"Well, I have had it brought here for use in the quenching tank. I use it to temper armour. I am sure this fellow hasn't produced much of it, unless he has a prodigious great bladder."

"Well 'e can't be b'aht piss an 'e as reights on it," said Gavin. The fuller nodded vigorously in agreement while scowling at the armourer.

"It seems that the fuller has the rights to take the piss for use in his trade. I think you know it is used to process woollen cloth," explained Tyrell.

"But I didn't take it without paying for it." The forge master looked at the fuller then turned his attention to Laurence.

"'E has reights on it," he repeated.

"Well it cost me a penny for two buckets paid to the chancellor's clerk," Laurence declared stoically. The fuller gasped in surprise.

"A' can't thoile payin' that!" he exclaimed angrily. "A' gets four for ha'pence."

"You might find yourself in trouble here," said Tyrell. "Piss is a marketable commodity and you have just quadrupled it in value!"

"I thought it was expensive but I have no idea what to pay in England. This isn't London, which is overflowing with piss, and shit for that matter, besides there is only one alehouse in the village. How much can it produce?"

"Which is why the castle supply is so valuable," laughed Tyrell. "An while I think on it, shit goes on the fields so don't go buying that either, at least until you have determined its proper market value."

Laurence realised the problem, but as he had approached the chancellor of the castle with a request to purchase the commodity, he hardly felt he was to blame, even less so as he had clearly been grossly overcharged.

"I shall talk to the chancellor about this," he told the fuller. "It is unlikely I shall need more of the supply though I am aggrieved that I have been over-charged for what I have bought." The fuller had no choice but to agree to let the matter drop and he went off with Gavin the smith disgruntled but pacified.

Tyrell laughed as he walked off and Laurence was left to reflect on the strange problems this impossible land imposed on him. Even so, he was amused at the different dialects and expressions he had to deal with. The nobles and knights all spoke French so there was no problem with them. The common people, though, had their own language, which those brought up in England, be they base or noble, had little trouble in interpreting. His own English had improved immeasurably in the short time he had been in the island, but the regional accents had confounded his best attempts at learning the language.

He followed the crowd of soldiers and castle servants through the east gate into the bailey, the outer courtyard of the castle. Here in the centre of the enclosed bailey a wooden block had been placed. There was no scaffold because there would be no ceremony. The Bastard of Fauconberg was brought to the block. His face was pale and defeat was etched in the lines of his face. He was no longer the haughty and clever noble who had walked grandly down the gangway of his ship to confront the duke of Gloucester at Sandwich. The duke was here, surrounded by his henchmen, seated on a simple stool over which a velvet cloth had been thrown as a tacit declaration of his rank.

The prisoner was pushed roughly forward. The sergeant of the castle guard, who was to carry out the execution, kicked him behind his knees causing his legs to collapse. His hands had not been tied so he was able to prevent himself falling upon his face. He raised his head just once to gaze pitifully at duke Richard before being pushed down so that his neck rested on the block. At a nod from the duke, the sergeant raised a heavy curtal axe and struck a blow at the Bastard's neck. Though it severed most of the neck, it took a second blow to free the head from the body.

"The first must have been a practice stroke," someone in the crowd muttered.

The sergeant took up the head and showed it to the assembled crowd, who dutifully cheered at the death of the traitor. The pathetic body was lifted and dropped into a wooden chest and the sergeant threw the head in with it. The castle carpenters nailed down the lid and the chest was taken away to be buried in some remote and unhallowed spot.

Laurence reflected on the fate of Thomas Neville, the Bastard of Fauconberg. The captains of his invasion force had met a more protracted and awful fate yet their heads had been displayed over the gateway of London bridge, or at Canterbury. They had, at least, achieved some sort of notoriety; a recognition of their deeds while Thomas would rot away with no marker and no monument, no matter how gruesome or fleeting, to mark his passage. He had been condemned as dispossessed from birth by his father's lust and he would thus lie in an unrecognised grave. Laurence had no particular sympathy for Thomas Neville, whom he knew as a pirate around the seas of his homeland, yet he would say a few prayers in the chapel of Middleham for the repose of his soul in the hope that it would not quite be lost to God.

Chapter 10 – Loyaulte Me Lie

Laurence the armourer had been left behind when the relatively small company of knights and men-at-arms rode out to quell the rebels on the Scottish borders. They were intended as shock troops who would strike quickly with deadly force wherever a group of rebels were encountered. A baggage train with heavy forge equipment and the supplies it required would slow progress so just a light train had set out from Middleham with provisions for the army. This was not a war with Scotland because the Scottish king, James III, was engaged in trying to negotiate a peace with England, a policy that did not find favour with many of his nobles. It was these who were raiding into England, and because they were not coordinated, as a national army would be, were a nuisance rather than a peril. Nevertheless, they had to be dealt with and that is what the duke of Gloucester was about.

The armourer used the relatively quiet period to repair a variety of harness left with him by the men-at-arms and to help with the refurbishment of arms at the castle armoury, which was over the north gate in the room above the portcullis and extending into a chamber next to it. The castellan had his chamber in the north range on the other side of the armoury and the two men frequently met and exchanged greetings, though the castellan maintained a measure of aloofness commensurate with his authority. Another captain of the castle defences was that of the artillery, Miles de Montford. He and Laurence struck up an immediate rapport. They were fellows in similar positions. Laurence as an armourer had particular skills that were necessary only to the noble elite. Smiths would take care of the armouring needs of the common soldiery and a master armourer such as Laurence would only be engaged by those who could afford his charges. Both had been left behind as the shock troops had ridden for the Scottish borders.

The artillery was regarded by most of the garrison somewhere between amusement and contempt. The men-at-arms and the archers were elite, being fast, highly mobile and deadly to the enemy. Guns were clumsy, difficult to transport, and dangerous to those detailed to fire them. They were useful as siege weapons that would pound at fortress walls or gates. They might be used in battle to reduce an opposing force, but were of little use once the combatants had engaged hand-to-hand. Not only that but the accidental ignition of the unstable gunpowder could reduce to rubble that part of a fortress where it was stored. Laurence was pleased when he met Miles, who, it turned out, was a Frenchman from Normandy. He had been part of the earl of Warwick's company, but being a Frenchman, and like Laurence having no particular quarrel with either of the contending houses in England, had remained at Middleham after his return from the battle of Barnet.

"The problem I find with the nobility regarding guns is that they think it is low-skilled work," said Miles as he stood with Laurence in the tower above the north gate regarding the bronze gun mounted in its cradle. Its muzzle nestled in an orifice in the tower wall and an extended slot above let the gunner spy out his target. "My lord of Warwick was enthusiastic and always had plenty of guns in his army, but most of the other nobles regard us with contempt." Laurence had an ambiguous attitude to artillery, he recalled the old gunner at the Tower of London who had lost an eye mixing gunpowder, yet the intricacies of gun manufacture and deployment interested him.

"Great lords often have particular passions, yet it appears that the duke of Gloucester has some interest in your art, and king Edward had some guns in his army." Laurence remembered the gunfire at the battle of Barnet where the Kingmaker's ordnance fired throughout the night, over the heads of Edward's opposing army with no effect, Edward being so close and invisible in the mystery of the fog.

"Duke Richard lived as a boy here at Middleham and the interests the earl of Warwick had in gunpowder would have influenced him. The earl was most enthusiastic and he had used cannon as siege weapons. I remember he had Flemish hand-gunners at one of his battles, St. Albans I think it was. That was before I joined his company. The duke is a modern prince with fresh ideas, though it must be said, he relies rather too much on the physical force of arms."

Miles de Montford was an elegant man, about the same age as Laurence, in his early twenties. He was dark complexioned with a short pointed beard and dark brown eyes. Laurence had seen him around dressed in a green woollen robe tied with an embroidered rope belt over which he wore a tabard with the white boar blazon. Today he was dressed in shirt and hose as he was about to fire off a few shots with the cannon. This was, Laurence knew, extremely unpopular with the village located directly under the north range of the castle, but the fields beyond had been cleared ready for the testing of the gun. Laurence had come to witness the procedure and was most interested to see how the whole thing worked.

Shot was cast iron, carefully selected to ensure it fitted through the annular wooden gauge corresponding to the bore size of the gun. Six of the verified shot were placed by the gun. "Of course, we can fire scrap from the gun but that is only of use at close quarters in the field against massed troops," Miles informed him. "Firing from here we would use iron shot as these you can see."

Today Miles had two men to help him as there was no urgency regarding the rate of fire. In battle there would be a crew of six. The breechblock had been removed and stood on end so that it could be loaded with powder and shot. Miles had already measured out a quantity of the grey gunpowder from a barrel located in the guardroom under the firing platform. Powder was brought there to prevent the barrel being ignited by a stray flash from the gun when it went off. The main store was in the cellar below the great chamber of the keep. Using a copper scoop, he had carefully measured out the powder and brought it to the gun. The powder charge was then poured into the breechblock and wool wadding put in and rammed down with a pole. The iron ball was dropped into the breechblock then more rough wool was rammed down over the ball. The gun servers tipped the breechblock over and laid it down on the floor. Finally, they lifted the breechblock using a pole inserted through two handles provided in the casting for the purpose and fitted it into the main breech of the gun.

Miles gave a nod to the gun servers who took up the ropes that were tied off to the gun carriage and hauled the gun forward until the muzzle just pointed through the orifice in the castle battlements. Laurence stood to one side of the gun and looking through an arrow slit in the wall, saw the target about five-hundred yards away in the fields beyond the village. It was a simple wooden palisade with a white circle painted on it. The target had been propped on staves and the area all around and behind had been cleared of people. Villagers were standing well to one side in anticipation of the spectacle. The castle guard were there ostensibly to keep order, but mainly to stop children or the plain careless wandering across the field of fire.

Under the direction of the master gunner, two yeomen gun servers levered the gun carriage around, and tapped at a wedge under the breech to alter the elevation of the muzzle. Presently, being satisfied with the adjustments, Miles took a horn of fine powder and poured it down a small hole in the top of the breechblock and onto the charge in the breech. One of the servers signalled to someone on the battlements who raised a black flag to inform the crowd the gun was about to fire. Miles ordered the servers to stand back and took a long stick, split at the end where a glowing taper was fixed. Standing well to one side he touched the ember to the powder. There was a sudden flash as a jet of flame shot up from the breech followed by an almighty bang. The cannon jumped backwards and had it been not secured to the heavy wooden cradle would have gone through the door in the wall of the tower and dropped into the castle courtyard. However, the gun and carriage was restrained by the heavy ropes and tackle. Wreathed in gun smoke and coughing in the sulphurous fumes, Laurence stuck his face into the arrow slit, something he found necessary in order to breathe in the confines of the tower. He had missed the fall of the shot, which had been obscured by smoke from the muzzle, but noted a scar had suddenly appeared in the field just beyond and to the right of the target.

"That was good for a ranging shot," declared Miles, who was grinning broadly. "If I can pitch the next one lower and more to the left, then even if it falls short it will strike on the bounce."

"How many shots before you hit it square?" asked Laurence, thinking he might make a wager.

"I should do it either on the next shot or the one after," replied Miles. "I am not too bothered about a direct hit for the moment. I am just getting a feel for the range and direction of shot from here. If an enemy attacks I will then have a good idea how to set the gun on his positions."

"Can you hit a target repeatedly once you have the settings for the gun?"

"Up to a point. Each shot weighs differently and the powder varies in quality. I mix my own powder and also I have made a series of powder measures for different ranges but even so there is still some error. One problem is the shot seems not to leave the muzzle with exactly the same force each time the gun is fired, even with the same measured charge."

"Well I can see how the weapon might be used against castle walls or a massed army, but it is no wonder that the archers are disparaging of your guns. They can fire a second arrow while the first one is in flight and strike exactly their target."

"Yes but one ball can take down a dozen or more men at one firing and there is no protection. You cannot hide behind a shield or armour when a ball strikes!"

"Yet I know of several explosions where the gun crews were destroyed by the bursting of their own cannon. I remember hearing how king James the second of Scotland was killed by an explosion of one of his own guns - at the siege of Roxburgh castle back in 1460, I think it was."

Just then a small figure came into the tower chamber. It was the boy Laurence had seen with duke Richard. He had obviously been attracted by the noise and smoke of the cannon and had somehow slipped his charge nurse and come up here. He could have been no more than five years old and looked up eagerly at the gun crew.

"Get the boy out of here," commanded Miles. "This is far too dangerous a place for a child. Besides, if anything happens to him we shall answer to duke Richard, probably with our lives."

Laurence reached down and took the boy's hand.

"Who is he?" he asked Miles.

"That is John of Pomfret, duke Richard's bastard son."

Laurence was astonished and looked at the boy anew. Yes, he could see the familial resemblance.

"I want to see the gun," piped the boy imperiously.

"Let him look at the cannon," said Laurence, "then I will take him onto the battlements to watch safely out of the way." Miles nodded and then smiled down at the boy. Holding him firmly by the hand the two men let him walk around the gun, which was warm after its first firing but not yet hot. They sat him astraddle the muzzle so he could look out over the fields to the target in the distance. Miles showed him the pile of cannon balls and let him try to pick one up,

192

which proved too heavy for him. He explained the use of water and vinegar for sponging out the breechblock and barrel after each firing. The two yeomen gun servers stood respectfully to one side while the infant captain inspected the gun. Presently Laurence took over and led him to the spiral stairs in the corner of the tower.

"Do you think you can climb to the top of the tower?" he asked the boy.

"Of course, I have been up there hundreds of times," came the boastful reply.

"Then you lead the way." The boy slipped his hand and began clambering upwards, his little legs barely long enough to make the steps. Laurence gave a nod to Miles who turned back gratefully to resume his gun practice.

Miles' second shot did indeed fall short and strike the target on the bounce to the delight of John who watched while sitting aloft on Laurence's shoulders so that he could see over the battlements. Laurence thought it fortunate he had not tempted the master gunner with a wager – he would have lost. They could see as several churls from the village ran past the remains of the target with another palisade, which they would erect further away. Gun smoke blew back over the battlements causing the boy to cough and his eyes to water but did not diminish his joy as he gave out a great hurrah and waved his arms about when he observed that the target had disintegrated.

"Dear God! Whatever are you doing with that child?" Laurence turned at the angry sound of a female voice. He saw a young girl dressed in the finery of a gentlewoman hurrying along the battlements towards them, her robes flying behind and her face flushed with anxiety. "Put him down at once!" Laurence obediently lifted John over his head and gently lowered him to his feet. She took hold of the boy by his shoulders and gave him a mild shake. "What do you mean running off from your prayers. Lady Montgomery is most distressed."

John thrust out his lower lip truculently. "I heard the gun mother, and anyway I have said enough prayers today."

"Indeed you have not," his mother informed him brusquely. "In fact you now have a penance to add for disobedience." The boy set his face in a stubborn scowl that did nothing to pacify her. She looked up at Laurence: "Who are you?" she demanded.

193

"Laurence de la Halle, a votre service, madam." He swept her an elegant bow. The sound of his cultured French made her pause and regard him curiously. She saw a tall, dark fellow in the rough attire of a workman, with a leather apron over his jacket and hose, yet his accent and manners belied his appearance. He saw a small, beautifully formed woman, probably around the age of nineteen or twenty, dressed in a yellow silken robe with a headdress that denoted she was of gentle rank. The gauze veil that might have obscured her face was swept back. He could just make out wisps of light brown hair that played across her shoulders. Her eyes were pale blue, which made him think of the far north where the inhabitants were fair and blue-eyed. For a fleeting moment he imagined the cry of seabirds and the wash of water over stone, then a breeze came over the battlements carrying with it the residual pungent smell of gunpowder, which returned his attention to the boy. "He was quite safe, madam," he said apologetically. "It is normal for a boy to find interest in such things." He swept his arm directing her gaze across the fields where the new target was being assembled."

"I have no doubt, monsieur, that you are right," she answered, "but the boy has run from his instruction with Father Bassant who is most displeased. You have earned him a beating by keeping him here." He noted that though she had begun by addressing him in English, now she spoke in French.

"I am most sorry for that. Perhaps I might speak to the priest on his behalf?"

"Thank you, sir, but no. He shall be returned to his nurse who will know how to deal with him properly." She looked down sternly at the child who stood crestfallen. Laurence placed a gentle hand on the boy's shoulder, and he was pleased she did nothing to prevent him.

"Perhaps you will visit me at the armoury," he said to the boy, "and I can show you the arms and guns at a proper time. Is that permissible, madam?"

"We shall think on it," she replied, her face softening somewhat. "You have a place here at Middleham?"

"Oui, madam. I have a place by the castle forge where I work on fine arms for his grace the duke of Gloucester." She raised her eyebrows when he mentioned the duke and regarded him curiously. Finally she took hold of the boy's hand and bidding Laurence good day, took him off to find his nurse.

He watched as they walked along the top of the castle walls by the roof towards the north-west tower. The boy walked upright, bearing himself proudly in spite of the trepidation he would be feeling as he was taken to confront his nurse.

"Has she gone?" He turned and looked to where Miles de Montford was peering up the final steps of the north-east tower.

"She has," replied Laurence. Thus reassured, Miles came up the steps and emerged onto the top of the wall.

"The fellow on the flagstaff told me she was here. Had I known she was on her way I would have warned you."

"Who is she?"

"She is Katherine Hepton, one of the daughters of the castellan at Pomfret castle and the long time lover of his grace of Gloucester. They played together as children; now they play together as adults."

"I wondered about the boy when I saw him with his grace in the great chamber. Just now he called her mother, and you had already told me he is Richard's bastard."

"Well his grace is quite open about him," said Miles "Everyone understands he may not marry the boy's mother due to her lowly rank, he is a prince of the blood after all, but he has not turned away from her as many would." Laurence thought how this reflected duke Richard's personal motto: *Loyaulte Me Lie*.

"I judge the boy to be about four or five years old, yet his mother cannot be more than twenty herself. She must have been no more than fifteen when he was born."

"Yes, she is a year older than his grace. It is well known that the air here in Yorkshire stimulates the appetite."

Laurence pondered on the situation with Anne Neville. He had mistaken duke Richard's hurried passage to Middleham as a wish to get the present business with the Scots over with so he could return to London and the lady Anne. Richard of Gloucester had asked the king for her hand in marriage. How would that work out should they come to live at Middleham after their marriage? It might not come to marriage, however, if the duke of Clarence has his way. He was very much opposed to a match that would prevent the whole of the duchess of Warwick's inheritance coming to him

195

through his own wife. That might still be the case, though for different reasons. Obviously Richard had sent ahead to inform the mother of his son he was on his way north. He thought back to his first day at the castle and the lady who had entered by the north gate. He now knew her to be Katherine Hepton and her son must have travelled in the wagon that came in with her. She certainly was a beautiful young woman and it was easy to see why Richard was enamoured of her and would not readily give her up, even though their legal union was impossible. The boy was strong and healthy. He would have been ideal as the duke's heir had he not been barred by the laws of bastardy.

It wasn't long before John turned up again at the castle forge. It was two days later and this time he came with his nurse, lady Montgomery who, Laurence had learned, was the wife of Sir Thomas Montgomery, the elderly knight he had first encountered at the entrance to duke Richard's private apartments in the Great Chamber. The boy was dressed in a plain red gown tied with a silken belt. Lady Montgomery explained that he was permitted to look around the forge and particularly wished to see how a sword was made. Although Laurence had no unfinished sword immediately to hand, he did have something that he hoped would please the lad. Before that, though, he took up a strip of iron and heated it in the furnace until it glowed white hot. He then took it and beat it on an anvil, explaining that the sparks flying off were impurities in the iron. He showed him how repeated beating and quenching of the iron would eventually produce steel that could be ground to take an edge. The boy delighted in the explosion of steam as the hot iron was plunged into the quenching tank.

Taking down a completed sword from the harness room he let the boy try it. He had deliberately chosen a heavy two-handed blade, knowing that the child could not wield it and so had little chance of causing damage to anyone.

"When I grow I shall have a sword like this one," he declared as he dragged it in a circle being unable to lift the point from the ground. Lady Montgomery stepped back discreetly out of his way.

"I think we might find something more your size," said Laurence and reaching under a pile of sackcloth, drew out a miniature sword and shield. John's eyes lit up and he dropped the full-size weapon and reached for the small one. Laurence had made it for him, carefully ensuring there was no effective cutting edge. The shield was a simple curved plate of iron hammered to thin it out and painted with Gloucester's emblem of the White Boar. "A knight must have his own arms," he said with mock seriousness. John immediately ran out into the bailey and began attacking one of the practice posts that was erected there. The castle guards watched with amusement as the boy danced around the post, hitting it with the shield and striking with the sword.

As they watched him thrashing away at the post, Laurence saw that his mother was on her way over. She ignored Laurence but addressed lady Montgomery.

"Where has he found that weapon?" she asked. Lady Montgomery indicated Laurence with a sweep of her hand. The lady Katherine regarded him with interest then raised an eyebrow quizzically. He swept her a bow, then stood upright.

"It is quite safe, my lady," he said politely. "The edge is dull so he can do little damage to anyone."

"I take it, then, that this is your doing?"

"A trifle, my lady." She regarded him for a moment as if wondering whether a rebuke should be given. Then she smiled and looked to her son.

"I suppose lady Montgomery will have little trouble getting him to sleep tonight. He is certainly using up some energy." She turned towards the forge where the castle smiths were watching. At once they returned to their work. "He has done nothing but talk of guns and fire-powder since his last encounter with you. Now I suppose you will have him in harness?"

"Oh, no my lady," he said with a chuckle. "He will outgrow any armour faster than I can make it."

"I suppose his grace of Gloucester will approve. He would have him trained to arms." She spoke wistfully, with resignation. She was showing a mother's concern for the well-being of her son, though she realised that his birth and status as the duke's favoured bastard son would require him to find a place among the retinue of a noble household, the males of which would all be trained to arms. Her face suddenly took on a sombre expression and she raised her face, her eyes expressing some deep anxiety. "You have made armour for his grace?" she asked rhetorically.

"Just a small portion, my lady, not the whole harness."

"Yet it is strong, his armour?"

"It is of the very best German manufacture."

"I would have his grace well protected." She paused for a moment in deep and melancholy thought then gave him a slight inclination of her head. He bowed to her as she turned to lady Montgomery. "Call John away now," she instructed. "It is time for his lesson."

He watched as they walked towards the stairway up to the Great Hall, the boy in front attacking an imaginary foe with his sword. Her obvious concern for the duke had caused him to think on Joan and he too lapsed into melancholy. The castle had some news of duke Richard as he caught up with rebel groups on the Scottish borders. He had been teaching them a hard and bloody lesson and it was generally believed it would not be long before he returned to Middleham. Laurence's hope was that his grace would then go back to London to pursue his suit for the hand of Anne Neville, which meant he would have the chance of returning too. At least his journey would be towards his love. Richard would be torn by leaving the lady Katherine behind, who no doubt would return to her family at Pomfret castle, and the prospect of having to espouse the lady Anne presently tucked away out of sight in Clarence's house.

* * *

The moment he entered the apothecary's shop and was greeted by Joan he knew his suit had been granted. He could see the white of her undergown through the parting of her unlaced overgown, which was a long-sleeved kirtle of blue wool. It was turned back to reveal a lining of pine-marten fur. Her hair had been carefully brushed and arranged through a wool headband that let her black hair hang down her back. The diamond jet in her eyes sparkled with joy. She must have heard of the arrival in London of the duke of Gloucester with his entourage and guessed that Laurence would come to her as soon as he had been released from his duty.

He too had taken some trouble with his appearance. His first visit had been to a bathhouse where he immersed himself in a hot tub. Though at any other time he might have been tempted, on this occasion he fended off those ladies who expressed a desire to share it with him. He trimmed his hair and beard and put on a clean shirt

198

under his best doublet. This was of the Italian style, which he favoured because the excessive stuffing of the English doublet made him look top heavy. The flatter form of the Italian style was all that was necessary over his broad upper frame. His drawers were of good linen and his hose, suspended from the skirts of the doublet was light brown, a little understated, but tasteful and his boots calf length in dark brown. Over all he had donned a gown of green velvet. He had acquired a short sword, useful for a man in the town, and this was suspended in a hanger from a new leather belt. On his head he wore an acorn hat with a white plume. It was in this state that the gallant presented himself to his lady.

Cornelius had come from the inner shop to stand behind his daughter and he too was beaming with delight. He came to Joan's side and taking her hands in one of his, reached out to Laurence and took his hands also and joined them all together.

"I think you have guessed which decision has been made," he chuckled as he withdrew his hands so that just those of the young couple remained joined. He handed Laurence a letter. "This is from your father. I know the contents and we will discuss them as soon as you can tear your eyes away from my daughter." Reluctantly, Laurence freed one of his hands, yet still gazing into her eyes took hold of the letter. Slowly he drew her to him until their bodies were close enough for each to feel the other's warmth. Still clutching the letter, which he held between them, he kissed her for the first time. It was a tender kiss, as was befitting the presence of her father, but it was pregnant with future promise. They held the moment then drew apart, still gazing at each other. It occurred to Laurence that neither had spoken. Cornelius had done all the talking and so they let their hands part while they walked through into the inner room of the shop.

There he saw Goodwoman Wood who bobbed him a greeting. Her round face was glowing with delight and clearly she knew what was going on. She had brought her husband Able with her. He too had a smile on his face. Unlike his wife, he was thin with spindly legs whose knobbly shape his red hose did little to enhance. The doublet he was wearing swelled his upper body giving the impression of a great wading bird. Laurence knew the couple to be good friends and neighbours of the apothecary. He inclined his head in greeting to the couple. Settling themselves before the fire,

Cornelius, Joan and the Woods waited patiently while Laurence read the letter from his father.

"My father is quite happy in the match," he declared, once he had read the letter. "However, my mother wants us to have the church's blessing ceremony in Brittany and he concurs with her view." He looked at Joan. "Personally, it is my wish that they meet you. I am sure that the decision for our marriage will gladden their hearts as it has mine. Yet all this is premature. I have yet to ask my lady if she will consent to be my bride." Everyone immediately jumped to their feet; Able Wood slipped an arm as far as he could around his wife's waist. Joan wriggled with delight but then, remembering the conventions, feigned coyness. She stood looking down at the ground, her hands clasped in front of her.

"I shall be interested to hear your suit," she whispered. He wondered at how her demeanour had changed from the confident and witty girl he had first encountered and who had dismissed his first clumsy attempts at courtship. Perhaps it had been part of her defence. His craft had taught him the value of armour and the heart is a most vulnerable part of the body. No doubt she had constructed a shield that now she was willing to let slip to expose her most tender part. He knelt before her.

"*Je pose mon coeur devant vous. Il est mon voeu le plus cher que vous devenir ma femme.*" He was delighted at her response as the tears that sprung from her eyes signalled her acceptance, confirmed by a gentile nod of her head and a whispered but clear "I will marry you." The Woods gave a clap of their hands.

"Let us thank God that the matter is now decided," intoned Cornelius in a pious manner. The couple bowed their heads while Cornelius conveyed his blessing upon their union, as was proper. "We can look over the marriage contract and if all is in order, you can sign and our friends will be your witnesses." The group went over to the table where the contract had been laid out for Laurence to look at. Simon de la Halle and Cornelius Quirke had been exchanging letters of negotiation while he had been away and Cornelius had settled on Joan a generous dowry that would allow Laurence to set up a forge and armoury in England, if he so desired. The marriage settlement included a house and garden in Brittany, donated by his family, with spare land to build a workshop. That meant he would have to go back there but he had begun have some affection for his mother's homeland. He would have to think on it, though he had no particular need to set up in Brittany. There would be a considerable advantage to his family in having a business in both countries. He would talk to his father about it. Having read through the contract he took up a pen that had been placed conveniently with a pot of ink. He placed his signature on the document then handed the pen to Able Wood who duly signed as a witness. His wife then made her mark and finally Cornelius signed. Laurence and Joan were now properly betrothed and henceforth would regard each other as man and wife.

The formalities concluded, Joan found a flagon of wine. Each took a glass and drank to the future, whatever that might hold. They stood and chatted gaily to each other for a while, enjoying the wine, a particularly fine one of Burgundy. Laurence was pleased that for once he was not compelled to drink ale. He had acquired a taste for ale, yet his palate was more suited to the softness of the grape. Presently, as evening drew on the Woods took their leave. Joan hugged Goody Wood and kissed Able on his cheek. Goody Wood wiped a tear away as she left, her husband grinning and shaking his head at her foolishness.

"His grace of Gloucester made short shrift of the Scottish rebels, I hear," said Cornelius, settling himself cosily into his favourite chair by the fire.

"Indeed he did and now he has returned to claim a bride," said Laurence.

"Is that what gave *you* the idea," Joan said archly.

"Of course, I would never have been so bold else," he responded. "Mind you, his grace has another tucked away in Yorkshire so he is not in so desperate a state as I am."

"So you are to marry me out of desperation?"

"No of course not; it is for your dowry, what else?" They all laughed together. "All is not well at court, I fear," said Cornelius. "The duke of Clarence is determined that his brother Richard will not get his hands on Anne Neville's half of the Warwick estate."

"It seems we are to consider her mother, the countess of Warwick as having no rights in the matter. It is almost as if she were dead, yet she lives," said Joan indignantly. "Countess Anne is in sanctuary at Beaulieu Abbey where king Edward is keeping a close eye on her." Laurence nodded in understanding.

"I wonder if his grace of Gloucester will pursue the matter vigorously. I have met his paramour and she is a most attractive and delightful lady who is the mother of his son."

"A bastard son," declared Cornelius, "who cannot inherit from his father."

"Yet he has not dismissed her and that must surely have an effect on his determination to gain the hand of Anne Neville?"

"You are confusing matters of the heart with those of government," said Cornelius.

"Well, a prince is still a man," Laurence retorted. He was in a state of euphoria being with Joan, and could see only one woman for a man. Cornelius smiled sagely and shook his head.

"Richard will prosecute his suit to the utmost, you will see, and it is right that he does so. He is a prince of the blood and must produce legitimate heirs. No doubt his paramour in Yorkshire will understand this too. However, he might find it difficult to obtain his bride. Clarence has Anne closely mewed up at Le Heber and he is not about to release her to the tender embrace of his younger brother."

"Le Heber! I can easily discover what is going on there."

"Why is that?" Joan interjected.

"Oh, I have friends in the servants there. I think I know where to find some of them and, with care, it shouldn't he difficult to discover at least something of what Clarence is planning."

"Why should Clarence be planning anything?" asked Joan. "It seems to me that for the moment he has only to keep hold of the lady Anne. It is the king who is the final arbiter in the matter. Surely Richard will petition him and all will be settled?"

"I cannot argue with the logic of what you say," agreed Cornelius, "yet I feel that having intelligence of what is going on in the duke of Clarence's household will do no harm." Laurence wondered why Cornelius should be so keen to involve himself in the matter, but then he had yet to penetrate the apothecary's darker side.

"I can ask my friends what they think," ventured Laurence, anxious to please his new father in law. "No harm can come of it."

"Then do so," said Cornelius. "Now let us eat. You will find it is not only potions that my daughter can concoct. She has a most prodigious roasted fowl waiting for us. I think that you are about to discover there is a most satisfactory codicil to her dowry."

* * *

Though he had yet to penetrate Cornelius' darker side, he soon discovered a most delightful aspect of Joan's character. After their meal a servant man called on Cornelius and the apothecary had gone off with him to tend to a wealthy merchant who had sickness in his family, leaving Laurence and Joan together for the first time. His request for her to marry him and her acceptance in front of two adult witnesses meant they were legally married. Consummation would render the contract dissoluble. The blessing of the church would take place in Brittany but that was just a formality. He was about to approach the subject of their cohabitation, now that they were properly contracted to each other, when Joan pre-empted the issue. She declared that her father would probably be away most of the night, which made her nervous, there being just the one servant girl in the house, and would he stay. He, of course, the consummate gentleman could hardly refuse a lady.

"I wonder if you intend to take advantage of me under the promise of our contract, as some have been known to do," she chortled, her face impish in the firelight of the room.

"I would never dream of doing so if you were unwilling," he replied with mock offence at the slight on his integrity.

"You know king Edward tried that particular ploy on queen Elizabeth. She, wise soul, made sure they were properly contracted in marriage before letting him into her bed."

"Perhaps, as you are unsure of me, I might sleep behind the door in the corridor, where Cerberus used to lie, if my lady would prefer?" She laughed and took his hand.

"How can you think I would let you sleep in Cerberus' old lair? I have a place on the floor at the end of my bed. You can have that." Her eyes suddenly became soft and she stroked his cheek with her fingers. He pulled her to him and kissed her as he had longed to do all evening. She responded avidly and moulded herself to his body. After a while she stood back a little and tugged at her kirtle and then his shirt. "We have much clothing here, monsieur, she whispered. Now we are betrothed surely nothing should come between us?" He smiled down at her and gently framed her face in his hands.

203

"My love," was all he said. She closed her eyes letting her expression signal deep satisfaction then opened them and smiled back at him.

"Am I to walk to my chamber or am I to be carried?" His answer was to lift her into his arms and then he stood stock still, looking around in confusion.

"I have no idea where is your chamber?"

"I shall direct you, after that I expect you to find your own way."

* * *

His opportunity for discovering what was going on at Le Herber came sooner than he expected and from a familiar direction. Sir James Tyrell sought him at the Tower armoury. He was still working under Nicholas Olds who was clearly losing patience with him due to his frequent absences. Normally Olds would simply command one of his armourers to keep at their work, but Laurence had come to the notice of some powerful nobles. Olds knew how he had been with king Henry in the Tower and at the battle of Barnet, he knew he had gone to Sandwich with the duke of Gloucester and then on to Middleham. More particularly, he thought on the battle armour Laurence had produced for earl Rivers. Jack Snipe had been especially virulent in his condemnation of Laurence, though there was little Olds could do about it. The order for the earl's armour had come through him and Laurence had been paid only after he had taken his share. He had opposed Laurence's application to the city merchant's guild for the setting up of an armourer's shop in London. He knew that his objection could not hold and that Laurence, should he push the matter, could set up independently. He was rapidly coming to the conclusion that he would be well rid of Laurence the armourer.

"I believe you have some friends among the servants at Le Herber?" said Tyrell. Laurence was mildly surprised that Tyrell knew this. So far as he could remember he had not mentioned Anna had moved in and she was the only one he actually knew there.

"I have a casual acquaintance with one or two servants," he answered. Tyrell regarded him with tolerant amusement.

"His grace of Gloucester has a need to discover the exact whereabouts of the lady Anne Neville. He knows she is in the house somewhere, but his brother George is being difficult and denying him access to her. He reckons as how the affairs of the Nevilles are entirely in his hands."

"I understand the king has given permission for Richard to marry the lady Anne?"

"He may well have done, but the king is less than forceful in the matter and brother George is being difficult."

"Then what is to be done; the decision is surely entirely in the king's hands?" Tyrell looked around. There were too many ears at the Tower armoury and quite a few were tuned in to their conversation. Jack Snipe in particular had moved casually into earshot.

"Let us go somewhere more discreet and I will explain the matter." Laurence put down the sallet he had been working on and removed his leather apron. That was the signal Nicholas Olds had been watching for. He came storming over and confronted the two men.

"Where do you think you are going?" he demanded. Laurence opened his mouth to speak but Tyrell got in before him.

"We are about the business of the duke of Gloucester, which is no business of yours," he snapped.

"His duties are here at the armoury, which is where he has work to do. I will not tolerate his constant going off at the whim of duke Richard."

"You have no choice, master Olds. I am here at the duke's command."

"Why, you are just an upstart, an adventurer who has wheedled himself into Gloucester's favour, as indeed, monsieur de la Halle seems to have done. His Grace has surrounded himself with the low and base. You do not command here, master Tyrell, I do!" Tyrell remained unflustered by Olds outburst.

"It is Sir James Tyrell, and I have his grace of Gloucester's authority to remove master de la Halle from your service as and when he is required. We have work to do which you know nothing of and you will not obstruct us." Nicholas Olds bristled with indignation. He turned angrily to Laurence.

"You must make up your mind what you intend to do. I will not tolerate this kind of thing any longer." Laurence was uncertain what to do. Recently betrothed, he needed to build a future for himself and his family. He did not want to fall foul of Nicholas Olds who was a master armourer to the king and therefore had a powerful influence of his own.

"I need time to think about this," he informed them both. "I am grateful to you, master Olds, for taking me along with you. You have been most tolerant so far yet I feel it is unwise for either of us to deny the orders of duke Richard. I think I should go with sir James now and afterwards we can properly consider our respective positions." Nicholas Olds thought about it for a moment. He was indignant at the treatment he had received and the callous disregard Tyrell had displayed yet he did not wish to offend the king's brother.

"Then go now and when you have finished with the duke's business, you might inform me as to your commitment to mine. Good day to you both." With that he turned and stalked off.

Tyrell watched him walk away and nodded in satisfaction as if it had been he who had dealt with him.

"His grace of Gloucester is not inclined to tolerate his brother George's intransigence," murmured Tyrell. They had found a convenient tavern with a discreet corner where they would not be overheard. "The king has informed Clarence he is not to interfere with duke Richard's suit so his grace went to Le Herber with a group of his retainers and demanded his promised bride."

"Where do we come into it?" asked Laurence.

"When duke Richard got there, Clarence told him the lady Anne was not in the house. A brief search confirmed she was missing. Duke Richard demanded she be produced but Clarence, slippery as always, simply said that as he had no jurisdiction over her, he could hardly be expected to know where she was. Clearly she has been spirited away somewhere. Your job is to discover her whereabouts."

"Why is it my job? How can I possibly find her?" said Laurence, slightly aghast at the demand.

"Because your prospective father-in-law has certain contacts in Clarence's household and you are thus in a position to find out where the lady is." Laurence was at a loss for words. How could Tyrell know of his relationship with Cornelius Quirke let alone his recent betrothal to Joan? Tyrell was regarding him with an

206

expression of sardonic amusement. Thinking about it, he had taken no particular precautions when calling at the house of the apothecary, he had not needed to, but he was troubled by the accuracy of Tyrell's information. It was almost as if he had been privy to his recent conversation with Cornelius and his declared intent to probe the secrets of Le Herber.

"What do you know of Cornelius' business?" he got out at last. Tyrell's face relaxed and he gave a reassuring smile.

"When the king was in Burgundy he needed information from England. As you know, the apothecary operates a courier service, which the king and his grace of Gloucester found and still find most useful. When duke Francis sent you over from Brittany to England with instructions to contact Cornelius Quirke he did so that he could claim favour with whoever won the throne. The arrangement was fluid. It is often the best way because the times are subject to unexpected change. You have experienced that for yourself. Having used his services before, naturally his grace, has turned to the apothecary for help in his quest to find the lady Anne Neville so things have worked out well." Tyrell regarded him with a quizzical look as if expecting further questions.

"So Cornelius is working for Gloucester's cause?"

"You might say that," came the tentative reply. "Master Quirke is in the peculiar position of being trusted with secrets that only the highest in the land are privy to. He makes himself useful to those in power and they, in turn, require someone remote from Court to make certain . . . arrangements." He let the implication of his words take root in Laurence's mind.

The armourer had begun to wonder where Joan fitted in. She obviously knew some of her father's business. He had noted her perspicacity regarding political matters. It had struck him as unusual in one of her class. It was normally only noble ladies who dabbled in political subterfuge, though most confined themselves to more amorous adventure. Joan was in no position socially to enter their world so it was likely she knew little of her father's more intimate world.

His mind was awash with questions and he badly needed time to think. He had always known he was in England for a purpose other than his own business of making fine armour, but this subversive work was something he had not thought on. His thoughts had all been centred on Joan and his future family. He needed to clear his head.

Chapter 11 – The Rescue

"Apparently you have underestimated George of Clarence," said Laurence with a note of bitterness in his voice. They were standing in the front shop and Joan was bustling somewhere in the back of the house. He had been ruminating over his meeting with Tyrell and considered he had been manipulated by Cornelius, the man who was to become his father-in-law. Moreover, he was disgruntled as to what Joan knew that she hadn't told him. Such is the mind of a lover on the discovery of what appeared to be subterfuge on the part of his paramour.

Cornelius nodded in understanding and stood in contemplation, as one trying to choose his words carefully. "I had told you that Clarence was transparent in his doings, and that remains true. Recent events do not change that, but we now need to discover where is the lady Anne."

"How did Sir James Tyrell find out I know some of the servants at Le Herber?"

"You might remember a fellow who you saw briefly leaving the shop as you arrived shortly after your return from Canterbury?" Laurence remembered the incident and acknowledged with a slight inclination of his head. "That was John Thursby, a servant in Clarence's household. He had asked me about you and it is likely he has passed the information to Sir James. Thursby is an old retainer of the earl of Warwick and favours Richard of Gloucester, whom he has known from youth, so he is quite safe. As you know, Richard was brought up in the earl's household. It is probable that Sir James sent Thursby to me in the first place."

Laurence thought on this new information. It is likely that Thursby had discovered his relationship with Anna and perhaps knew of his meeting with her and her fellow servants in the tavern. That meeting was entirely accidental and innocent, but if Thursby had informed Cornelius, it was fortunate he had volunteered his connection with Le Herber otherwise the apothecary might have suspected him of something that might have prejudiced his suit for Joan's hand. Clearly that had not happened but nevertheless it came to him how easily suspicion and misunderstanding is engendered in those who work on the clandestine business of the state.

"And has this Thursby no idea where the lady Anne is hidden?" he asked.

"No. He has to tread carefully. Clarence is aware that some of his servants have divided loyalties. Like Thursby, many have worked in various houses both of Lancaster and York. You can be sure he will only entrust her keeping to those few whose loyalty he can be certain of."

There were some such in that house, Laurence knew. He remembered the fervour in which Barrett and the other servants of Clarence had defended their liege lord. They had refused to drink the health of the king in a public tavern, which was extremely risky and would have caused a fight if they had been noticed. Fortunately he was the only one who had. Perhaps he should try to meet with Anna and try to find out if she knew anything. Immediately he realised that he could say nothing of this to Joan for fear of arousing her ire. Following on from this came the thought that he had suspected her of holding something back and now here he was contemplating exactly the same. His confusion must have reflected in his face, for Cornelius placed a gentle hand on his shoulder in reassurance. Later the apothecary would instruct him on how to keep a straight face, but for now the young man needed time to reflect on the business in hand.

"How much does Joan know of this business?" he asked tentatively.

"Pretty much as we do," came the reply. "She has always been in our company when we have spoken of the matter and she talks to people in the market place, especially servants of the great. She knows what questions to ask and lets me know the latest gossip."

This was something of a relief to Laurence. Joan had, indeed, been present at all their meetings, entering into the discussion and venturing her opinion, something he had thought unusual at the time. Given the nature of her father's clandestine business it was just as well otherwise ignorance might cause her to let something slip by a careless remark.

"The only thing I can suggest is that I have a walk by Le Herber and get the measure of the place," said Laurence. "With luck I might see someone I know and engage them in conversation. Beyond that I have no idea how to proceed."

"That is by far the best way to proceed for now," replied Cornelius. "To be sure I have there no other contact than John Thursby and in this matter he is helpless."

It was a two mile tramp from Cripplegate to where he believed Le Herber to be, which was near the river at Dowgate so he headed in that direction. He navigated by churches, these being the easiest to ask directions for. He passed St. Alban situated on Wood Street, a church he was already familiar with, then reaching the church of St. Peter, crossed over the busy Watling Street and walked along until he found St. Mary Bothaw. There he asked a passer-by for directions to Le Herber and was pointed down Go Fair Lane.

Of the tenements along Go Fair Lane, Le Herber was the grandest. The gatehouse was timber framed with brick infill on the street level and wattle and daub in the upper two floors, which protruded over the lane. Shuttered windows were set at intervals in the upper floors overlooking the street. A massive oak double gate filled the arch of the main portal into the building. A wicket gate set into the right-hand side must be the normal entrance for foot visitors. It was fitted with an iron grill closed behind with a wood panel. He guessed there would be a porter to tend the gate. Laurence could see that wagons or coaches had passed through as the ground was rutted where wheels had passed over the cobbles that could just be seen in the immediate entrance to the gate. As he stood there a party of horsemen came along and after communicating through the panel with the porter, the gate was opened and they rode through. Laurence caught a glimpse of a stone courtyard within before the gate closed again. Two massive sconces were fixed to the wall either side of the portal and no doubt these would be provided with torches and lit at night so that the porter would be able to have sight of any visitors. He walked by the house and turned down a lane on the south side. Just where the house ended, a stone wall extended the bounds of the property, which would most likely enclose a garden. In fact, he conjectured that this might be from where the house had its name. Menacing iron spikes were ranged along the top of the wall, which was about eight feet in height.

211

He crossed to the far side of the lane in an attempt to see something of the house, but the lane was too narrow to let him stand back far enough. As he reached the end of the wall and looked back, he found the depression of the lane further obscured a view of the house. Whoever had built it must have had a need for privacy. Go Fair Lane seemed to be something of a cut through to the thoroughfare at the far end of the lane. He was constantly jostled by people hurrying along or by vendors with handcarts trundling past with little regard for the feet of anyone who got in the way. The thoroughfare thronged with people, horses, carts and wagons. On such a street he might expect to find an alehouse and sure enough there were several and a couple of bawdy houses too. At first he had been reluctant to enter such a place as he would be unable to observe the people in the street. However, after being accosted several times by the denizens of the bawdy houses, he realised he might be drawing attention to himself by constantly brushing them away, so he ducked through the door of the nearest alehouse where he could get a view of Go Fair Lane.

This hardly improved matters. The doxy who came to serve him was obviously a sister of those he had dodged inside to avoid. The establishment served more than ale and she was affronted when he declined her offer to go with her behind the curtain that hung before a niche at the back of the room. The alehouse keeper was not too pleased either, seeing that there was little profit from a mug of ale and he pocketed a farthing with a disapproving sniff as he handed Laurence his ale. Fortunately a man came in who was obviously a regular and the doxy immediately clamped herself to his arm. Laurence saw a three-legged stool lying on its side by the door. He extracted it from a clump of dirty rushes, set it upright and sat on it where he could look through the opening into the street.

He sat there for the best part of an hour idly crushing the insect life that lived in the rushes on the floor and in the very fabric of the building. He had no doubt that some of it would have moved residence into his clothing. Hundreds of people must have passed by yet there was nobody he recognised. The alehouse keeper was getting annoyed. He had taken his time over the ale, which was hardly surprising as it was sour and tasted vile. Either he would have to order some more of it or leave. He decided to leave and take one more turn past Le Herber, then go back to report his failure to Cornelius.

"Why, bi 't mass! What's a fine fellow like you doing in a place like that?" He had just stepped out of the alehouse into the street when he bumped into Angelica, the buxom wench he had met with Anna and her friends. "If I'de 'ave known you were that frisky I would have obliged you meself," she giggled and cheekily jiggled her breasts at him.

"Why good day mademoiselle," he said giving her a slight bow. "I think, though, you are mistaken in me. I have been waiting for a friend who, it seems, has been detained elsewhere." It was a lame excuse but the best he could think of. It mattered little to Angelica who didn't believe him anyway but who was willing to go along with anything he said. "I see you have been to market?" He nodded to the basket that was slung over her right arm.

"A great cheese," she said tugging at the cloth that covered the contents. The kitchen was short in the order and I have been sent to fetch it from the dairy." He was new to the game of subterfuge and he had been slow in realising what Angelica's job had been.

"The kitchen!" he snorted. "I thought you were attending on the lady Anne Neville at Le Herber? What are you doing running errands for the kitchens?" Angelica took on a sober expression.

"The lady has gone I know not where."

"Without a tiring woman?"

"Unless there is one where she has gone. To be sure nobody from the house went with her."

"But surely someone must know. Do none of the servants know where she is?"

"Not a soul. I saw her to her bed one night and settled down on the floor by the door when the duchess Isabel herself came and awakened her. I was ordered to help her dress in a plain gown and then sent away. That was the last any of us saw of her."

"Did you not ask where she was?"

"Yes and was beaten by one of my lord's retainers for my concern. Afterwards I was ordered to the kitchens where I have been ever since. In fact, this is the first time I have been out of the house." As she related her experience her demeanour changed from her usual jolly self to sadness tinged with apprehension. Suddenly she seemed to consider her position and glanced around her as if fearful of being observed talking to a man in the street. Laurence sensed her concern and moved to console her.

"Do not worry, Angelica," he said tenderly, "I shall not disclose our chance meeting." Angelica nodded, hardly daring to speak for fear of breaking into tears. "There is one thing you might do for me, perhaps?"

"I hardly dare."

"Could you get a message to Anna for me? I hope she will respond." Angela gave him a broad grin.

"I should think she will want to see you," she chuckled. Laurence was puzzled by her sudden change of attitude.

"Just get a message to Anna for me. If you are discovered you can say you are simply passing a message between lovers and attention will be diverted from you." She looked around again then nodded.

"I will tell her I have seen you."

"Tell her to meet me outside the church on the corner by here, St. Mary Bothaw. I shall be there in the morning at the time of the bell for tierce. If anyone sees us she can say we have been at prayer there and were simply recalling old times."

"I will do that." Suddenly she brightened at a sudden thought. "If she will not come, then I shall, but I think somehow she will be there," giving him a knowing wink.

"That would be most delightful, but I really must talk to Anna. I have some information for her from a friend." It was a poor excuse, but he knew it would suffice. Angelica nodded with resignation. "Promise me you will tell no other of the meeting."

"You can absolutely rely on me for that," she replied with a laugh.

He offered her his arm and, with a final glance around her, she put her arm through his and let him escort her back to Le Herber. She left him at the end of Go Fair Lane and once he considered she would be safe inside, walked one more time past the house and returned to his new home where Joan was waiting for him. He felt a little guilty in trying to elicit a meeting with Anna, but he needed to try a new approach. He knew she was friendly with Clarence's trusted servants. Perhaps she could give him a clue. It was worth a try.

* * *

214

The morning was chill now that the year had turned into September   and Laurence wrapped his cloak tightly around him as he waited in a niche behind a buttress of the church with a clear view of the street. London woke at prime and had been about its business for some time before the bell for tierce sounded. Few took notice of him except for a legless beggar who had squatted by the door of the church. The man kept staring malevolently at him and rather than endure the malicious scrutiny, he pushed himself away from the wall and strolled to the other side of the building. At once the beggar hutched himself along using his arms for propulsion and installed himself in the very niche Laurence had vacated. Clearly this must be his regular pitch. After settling down with his begging bowl he took no further notice of Laurence who was, in any case, out of sight behind the church portal.

People were constantly hurrying through the churchyard and he kept a wary eye open in case any of the servants from Le Herber were about. They could very well be for all he knew. He had only met three of them besides Anna, so he was unlikely to recognise one unless dressed in Clarence's livery. After a while he guessed that the brothers' prayers had finished inside the church and wondered if Anna would come. Perhaps Angelica had been unable to talk to her? He was just wondering how long he should keep his vigil when he spied her hurrying through the churchyard towards him. She was clad in a voluminous cloak to keep out the cold wind and the hood was pulled over her head. Whether this was for warmth or an attempt at discretion he did not know.

"Hello, Laurence," she said looking up at him, her voice and face expressionless.

"Bonjour, Anna," he greeted her with a smile, genuinely pleased to see her. She looked around then led him to a place beneath a tree that grew against the churchyard wall away from the course of those cutting through. She threw back her hood and he was at once struck by how lovely she looked.

"It seems that the trade of Brewster is agreeable to you," he said admiringly. She gave a toss of her head but remained tight lipped. Clearly she was worried about something, the clandestine tone of her meeting with him, perhaps. "How is Barrett?" he ventured.

"He is most contented," she replied without emotion.

215

He sensed there was something wrong. If there was trouble in the house due to Clarence's dealings with Anne Neville it was not surprising that she would be reticent. If she were caught giving information away she would be in serious danger. He did not think he would be known to anyone in the household as having a connection with Cornelius Quirke, so she had little to worry about there. If they were seen and reported, then he had already given a perfectly reasonable excuse to Angelica, which would suffice.

"Why have you asked to see me?" she asked quietly. He supposed she had detached herself from her affection for him and was now unhappy at reawakening an old passion. "What have you heard?"

He was puzzled by her question. Did she know that he wanted information on Anne Neville; but that was impossible? He hadn't mentioned his quest to anyone and he certainly had not revealed his purpose to Angelica.

"The matter is most delicate." Her head shot up and she scrutinised his face frantically. "Anna, what is it that is troubling you?" he asked suddenly alarmed. She stepped away from him and when he moved to follow her she put up an arm, palm outwards to stop him. Slowly she opened the cloak that enveloped her. She stood before him dressed simply as usual, but there, to his shock, for all to see was a swelling - she was plainly pregnant!

"Whose child is it?" He asked the question but felt he already knew the answer.

"I am four months gone."

His head was in a spin. Four months ago! In a fraction of a second he imagined he could recall the stars whirling above the wagon in Warwick Town where they lay together while the soldiery caroused all around. There were the other times, too, on the great march after which he had had to go to the priest to confess the sin of fornication. He had thought his sin slight because he was genuinely fond of her. He had not expected the relationship to be more than casual, and he thought she would understand that too, given her background as an alehouse doxy.

Joan! The realisation and full portent of this new situation descended on him like an announcement of Armageddon. Events were travelling at a pace his thoughts could not match. His courting and betrothal to Joan had been so swift that even his friends at the Tower armoury were yet to learn of it. This had been due to his constantly being taken away from London on the business of the king and the duke of Gloucester: Canterbury, Middleham and now this quest to find the lady Anne Neville.

Anna, observing the pattern of emotions that were chasing themselves over his face was in similar confusion. "You have no need to worry yourself," she said bitterly. "Barrett believes the child is his."

He concluded, from her tone, that she had harboured some hope that he might cleave to her now that a child was in the offing. Obviously, she knew nothing of Joan or that he was in any way attached to someone else. Why should she; the time between his coming to London and his betrothal was barely three months. It had even taken him by surprise and it was only now he realised how extraordinary the events had been. He decided she must know his situation.

"Anna," he said gently, "I am betrothed." He had no idea what reaction to expect. Later, in his mind's eye, he would think of her cloak sinking to the ground her corporeal body deflating to nothingness. He had no idea she felt towards him so intensely. He saw her visibly shrink before his eyes as if some spell had been cast to send her soul towards some unimaginable oblivion.

Anna trembled and felt the cloak slip from her shoulders to the ground. She was too distraught to catch at it. When Angelica had brought the news of her meeting with Laurence and his wish to see her, she had imagined that he, somehow, had learned of her condition and wanted to acknowledge his child. Hope had flooded her heart and all other possibilities were purged from it. Now, suddenly she realised how false her expectations had been. She felt a fool, to believe that he would know and want to take her for himself. It had been from the start a false hope, and at least she was sensible enough to ensure the child had a father. Barrett was not a bad catch as a husband. She would make him a good wife, but she would never feel that fathomless something that God allows just a very few men and women to have between them. She had felt that with Laurence and had thought that there was something of it too in him. Apparently she had been so wrong.

Laurence reached down and took up her cloak. She snatched it from him and wrapped herself in it as if putting on armour, which,

217

in a sense she was. She choked back the tears that were welling up in her and looked him defiantly in the face.

"I wonder, monsieur, what you want of me?"

He was taken aback by her use of "monsieur". That was how Joan referred to him, though with her it was meant as a term of endearment, her fond name for him; Anna pronounced it with cynicism. He didn't understand why, but it was that, more than anything, that caused him the deepest pain.

He decided he could not go on with his quest for now; he would have to find another way. He reached out to take her hands, but she snatched them away.

"I cannot ask anything of you, Anna. Please accept by profound apologies for asking to see you. I had no idea I should cause you such distress. I have no idea what to say to you." She raised her head and glared at him.

"Perhaps, monsieur, you can partake of a penance. I seem to remember you have a taste for such." The monsieur again – it was as if a corner of his heart had broken away and drifted off somewhere he might never find again.

"You have only to ask," he said enthusiastically. She snorted but gathered her dignity and raised herself to wholeness.

"What is it you came here for?" she snapped impatiently.

"I am on an errand for his grace of Gloucester. He is seeking the lady Anne Neville who, until recently, was residing at Le Herber." She stood away from him, sudden fear showing on her face.

"You will do well to keep out of the affairs of his grace of Clarence," she said, her voice trembling slightly. "He does not take kindly to anyone interfering in his business."

"I am aware of it," he replied, "but I am instructed by his grace through Sir James Tyrell – I think you know him." She regarded him carefully, her face now troubled with something quite different from her own concerns.

"I know nothing that can help you," she said eventually. "Besides, Barrett is faithful to his lord and he certainly would not like it if he found out I had been conversing with an agent of Gloucester." Laurence nodded in understanding. He was decidedly uncomfortable at pressing her for information now he had discovered her - no, their secret.

"I understand, but surely you must have some sympathy for the lady Anne. Fate has suddenly turned against her and she has been cruelly used by Clarence; surely you can see that?"

"I don't see how she is worse off than any other woman who is trade goods," she said bitterly. "What makes you think Richard of Gloucester is any different from his brother. In fact, he isn't. They are both covetous of her share of the Warwick estate." He noted how readily she understood the politics of the business. That could only be the result of servant chatter. He began to wonder what else the servants had been gossiping about.

When I spoke to Angelica yesterday, she told me nobody at Le Herber knew where the lady Anne had been taken. I don't suppose you are any different, though I hoped that your relationship with Barrett, who I understand is completely loyal to Clarence, might have given you a clue?"

"If that were so I could not possibly tell you," she snapped. She shrank into herself and began to think the matter through. "As it happens, Barrett has not confided anything to me; I do not believe he knows more than anyone else though he is friendly with some of the duke's personal servants." She paused again in deep thought. "I have some sympathy for the lady Anne," she said pensively, "as I have for any woman in this world who has no man to protect her." With this she looked him directly in the face and he felt himself withering away inside. "There is one very remote possibility that there is someone who might have an idea where lady Anne has been taken. I do not expect you will like it much if I tell you who it is?"

"Anna, I should be glad of any help. So far the matter is completely hopeless. I have few contacts in England yet I have been tasked with finding where is the lady."

She looked up at him and a sly smile crept around her lips. "Then come with me. I hope you are ready for this and prepare yourself – you might have to protect me where we are going, and yourself too." He nodded and loosened the dagger at his belt. He also wore a short sword and wondered if it would be needed.

They took a route well clear of Le Herber then turned towards the river. As they walked through the narrow streets where the destitute lay against walls or lurked threateningly on corners she asked him about his betrothal. He told her of Joan and that she was

219

the daughter of an apothecary. He told her that he was to be married in Brittany. At that she stopped for a moment and looked down in contemplation. He stood patiently, wondering what had arrested her perambulation, but hardly daring to ask what the problem was. Presently she looked at him with something of guile in her face and stepped out with rather more vigour.

As they drew close to the river the district became more dirty and dangerous. Had it not been for the fact he had dressed sombrely, so as not to attract attention to himself, richer clothes would have provoked an attack by now. As it was he steered them both along the centre of the narrow streets and kept a wary hand on the hilt of his dagger. He held himself confidently erect and demonstrably alert. It was like dealing with savage animals. Any sign of fear would have the whole pack onto him.

Presently they could go no further as they had reached the muddy bank of the river. They came to a quay backed by a warehouse, under which dirty cloths were nailed between the stanchions to give some sort of protection to the wretches that dwelt there. Somewhere just above the high tide line slats of wood were nailed together under the quay where it ran into the bank to construct a hovel that the meanest village churl would balk at. To his uttermost dismay Anna steered him to where a huddled figure sat outside the hovel sorting through a small pile of rubbish. As their shadows fell over the wretch, it looked up at them and he thought he recognised something familiar, then it came to him – it was Mother Malkin! The old crone, on recognising Anna, held out a scrawny arm terminated by a clutch of knobbly fingers. Anna delved into her cloak and drew out a crust of bread and a morsel of cheese. The old crone snatched them and immediately began cramming them into her mouth. Anna looked at him, clearly expecting some sort of reaction. Laurence was horrified. The stench that came from the old woman competed with that of the riverbank mud where the ordure of London fetched up at low tide. The old crone was winning the contest. He looked at Anna aghast with horror.

"What corner of the infernal regions have you brought me to?" he gasped, his breath almost stifled by the foul miasma.

"You look as if you are horrified, yet she is just one step from heaven," stated Anna. "What price your prating priests now?"

Laurence frantically crossed himself. "You speak blasphemy," he struggled to say. "What better demonstration of the wages of sin than this."

"Well, if she remains in this state, she will soon find release. Be careful, monsieur, you might find yourself sitting beside such as she in heaven at the last."

"I have seen images such as this, not in heaven, but hell." He recalled the gargoyles, the painted walls and images in glass displayed in every church, reminding sinners of the fate awaiting them. All those depicting hell were characterised by monstrous ugliness and filth. "How can she possibly know anything of the lady Anne Neville?"

"She may not, but she remains your only hope."

"How can that possibly be so?"

Anna regarded him with a supercilious smile. She was extracting some sort of revenge for his treatment of her, though she could not bring herself to condemn him utterly. In her inner self she knew the stations in which they had been born separated them. They were not so far apart as commoner and noble, but there was still a gulf between the son of a rich tradesman, the armourer to princes, and an alehouse doxy. Yet she knew, the king himself had married beneath him. It was not unprecedented. She shook off the idea – distinctions of class were much stricter in the lower orders than that of the nobility.

"When I first entered the household of the duke of Clarence, by the influence of Barrett, I was able to find some support for Mother Malkin too. Clarence has a large household; in fact it is virtually a court. There are many amongst his servants and entourage who need the ministrations of a cunning woman, especially one as skilled as Mother Malkin. Though she was treated with indifference most of the time, there were many who were glad of her remedies. Many wives have skill with herbs and such, but Mother Malkin has ranged afar and knows so much more. Word of this got through to his grace and even the duchess Isabel had occasion to use her potions." Laurence looked down on the old woman as she chewed at the bread and cheese. It was difficult, at this moment to see evil in her, only disgust, but who knows what devious matters lurked in her cunning brain.

"I still cannot see how she can be of any use in my present quest?"

"It concerns her present plight. How, think you, given that she had found favour with the duchess Isabel she has ended up here in this state?" He became more attentive.

"Please enlighten me." Anna took on a more sombre aspect.

"Soon after the lady Anne was taken from the house, and remember nobody knows where, it seems she was taken ill. This was not unexpected. She is not a robust lady and the strain of her circumstances up to that time must have weakened her. Anyway, Mother Malkin was brought in to brew up a potion for her. Now I do not know what that was, but I do know that she would not have done so without first looking at the lady herself. She was taken off somewhere and never returned to Le Herber. Afterwards, as a nobody she was turned out and disregarded. It was only by chance that a servant at the mansion happened to see her picking rubbish along the shore and mentioned it in the kitchen. It was hardly a topic for general discussion, but I noted it and decided to seek her out. It is only by my bringing her food she has managed to survive at all."

"And you think she knows where the lady Anne is being held?"

"I cannot say, and neither can she in this condition."

"Then the situation is hopeless."

"Unless you can get her to recall where she was taken."

"How can I do that? The woman seems to have lost her mind."

"Can you be sure of that? In any case, she remains your only hope." Laurence was at a loss as to how to proceed. Clearly the old crone must have some information locked away in her confused brain, but how to extract it was completely beyond him.

"I have a suggestion," said Anna quietly. "Are you interested?"

"Anything."

"Take her with you to your little apothecary woman."

"She is not an apothecary, her father is."

"It matters not. An apothecary uses simples and herbs for cures and Mother Malkin has much skill in that respect. Present her as a substitute for your betrothed. You are leaving for Brittany soon, so you say, and the apothecary will have need of her skill when he loses his daughter."

"I cannot do that. How would I explain who she is?"

"She is a woman you met on the great march. Your betrothed should not be too concerned that you might have had designs upon her virtue." Anna spoke with an eloquent raising of her eyebrows.

"But she knows of us."

"That is a chance you will have to take. She will probably keep her own council, but you must decide, for safety sake, whether or not to tell your betrothed about me."

Laurence's mind was once again plunged into turmoil. He gazed down on the bundle of rags, which, it seemed, was the only chance he would have of discovering where the lady Anne was being held. He could not believe others were not searching also, but so far nobody seemed to have a clue where she was. If he were to be the one to solve the riddle then he would be in high favour and the chances of him setting up as an armourer in London would be virtually assured. It was with some trepidation that he made his decision, in truth, the only one he could take. Crossing himself, he decided Mother Malkin would accompany him to the apothecary's shop at the Cripplegate.

It was with some difficulty they got Mother Malkin through the narrow streets by the river. As they reached a thoroughfare Laurence managed to persuade, using a few coins, a waggoner to let her ride on the back of his wagon, which was on its way along Watling street towards Newgate. He left Anna at the corner of the church where they had met and he watched as she turned away and walked back towards Go Fair Lane. The coin was sufficient to encourage the waggoner to divert along Wood Street towards the Cripplegate. Laurence certainly did not want to be seen walking along with the crone, especially in her present state. He could not think what Joan's reaction would be and he only hoped the possibility of getting some information from the old woman would mitigate his action.

Joan had smiled as she saw him in the doorway, but she clapped a hand to her mouth when the old crone shuffled into the shop with Laurence. Unfortunately, she brought her river stench in with her. He raised both hands in an attempt to stay her reaction, hoping to get an explanation in before Joan had the chance to say anything.

"Hear me," he said quickly, "I have rescued her from the river."

Joan looked in horror between the two, speechless. Presently she gathered her wits.

"Who is she and what are you doing bringing her here in that condition?" she demanded, though there was no anger in her voice, which he found encouraging.

"It is something of a long story, but the crone could have some knowledge about where the lady Anne has been taken."

She looked at the old woman who had remained silent, her destitution having reduced her to absolute subservience. "Has she a name?"

"Aye, Mother Malkin."

"None other?"

"Not that I know of."

"And you have rescued her, you say?"

"In a manner of speaking."

Joan fixed him with a grim stare and placed her hands on her hips, a stance that demanded a further explanation of him.

"I, I know her from the great march," he stammered. "She is a cunning woman and tended to the sick and injured in the army." Joan looked at the crone with some interest. "I found her living in squalor, just where the Wall Brook discharges into the river."

"What in God's name were you doing there?"

"My enquiries had led me there."

"I thought you were trying to contact some of the servants at Le Herber?

"Quite so, and one of them told me of Mother Malkin. Nobody at Le Herber knows anything of where the lady Anne might be, at least those it is possible to ask without suspicion."

"Then what does this woman know that the others do not?"

"I have no idea as yet. We shall have to question her. It is possible she treated the lady Anne for some ailment at the place where she was taken, then cast out to fend for herself. This is the state I found her in."

Joan's face immediately softened and she looked at Laurence with a hint of tears in her eyes. "Whatever else your motives it was an act of great kindness to bring her here."

Laurence immediately brightened and the trepidation he had felt before he entered the apothecary's shop melted away. Apparently Joan saw his actions as an act of charity and thus he had won her respect. He would not tell her whose idea it really was to bring her here. Her concern for the old crone had diverted her attention from

224

asking questions about who it was he had contacted at Le Herber. It would be prudent to leave things as they were and let Joan take over.

"The first thing is to get her out of those filthy rags and burn them. I shall find some clean clothes for her; after we have scrubbed her clean of the river filth."

"We shall scrub her?"

"Not you," she chuckled. "I shall have Jennet to help me." Jennet was the maid who helped around the house. "I expect she will need a good meal also. When we have tended to her immediate needs, perhaps a gentle question or two might be tried." She looked down at the pathetic bundle of rags. "We might not get very far, but we shall try." She reached out a hand to the crone, who looked up with rheumy eyes and nodded an ingratiating greeting.

"I hope you can understand her, she speaks a strange tongue and I am not sure if she is a caster of spells. Make certain you wear a charm against the evil eye as you tend her, just to be safe." Joan looked at him with concern.

"She is in too pitiful a state to do anyone harm." The crone tentatively placed a grimy gnarled claw into Joan's soft white hand and let her lead her from the street shop to the apothecary's chamber.

They passed by the entrance to the passage where the dog Cerberus used to lie and Laurence wondered how the animal would have reacted to the smell. Perhaps it would merely find it interesting. Cornelius Quirke was dozing near the fire as Joan passed through to the rear gently leading the old woman. He sat bolt upright in his chair, gasping as the miasma that surrounded her assailed his nostrils.

"God's blood! What was that?"

Laurence, now he was relaxed having got the introduction to Joan safely out of the way, laughed at the apothecary.

"Unless you have some new intelligence, she is the only one who can help find where is the lady Anne. We must wait until Joan has restored her to human shape, then see what we can discover."

It was some time before Joan presented them with the refurbished Mother Malkin. Laurence was astounded at the difference – he would not have recognised her. She was small and looked frail, not surprising given the ordeal she had been through. He supposed her diminutive appearance was due to the removal of the incrustation of dirt that had formerly covered her body. Her hair was pale grey, tied back and only partly covered by a linen cloth. Joan had dressed her in a plain brown dress tied with a simple rope belt. She had a woollen shawl over her shoulders. The toes of a pair of red slippers peeped out from the bottom of her dress. Only the smell of soap, which mingled with the scent of herbs in the shop, could be detected.

"I have burned her old rags and a multitude of fleas with them." Joan informed them. "Her hair is washed with Camomile and fine-combed. I believe she is mostly free from vermin now."

Cornelius, who by now had been apprised of her circumstances, stood and offered her a seat in a chair by the fire. Mother Malkin looked around then, with some uncertainty, placed herself in the seat. She looked desperately at Joan, as if to reassure herself she was still with her. Joan nodded and smiled comfortingly at her, then drew up a stool and sat beside her. The two men resumed their seats and the small group huddled intimately around the fire.

"I understand that you tended the lady Anne Neville recently?" ventured Laurence while scratching at his armpit. Mother Malkin looked at him quizzically.

I knows you," she said after scrutinising his face. "Youme be that gurt felly fro' t' march wi't' king." Laurence's heightened degree of concentration let him work out what she was saying.

"Yes, but never mind that for now. We are interested in what happened at Le Herber." He needed to steer her away from tales of the great march in case she said something he might regret.

"I think it would be better if we let her tell her tale her way," intoned Joan innocently.

"There is hardly time for that," he replied in desperation. "His grace of Gloucester will not thank us for any delay in finding the lady Anne."

"Tosh," Joan replied. "He has no idea himself and is dependent on us. It is better to get the information eventually rather than driving the memory from her by aggressive questioning." Laurence had no choice but to draw back and let her talk. Hopefully Joan would have as much understanding of her dialect as he had. She leaned towards the old woman and spoke gently to her.

"We are looking for a lady we think you tended at Le Herber. Do you remember her?"

"There were many gurt ladies i' th' heawse."

"Yes, but we think this one was taken away and that you were sent to tend her."

"Aye, there wur one sich hoo did mich scwarkin'" Joan looked expectantly at Laurence who stood there confounded having understood not a word.

"And what was wrong with her?" continued Joan, gently.

"Nobbut melancholy aw reckon. I gin hoo some remedy." The old woman looked around and pointed to a bunch of dried leaves that were hanging from the rafters near the mixing table. Joan looked and identified the plant.

"She gave her borage, as I would have done," she said to the men. "There seems nothing seriously wrong. The lady is naturally upset but otherwise healthy." Cornelius nodded in understanding. All this was going over Laurence's head.

"But where had she been taken?" he asked in frustration. Joan impatiently waved him to silence.

"Where were you taken to see her after she left Le Herber?"

"Aw dunno, Londin is strange to mi."

"But she was no longer at Le Herber?"

"No. In a great heawse bi 't church."

"Which church?" There were so many in London it would be impossible to identify a particular house near a church unless they could discover which church.

"Magdalene, hoo was a paramour too." Joan sat back, puzzled. Laurence thought he knew what was going through the old woman's mind and panic began to well in his breast. The Magdalene had been a close companion of Christ on his journeys, though to think of her as his paramour was blasphemy. He hastily made the sign of the cross.

"Just a moment," interrupted Cornelius. " There is a church – St Mary Magdalene on Old Fish Street. That street leads from the corner of Watling Street where St Mary Bothaw is, towards Blackfriars. I think I am right in believing Sir John Poyners has a mansion there, or in that area, and he is a friend of George duke of Clarence."

"So it is not that far from Le Herber," Laurence inserted quickly, keen to divert attention away from the garrulous old woman.

"I think you should have another walk, Laurence," said Cornelius.

"I shall go there right now."

"It's too late, the evening is drawing in," Joan said with concern. "The streets are not safe after dark." Laurence agreed with her. In any case, the house would be closed for the night and it was unlikely he would learn anything useful until the servants were about at daybreak. Joan stood and took him to one side.

"I cannot think what to do with Mother Malkin, but for now I shall find a bed for her in the kitchen. Let us see what the morning brings." Laurence could only nod in agreement. At least while the old crone slept she wouldn't be gossiping.

* * *

He identified the house of Sir John Poyning by simply observing the servants who bustled around the streets leading on to Old Fish Street. Most of them wore the livery of their masters and Cornelius had told him which to look out for. He spotted one who led a horse to a farrier and was waiting for a loose shoe to be secured. The farrier soon fixed the loose shoe and Laurence had merely to follow the groom at a discreet distance to discover the house. It was on Old Fish Street and sure enough, nearby was the church of St. Mary Magdalene. The house was set back from the street and built behind a high wall. He caught a glimpse of it as the groom passed through the gateway leading the horse. The gate slammed shut as soon as the servant passed through. If the lady Anne Neville were in there then he would have the devil of a job getting to her. He was just about to leave when he saw a familiar figure coming down the street. It was Barrat, who curiously had discarded the murrey and blue livery of Clarence and was in plain dress. This was suspicious, as he had worn Clarence's livery proudly in the tavern where Laurence had met him. Other servants were wearing theirs, so why had he discarded his? He had not noticed Laurence and may not have remembered him anyway. He knocked on the gate and the face grill was drawn back. He said something to the porter and a wicket gate was opened, which he stepped through, and which closed firmly behind him.

There could be little doubt that there was a connection between Le Herber and the house of Sir John Poyner. He decided to get back to the apothecary's shop and inform Cornelius. Then they would contact Sir James Tyrell and let him deal with it. It was highly likely that the lady Anne was concealed somewhere in the house, but it would take a troop of armed men, backed by the authority of the duke of Gloucester, to get in there. Nothing was certain, of course; the lady might have been removed to one of Clarence's estates, but that would have required some organisation and the chance of detection. It would have been simpler to move her just a short distance and hide her among the crowded streets of London. If it had not been for his relationship with Anna, and the involvement of Mother Malkin then she might never have been found.

* * *

Crosby Place on Bishopsgate Street was a superb house, exactly what was expected of the town residence of a prince. Rented by Richard from Sir John Crosby, a wealthy merchant, it was fairly new, as grand as Le Herber but with more coming and going of servants and others who wished to petition his grace. The gates stood open, though guarded by pike-men, but passable by those having business with the house or the duke. Laurence and Cornelius had been led through a great hall with a fantastically decorated ceiling where they passed under a minstrels' gallery into an ante-chamber. Splashes of colour were everywhere, from the splendid tapestries to the bright clothes of the servants and blue, crimson and green gowns of the merchants who waited on the favours of the duke. The house was lighted by grand windows and ornamented with rich carvings and panels. It was almost as if they were entering a college, such as at Oxford. In his privy chamber, Richard of Gloucester stood facing them, resplendent in his brilliant court dress, his face set with determination. Beside him stood Sir James Tyrell. Laurence and Cornelius fell to their knees in obeisance.

"Sir James informs me you have discovered where the lady Anne Neville is hidden," the duke intoned without preamble.

"Indeed we hope so, your grace," said Cornelius hesitantly.

"You are not certain?" snapped the duke.

"The evidence is circumstantial, but convincing, your grace."

"Then let us hope you are right. If I go charging in to no avail, then I shall be made to look a fool. Do you understand me?" Both men bowed their heads.

"Yes, your grace," muttered Cornelius, " but it is all we have." The duke spun around and paced the room, his feet idly shuffling in the rushes on the floor. Presently he stopped and turned to them, indicating they should rise. Cornelius and Laurence got to their feet and waited for the duke to speak.

"I have several agents working on this right now, yet you are the only ones to come up with anything remotely plausible. I confess your tale has given me hope. We shall go this very evening and search the house from top to bottom. If the lady Anne is there we shall find her. If she is not, then I shall have some explaining to do to the king." He glared at them coldly and both men feared what retribution might follow such an abject failure.

It was apparent that the duke would lead the expedition himself rather than leave it entirely to his henchmen. This was rash behaviour for a prince. He had already told them the consequences of failure and his personal presence would cause him even greater embarrassment should he not find the lady there. Laurence wondered if the duke wished to be seen by the lady as her rescuer. If so, he was showing a spark of romanticism that belied the idea he was simply after her inheritance.

"Master armourer, you will attend Sir James here and get ready to come with us," commanded the duke. "We will start out after curfew when the streets are deserted. I may have to move fast to get the lady Anne away and crowds will only hamper us. Apothecary, you will come too, at the rear in case the lady requires your assistance." With that the duke turned to a table and began examining some documents that lay there. His secretary, who had been standing discreetly behind the duke, stepped to his side. Sir James Tyrell indicated the door and the three men backed respectfully from the room.

"You will remain here until we leave this evening," Tyrell informed them once they were clear of the duke's presence. "There must be no chance that our plans leak out, so make sure you keep close council. The servants here are loyal, so far as we know, but you can never be sure." Both men nodded in agreement.

Sir James Tyrell took them down to the servant's quarters where they were bid to sit and take some food. Their table was at the end of the room by the larder away from the kitchen servants. It was mid morning and they would have to wait some hours before starting on their expedition. Tyrell left them after a while, but returned later towards evening and signalled for them to follow him. He took them into the cellar where the armoury was. The room was almost crammed with the duke of Gloucester's armed henchmen. All wore cuirass with chapelles de fer for head protection.

"Find yourself some armour," Tyrell told Laurence. "You too, master apothecary, just to be on the safe side." Laurence chose the same as the other men. None would wear full harness, it seemed, probably so they could move swiftly through the streets. All were to wear the white boar badge of Gloucester and they slipped a blazoned tabard over their heads. Laurence strapped on his own sword belt with his sword and long dagger. Some of the other henchmen were similarly armed and some had pikes. They all sat around, waiting for the appearance of the duke.

Richard of Gloucester came down to the armoury after darkness had fallen and the curfew had sounded to close the city gates. He alone was dressed in full harness. His visor had been left off his helmet so that his face could be plainly seen. His surcoat had the royal arms on it, three leopards of England quartered with the *fleur de lis* of France and a label of difference denoting his rank as the king's brother. All the men got to their feet. There were two dozen in all, not including Laurence and Cornelius. Duke Richard stood on the steps of the cellar and beckoned them to get close so he could talk to them.

"When we get to the house we must work quickly," he told them. "It will be likely that someone will get a message to my brother Clarence that we are on the move. Crosby Place is constantly watched. We shall go mounted because of the distance across the city. Surprise and speed is our best advantage. Nobody knows we have discovered the house where the lady Anne is being held, but Clarence will not be long in working it out. When he does he will move to stop us. We must find the lady then get her to sanctuary

where she will be beyond his reach. I shall then report to the king."
He looked around and nodded in satisfaction at their readiness.
"Pikemen, you shall lead and when I demand entrance your job
will be to keep Sir John's servants and retainers in their places.
The rest of you will search the house. I shall go directly to Sir
John's privy chamber and see if the lady is there. If she is, we will
get her away immediately despite any protests from any quarter."

There came a murmur of understanding from the
assembled men.

The duke ordered the cellar doors opened whereupon he led the
troop from the chamber and into the courtyard where Sir James
Tyrell had the horses ready. They mounted swiftly and as soon as
they were all ready, the duke led them out of the house gates and
away through the dark streets. A full moon shone, which gave
some light and they were able to trot the horses at a reasonable
speed. Laurence and Cornelius were at the front of the troop
directly behind Tyrell. Cornelius was plainly enjoying the
adventure, though Laurence hoped he would not have to engage in
a fight. In that case he would be obliged to look to his father in law
as well as himself. The only persons who were supposed to be
abroad after curfew was the Watch, and when these were
encountered they soon got out of the way when they saw the royal
arms on Gloucester's surcoat. Every now and again a shadow
would duck into a side alley, some felon on dubious business,
fearful of a troop of armed men.

The duke took them the nearest way along Cornhill towards St
Paul's where they turned left before they reached the cathedral and
rode down Bread Street. At Old Fish Street they turned right
towards the church of St. Mary Magdalene opposite which was the
town house of Sir John Poyner. The house was not large or grand
as Le Herber but it was still large enough to contain a sizeable
household of servants.

Richard threw himself out of the saddle and drew his sword, the
hilt of which he used to beat on the door. Tyrell was right behind
him shouting for the house to be opened by command of the duke
of Gloucester. Presently they could see glimmers of light as
candles were lit. Presently the hatch in the door was opened and a
frightened face stared whitely out at them. The duke stood back so

232

that the royal arms of his surcoat could be plainly seen in the moonlight.

"Open immediately for his grace of Gloucester!" shouted Tyrell. The hatch in the door slammed shut and they could hear shouting behind the stout timber. Tyrell was just about to order the door broken down when they heard the bolts being drawn and the door opened.

The duke pushed his way in and demanded the presence of Sir John Poyner. Tyrell was at his side and Laurence came in after. He had gently pushed Cornelius to one side telling him to wait outside until called. Pike men entered and arranged themselves around the spacious hallway. The gentleman of the house was half way down a staircase with a fur cloak wrapped around him. With him were two burly serving men armed with cudgels. As soon as they saw Gloucester's blazon they hesitated and looked to their master for instructions. Sir John was a young man, just a little older than Gloucester and his fellowship with the duke of Clarence had made him arrogant. He was not easily intimidated by Gloucester's display of heraldry.

"What is the meaning of this intrusion, your grace?" he demanded, his voice tinged with anger.

"We are here for the lady Anne Neville who I believe is being kept here against her will," said Gloucester imperiously.

"For a fleeting moment Sir John's face showed consternation, but he recovered himself quickly and presented an aspect of indignant innocence." He exchanged a glance with one of the serving men who gave an almost imperceptible nod in return.

"I have no idea what you are talking about, he said.

"We have good reason to believe she is here and my men will search your house until we find her. I will begin with your privy chambers. I expect that a noble lady will be held somewhere there. Sir John stood back and his serving men came down to stand with the pike men. With a nod to Tyrell, Gloucester began mounting the stairs. The other henchmen entered and began looking through the rooms. In the confusion, Laurence noticed that one of the serving men had gone through a door that led to the back of the house. He told one of Gloucester's henchmen who took a couple of his companions and followed after the servant. He was probably trying to get away to inform Clarence. Laurence decided to follow and supervise the search in that part of the house. He had a real need for the lady Anne to be found.

He entered what was the kitchen and saw that the serving man was standing protectively in front of the cook and her female staff. All of them were terrified with no idea what was happening. One of them was clearly hysterical as the serving man was holding her head into his shoulder where the poor woman was sobbing. It was soon clear that there was nobody else there and they left to get on with the search. Laurence posted one of the men as a guard to ensure no other could sneak into a part of the house that had been searched.

The sounds of shouts and female hysterics could be heard and Laurence wondered if the lady had been found in the family chambers. Apparently not and it was with a face like thunder that Gloucester came down and stood in the hall. One by one his men returned and declared the house had only those who were supposed to be there. Sir John stood in his former place on the stairs gloating in satisfaction. His serving man returned and stood next to him holding his cudgel aggressively now that his master had the upper hand. Tyrell came down and looking at the duke shook his head hopelessly.

Gloucester stood in silence, glaring at Laurence under hooded eyes. Clearly he was going to be blamed for the fiasco, yet he had been so sure the lady would be here. He frantically looked around the entrance hall hoping to see something that would help – a secret passage, perhaps. Then he noticed something. The serving man with Sir John was on his own. The other, he remembered had remained in the kitchen with the cook and her servants. There was something odd about that. Shouldn't he be here with his master, as the other lout was? Perhaps there was somewhere in the kitchen that hadn't been properly searched. It was a faint hope but a last try was better than nothing.

"Your grace," he said tremulously. "There is still one place I believe was not searched properly."

"What do you mean, we have been into every room, nook and cranny," threw back Gloucester angrily.

"Yet there is something I have thought of, if your grace will permit?"

"Where do you propose to look?"

"The kitchen." As he said it he knew he had hit on something. Sir John had stiffened and the serving man gripped the cudgel tightly, his knuckles showing white. The duke sensed it too.

"Lead on," said the duke firmly.

Laurence addressed the pike man who guarded the door to the kitchen. "Has anyone entered or left here?" he asked him.

"Not a soul," was the reply. That meant Sir John's other lout was still in there.

He pushed back the door and entered by way of a short passage into the kitchen. Tyrell followed behind and duke Richard brought up the rear. The serving man must have heard them coming and had the kitchen staff bundled into a corner where he stood protectively before them. Laurence looked around the room. It was built entirely of brick and even a cursory glance made it certain that there was nowhere that could conceal a secret opening. The only place that was obscured was immediately behind the huddled servants. It was the last chance of finding a place of concealment. He stood before the serving man who showed no inclination to move, but clearly was suffering from nerves. His eyes had lost the arrogance they had when he first searched the kitchen. He reached out and attempted to thrust the man aside. The lout took hold of his arm and began to wrestle Laurence back. Both men struggled for a moment before they both lost balance and fell over. The women servants screamed in panic and fled leaving just one who had been pressed up against the wall at the back. She stood there in confusion, a small girl with her long fair hair plaited over her shoulder.

"Anne!" cried the duke of Gloucester triumphantly. The servant girl flung herself sobbing into his arms. Tyrell looked at her in astonishment. It was indeed the lady Anne Neville dressed as a kitchen servant. The serving lout crawled away under a convenient table while Laurence scrambled to his feet. The young couple embraced and Tyrell had to grunt a warning in Richard's ear.

"We should leave quickly, your grace."

"Quite so, Sir James." He turned to Laurence. "I owe you a great debt, master armourer; you shall not find me ungrateful."

"We have still to get my lady clear of this house," Laurence reminded him. With that, duke Richard took the lady Anne by the hand and led her from her captivity. Outside he mounted his horse and Sir James Tyrell lifted the lady behind him where she clung to him.

Laurence felt a tug at his sleeve. It was Cornelius who had been patiently waiting outside.

"Yes, we found her," he said, "but can we keep her." Already the sound of galloping horsemen was heard coming along Old Fish Street. It could only be Clarence's men. They would have to get away swiftly. The duke of Gloucester trotted off with the lady Anne in the direction of St. Paul's churchyard followed closely by Tyrell. Laurence got Cornelius onto his horse them mounted himself. The troop would deliberately lag behind Gloucester and Tyrell to slow down any pursuit. It wasn't long before they were caught up with.

Laurence was near the front of the troop, which turned to confront Clarence's men. He noted that half a dozen or so pursuers turned off and were riding with the intent of cutting off duke Richard, who he knew was heading for the sanctuary of St. Martin le Grande somewhere on the other side of St Paul's. Leaving the troop to deal with the main body, he galloped off in pursuit when, to his dismay, Cornelius followed. Clarence's men had cut off the duke of Gloucester just at the entrance to Fauster Lane, a short distance from the safety of sanctuary. Gloucester and Tyrell rode straight for the troop, which numbered six men. They held their ground and Gloucester was forced to stop for fear of the lady Anne coming to harm. Screaming "A Gloucester" and brandishing his sword on high, Laurence galloped his horse straight at their flank, with Cornelius behind, his cloak flying looking for all the world like a demon. They had charged out of a side street and the hostile troop had no idea how many were following. Gloucester and Tyrell rode at them too, which caused Clarence's men to break and ride off. Gloucester gave Laurence a grateful wave and trotted towards the sanctuary of St. Martin le Grande, the diminutive form of the lady Anne Neville clinging on behind him, her blond plait tossed carelessly by the rhythm of the horse.

Chapter 12 – The Outcast

Laurence and Cornelius were both contemplating that it might have been easier to confront a dozen of Clarence's henchmen than the angry young woman they were now facing.

"You would have me in the same condition as the lady Anne Neville," she spat at them, "where I had lost my husband and my father at once!"

"We had no choice," ventured Laurence. "We were ordered by his grace of Gloucester."

"I cannot think that his grace would order a man of my father's years into battle," she returned sharply.

"Lord Wenlock was well into his seventies at the battle of Tewksbury," argued Laurence.

"Yes, and he was riven from skull to chops," she returned.

"Our exploit was hardly a battle, daughter," said Cornelius placatingly, "besides, I was left outside . . ."

"Where you could have been murdered when Clarence's men came along," she interrupted. Clearly the two men were not going to get the better of the argument, but the issue had been resolved now and she would calm down eventually.

Joan stamped her foot and flounced into a chair at the table in the apothecary's shop. She had been up all night pacing the floor having no news of where they were. Gloucester had not allowed them to send out any kind of message for fear it would be intercepted by Clarence. They all knew it was the sensible thing to do, but it had caused Joan to worry about them. While they had told her of the search and rescue of the lady Anne, neither felt it necessary to tell her of the final charge, when the two of them had hurled themselves towards Clarence's henchmen. Their desperate strategy had worked, though if Clarence's men had decided to fight, things might well have turned out as Joan feared.

She grabbed at a pestle and started pounding away in a mortar at something she was concocting. Mother Malkin was seated quietly at the far end of the table, keeping silent in what was a family dispute. A pregnant silence followed, only to be broken by someone coming into the outer shop. Joan went to see who it was.

They heard her give a familiar greeting, replied to by a gruff male voice then Joan returned clutching a letter, which she handed to her father. Cornelius broke the seal and read the contents. Presently he sat back, his brows knit in deep thought.

"I hope you are not contemplating more distractions," muttered Joan as she pounded vigorously with the pestle into the mortar.

"For once, daughter, the king's business and our own are in harmony." She regarded him with a doubtful expression. "We know that in June, the Tudors escaped from Tenby, where they were holed up, and landed in Brittany where they are in the care of duke Francis. They arrived at the port of Le Coquet and were taken to Brest. After that the king lost track of them." Cornelius smiled quietly to himself. "Apparently, duke Francis has welcomed them kindly, no doubt conscious of their value to king Edward. The king, though, is keen to get them back. He is offering a large reward. King Louis XI of France is also asking to take them into his protection so it seems the situation is uncertain. King Edward is most concerned and he requires me to discover the exact whereabouts of the Tudors, and which way duke Francis is likely to turn."

"Why you in particular?" asked Joan with some annoyance. Cornelius regarded her with self-satisfied humour.

"Through my contacts at Tenby, the king knows I had the Tudors, Jasper and Henry, diverted to Brittany. Edward thinks I can discover where the Tudors are now. Duke Francis has not been exactly forthcoming with specific information. Louis has sent a delegation to Brittany meaning that the French are seriously planning to get hold of the final Lancastrian hope. Edward would rather have the whelp Henry back in England where he can keep him secure, but if that is not possible, he needs to know the Tudor is secure in exile."

"The king must know our immediate plans are to go to Brittany ourselves," mused Laurence, "where Joan and I shall be married. Once there we will be well placed to find out exactly what is to happen with the Tudors."

"You can leave from Southampton in just a few days, if you bustle," said Cornelius. "There is a vessel bound for Brest that will take you as passengers. That is where the Tudors were last seen, so ask around and see what you can discover. Then you can go to

Nantes either by land, or down the coast by sea. I shall give you a letter to present to either duke Francis or his close advisor and chancellor, Guillaume Chauvin."

"Are you sure you will not come too?" Joan inserted. Her father had his business to attend to in London and could not go with them, though he dearly wished to.

"I cannot, daughter, but I shall miss your skills around the shop."

"You might have done, father, but we now have a further concern." Joan nodded to Mother Malkin. "Are we to turn Mother out into the street?" Neither Cornelius nor Laurence had given that any thought. Laurence was surprised that Joan wanted to take responsibility for the crone. The beldam had barely been in the house a couple of days, yet Joan was already regarding her as part of the household. There was also the possibility she would place some sort of charm on the house. Perhaps she had already enchanted Joan, otherwise why should she move to protect the crone after such a short acquaintance?

"What are you thinking on, daughter?"

"I have an idea which should benefit us all." Joan stopped her mixing, put down the mortar and stood beside Mother Malkin. "This dame has much skill with simples and cures," she said. "I have been talking to her about her travels with the army and she knows how to treat illness and injury in ways I had not thought on." Laurence began to worry that the old crone might have mentioned his relationship with Anna, but Joan's demeanour argued against that.

"Can you understand what she is saying?" he asked, astonished that anyone could comprehend the weird cackling that passed for speech.

"Mainly yes. Sometimes I have to ask her to repeat what she says, but once you get used to her accent she can be understood. She has some strange names for the herbs and plants we use for healing, but I can identify these when she points them out. We have a large herb garden here, which requires attention. It is where we grow many of the simples for our cures. Mother can tend the garden while we are away, with the help of Jennet, but even more, she can mix up the usual remedies our customers come here for."

"Does she have the skill, though?" mused Cornelius, clearly considering the idea.

239

"Mother has much experience not only in making up remedies, but in surgery, too. I have spoken to her at length and I feel sure she would be of great advantage to us."

Laurence remembered how the old woman had dealt with illness and injury on the great march. Certainly she had much skill, and as a bonesetter had been in demand by the common soldiery, amongst whom the word of her cures and treatments soon spread. There was nothing focused the mind more than pain, nor more appreciative of its relief. Then he recalled the words of Anna, who had suggested such a course to him after they had extracted the crone from the mire of the river Thames. The least said about that the better, yet it was strange how Joan had immediately come to the same conclusion. It was almost as if the two women were in collusion, but he knew that was not possible.

"She has few needs, mainly a proper roof over her head. Jennet can take care of the housekeeping."

"Yet how do we know all her cures come from the use of simples and such?" he persisted doubtfully. "For all we know, she might use her cunning powers to help her. Would you risk the house being tainted with the suspicion of magic or worse?" The thought had come to him that Joan might come under some malevolent influence as reward for her charity.

"I have some knowledge of cures myself," replied Joan, suppressing her annoyance at his attitude, though she understood he was being quite reasonable. There were even some in her father's trade who practiced the black arts to be sure. "Her skill is quite genuine; she has no need of enchantment. I believe there is a clear advantage to us leaving her here. It is far better than leaving father with the extra work until we return."

Cornelius, who had been listening to the exchange, nodded his head in agreement with Joan. He had been concerned about running the shop for the couple of months they would be away. Mostly people called with relatively minor ailments that could be served with the potions and herbs mixed by Joan. The apothecary personally attended wealthy patients at their own homes, so he often spent time away from the house when called by sickness or some other more discreet matter applicable to the king's government. Then there was the likelihood that contrary winds this late in the year might delay the couple's return possibly until the spring. It was something that he had been thinking on and Joan's suggestion brought him much relief. Almost as if fate was taking a hand, that moment someone entered the front shop and Joan went to attend them. She soon returned and asked Mother Malkin to come to her.

"We have a boy with a shoulder out-of-joint to tend," she said. "Mother is an excellent bonesetter and here is her first patient." The old woman, who had been listening stoically to the discussion regarding her fate, grinned her joy at being called on to tend the injured boy and trotted along behind Joan into the front shop.

"Well, it looks as if things are decided," said Cornelius. Laurence could only indicate his agreement with a casual shrug of his shoulders.

* * *

Nicholas Olds was fatalistic about Laurence's departure from the forges at the Tower of London. He had resigned himself to the loss of a potentially profitable craftsman. Even the king had casually enquired of the French armourer who had given earl Rivers his warrior armour and the duke of Gloucester his modified pauldron. Small issues it was true, but the skill of the Frenchman was apparent to all those who had sought him out to modify or repair their harness. He had detected there was more to what he thought of as the Frenchman than simply his trade, and it was with some relief that he accepted his decision to return to Brittany to marry. Of course, Laurence had informed him of his intention to return to England and set up business independently but that would be some months hence, if at all, and much could alter in these times. Nicholas Olds was not one to worry about a projection of the future that would most likely never arrive. For now he would clap him on the shoulder and wish him all happiness in his marriage and his prospects for the future.

John Fisher and Will Belknap wished him joy in his new wife. Both were highly amused to discover what they chose to believe had been a clandestine love affair. Laurence tried to explain that it had only been circumstances and his constant adventures away from the forges that had prevented him telling them of Joan, but he soon gave up trying to convince them.

241

"Is she with child?" chortled Will with a sly wink while John grinned at him waiting expectantly for what he was sure would be a reply in the affirmative. Laurence stuttered a denial, his tongue stumbling by the knowledge of his real secret, that it was Anna who was carrying his child. This only served to convince the two that they were right in their appraisal. He made arrangements for John to care for his tools until he returned. Taking a fond leave of his friends, he went to the Tower stables where he settled his account for the stabling of his horse. He then saddled up and rode back to the apothecary's shop where he had prepared a stall for the mare in the stable there. Cornelius promised to exercise her, though when he went any distance on business he usually rode a mule side-saddle to accommodate his gown and keep the hem from the mire of the road.

They had made arrangements to go to Southampton along with a company of merchants who had with them a small band of armed men. Laurence would be carrying a substantial purse and he could not risk a swift but hazardous journey in lesser company. Joan would ride in one of the wagons while he would ride a hired mule belonging to one of the mercers who was returning to Southampton having sold his imported cloths in London. They assembled near to London Bridge and the young couple, along with Cornelius went into the nearby church of St. Magnus to pray together for a safe journey. As the wagons, horses and mules set off they left Cornelius at the end of London Bridge and he was soon lost to sight as they crossed between the shops and houses where there was a confused throng of people, horses and carts of all description. They left the bridge under an array of heads spiked on the top of the bridge gate. Laurence resisted the temptation to look to up see if there were any he could still recognise. Soon they were pushing on through the hovels of Southwark and then, having passed the Tabard Inn, took to the open highway.

* * *

The quayside at Brest was full of noise from the cry of seabirds constantly on the lookout for scraps to the noise of seamen and merchants busily chattering and gesticulating with each other. Laurence and Joan stood together waiting while their chattels were unloaded from the ship that had brought them from Southampton. Laurence saw that a merchant was checking over the heaps of goods in barrels and chests that had already come from the hold of the ship. He decided to engage him in conversation to get some local news before they travelled onwards to Nantes. It was as well he did so. He learned that duke Francis had moved the court to his chateau at Suscinio, further down the Atlantic coast. That meant his father would probably be there also. He wondered if his mother had gone with him. Their main business was at Nantes and it was unlikely the whole family would have followed the duke to Suscinio. The merchant told him of a tavern where they could get a room while they decided what to do next.

"In a way," said Laurence, "it is fortunate that the duke has moved to Suscinio. It is not so far as Nantes. We should be able to find a vessel here to take us down the coast. It is barely a day's sailing."

Joan pulled a face. She had not enjoyed the voyage to Brest hating the strict confines of the ship and the sullen glances of the sailors who were always nervous when a woman was aboard. She had been sick at first but recovered somewhat after a couple of days though her stomach had never entirely come to terms with the sea. Soon they were busy extracting their belongings from the rest of the goods coming from the ship. Laurence found a paysan with a donkey cart and he guided them to the tavern recommended by the merchant, Le Lapin Triste. Le patron, well used to the requirements of casual travellers, let them place their belongings into a secure locker by his living space. Having paid for their lodging the couple went across the street to where a small chapel stood, clearly well positioned for serving the fishermen and seamen of the harbour.

The door creaked open and they kneeled before a statue of the Virgin and gave thanks for their deliverance from the sea and asked her blessing on their continuing journey. They lit a votive candle and as they turned to go, a short man, tonsured and dressed in priestly habit emerged from behind a screen and greeted them.

"Good day," he smiled at them. "It is not often we have persons of quality visit our humble chapel." Joan was flattered to be called such though Laurence accepted the accolade with aplomb. The priest spoke well, though his accent was overlaid with the patois of the region. His habit was threadbare and his feet, which protruded from the hem of the garment, were bare. Laurence offered him a coin, which he took with great pleasure and dropped into the scuffed leather purse he wore at his belt. He asked them about themselves, politely curious without probing too deeply into their business. Laurence decided it might be a good idea to ask him if he knew anything of the Tudors, who must have passed through Brest from Le Coquet.

"There were two such as you describe," he said after a few moments consideration. They were met in the market here by duke Francis' men and went off with them. We wondered who they were and all that is known is they had escaped from Edward of England."

"You have no idea where they were taken?" Laurence asked.

"No, except they were escorted by men in duke Francis' livery so I assume they were taken to him." The priest stood as if in thought. "There is something that was curious, though."

"What was that?"

"Two days or so later a man was heard asking questions, much as you are, in the taverns and inns of the town. I suppose he was told that which I have told you and he disappeared. However, it was reported by a local paysan that a troop of horsemen without livery were encamped in the woods just outside town. They too disappeared at the same time the enquirer did, so I presume they were together."

"Thank you father. We are on our way to duke Francis as soon as we can find a vessel to take us down to Suscinio. I shall pass on the information you have given me." The priest beamed with pleasure.

"I am pleased to be of service to the duke. May God go with you," he intoned as he blessed them.

"Did you understand that?" he asked Joan. Her French had been rudimentary but in the few weeks since their betrothal he had been coaching her and her ear had improved much. However, she now had the same problem that had plagued him in England. His was cultured French while that of the priest was Breton French and difficult for an untuned ear to interpret.

"I think I caught most of it," she said doubtfully. "If the Tudor's were taken away by duke Francis, then who were the others?"

"They might have been Edward's men," mused Laurence.

244

"Possibly, but surely we would have been informed if there were any such after the Tudors?"

"Yes, your father would have told us so we could make contact. We must assume they are king Louis' men. He also wishes to get the Tudors out of Brittany."

"We must inform the duke as soon as possible," she said resignedly. "It looks as if we might be embroiled in another of king Edward's problems. Shall we never marry?"

"Once we reach Suscinio we can unburden ourselves and attend to our own business for once."

"Oh, I do hope so, my love," she whispered.

* * *

The sail down to the small port of Suscinio was rough and the small coastal vessel had tossed and pitched on the choppy waves causing both a return of sea-sickness. To add to the misery, Laurence began to worry that his father might not be with the duke; he had made the assumption he would be, knowing that Simon de la Halle usually followed the duke as he moved around the country, but that did not mean he would always do so. He consoled himself with the thought that if his father was not at Suscinio then they could continue down the coast and up the Loire river directly into Nantes. He dreaded what Joan's reaction would be to that idea. In any case, they must go to Suscinio first because he had the letter from Cornelius to deliver to the duke, so the decision had really been taken out of his hands.

They sat together outside a small inn by the quay in the weak sunshine of the forenoon each with a comforting cup of wine, their baggage heaped by. He had decided to send to the chateau with a message for his father, rather than chance a problem with the duke's guard should they turn up unannounced. The chateau was close to the harbour within easy walking distance. They watched as supplies and victuals were loaded into carts to be trundled away clearly intended for the garrison.

Presently they heard a shout and Laurence got quickly to his feet. His father was hurrying down the road to the harbour, his robe flowing around him and the brightly coloured ribbons of his hat

245

flying. The two men embraced and gripping their extended arms appraised one another.

"You are looking well, my son. It seems England has been good to you."

"It has father, rather better than I expected." Laurence turned to Joan who had stood up close behind him. Simon gazed at her, his face alight with pleasure. Before his son had the chance to make an introduction Simon spoke.

"You are Joan, of course," he said gaily. "I had expected that my son would choose a beautiful woman, but you exceed my expectations." Joan blushed and bobbed him a greeting. Simon held out his hands and took hers, gazing happily into her eyes. "I cannot wait to show you off to our family and friends," he said.

"You do me much honour, sir," she replied, slightly overwhelmed by the enthusiasm of his greeting. Simon lifted her hand and kissed it. Laurence grinned at her.

"Remember, he is a Frenchman, it is my mother who is English."

"Come, let me escort you up to the chateau." Simon offered her his arm. "There is not much room, I'm afraid, with the duke being in residence, but I shall find somewhere to squeeze you in. My wife, Laurence's mother is not here, of course. She is not fond of being cramped in a ducal chateau, no matter how grand, when she can command freely her own household. I shall request permission from the duke to go to Nantes with you for your marriage and I have no doubt it will be granted." His father was clearly charmed and for the moment it was as if Laurence was no longer there. With a huge grin on his face he followed them along the road to the chateau.

The chateau of Suscinio stood within a set of earthworks. Inside the earthworks a moat surrounded the chateau, which was accessed by a single bridge that ended with a gap that was crossed by lowering a drawbridge at the gate. Guards in the livery of Brittany stood at both ends of the bridge. They had to wait while a troop of richly caparisoned horsemen trotted over the drawbridge from the gatehouse and galloped away into the country. The guards knew Simon so they had no trouble crossing the stone bridge and wooden drawbridge. Simon had instructed one of the loungers around the harbour to bring their possessions on a handcart and the small group entered through the gate. The chateau comprised a series of round towers linked by walls of apartments for the many retainers and guests. The stone was washed with lime and shone white in the autumn sun. There was no donjon but a large palacial building dominated the north-east range that blended into a huge round tower topped, as the other towers, with a conical roof of blue slate. The courtyard was spacious but crowded with horses and men gaily dressed in court dress, their servants running to and fro according to the demands of their masters.

Simon led them to the base of one of the towers and took them inside. It was on the first floor where Simon had his quarters in a small chamber and he informed them they could have that while he found a place for himself with the duke's retainers in the great hall. Fresh rushes were on the floor and there was a capacious bed and a large locked chest in which Simon kept his belongings.

"You are most generous, sir," said Joan thankfully. "I fear we are depriving you of your own accommodation."

"Not at all, my dear," he replied. "I spend a good deal of my time between the armoury and the great hall so it is no hardship for me to sleep there. In any case we shall depart for Nantes in a few days, so please make yourself as comfortable as possible." While Joan busied herself taking her gowns and dresses from the chests and smoothing out any creases, the two men stepped out into the courtyard to talk.

"I understand master Quirke has given you a letter for the duke's attention?"

"Yes, it is sealed but I think it concerns the whereabouts of Jasper and Henry Tudor. We know they are somewhere in Brittany in the care of the duke, and Edward wants Henry returned to England. Do you have any idea where the Tudors are?"

Simon raised an eyebrow and smiled. "As a matter of fact I do; they are over there," and he pointed across the courtyard to where several courtiers stood casually chatting together. "He in the blue gown is Henry; Jasper is the one in scarlet doublet and hose. Laurence studied the two men carefully. Jasper was of medium height and thick-set. He was clean-shaven and wore a black tapered acorn hat over his dark brown hair. Henry seemed to be of slight build, according to the way the gown hung from his drooping shoulders. His face was thin with a tight drawn mouth and slender neck. Long brown hair descended from under a plain cap that was embellished with a jewelled medallion. Laurence could not help but compare him to Richard duke of Gloucester. He too was spare of frame but whereas Richard was lean and strong, Henry looked bookish and more of a clerk than a fighting noble. If this was the bastard Lancastrian hope, then king Edward of England had little to fear from him.

"From what I can see he hardly deserves king Edward's attention," said Laurence.

"I think it is more the capacity for the French king to do mischief than any danger the youth might present by himself," replied Simon. "There is a delegation from king Louis here right now. The French have been appealing duke Francis to place Henry in their hands so he can be taken to France. Henry, it seems, is more than willing to comply with the French. He fears that there is always a chance a request from Edward might persuade his grace to return him to England."

"And duke Francis, what are his thoughts?"

"He is likely to keep hold of Henry for now. He fears the ambition of Louis XI of France and Edward's desire for his return to England means duke Francis can play one king against the other."

"So there seems to be an impasse?"

Simon nodded and sighed hopelessly. "I shall take your letter to the duke's chancellor, Guillaume Chauvin. Hopefully the information it contains will free us up. I have no wish to become embroiled in the duke's schemes. Your mother will not approve if there is any delay in her meeting your bride."

"Your timely information gives us cause for great concern," said Guillaume Chauvin. "It informs us that there is a French plan to get Henry Tudor out of Brittany and into France, should king Louis' diplomatic appeal fail. That it will fail, I can tell you, is almost certain." He was standing apart in a corner of the great hall of the chateau with Simon and Laurence de la Halle. The hall was buzzing with sound from the muted hum of conversation to the persistent scratching of pen on parchment as a multitude of clerks scribbled away at the tables around the hall. The ducal throne was empty at the moment, duke Francis being in his private apartments, which meant that there was a crowd of courtiers and petitioners waiting for audience.

248

"Do you think, my lord, that such a plan is possible?" said Simon. "I know that the Tudors are not imprisoned here but the chateau is quite secure. I am sure that they will not be allowed out without an escort."

"You are probably right, but at least now we can take greater care of our guests than was our wont," replied Chauvin pointedly. He turned to Laurence and clapped him on the shoulder. "Many thanks for your help in this, monsieur. His grace tells me he has need of your father for one or two days, then you are both given leave for Nantes. Please avail yourself of the duke's hospitality in the meantime and I expect it will not be long before you are on your way."

"Many thanks, my lord. My lady will be most glad, though that is not to say we are ungrateful for our accommodation here, but for a lady there are matters of greater importance." Chauvin laughed with them. Simon and Laurence bowed to the chancellor and backed away while he turned around and walked into a throng of courtiers who immediately surrounded him, clamouring their appeals.

* * *

The countryside around the chateau at Suscinio was breathtakingly beautiful, even at this late time of year when the leaves were falling in abundance from the trees. It seemed to the couple riding together in the morning that the slanting rays of the sun were exposing nature through her bright vestments of colour. Just the lightest breeze caused a swirl of brilliance about their heads and their horses kicked up golden leaves as they made their way through the trees. They had been at the chateau two days and Laurence had managed to persuade the duke's master of horse to lend them a couple of mounts. As there were always horses that needed to be exercised that was a small matter and this afternoon they were riding in the woods that were all around. Soon they emerged above pasture where skeins of wood smoke drifted from the autumn fires in and around the cottages of the paysan farmers. It seemed as if the whole of Brittany was laid out before them.

Below them was a road that wended its way through the countryside, connecting village with chateau and town. Lesser pathways diverged towards the farms and hovels of the paysans. They brought their mounts close together then leaned across and kissed each other. Tomorrow they would be on their way to Nantes and their wedding and neither of them could bear to wait any longer. Though their union had been consummated and the legal niceties complied with, yet they both felt that the blessing of the Church was necessary to complete them as a couple. Joan was eager to meet Laurence's family who were prosperous artisans with good future prospects in which they would bring up their children.

Suddenly, Laurence stiffened in the saddle and fixed his gaze on a spot below and to the left of them.

"See there," he said and pointed to a corner of the woods above the road. "Is that a troop of about ten horsemen?" Joan looked to where he was pointing.

"I do believe it is," she replied in a puzzled tone. "Why are they lurking there? I suspect they are up to no good."

"It's too close to the chateau for brigands," he murmured, thinking out loud. "I cannot see any livery; they are plainly dressed and armed too." He felt for the sword at his side. Nobody rode abroad unarmed, but his sword was a light one, intended for defence in a town, not for battle with armed horsemen. Just then there was further movement as a group of horsemen in bright courtly dress casually emerged from between the trees that screened them from the chateau. They had pages running on foot along with them.

"There is a hawking party, I think," said Laurence. "Surely they are not about to be attacked. For one thing they are unlikely to be carrying much in the way of plunder."

"Isn't that the Tudor with them?" said Joan, squinting her eyes to get a better view. Laurence studied the group and picked out the slender frame of Henry Tudor and the thicker set of Jasper, his uncle.

"I do believe you are right." Suddenly he recalled what the priest at Brest had told them. There had been a mysterious troop of riders who he suspected were searching for Tudor. They too had been lurking in the woods outside the town. Could this be the same group?

"We need to alert the garrison as Suscinio. I believe these are about to take the Tudors away. The French delegation left yesterday, having failed to negotiate the Tudor's release to them. This must be the part of the plan your father got wind of!" As they turned their horses, one of the troop spotted the movement and pointed them out to the others. Laurence had intended to return to the chateau by the way they had come through the woods, but now they had been seen, a better plan would be to ride directly by a pathway he had noted by the fringe of the woods, taking them down the hill to where the hawking party were sporting, still unaware of the danger. Laurence urged his horse onward closely followed by Joan, riding side-saddle.

One who seemed to be in command of the strange troop sent a couple of riders across the fields to cut them off. This attracted the notice of the hawking party, which was thrown into confusion. The Tudors, who were clearly ready for the situation, suddenly galloped away from their companions. The remaining riders of the foreign troop burst out of their concealment and galloped down the hill to place themselves between the Tudors and their erstwhile companions. Laurence realised that the Tudors would need time to get clear away and disappear into the countryside before pursuit could be organised. The hawking party were turning to face the threat from their attackers and were unable to send for immediate help. That meant it was essential for Laurence along with Joan to get word to the chateau. The two soldiers who were galloping to cut them off from the chateau realised this too and were closing in fast. It would be impossible to get by them without a fight and he noted, with alarm, they had lances. His only weapon was his sword; he had no shield or armour meaning it was impossible to defend himself from the lancers, and he had Joan to protect too!

His brain racing, he stopped while Joan caught up then directed her into the trees. It would take them away from the chateau, but the lancers could not charge at them as effectively as they could in the open pasture. The tangle of undergrowth meant the couple could not gallop or even trot safely without danger of being unhorsed. The two lancers had entered the wood also and were closing in on them, their horses being heavier and more able to burst through the bracken, though their lances were now of less use. The two horsemen had spaced out intending to take them from two sides. Laurence remembered there had been a granite outcrop in the wood where rock was heaped on rock and covered in moss. He had

251

fancied it to be a fairy spot and shied away from it earlier, but now it might offer some refuge. He pushed Joan ahead of him to where he thought the rocks to be.

They got there just ahead of the lancers. A bush was growing from a niche in the rocks above his head. Laurence reached up and hauled himself onto a ledge, kicking free of the stirrups while his horse skittered away. Hanging on to a branch, he reached down and took Joan by her uplifted arms and pulled her up behind him. Just then the lancers burst through the bracken and skidded to a halt at the base of the rocks. Laurence and Joan scrambled higher, just out of reach of the stabbing points of the lances. Laurence had entertained the thought that now they were, in fact, neutralised so far as raising the alarm was concerned, the lancers would be content to remain where they were, thus preventing them climbing down. The two men circled their horses in consternation then, throwing down their lances, got down from their mounts and began to climb the rocks. Both had drawn their long-bladed murderers and clamped them between their teeth.

The places where purchase could be made on the slippery rock were limited and this meant that the two men had to climb more or less together until they managed to get higher, when they could spread out. Laurence drew his sword and looked around for anything else that might be used as a weapon. He found a small boulder, which he lifted and heaved down on the pair. They ducked out of the way, but one of them lost his grip and tumbled over the stones and fell to the ground. He was holding on to his foot and grimacing in pain so it seemed he had damaged something. The other threw himself onto a ledge and shouted down to his companion, who waved him on upwards. That had reduced the odds, but the second man was well armed and clearly unwilling to give up until his victims had been dealt with. There could be no doubt that both would be murdered if he got within striking distance. Laurence would expect to put up a fight, but he had Joan with him. He needed to get her into a safe position where he could defend her without her being in danger of harm. He had spotted a crevice in the rocks just a little higher. He could place her in there and take up a position in front, but that would severely hamper his movements. He could never move away without exposing her. However, the ledge in front of the crevice was narrow so that meant his attacker could not come in from the side and drive him away from Joan.

They scrambled upwards, Joan in front, when suddenly she lost her footing on the slippery moss. Her right leg dropped into a crack between the rocks and she cried out, her face frightened and twisted in pain. Laurence lifted her skirt and pulled her leg out. It was badly lacerated and he could not tell if it was broken or not. She leaned against the rock face unable to put weight on the injured leg. Frantically, he looked around and found a stout length of broken branch that had fallen from one of the bushes whose roots found a precarious home in cracks and crevices. With his sword, he hacked away superfluous branches until he had a rough staff. She took it for support and nodded through gritted teeth for them to go on.

When they reached the spot he had been aiming for, they found they had to cross what amounted to a stone bridge across a deep split in the rock. It did not seem very secure and he thought he detected movement as he crossed onto the tiny ledge in front of the crevice. He reached out and helped Joan across, supported by her staff. He installed her in the crevice, then, with sword drawn, stood at bay waiting for their nemesis who could be heard scrambling up towards them.

Laurence immediately recognised the type of fellow who appeared over the lip of the rocks. Any army was full of them, mercenaries, desperate men who depended not on the meagre pay of a soldier, but plunder and pillage. They casually murdered men, women and children. Women in particular were subjected to rape before having their throats cut. Laurence's heart lurched, not from the thought of danger to himself, but for Joan who, once he had been removed, would be helpless. It was one such as this who had broken into the shop of the apothecary in London and sooner or later he would meet a similar fate, but for now the mercenary had the upper hand. He wore a helmet, a salet of a quality that meant he had plundered it from some battle or fight. He also had on a breastplate and Laurence knew he had little chance of causing him serious injury. He drew from his scabbard a heavy sword with a length that outdistanced Laurence's reach by nearly a foot.

He stopped and glared at them, quickly appraising their situation and recognising their helplessness. Clearly an experienced mercenary, he did not charge immediately to attack but took his time. Such men survived by making sure their victims were helpless and no harm to themselves before despatching them. He drew the dagger from between his teeth and clutched it in his left hand. Laurence drew his own dagger, a small blade just six inches long. The fellow laughed when he saw it, but Laurence did not intend it for a *main gauche* but handed it behind him to Joan. It was no defence, but she could take her own life if it came to it. That was the only choice he could offer her. He took the staff from her. It was much longer than his sword and he had the idea he could fend off the fellow who had to approach across the narrow way, though it would be cumbersome in the confines of the small ledge. He placed his sword ready to hand against the rock face and gripping the staff in both hands waited for the attack.

The fellow spread his legs for balance and edged onto the stone bridge his sword ready. He tried a couple of lunges, which Laurence easily parried, knowing his enemy was merely testing him. Suddenly the man leapt forward and struck heavily hoping to take Laurence by surprise. It almost worked and Laurence barely managed to parry the blow. He knew he would not be so lucky the next time. The mercenary attacked again immediately giving his opponent little time to recover but he managed to parry this blow too. The man edged closer, his cold eyes glittering fiercely. Laurence knew the situation was hopeless, yet there was one more thing he could try. He jammed the end of his staff into a crack in the side of the stone bridge and, using it as a lever, heaved on it. The bridge began to slide sideways and the mercenary, realising his danger, tried to step backwards but lost his balance. The stone bridge slipped into the split in the rock taking the man with it. This dislodged further rocks and soon boulders were crashing all around the fellow who was carried down to be crushed against the ground, a great boulder across his pelvis. His screams were hideous in the quiet of the woods and it was clear he was not going to die easily. Joan stood with her hand to her mouth in shock. Laurence took her in his arms and gazed down. Then the realisation came to him they were trapped. They were about thirty feet up on a tiny ledge with no way down now the stone had carried away their means of descent.

Then, to make matters worse, the mercenary's companion came limping into view leading their horses. He looked to his companion and realising there was nothing he could do to help him, took out his dagger and slit his throat, thus silencing him forever. He was about to mount his horse and ride off when he looked up and spotted the young couple trapped on the ledge above. He paused for a moment looking down at his companion then took from the saddle of his horse a crossbow. Laurence and Joan were both horrified. They were as rats in a barrel with no possibility of escape. The crevice was far too narrow for them to squeeze back into though Laurence had the idea that if he could jam them both into the crevice, with Joan behind him, though shot through he might not fall away. He thrust the staff into the ground and laid it across the crevice and into a crack hoping that would prevent his falling away. The mercenary could not get to her and sooner or later she would be found.

Slowly, as if relishing his moment of revenge, the mercenary took a number of quarrels from his supply and pushed their points into the ground in front of him. Next he took the pulley and hooked the cord of the prod and wound it back until it latched into the trigger. Slowly he removed the pulley and placed a quarrel into the weapon. He lifted the crossbow and took sight. Laurence braced himself for a hit and muttered a prayer to St Barbara for the last time, fingering the reliquary he always carried around his neck. Behind him he could hear Joan sobbing hysterically.

He heard the snap of the bow as it released its missile and wondered why he had not been hit. Something had sent splinters of rock into his face and it was only the strike of the quarrel that could have done it. The fellow was either a bad shot or was playing with them. He looked down and saw the mercenary standing with his mouth wide open in surprise, an arrow protruding from his chest. Slowly he collapsed almost gently into a soft bed of leaves.

* * *

"It took you long enough to get us down," Laurence complained jokily.

"Have you ever tried getting a forty-foot siege ladder through a dense wood?" grinned his companion. "We got you down before

255

dark, so thank the saints otherwise you might have been up there all night." The speaker was Jean Marquand, captain of the duke's own guard.

"I have never been good on ladders, but I must confess I was grateful to shin down yours." Laurence was in buoyant mood in the aftermath of his and Joan's brush with death. She was sitting beside him with her leg stretched out before her. It was not broken, but her ankle had been badly twisted and her skin grazed. Both were laughing with their rescuers and only later when the full realisation of what had happened came to them would they become quiet and reflective. They were sitting in an anteroom of the great hall themselves the object of great interest to the court. Several courtiers had engaged them with questions as to what had occurred. Their brief adventure had been better than any arranged entertainment. It had been a company of Jean Marquand's men who were attracted by the screams of the injured mercenary. One of their ancients, seeing what was happening and recognising Simon de la Halle's son, sent an arrow from his crossbow into the chest of the man just as he fired. The ancient's quarrel struck a split second before the other fellow released his, which was enough to deflect his aim.

"How were you able to get to us so quickly?" Laurence asked. "We thought we were the only ones who could warn the chateau garrison what was happening." The ancient, who was sitting with them interjected:

"If you recall your conversation with Chancellor Chauvin, he did say he would be watching the Tudors more carefully."

"Yet they were riding in the countryside with a lightly armed group of hawkers whose attention was on their sport?"

"That is so, but following at a discreet distance were the duke's own guard. The Tudors had expressed a wish to go hunting, but seemed set on that particular day, which made us think something might be amiss. The French petition for Henry Tudor to go into France with them had been denied, and because of the warning carried in your despatch from master Quirke, we thought it prudent to watch them."

"But that action took place on the roadway; we were out of sight in the woods."

"You were seen galloping to warn the garrison here and then divert into the wood followed by those two. Our captain had no idea if there were any more mercenaries in the woods so he despatched a few men to investigate. We might have missed you had we not been attracted by the screams of the man you dropped a rock on."

Simon de la Halle had been sitting quietly listening as the tale unfolded. He came over to them and arranged the mantle over Joan's shoulders.

"I wonder what I shall say to my wife, and your father, too. You have been with me just three days and I almost lost you both."

"I think we should say as little as possible," advised Joan. "I can say my leg was injured in a rabbit hole or something." Simon considered her suggestion while stroking his chin thoughtfully.

"Hey, come this way," called one of the guards who had been looking out into the courtyard below. "Here is a sight." Laurence helped Joan to her feet and holding her firmly, helped her to the window. It had begun to rain and the courtyard was empty of the usual crowd other than a few ostlers who had hurried from the stables to take care of the horses of the small band that had just entered the chateau. It was a troop of the duke's guard and they had with them two melancholy figures, one scrawny and bedraggled, his thin face pale and miserable, the other looking as though he had had a fall and was patched with mud.

"The Tudors are back with us, I see," said Simon de la Halle. Laurence tightened his grip around Joan and reflected on the sad pair of nobles. It seemed to him that Henry Tudor caused rather too much trouble for one of such insignificant hopelessness.

End Of "ON SUMMER SEAS"

Continuing In: "A WILDERNESS OF SEA."

Glossary

This story is told through the eyes of Laurence de la Halle, a Breton armourer. Because the terms used to describe medieval armour may be unfamiliar to some readers, this glossary, arranged alphabetically, will explain those that are used in the book.

Armet á rondelle – a later development of the bascinet having a round form and favoured by Milanese armourers.

Arming nails – the modern term is rivet.

Aventail – mail that is attached to a helmet and draped over the shoulders to protect the neck of the wearer.

Barding – armour for horses.

Barbute – a visorless helmet for protecting the head. It was open at the eyes and down the front. Italian in design after the ancient Greek model, it was rare in England.

Bascinet – a helmet with a pointed skull, worn with a visor. Old fashioned in the 15th century and largely superseded by the sallet.

Bevor – protection for the neck made of plate and extending up over the chin. This would be worn as a pair with a helmet, usually a sallet.

Brigandine – a leather coat fitted inside with metal plates to form effective body protection.

Cap à Pied – the term used to describe full harness (from head to foot).

Caparison – the colourful cloth covering of an armoured horse.

Chamfron – armour fitted to the face of a horse.

Chapel de fer - an iron domed helmet with a broad rim worn by common soldiers.

Couter – metal protection shaped around the elbow (see lames, rerebrace and vambrace).

Criniere – a series of lames formed and fitted to protect the neck of a horse.

Croupiere – armour that protects a horse's hindquarters.

Cuirass – This is a term that describes a set of upper body armour comprising breastplate and back plate.

Cuir bouilli – leather boiled and then shaped into a hard plate as a means of providing protection.

Cuisse – Armour for protecting the thigh.

Curtal axe – A heavy curved sword with a single edge.

Faulds – articulated plates similar to lames for protecting the hips. Attached to the bottom of the breastplate and the backplate (cuirass).

Jupon – a quilted jacket to which armour is tied.

Harness – the term for full armour worn by a man at arms and used when referring to this.

Haubergeon – a mail shirt to protect the body and extending to the thigh.

Hauberk – similar to haubergeon, but completely covering the body including the arms and legs.

Gardebrace – a plate that covers over a pauldron to give additional armoured protection to the shoulder. Usually fitted on the left side as this is where a lance is most likely to strike in the joust.

Gauntlet – a leather glove covered with armoured finger and hand protection. The palms were usually bare for better grip.

Gatlings – the finger joints of a gauntlet.

Lames – strips of formed metal over and under joints at the elbow (couter) and at the knee (poleyn). Also used in the flexible neck armour (criniere) for horses. They are made to pivot so that the joint can move.

Latten – the old name for brass.

Mail – links of metal formed into a body shape according to where it was being worn. Often worn under plate armour where a gap might offer an entry point. The term comes from the French for chain: *maille*, thus chain-mail is a tautology.

Pole Axe – an axe having a single blade on one side and a hammer, or spike on the other. There would also be a spearhead on the end for thrusting at an enemy. Usually fitted to an extended shaft for use on foot, though mounted knights sometimes carried a shorter version.

Poleyn – metal protection shaped over the knee (see lames). Usually fitted with wings for extra protection of the joint.

Pauldron – articulated plates that cover over the shoulder.

Prod - the "bow" of a crossbow.

Quarrel – the missile fired by a crossbow; also known as a bolt.

Rerebrace – armour for the upper arm.

Rondel (1) – a round plate typically fitted over the front of the shoulder joint (pauldron) to protect the armpit. Usually embossed, ornate and embellished with latten or chased with a pattern. Also fitted to the chamfron of a warhorse with a spike fitted to the centre.

Rondel (2) – a round spiked dagger with a haft and heavy round pommel. It was used to force entry between armour joints, visors, etc, while the heavy pommel was a useful club. It also let the soldier strike hard with the palm of his hand to drive the point home.

Rouncey – a horse chosen for stamina and speed, much favoured in the middle ages for scouting work and for hunting.

Sallet – a helmet with curved edges sweeping to the tail.

Stake (arming) – a shaped metal device with a post that fits into a Stake Plate. The armourer selects the shape relevant to the profile of the piece he is working on, which he then hammers over it into the shape he requires.

Stake Plate – a heavy iron plate with various shaped holes into which is fitted a stake.

Sumptuary Law – laws that set down the kind of clothing allowed according to rank. For instance, only princes of royal blood could trim their clothes with ermine.

Tassets – The plates suspended from the faulds to provide additional extended leg protection.

Vambrace – armour to protect the forearm.

Author's Notes

Although the story is conjectural, it is told within the actual events of spring to autumn in a single year, 1471, during the second reign of Edward IV, a period when kings went into battle personally. Edward IV had deposed Henry VI in 1461 and was himself driven from England in 1470. He returned the following year and landed at Ravenser, a port on the Humber now lost to the sea. The story of how Edward IV reclaimed his throne is almost too fantastical for literary invention, yet he actually did so as described in these pages. His youngest brother, Richard duke of Gloucester was eventually to become king Richard III, but early in this year he was a youth with little military experience. By the end of the year he had acquired more than enough for several normal lifetimes.

So far as the history is concerned actual persons and events are depicted with reference to factual records, though their words and personalities are, of course, to some extent, invention. Others are entirely fictional, placed in there as glue to hold the story together. Many records of the time are highly subjective, often written with regard to a particular faction in government, so this allows some license in describing them. I have, however, tried to place the action within those actual events familiarly known to historians. The interpretation of those events is, of course, my own. The story of Laurence de la Halle and his association with Richard of Gloucester will continue in the next novel of the series: A Wilderness of Sea.

Notes on the Text

The Pilgrim – This was the earlier name of the oldest inn in England known since the sixteenth century as Ye Olde Trip to Jerusalem, still open today under the castle walls at Nottingham. The castle was under-used until the second reign of Edward IV. He proclaimed himself king there in 1471, and later ordered a new tower to be built along with royal apartments.

Three suns – The Sunne in Splendour was the device of Edward IV. This is a natural phenomenon caused by refraction of the sun's rays through frost particles when the sun is low on the horizon. It was this that was seen before the battle of Mortimer's Cross. Known today as Sun Dogs, there are many images of them to be found on the internet.

The peculiar fog at the battle of Barnet and the way in which the battle was fought is described as it happened. Henry VI was taken along with Edward's army to ensure he would not be used as a rallying point in London.

The Cunning Woman – Every town and village had one or more cunning women who were consulted mainly by poor people who could not afford a doctor. Their ability varied enormously, but there is no doubt that some of them did more good than the medical profession when dealing with common ailments. Their remedies were mainly herbal while a doctor attending a rich patient would prescribe according to the patient's wealth. Apothecaries, too, sold patent medicines containing powdered emerald or other precious stones, along with gold and silver coatings, in the belief that the more expensive the medicine the more likely a cure. Cornelius Quirke would have done this, though his daughter is clearly a cunning woman.

Elizabeth Wydville and witchcraft – It was certainly rumoured at the time that queen Elizabeth used witchcraft and also her mother, Jaquetta of Luxembourg. Modern minds are generally dismissive of these beliefs but they were quite acceptable at the time, thus it is difficult to extract the actual from the political. Though the church prescribed punishments for witches, the great persecution would not happen until the 17th century. Nevertheless, 15th century superstition reluctantly tolerated witchcraft, yet executions for witchcraft did take place, as we shall discover in the next novel of this series.

Death of Henry VI – It is often assumed that Henry VI was murdered in the Tower of London on the orders of Edward IV, but this is by no means certain. The defeated Lancastrians could not contend militarily with Edward any more, so they resorted to a propaganda war, which means the contemporary accounts are untrustworthy. Henry's death was certainly fortuitous for king Edward, which made the job of the propagandist so much easier. There are difficulties with the circumstances of the supposed "murder" and the story in this book sets some of them out. It is unlikely a modern jury would pronounce either Edward or his brother Richard of Gloucester guilty of murdering Henry VI.

Bastard of Fauconberg – Thomas Neville, illegitimate son of William Neville of Fauconberg, earl of Kent, was a colourful and piratical character who was unfortunate enough to be born on the wrong side of the blanket. He was loyal to his cousin, Richard Neville, earl of Warwick known to history as the Kingmaker. Thomas, along with Warwick had helped Edward to the throne in 1461 and was given the freedom of London for helping free the Channel of French pirates. After his surrender he was pardoned by Richard of Gloucester and then went with him to the north where Scottish rebels were plundering over the border with England. He seems to have reneged on his oath of loyalty to Edward and was summarily executed by Richard's order.

Richard of Gloucester's Bastards – The duke had two, John of Pomfret and a daughter, Katherine. Their mother is unknown to history so the lady here is an invention.

Anne Neville – the story of Anne Neville's disappearance and her subsequent rescue is true historically, but where she was actually hidden or how duke Richard found her is unrecorded. All that is known is she was discovered in the house of one of Clarence's friends disguised as a kitchen maid.

Henry Tudor – The details of his escape from Pembroke Castle and concealment in the tunnels under Tenby are described as they happened. The mayor of Tenby was a merchant and it was his ship in which Henry and Jasper Tudor sailed intending to go to France. The captain was indeed a Breton and historians are uncertain if his voyage to Le Coquet in Brittany was deliberate or simply due to contrary winds. In any case the actual circumstances were too tempting to ignore, so I made him an agent of Cornelius Quirke. The tale of the Tudors' attempted escape from the chateau of Suscinio is pure fiction. Henry did attempt unsuccessfully an escape from Brittany some years later.

Author's Web Site: www.quoadultra.net

20739170R00147

Printed in Great Britain
by Amazon